*Books by Thomas Block available
from New English Library:*

MAYDAY
ORBIT

ORBIT
Thomas Block

NEW ENGLISH LIBRARY

To Eileen, as always, as we take another step.

First published in the USA in 1982 by Coward, McCann & Geoghegan

First published in Great Britain in 1982 by New English Library

NEL Open Market Edition January 1983

First NEL Paperback Edition August 1983

NEL Books are published by
New English Library,
Mill Road, Dunton Green,
Sevenoaks, Kent,
Editorial office: 47 Bedford Square, London WC1B 3DP

Typeset in Times by Fleet Graphics, Enfield, Middlesex
Printed and bound in Great Britain
by Cox & Wyman Ltd, Reading

Block, Thomas H.
  Orbit.
  I. Title
  813'.54[F]   PS3552.L634

ISBN 0-450-05556-8

I'd like to thank the people at NASA who were kind enough to show me their wares; my doctor, lawyer and Indian chief friends who gave their expertise whenever I asked; and the three wise editors — R.M., R.C., N.W. — who steered and steadied me along the path.

Now it is autumn and the falling fruit
and the long journey towards oblivion . . .
Have you built your ship of death, O have you?

D.H. LAWRENCE

Chapter One

'THEN WE'RE finished with the checklist except for the fuel?' Captain Donald Collins asked, although in his mind there was no question about it. He looked down at the instrument panel in front of him, his eyes darting quickly from one instrument to the next. He scanned rapidly from left to right across the cockpit. He turned in his seat so he could look to where the flight engineer's panel was mounted against the wall behind the copilot.

'Yessir. Just about ready,' Flight Engineer Katie Graham answered when the captain faced her. She pointed toward a large gauge in front of her, near the middle of the console. 'They've finished with the jet fuel. Twenty-four thousand pounds. They're still working on the rocket fuel. It'll be done in another minute or two.' As she spoke the thin white needle crept another quarter of an inch across the black face of the instrument.

'Good. Let me know.'

'Certainly.'

Satisfied, Collins sat further back in the captain's seat of the *Star Streak* hypersonic airliner. He watched the rain fall on the asphalt ramp for a few moments, then glanced down at the digital panel clock. Its luminescent numbers glared up at him. Eight fifty-one. Nine minutes to go.

7

Collins had completed the cockpit check fifteen minutes earlier, and had then taken a few minutes out to introduce Paul and Chris Diederich to the cabin staff. The more Collins thought about her, the more pleasant things he remembered. Chris had been a stewardess with the airline 14 years before, and had flown with Collins often. She had quit to get married, and now she was on her way to Australia with her husband to attend a science symposium. All things considered, Collins was happy to have run into them in the terminal.

Eight minutes more before it would be time to start engines. Until then, there was nothing else for Collins to do. He looked across the small cockpit. Copilot Ernie Briscoe sat sullen and brooding, his shoulders hunched forward and his head down.

Out of the corner of his eye, Briscoe saw that the captain was staring at him. *Screw you.* Briscoe was still upset over Collins' instructions to reprogram the navigation computer manually. It was unnecessary, pure bullshit, just another example of Collins' asinine, bizarre behavior.

Collins shook his head imperceptibly. He realized too well what the copilot thought of him. 'Just about finished, Ernie?' he asked. Collins' voice was a blend of forced friendliness and exhaustion. The day already seemed a hundred years old, yet it had hardly begun.

'Almost.' Briscoe did not raise his eyes from the chart on his lap.

Katie Graham flipped a switch on the engineer's panel, then turned to the two pilots. Both men sat rigidly tense, pretending to be oblivious of the other. They looked like animals in battle who, for the moment, had taken a mutual rest to lick their wounds. She knew that they'd be at each other's throats again shortly. Of the two of them, Katie felt more comfortable with Ernie Briscoe. What Briscoe had told her about Captain Collins was exaggerated – he was not impossible to work with, nor was he belligerent or overbearing. Yet he was obviously insecure. Regardless, he was still the captain and, as such, he had to be dealt with on his terms. Katie wished that Briscoe would simply accept Collins the way he was and let that be the end of it. But she knew that Briscoe wouldn't, and she also knew that she had to do something to ease the tension in the cockpit or she might get caught in the emotional crossfire between the two pilots. Anything would be preferable to this sullen silence. 'Do either of you men know much about the X-15?'

'Sure,' Briscoe said. He flashed a provocative smile. Even seated, Briscoe could see that Katie's tailored uniform jacket curved sensually inward at her waist. Beautiful Katie. She had shoulder-length auburn hair that flared out in long strands of complex swirls, and her tanned skin appeared incomprehensibly smooth and luxurious. She had a childlike face, with hauntingly dark eyes and a small, upturned nose. 'What would you like to know?'

'I've read a great deal about the X-15,' she said directly to Collins. More than Briscoe, she wanted the captain to be part of the conversation. 'It always amazed me. It was so far ahead of its time.'

'I guess it was.' Collins struggled to remember something about the airplane. A rocket-powered test ship with short, stubby wings and a needle nose. It was all-black, almost evil-looking. It was flown from Edwards Air Base in the California desert. 'The early sixties, wasn't it?'

'Yes. They flew the X-15 to 314,000 feet in nineteen sixty-three. Six times the speed of sound. Isn't that incredible?' Katie's voice was laced with enthusiasm, some of it real, some of it forced. 'They went twenty miles higher than we do in the *Star Streak,* and several hundred miles an hour faster. All that, twenty years ago.'

Briscoe smirked. It was funny to watch her get worked up over an airplane. He tried to imagine what her room must've looked like while she was growing up. Pink pillows embroidered with X-15 rocket airplanes. She was the most luscious creature he had ever set his eyes on, and a hard piece of fast iron was what got her going. He almost laughed out loud.

'I remember it,' Collins said kindly, but with little apparent interest. Test aircraft. Records. None of that meant a thing to him. 'The X-15 received very little public notice. The space program overshadowed it.'

'Yes. Yet the X-15 program came up with a lot of new things.' She pointed to the small pistol grip on the center console, a few

9

inches left of the throttles. The device looked more like the black grip on the end of a bicycle handlebar than a sophisticated flight control. 'The peroxide thrusters. They had a similar arrangement in the X-15.'

'Really?' Collins looked at the black plastic grip. It stuck six inches above the console, its base buried in a polished-steel gimbal that allowed it to swivel freely in any direction. Collins would use that small grip instead of the normal flight controls to steer the *Star Streak* once they climbed above 80,000 feet. Up that high, the air was too thin for their normal flight controls to have any effect. 'Did they have problems when they first used it?'

'Sure. Plenty.' Katie laughed. 'That's why we don't. They took the bugs out.'

Collins opened his mouth as if he were about to add something, but changed his mind. 'What about wing cooling?' he asked instead. 'Did they have the same arrangement on the X-15?'

'The ablative tiles? No. Those came from the original Space Shuttle program.'

'I mean the liquid-hydrogen cooling system.' Collins pointed at a gang of covered switches on the flight engineer's panel. They activated the pumps that allowed super-cooled liquid hydrogen to flow through pipes in the front edge of the aircraft's wings and tail. 'Is that what the X-15 used?'

'No. The designers weren't worried about cost, weight and fatigue life. The X-15's leading edges were made of special metals. Very heavy. Very exotic.'

'I see.' Collins nodded, then turned away to face the windshield again. He was quickly lost in his own thoughts.

Katie looked closely at the captain's face, which was etched in uncommonly deep wrinkles. The skin around his eyes seemed drawn down by invisible weights. He was obviously uneasy. Collins was a textbook example of the apprehensive pilot, and he wore his burden as openly as most airline pilots wore their sunglasses and stripes. She had seen fear envelop pilots before. Like an uncoiling spring, their courage would continue to wind down until they were left with none at all. A psychological cancer that attacked and destroyed their spirit. Katie also knew that those who became afraid to fly usually remained that way. It was

10

untreatable. She glanced back at the engineer's console and noticed that the gauges had finally reached their marks. 'Captain, the liquid oxygen is onboard,' she said softly. 'Two hundred and twenty thousand pounds. The system checks normal. All the valves are closed.'

'Thank you.' Collins forced a smile in response to the routine information. *The liquid oxygen is onboard.* They weren't an airplane anymore, they had become a damn missile. Ablative tiles on the belly and the bottoms of the wings. A liquid cooling system that used one of the elements of their rocket fuel – liquid hydrogen – to keep the front edge of the wings from warping in the blistering heat of the ultra-high speed. Two rocket engines in the tail of the *Star Streak,* which were used in place of their four jet engines once they began the hypersonic portion of the flight. More than any other element, the rocket engines were what Collins had become more uncomfortable with. They were hardly more than two giant Roman candles, with his ass perched on the front end. Collins had hoped that his newly developed discomfort would pass after a few months – he knew damn well what was behind it, but his attempts to overpower it with rational thought hadn't made the slightest difference. Instead, it seemed to have gotten worse. He wished he could get himself to enjoy his job again, as he had for so many years before.

'The liquid hydrogen also checks,' Katie announced as she eyed another gauge. 'Thirty-seven thousand pounds. That includes eight hundred pounds reserved for wing cooling.'

'Fine.' It wasn't the rocket engines themselves that bothered Collins. They seemed well designed and well monitored. It was something far more basic about the *Star Streak.* Lately, every time Collins took the airliner up to its maximum speed and altitude, he felt outside his element. Thirty-nine hundred miles per hour and 200,000 feet. Forty miles high. He was no longer a transport pilot, he had somehow become an astronaut.

'The way points are programmed,' Briscoe announced dryly.

'Thank you.'

'Captain, they're ready to start,' Katie reported as she received the message over the ground interphone.

'Okay.' Collins glanced around the cockpit. Everything was

11

still in order. 'Normal start sequence.'

Briscoe read the items on the checklist. The captain and the flight engineer responded methodically. Each of them had become immersed in the long-practiced drill to get the ship under its own power. Clipped phrases that to the uninitiated would have seemed another language were exchanged by the three of them. Lights flashed, and needles rose to their proper positions. One by one, the four jet engines were brought to life.

'After-start is complete,' Katie said.

Briscoe spoke into the radio as Collins concentrated on wheeling the *Star Streak* out of its tight parking slot. The tip of the left wing swung within a dozen feet of the terminal building as they moved slowly toward the open ramp.

'Follow the USAir Boeing.'

'Where is he?'

'On the outer taxiway.'

Collins looked in the wrong direction. 'I don't see him.'

Briscoe smiled maliciously. He enjoyed having any edge over Collins, even an insignificant one. Briscoe had mildly disliked Donald Collins from the first time they had met in the crew room years before, but that dislike had lately turned into an obsessive hatred. Collins would eventually do something to endanger them all, and Briscoe would be forced to take command and save the ship. That piece of wishful thinking was all that made working with Collins even mildly tolerable. 'Over there,' Briscoe said in a taunting voice as he pointed toward the Boeing on the taxiway with an exaggerated gesture. 'Red and white. Silver wings. Black tires.'

Collins ignored the copilot's sarcasm. He spotted the Boeing and steered the *Star Streak* behind it. They worked their way toward the end of the runway, all the while finishing the tasks on the pretakeoff check. Collins edged the throttles a fraction of an inch forward to increase their taxi speed. The air frame quivered from the added throbs of thrust.

Katie put down the cabin interphone. 'Captain, the cabin is secure. The passenger count is correct. Ninety-one adults, six children, one infant.'

'Thank you.' The rain had increased. It fell in straight, heavy sheets. The New York area had been blanketed by overcast for nine of the last 14 days. Today's clouds hung even-handedly low, as if they were the bottomside of a canvas tent. The airport was shrouded in a wearisome October gray that made the early morning seem like late afternoon. Collins looked at the clock. Nine-o-six. He peeked out at the long expanse of concrete that made up the northwest runway. The far end was obscured behind the curtain of water. As the Boeing in front of them began its takeoff roll, Collins moved the *Star Streak* into the number-one position.

'Ready?'

Collins looked at his copilot. Young. Brash. Arrogant. His long and unruly red hair seemed an appropriate addition to the smirk that was always on his face. A 37-year-old teenager. A real bastard. There was no longer any doubt in Collins' mind that toying with rocket-powered airplanes on the fringe of outer space was more properly the province of people like Ernie Briscoe, not men like himself. You had to be either crazy or childish to enjoy it. 'Yes. Ready.'

'Roger, Consolidated Flight fourteen is cleared for takeoff,' Briscoe repeated to the tower.

As Collins steered onto the runway, he glanced at his control column. The words 'United Aerospace' were stenciled in bold black letters on its white faceplate, with the phrase *'Star Streak'* emblazoned below it in bright red.

Even though the engines responded rapidly, the sleek delta-winged *Star Steak* began its takeoff roll with apparent reluctance. With a full complement of jet and rocket fuel in its tanks, and nearly a full load of passengers in the cabin, there was a total of 347 tons to be carried aloft.

As Collins pushed forward on the throttles, the four jets began to suck in thousands of cubic feet of air. The titanium-and-steel engine compressors packed the air tightly. The jet fuel was poured in, and the mixture was ignited. The force of superheated exhaust speeding out through the red-hot tailpipes produced a shock wave that filled the surrounding sky with the rumble of continuous thunder. The airport buildings shook from the noise and vibration.

As the airplane continued its roll down the runway, it pushed through several deep puddles. A wake of churned water sprayed up in large circular swirls behind the fuselage. The jet engines gulped in hundreds of gallons of rainwater that evaporated harmlessly in the hot cores of the engines.

The ground roll of the *Star Streak* seemed to go on too long. Just before the available runway had nearly all been used, the *Star Streak* rose abruptly. The airplane's streamlined nose section, built at a canter that was already pointed several degrees toward the sky, pitched to an ungodly angle. Yet the power and performance of the hypersonic airliner was so immense that it could take in its stride what would have been a suicidal maneuver for a lesser machine.

Nearly as fast as Donald Collins could read them, the numbers on his electronic altimeter whirled past. 'Gear up,' he commanded, just as Flight 14 was enveloped by the base of the clouds. One thousand feet. Collins took a brief glance around the cockpit to verify what his instincts already told him: all was well. No flashing lights, no oscillating needles. 'Climb power.' He could sense the reduction in thrust made by the flight engineer, even before it showed up on the gauges.

Two thousand feet. 'Flaps are up,' Briscoe reported. Now they could begin their maximum performance climb. Four thousand feet. Six thousand feet. Eight thousand feet. At the rate they climbed, they would match the height of the world's tallest structures once every ten seconds. They were a super-express elevator to the top of the sky.

The *Star Streak* entered a patch of heavy rain, and the oversized drops battered loudly against the windshield. The wings rocked from the increased turbulence. 'We're cleared on course,' Briscoe said in a bored voice.

Collins nodded. He played tentatively with the control wheel. The ride through the dense clouds remained generally smooth, with only an occasional period of jumpiness.

Ten thousand feet. Four-hundred and seventy miles an hour. Still accelerating. Everything was routine, strictly by the book. Collins felt very good. With nearly unlimited power in one hand and obedient flight controls in the other, he could focus solely on this moment.

The rain ended and the clouds above them grew thinner. The gray outside the cockpit windshield had changed to an off-white. 'Soon,' Collins said as he spoke their shared thought. The three of them sat forward, each anticipating the same event. 'We're almost there,' he added. He looked at his altimeter. Twenty-two thousand feet ticked past.

Suddenly, as if someone had snapped on a light switch, the cockpit was flooded with sunlight. They had shot up through the top of the cloud deck and into the full brightness of the day. The dazzling midmorning sun hovered above and behind them, and it caused the *Star Streak* to cast an angular black shadow on top of the sea of white clouds beneath them.

They were ringed by scattered columns of thick, billowy cumulus that poked up measurably higher than the flattened overcast. The closest group of them, hued in blotches of white and dark gray, lay a few miles ahead. 'Tell air traffic control I'm going to maneuver around the buildups,' Collins said as he turned the *Star Streak* westbound. His ostensible reason to circumvent the towering clouds would be to keep the ride smooth, but that idea was not his sole one.

'They say that course deviations are okay,' Briscoe said as he placed his microphone back in its holder.

'Good.' Donald Collins was about to indulge himself with a whim that was too tempting to let pass. He waited until the first of the vertical clouds looked almost close enough to touch, then he rolled the *Star Streak* into a moderate bank. The vertical wall of puffy white swept past them with startling speed. The sense of relative motion – something that modern transport pilots seldom experienced – was exhilarating. Like a skier going down a slalom, Collins began to weave Consolidated Flight 14 through the course he had laid out. The columns of clouds were his marking flags. 'Nice, huh?' Collins asked with a grin on his face. He continued to toy with one after another of the vertical columns of cumulus, like a mythological god romping through the sky.

'Sure is,' Briscoe replied sincerely. The moment was an infectious one, and that made it easy to blur the distinction between those crew members you didn't like and those you did. Flight 14 had flown into one of those beautiful, ever-changing recesses in

15

the sky, and Briscoe knew that it would disappear before anyone else would get to see it. They had a private viewing of his three-dimensional canvas. The dynamic shapes and colors belonged entirely to them. 'Beautiful,' Briscoe said in a hushed voice. There was no other word that fit.

'Very nice,' Katie added after a short silence. She had also been swept up by the mesmerizing path, but now her thoughts were back on a more practical path. The altimeter showed that it was nearly time for another of their checklists. She wanted to remind Collins of that fact, but she also wanted the news to sound more like a suggestion than a challenge. 'Captain, I'm ready with the transonic checklist,' she announced.

'Yes. Okay.' Collins gradually turned the *Star Streak* back to its on-course heading.

'Let me know when you're ready,' Briscoe said tersely as he fiddled with one of the knobs on his navigation console. His brief spirit of goodwill – like the vertical columns of cumulus clouds – was behind him.

'Soon.' Collins reached reluctantly for the autopilot switch and flipped it on. His moment of reverie was over. Yet he was surprised at how much he had genuinely enjoyed himself. 'Okay, I'm ready for the transonic check,' he said as the *Star Streak* climbed through 42,000 feet. Collins knew that their flight plan called for them to penetrate the speed of sound at 65,000 feet. After that, they would turn on the wing- and tail-cooling systems, ignite their rocket engines and accelerate to hypersonic speed. Everything was going strictly routine. Better than routine, actually. It had turned into a beautiful day to fly.

'Mach one,' Briscoe announced matter-of-factly. 'We're right on target.'

Collins watched the symbols on his computer readout as they displayed precisely what the copilot had just confirmed. Within another minute they had passed Mach 2 – twice the speed of sound. They now traveled at 1400 miles an hour at 75,000 feet, with each of those indications rapidly rising.

'The liquid cooling valves are open,' Katie reported. She glanced at the gauges on her panel. 'The main pumps are on. Pressure is steady at eighty pounds in the wings, seventy-five in the tail.'

16

'Okay.' Collins took his right hand away from the four throttles that controlled the jet engines and moved in to the bicycle grip that was connected to the special thrusters. 'Okay. Tell me when we get rocket ignition.' The whole procedure would have been like threading a needle in a windstorm, except that it was totally automatic. *Monitor the system* was what the checklist said. It was a polite way of telling pilots to keep their damn meddling hands off.

'Ignition is on,' Katie confirmed. 'Here comes the fuel.' She watched as the instruments began to register the flow of liquid hydrogen and liquid oxygen to the chambers inside the two rockets.

Collins felt the familiar dull and muffled thud as it reverberated through the airframe. The rocket engines had ignited normally. 'Let's finish the checklist,' he said, since he knew that the rocket power would be stabilized in a few seconds. He glanced at his clock. Nine twenty-four. He was always glad when this part of the flight was over.

'The auto-controls aren't working.' Katie's voice had lost a portion of the mild and measured quality that she worked diligently to maintain. When events went other than strictly as planned, she always sounded nervous even though she wasn't. 'I'll try the auto-reset,' she said in a forced monotone. The mark of a truly professional pilot was his calmness during abnormal situations, and Katie knew that she was capable enough to be just that. Except for that silly cracking of her voice, she felt that she could keep up with the best of them. She reached out for the auto-reset button and pressed it. To her amazement, it seemed to have no effect. 'Captain, I might be having an indication problem,' she said, her voice half an octave higher again. She peeked at the label underneath where her finger lay. *Rocket Power Auto-Reset.* It was unquestionably the proper button.

'What the hell's happening?' Collins snapped. He kept his eyes glued straight ahead, at his flight panel. Airspeed and altitude had increased slightly beyond the predicted computer profile. Something was wrong. He could feel the aerodynamic forces as they grew slowly and steadily. He had flown for so many years that he was keenly attuned to even minor changes in motion.

17

'For chrissake!' Briscoe said angrily, also aware of being pressed further back into his seat. 'The power's too damn high.' He looked over his shoulder at Katie Graham. 'What did you set it at?'

'Normal. Twenty percent.' She pointed to the automatic controls. 'See,' she offered defensively, even though Briscoe was too far from the panel to read the setting. The hash mark on the dial neatly straddled the correct number. 'Should I go to manual?'

The rocket power output needles continued to drift up on the face of the instrument. Thirty percent. Thirty-five percent. A loud warning bell began to ring.

'Yes,' Collins said loudly. 'Go to manual.' He needed to shout to be heard over the noise of the bell. The continuous metallic ringing filled every inch of space in the small cockpit and pushed forcibly into his conscious thoughts. No matter how hard he tried, the sound of the alarm bell overwhelmed everything else. He couldn't think. It was like trying to play chess at a rock concert. 'Is the power reduced yet?' Collins asked.

'No.' It was Briscoe who had replied. He sat stark upright in his flight chair, his hands gripped tightly to the cushioned armrests, his eyes fixed on the rocket power gauge. Both of the rockets had risen to 45 percent of their power. Impossible. The rocket engines were totally independent and shared nothing whatsoever in common. Yet Briscoe knew that they had not experienced an instrument or indication failure. He had also flown for enough years to feel the elevated levels of engine thrust almost before it showed itself on the cockpit gauges.

The altimeters whirled past the 100,000-foot mark. Flight 14 had climbed 20 miles high, and the corners of the distant horizon had become visibly rounded. From here on up, the earth would resemble the globe that scientists for centuries had argued about. The line of demarcation between the rich blue tones of the sky and the chilled blackness of space was clearly visible. Beneath the passengers and crew of Flight 14 were clouds, moisture and breathable air. Above them was abject nothingness, an intractable and hostile vacuum.

The *Star Streak* trembled from the increased amounts of excessive thrust. Its nose section pulsed up and down in short, jerky movements. The panel gauges in the cockpit danced in their mounts, and it made them nearly impossible to read. 'Overpressure buffet. Christ Almighty.' Collins' hand was damp from sweat. He had a difficult time holding the bicycle grip steady, and he worked the special thruster continually in an effort to keep the aircraft under control. He kept the nose of the aircraft pitched upward as much as he dared. 'Abort the rocket firing!' he shouted, even louder than was necessary. 'Use the emergency override.'

Emergency override. The words hit her like a fist and they jolted Katie out of her transfixed stare at the rocket power gauge. She had never, except in training, been in an emergency situation. She remembered the procedure for emergency rocket shutdown – and simultaneously, she remembered nothing about it at all. It had jumbled in her mind. She turned and looked at the crowded flight engineer's panel. 'I don't see the override,' she said, in a voice too low to be heard by the men.

'Hurry. Shut it down.'

Katie floundered. Her eyes darted across the flight engineer's console. It was jammed with endless rows of instruments and controls, and each row seemed a carbon copy of the row above and below it. None of the panel labels made sense. As Katie searched frantically, she looked directly at the proper switch twice without realizing that it was what she hunted for.

'Hit the damn override!' Collins shouted.

'Wait!' Katie was nearly in tears. How could she have been so stupid? The delay, which had gone on for no more than a handful of seconds, seemed to her to be hours. Finally, she spotted it. 'Here!' With one rapid motion she flung aside its safety guard and pushed on the switch.

Senior Flight Attendant Gayle VanCroft sat in Flight 14's forward galley. Over the past 13 years she had gotten accustomed to riding backward, and her eyes stared absently down the long aisle toward the rear of the aircraft. She noticed that the majority of people onboard were businessmen traveling alone, although they also carried a scattering of couples, and even a few children. A young boy dressed in an expensive navy blazer with a school emblem on the breast pocket sat with his face pressed against the window. It was a normal cross section of passengers. They all seemed polite and well mannered – which was also a commonplace occurrence in the *Star Streak*. The ship attracted a wealthy, cultured crowd. None but the rich could afford to indulge themselves with hypersonic speeds, and fares to match.

'Did you see the November flight schedule yet?' Carl Tyson asked as he fidgeted in the small seat in the forward galley.

'No.' Gayle shook her head, then pushed back her long blond hair. 'Has it come out yet?'

'No. But it should be. Maybe when we get back.'

'Maybe.' Gayle stifled a yawn. Until the ship went hypersonic and they could begin the meal service, there was nothing to do. She glanced back into the cabin.

The interior of the *Star Streak* had a clean, antiseptic appearance. Sterile, actually. She preferred the old 747's, where at least the first-class lounge on the upper deck was done in real wood, with leather and brass trim. But those touches had been relegated to the past. Modern airliners were strictly functional. Strictly Fiberglas and plastic.

Except for two lavatories on either side of the aisle halfway down, the cabin was an unbroken expanse of rows of seats. The seats themselves, two on each side of the center aisle, were comfortable, deep-cushioned and upholstered in pleasant tones of blue. Above the rows of windows on each side of the fuselage wall was a long overhead luggage compartment. There was a third lavatory in the rear, and a coatrack up front.

'Are you off tomorrow?' Tyson asked.

'No. I'm working.' Nancy and Adrienne had been the lucky ones today. They had pulled assignments C and D, which meant that they got to work together in the back galley as they served the rear half of the aircraft. Gayle hoped to get a better partner for her next trip. 'Wait. Did you hear something?'

'No. What?'

'I don't know.' Something seemed wrong. The forward galley seats were near enough to the cockpit to hear some of the sounds that drifted out of it, and Gayle could faintly make out the ringing of a bell. That alone was not unusual. But something else was out of the ordinary. 'Don't we seem too steep? At too much of a climb angle?' she asked as she pitched the palm of her hand up to show him what she meant.

Tyson peered down the cabin aisle. 'No. Seems normal to me.'

'Okay.' Gayle looked at the passengers. The Diederich couple who were friends of the captain caught her eye, and she watched them as they sat quietly, each engrossed in the view out the window.

'Look.'

Gayle turned. 'What?'

'There.' Tyson pointed at the galley shelf a few feet to their left. 'Look at the vibration,' he said nervously. A large metal container filled with coffee jiggled in its mounts, to the limits that the tie-down straps would allow. An occasional drop of the scalding, black liquid popped out of a tiny overflow vent at the top.

'Yes.' Gayle frowned. 'That isn't right.' It was only her long years of providing constant reassurance to passengers that allowed her to automatically say less than she really thought. She felt the quivers of increased vibration as the entire airplane began to shake. *Something is definitely wrong. Drastically wrong.*

'It doesn't work!' Katie cried out. Her hand slammed repeatedly into the emergency shutdown switch, but it caused no change in their condition. 'What should I do?'

Briscoe searched his mind for a solution, but he rejected the ideas as fast as they popped into his head. 'The circuit breakers!' he finally said.

'Yes, yes,' Collins agreed quickly. 'Cut the electrical power.' That might work, as long as they left themselves enough power for control of the ship.

Katie turned to the enormous panel of electrical breakers on the rear cockpit wall. 'Which ones?' she pleaded as she scanned the hundreds of the round, plastic switches that controlled the flow of power to every component in the aircraft.

'The bottom panel. Down there,' Briscoe answered as he waved his hand furiously. 'Make it quick. We don't have much time.' He glanced at the power gauge. It had risen to 65 percent, which

21

was more than triple what they normally used. The airspeed had risen to 3200 miles an hour. The altitude was up to 170,000 feet – and still climbing.

Collins barely heard what the two of them said. Instead, his mind wrestled with the problem in front of him. The *Star Streak* was flying too fast for the altitude they were at. Collins knew that they had to go either higher or slower – and they had to do it very soon. Another warning bell had begun to ring, and its tone was even shriller than the first. They had only a few seconds left before the airliner would accelerate beyond the speed it had been designed for. The excessive airflow would blister and warp the aircraft's titanium exterior, and then the pressure of the wind would peel back the skin from the wings and tail as if the *Star Streak* were no more than an overripe piece of fruit. He could see from the warning lights on his panel that the liquid-hydrogen cooling for the leading edge of the wings had already been over-taxed. The auto-controls for the cooling pumps couldn't keep up with the rapidly building heat. If Collins didn't do something very soon, they would disintegrate in midair.

'I'm pulling up,' Collins said hesitantly. The checklist procedure was just the opposite. The official, printed words seemed incredibly naive. *Reduce Power,* the checklist said. The emergency page in the manual mentioned nothing about what to do when a reduction in power was impossible.

'No!' Briscoe said when he realized what Collins intended to do. 'Wait for the circuit breakers.' Experimenting with untried methods was too risky.

'We can't wait. Not anymore.' Yet Collins continued to wait. He shot a glance at his panel. Another red light glowed brightly in the corner, and he knew that he was the one who had caused that one. With his wild gyrations on the bicycle grip, he had already used much of their peroxide fuel for the special thrusters.

'We're running out of control fuel,' Briscoe said as his eye caught sight of the same red light. His voice was filled with fear. He reached for the flight controls once, then twice, but each time Briscoe pulled his hand back.

'There's no choice. It's our only chance to keep control.'

Even as they talked, Briscoe could see that their precious reserve was being depleted by the gross maneuvers Collins subjected the *Star Streak* to. Keeping the airliner pointed so far nose-up against the enormous aerodynamic pressures had taken all the output the control thrusters could provide. If they ran out of peroxide before the rocket engines cut off, they would go into an uncontrollable nose dive. At this speed, they'd churn a hole in the ground a thousand feet deep.

'I've found the breakers!' Katie shouted from the back of the cockpit. She reached for the lower breaker panel and yanked out each of the circuits that had anything to do with the rocket engines. 'They're all out,' she said as she turned to look at the power gauge.

It read 80 percent, and was still on the rise. The rocket engines had acquired a mind of their own, and they continued to function as if she had done nothing.

'Oh, my God. No.' Katie whimpered.

The flesh on Collins' face began to be pulled down by the tremendous aerodynamic forces. He felt the blood drain out of his head. Flight 14 had turned into a wild and hideous carnival ride. Through weighted eyelids Collins stole a glance at his airspeed indicator. The needle nudged through 4500 miles an hour. No *Star Streak* had ever flown that fast. 'I'm pulling up!'

'No.'

'Yes.' Collins yanked back on the bicycle grip. The airplane's nose pitched higher. As far as he was concerned, they had waited too long. They had nothing more to lose. The only way to keep from a further increase in speed – certain suicide – was to climb even more rapidly, like a truck driver steering a runaway rig up a hill. His pilot's instincts told him that pointing the *Star Streak* straight up was their only chance.

'You'll kill us!'

'Shut up.' Collins pulled the bicycle grip back as far as it would go, then turned his head and looked toward the left wing. The front edge appeared to glow deep-red like a poker stuck in a hot fire. Collins looked back at his airspeed indicator. The needle edged up to 4700, then 4800 miles an hour before it stopped. It then hung motionless for what seemed an eternity. Finally, the airspeed needle began to reverse itself. Forty-six hundred. Forty-five hundred. Forty-four hundred. 'We've got airspeed control!' Collins shouted. 'God Almighty. Yes.'

But Ernie Briscoe had focused on something else. 'The altitude.' The copilot saw that what they had given away in airspeed, they had acquired in an unwanted rate of climb. Briscoe watched in horror as Flight 14 shot up through its cruising level of 200,000 feet like a wild animal in a frightened gallop. The *Star Streak* continued its unbridled ascent without a pause.

Briscoe stared in disbelief at the panel gauges. The *Star Streak* was locked into a vertical path that was nearly beyond the measurement abilities of the cockpit instruments. The increased aerodynamic forces – now registered at five times the normal weight of gravity – pressed down on him like a giant invisible hand. His muscles struggled in vain against his own body weight, which had increased to over one thousand pounds. Briscoe imagined the helpless horror in the cabin as the passengers were crushed down in their seats by the violent aerodynamic forces.

Katie's stare was riveted straight out the cockpit windshield, into the bleak nothingness of space. After several seconds she dropped her eyes back to the altimeter. 'Three hundred thousand feet.' She knew they might be higher, because the altimeter had reached the limit of its scale. The intermittent cockpit buzzer had changed to a steady tone, and it caused her to glance at the flight engineer's console. 'We've run out of peroxide,' she said numbly. The indicator showed that none remained in the special tanks.

Before Collins could reply the bicycle grip went slack in his hand. 'Out of control.' He was surprised at how calmly he had managed to say those dreaded words.

Yet the *Star Streak* did not begin to tumble. The normal laws of aerodynamics had been left far behind. As Flight 14 climbed through 300,000 feet – 60 miles above the earth – they had slid into the edge of space. The sky that surrounded them still contained scattered molecules of air, but its substance was too insignificant to create any difference. Flight 14 had become a rocket-powered ballistic missile, locked into a trajectory determined entirely by the complex laws of orbital physics.

Seven, eight, then nine times the normal force of gravity

pressed down on them as the rocket engines continued to pour 100 percent of their enormous power into the vertical climb. Each of Collins' hands seemed to have 50-pound weights strapped to them, and his chest and shoulders supported what could have been measured at nearly half a ton. His breathing was labored, and his consciousness had begun to fade. Collins knew that the less-fit passengers must have already blacked out. They were the lucky ones. 'Ernie? Can you hear me?'

'Yes,' Briscoe grunted, not able to say more.

Collins was thankful that Briscoe had acknowledged him. The idea that he might be the only one of them still awake had startled Collins. It seemed a more horrible thought than dying. Collins tried to move his head, but couldn't budge against the overwhelming forces that nailed him firmly against his flight chair. His vision grew dark and blurred. There was nothing either one of them could do now but wait. Wait to die. Collins prayed that it would be over quickly and painlessly.

At first the rocket acceleration had seemed normal, but soon the noise from the *Star Streak*'s engines had increased to an intolerable level. Even passengers who seldom flew, like Linda Lewis in seat 20D, knew that something was terribly wrong. When the airliner had pointed its nose straight up into the blackest portion of the sky, Linda had screamed. Then others began to scream. The airframe vibrations had begun moments later, mild at first, and then so severe that Linda and the others had been tossed around in their seats. Those in seats by the windows were knocked repeatedly into the cabin wall. Linda's head and upper torso by their own weight and inertia, were battered several times against the Fiberglas panels that made up the interior sides of the *Star Streak*. Her chin was gouged by the handle of the plastic window-shade.

Michael Lewis sat in his mother's arms. His fingers were balled into tight fists, and his tiny arms were rigidly held in front of his chest. It appeared as if he intended to clap his hands. But Michael, at eight weeks of age, had no such intentions. His capabilities were few. His responses were totally automatic. His crying, which had become loud and sustained, was a direct result of the uncomfortable stimuli which acted upon his fragile body. The weight of the aerodynamic forces from Flight 14's continuous and unwanted climb had pushed further down on him. Michael's small body was pressed firmly, incessantly, against his mother's chest.

Linda held her baby tightly. During a momentary pause in the vibration, she picked up her head and looked around the cabin in terror. The passengers continued to shout and scream. A few of them mixed both sounds into a blend as horrid as the distress it was meant to convey. 'Michael. Oh, God, Michael,' Linda said out loud, as if the mention of her child's name might be magic enough to cause the horror to disappear, might wake her up from her incredible, frightening dream. She expected to find herself at home, Andy asleep next to her, the dog at the foot of the bed. Instead, the forces got worse.

'Help us! Someone! My husband is sick.'

The shout came from the row behind Linda, and it rolled across her like storm-tossed waves on an empty beach. But even if she had wanted to help, she wouldn't have been able. Linda, and all those onboard the *Star Streak,* were being subjected to enormous and increasing pressures from the unbridled acceleration. Linda suddenly discovered, to her agonized alarm, that she could hardly move, hardly budge her arms or turn her head. She managed, only with great effort, to wrap her arms more securely around Michael.

'Help me!' Linda's unheeded plea had joined the loud, perpetual chorus of terror-stricken cries.

The passengers irrationally pleaded for help that was not possible. In a matter of seconds, everyone onboard Flight 14 had seen their lives transformed from another dull, endless routine of modern technology into a macabre nightmare.

Linda looked down at her baby. She saw a puddle of red on his blue cotton bunting. It was her own blood. It poured from the large gash across the lower side of her face.

Linda held her baby tightly, the same way she had the first time the doctor had handed Michael to her. But this was no hospital. There were no doting nurses around, or doctors exuding competence. The passengers in the cabin had been left to themselves, without warning or explanation.

Linda continued to lose blood. The vibrations suddenly began again, and again her head and shoulders were slammed repeatedly into the Fiberglas wall panels. The pounding, coupled with the increased aerodynamic forces, had begun to exact their gruesome toll. Linda was lightheaded. She moaned half aloud. Her voice seemed to come from the other end of an empty tunnel. She was losing consciousness.

In a flash of lucid insight, Linda realized what might happen next. *Michael.* With the last of her strength, she attempted to get her infant's legs beneath the seat belt that was wrapped around her. She almost managed once, but Michael kicked his legs free. She tried a second time, but the aerodynamic forces pulled the belt too snugly against her lap. Linda's arms tingled as if a continuous electrical shock flowed through them. Her fingers no longer responded. Her hands quivered uncontrollably for several seconds, then dropped heavily into her lap. 'No. Oh, God.' Tears filled her eyes as she slid into the netherworld of unconsciousness.

For a short while, Michael Lewis did not move. He was pinned to his mother's chest by the continuous forces of the acceleration as the *Star Streak* climbed further into the black sky. But then the airliner's rocket engines ran out of fuel, and the sudden loss of thrust set an entirely different array of forces into effect. When the *Star Streak* abruptly ceased its acceleration, it was as if someone had slammed on the brakes. Every object that was not securely restrained was thrown forward. Michael Lewis had become a 12-pound projectile.

He tumbled upward off his mother's lap. His first impact was into the cushioned seat back of row 19. He bounced off that now, and was then propelled up and into the Fiberglas ceiling. The bones in both his legs snapped like twigs in a windstorm.

Coats, shoes, pocketbooks, luggage, pillows, magazines, books, pens, pencils, playing cards and loose objects of every imaginable shape and size were caught in the maelstrom of motion that propelled them through the zero-gravity condition. Michael's body was carried rapidly along with the barrage of debris. He tumbled head over heels several times, like a badly tossed football, over the heads of dozens of terror-stricken

27

people, most of whom had lost consciousness, or were very near to it.

Michael was aimed directly at the edge of the lavatory wall, at the midsection of the aircraft. His skull would have smashed into it, except that a pile of heavier debris beat him to the spot. His course was altered slightly as the objects pushed into him on their way to the front of the cabin.

Michael's head missed the wall by a fraction of an inch. He continued forward, still tumbling randomly, still locked in continuous, convulsive motion, until there was no place left to go. His body, along with the hundreds of large and small articles that had been swept up with him, smacked into the bulkhead that separated the cabin from the cockpit.

Out of the corner of his eye, Paul Diederich saw Michael Lewis' body as it flew past where he sat in seat 2B. But none of what swept past Diederich was more than a blur. He had, along with his wife, managed to retain a bare thread of unconsciousness. Diederich's vision was dark and shadowy, and his head ached.

As the last drops of the liquid oxygen portion of Flight 14's rocket fuel had finally poured through the high-velocity engine pumps, the rocket engines shut down automatically. In less than a snap of a finger, both engines had gone from full power to zero. The roar and vibration had ceased instantly.

'What happened?' Collins was only partially aware that he had spoken out loud. Without the roar from the rocket engines, the cockpit was filled with deafening silence, and his ears rang from the noise that was no longer there.

'God. I don't know.'

It was Katie's voice that Collins had heard. He tried to clear his head, but he couldn't. He felt as if his body were tumbling end-over-end, even though his eyes told him that their motion was relatively stable. He could make out a patch of earth as it rotated past the centerpost of the windshield in a gentle, slow roll. 'I'm disoriented.' He could no longer tell up from down, and he felt nauseous and dizzy. 'Take the controls.' Collins had forgotten that there were no longer any controls left for them to be

28

concerned with, since they had already run out of thruster fuel.

Briscoe, too, had suffered from the same sense of tumbling. But his military experience in high-performance fighters told him what the sensation meant. His face turned ashen white as he realized what their situation was. He glanced out the windshield to confirm what he thought, then turned to Collins. It took Briscoe several seconds to force the first words up through the bile that lodged in his parched throat. 'We're in zero G. No gravity.'

'What?'

'I told you not to pitch us up. You stupid, fucking bastard.'

'I don't understand.' Collins rubbed his eyes and looked down at his instrument panel. The indications were either wildly erratic, or far off their scales. The eerie green luminescent numbers of the clock – the only gauge that seemed to work – glared up at him. Nine thirty-five. 'Where are we?' Collins blinked several times. The severe nausea had passed, and his dizziness was nearly under control. He glanced out the window, but could make no sense of what he saw. 'What happened?'

Briscoe waved his hand at the Earth below them. As incredible as it seemed, he knew there was only one explanation for it. 'Orbit,' he said tersely. He glared at Collins, his expression a mixture of fear and anger. 'You bastard. You've launched us into some kind of low-Earth orbit.'

Chapter Two

BEN ROBINSON, vice-president of technical standards for United Aerospace, stood at the picture window of the large conference room that he had been ushered into half an hour before. His arms were clasped behind him and his body swayed rhythmically in a fore-and-aft motion. He gazed out from the high perch that the tall building in the Crystal City Office Complex provided him, across the flat terrain that surrounded the Washington, D.C., area.

But instead of looking in the direction visitors normally did, toward the northeast where the Washington Monument, the Capitol and the other government buildings were, Robinson had focused his attention further to his right, toward Washington National Airport. As he watched, one airliner after another taxied onto the runway and took off into the bleak overcast sky. Sally Robinson may have been pleased with the way things turned out, but he certainly wasn't. His thoughts drifted away from the details of the upcoming negotiations with the Astrex Corporation, and back to the memories of his days spent inside the cockpit. He did not notice when the door to the conference room opened behind him.

Ray Lee, United Aerospace's chief legal counsel, stepped quietly into the room. He glanced at his stack of papers that lay on the oak table, then walked toward the window. 'I'm back,' he said to announce his presence.

Robinson turned. 'That was quick. Did you find them?'

'No. Only the same secretaries, saying the same things. That young man that met us at reception – Mervis, wasn't it?'

'Something like that.'

'His secretary says that he's been unavoidably detained. It seems that all the people we've been scheduled to meet have been unavoidably detained.' Lee glanced over Robinson's shoulder and out the window. He watched an airliner as it climbed into the clouds. 'Sightseeing? An ex-busman's holiday?'

'Sort of.'

'Do you miss it?'

'No.' Robinson shrugged. His automatic lie had slipped out before he could stop it. 'Yes,' he corrected himself. 'I miss it like hell.' He glanced self-consciously around the oak-paneled room.

'It shows.'

'Very much?'

'Hardly.' Lee waved his hand in dismissal. 'If I didn't know I'd never guess. You're as bland as most of our vice-presidents.'

'Good. I don't want to buck the job description.'

'A valid point.' Lee looked out through the picture window, then back at Robinson. 'How are you feeling?'

'Better. It comes and goes.'

'Unpredictable, I understand.'

'Right.' As much as he tried not to, Robinson found that he always cut short any conversation about his illness – even with his good friends.

'I see.' Lee took the hint. He touched his hands together lightly, a gesture meant as a sort of punctuation. The previous thought was ended. Time for a new paragraph. 'It seems that nine forty-five is much too early to start a nine-thirty meeting,' he said as he glanced at his watch.

'They might have a good excuse.'

'They'll have an excuse, but not a good one.' Lee pulled out a chair and sat down. 'I predicted, if you'll remember, that we'd be left to simmer on a back burner for a while. Part of the Astrex Corporation's business philosophy. I hear that they actually paid a consultant a large fee to determine the most advantageous psychological approach to contract negotiations. He convinced them that products weren't as important as image and that they'd get better deals if the opposition became bored and irritable.'

Robinson pulled out a chair for himself. 'Being left alone doesn't seem so horrible.' He rubbed his hand along the side of his head, to pat down the thinning patches of black hair that remained as a frame to his increasingly bald skull. The dizziness from the attack of his Ménière's disease an hour before had passed, although he still felt slightly nauseous. At least the disorientation and the ringing in his ears had stopped.

'Most people don't think much of themselves. Solitude is a common method of inflicting misery.'

Robinson sat back, draped his arm across the rear of the chair and shifted the weight of his bulky, squared-off body. 'Sounds diabolical. I imagine it's Oriental.'

'I learned it from my father. After I had mastered the inscrutable expression, he felt I could be trusted with the remainder of the heritage. Being Oriental – even second generation – does have an occasional advantage.'

'I'd never trust you with my laundry.'

Both men laughed heartily, more because of the situation than the remark. If they weren't alone in the room and weren't good friends, nothing approximating an ethnic slur would have been tolerated by Lee. In his younger years, Lee had vacillated between being fiercely proud and embarrassingly distressed by his Oriental lineage. Now that he had turned 50 years old, he was simply tired of it. His Chinese appearance and Oriental manner and bearing were both comfortable and boring – like the Far Eastern rituals his 82-year-old father continued to observe. 'By the way, my father sends his regards. If Sally gives you another weekend pass, I hope you'll come with me again when I make the next quarterly pilgrimage to San Francisco.'

'She might. Is it time already?'

'Soon. Next month.'

'I'll try to come. I enjoyed meeting your father. Send my best.'

Robinson fidgeted in his seat. 'Doesn't it seem chilly in here?' he asked as he shivered involuntarily. He stuck his hands into his pants pockets. 'Is this part of their business psychology? Freeze our asses off?'

Lee smiled. 'Might be. I didn't hear about that part.'

Robinson glanced at his watch. Nine forty-nine. 'How much longer are they going to play this game?' There was annoyance in his voice.

Before Lee could answer, the telephone on the table rang. 'You expecting a call?'

Robinson scowled at the ringing phone. 'I'm always expecting a call.' Since he had taken the vice-president of technical standards job, anytime he was near a ringing phone he assumed it was for him. It often was. He leaned forward and yanked it off its cradle. 'Robinson,' he said tersely.

'Ben, is that you?'

'Yes.' Robinson recognized the voice instantly. It was his boss, Mike Ferrera, the senior vice-president of United Aerospace's Phoenix Division. 'Where are you?'

'Still in Phoenix. At home, actually. They reached me here, before I left for the office.'

'What's up?'

'A grim choice of words, Ben. Are you sitting down?'

'I figured it wasn't good news. Shoot.' Robinson grabbed a blank notepad off the table, scribbled Ferrera's name on it and shoved the pad over to Lee. Lee nodded.

'It's the *Star Streak*. An incredible accident.'

'Which airline?' Robinson pulled the pad back to his side of the table and began to take notes.

'Consolidated.'

Robinson stopped writing. 'Do you know the names of the crew?' There was a nervous edge to his voice.

'No. Not yet. I'll check into that and get the information to you. But don't get ahead of me. It's not a normal accident. It's not over yet.'

'I don't understand.'

There was a pause on the other end of the phone, as if the man in Phoenix couldn't decide whether or not to go ahead with the explanation. He cleared his throat and began hesitantly. 'Consolidated Flight fourteen. The rocket engines locked on while they were accelerating to cruise speed. Both engines went to one hundred percent power. I don't have to tell you how much raw thrust those rocket engines are capable of. It was enough to push the airplane to an altitude of approximately one hundred miles.'

'A hundred *miles!* Impossible.'

'Yes. I know. But it happened – and that's not the worst of it.' Ferrera paused again. He needed to run the next sentence through his mind one more time before he could bring himself to say it. He couldn't believe it himself. 'The airplane is still up there.'

'What?'

'It's trapped in a low-Earth orbit,' Ferrera added casually, as if he were reporting that the airliner had blown a tire while landing.

'God Almighty. Are you sure?'

'Unfortunately, yes.'

Robinson lowered the phone and stared blankly at Lee. In his mind's eye, he could suddenly visualize the *Star Streak* tumbling through the black, airless void of space, far above the atmosphere, far beyond the normal reaches of gravity. 'It's a *Star Streak,*' he said to Lee. 'Consolidated Airways. The rockets locked on. It's trapped in orbit.'

'Orbit? Like a space capsule?'

'Yes.'

'Christ.' Lee shook his head. As their legal counsel, he was accustomed to a daily diet of problems – corporate ones, normally – and an occasional tragedy. That exposure, plus his lack of technical knowledge, had provided him with a natural callousness. Nothing startled Ray Lee, and nothing ever amazed him. Whatever was about to be offered – asinine information, absurd coincidences, tragic news – Lee could buffer himself with the knowledge that he had probably heard something equally incredible a dozen times before. But the prospect of one of the company's giant hypersonic airliners becoming trapped above the Earth in some sort of ungodly orbit was a shock, even to Lee. 'Is that possible?' he asked incredulously, hoping that it was Robinson's idea of a joke – and knowing for certain that it would not be.

'I don't know. Yes. Evidently.' Robinson's brain whirled with snips of technical data. He had been the chief engineering test pilot at the beginning of the *Star Streak* program. Later, when the initial testing had been completed, he went on to head the newly formed flight sales division – a position that combined the best of his talents with the greatest share of his interests and enthusiasm. Robinson had lived with the *Star Streak* day and night during the inception of the project. He was a major part of every crucial design decision along the way. While other people at United Aerospace knew their specialties better than Robinson, no one knew the overall *Star Streak* better than he did.

'Ben? Hello? Are you there?'

'Yes. Go ahead.' Robinson pressed the phone firmly against his ear and tried to concentrate on the details that Ferrera had begun to give. But in the back of his mind, Robinson kept wrestling with the basic premise that he had been told was responsible for the accident. *Both the rocket engines locked on at 100 percent power.* He could not believe it. He wouldn't accept it. It was beyond being impossible. It was a contingency, he knew, that they had specifically designed against.

'Then you understand the situation,' Ferrera added as he finished summing up what little information they had. 'At the moment, the ground stations are out of communication with the flight. They received a distress signal and answered it. After that, communications were lost.'

'They might have broken apart.' Robinson was well aware of the enormous forces involved in high-speed hypersonic flight. He could hardly imagine how much additional strain the ship had been subjected to by the runaway engines.

'Perhaps. But they tell me it's not likely. The first distress message came after they reached their orbit altitude, so the most dangerous part of the climb was already behind them.'

'That's true.' Robinson remembered from his reading in technical journals that once a ship was in orbit, there was hardly any strain on its structure. It was the getting up – and, worse, the coming down – when the vehicle would be subjected to an enormous buildup of heat and pressure.

'One other point,' Ferrera added, 'is that I'm told the military

35

is currently tracking an unknown target in a low-Earth orbit. It's undoubtedly the *Star Streak*. It obviously hadn't broken up, at least not yet. The problem, as I understand it, will be to get them down. They evidently have enough oxygen onboard for several more hours.'

'Okay,' Robinson paused, unsure. 'What should we do next?'

'The last news I received from the airline was that coordination will occur at the NASA Goddard Center. They've got the best communications facilities for this sort of thing. We're fortunate for one small break, that Goddard is only twenty or so miles from where you are.'

'Sure. Lucky as hell,' Robinson said.

'Let me explain,' Ferrera said, more as an order than a request. He admired Robinson for his straightforward, no-nonsense attitudes – that was why he had sponsored the 47-year-old ex-test pilot for the vice-president's slot when his medical problems had knocked him out of the flying end. But sometimes Robinson could be shortsighted. Quick-tempered. 'We *are* fortunate. It's very important that we be on hand for every phase of the operation from here on. I hope I don't have to explain how legally liable we are.'

'No. I understand.' Robinson didn't understand, and didn't really give a damn. He was thankful that the senior vice-presidents could concern themselves with the legal implications because Robinson considered it nothing but bullshit. Law these days seemed more designed to make attorneys rich than to promote justice. Robinson was more interested in the *Star Streak,* and the people onboard it.

'There's one additional fact you're not yet aware of,' Ferrera continued. His tone had grown weary. 'The aircraft in question, Ship thirty-five, was here in Phoenix for fourteen days of service work last month.'

'What kind of work?'

'Repainting and electronic updates.'

'Shit.'

'My feelings precisely. We're distinctly on the defensive, liability-wise. Not only did we build the damn thing, but we were the last people to do any major work on it. Electronic work, too, if that isn't a kick in the ass.'

'I see your point.' Robinson was well aware that most every critical system in a modern airliner – including the *Star Streak*'s rocket engine controls – were electronically regulated. But a judge and jury – with the help of a fast-talking lawyer whose fee would take much of an award – would see only the similarities and draw the obvious but not necessarily valid conclusion that United Aerospace's handiwork the months before had caused the accident.

'A small break in our favor,' Ferrera continued as he attempted to sound positive, 'is that you and Ray Lee are in Washington. You're undoubtedly the best man we could get to handle the technical aspects, and Lee can monitor the legal situation for us firsthand. That exposure might prove significant later on. Is Ray in the room?'

'Yes.'

'Let me speak to him.'

'Right.' Robinson handed the phone to Lee, then rose from his chair and walked to the window. The rain had stopped, although the sky remained a leaden gray. Robinson watched as a McDonnell Douglas jet rose off the wet runway, pointed its nose up and climbed into the clouds.

Electronic updates. The words steered through the recesses of Robinson's mind as he tried to recall all the aspects of their latest program. While he was certain that the update work had nothing to do with the rockets, he also remembered that it would have taken place in the same lower-bay electronics compartment where the rocket controls were. Built into those rocket firing circuits in the lower bay were the safety devices that had been designed to prevent a runaway engine.

Robinson shook his head. The entire business had developed a sour stench. Coincidence. Robinson had survived his many years as a test pilot by learning to mistrust coincidence. The laws of cause and effect are what made aircraft function, not chance and luck. That was what he had patiently explained to Sally for years, even though she had never believed him for a moment. To her – like to most non-pilots – airplanes were no more than dangerous, unpredictable beasts that would bite you in the ass when you least

37

suspected. Robinson's entire life had been based on proving how false that premise was.

Robinson's instincts told him that the work in the United Aerospace hangar on that particular *Star Streak* a month before and today's double-engine runaway were somehow connected. He felt that Ferrera believed the same, hence their conversation about United Aerospace's liability. Yet the more Robinson thought about it, the more it seemed impossible to believe that an error – no matter how severe – could have resulted in a double rocket-engine runaway. The control circuits were too complex. Too delicate. The quality control inspections after any modification were computer analyzed and verified. If the rocket circuits had simply been damaged by sloppy workmanship, they wouldn't have checked out. The ship wouldn't have passed inspection during any of the dozens of preflight safety tests that had been conducted during the past weeks of airline service. Any disparity would have shown up, and it would have been dealt with. There was simply no way the accident could have occurred unless the control panels in the lower electronics bay of that *Star Streak* had been physically altered. The separate, independent panels had to have been deliberately wired together. It was an impossible occurrence – unless it was intentional.

Sabotage. The word exploded into Robinson's thoughts. The rocket engine controls must have been deliberately tampered with. In his mind he saw no other possibility, no other feasible explanation. He spun around and gestured toward Lee. 'I want to talk to Ferrera when you're finished,' he whispered. As he did, Robinson noticed that his heart had begun to pound and his hands were damp with sweat. The room suddenly seemed warm and stuffy.

Lee nodded, spoke for a few more seconds, then handed the phone over as Robinson stepped up to the table.

'Mike, there's no way this can be an accident,' Robinson said abruptly.

'What?'

'Those circuits must have been deliberately tampered with. I'm certain of it.'

'For chrissake, don't be an ass. Do you realize what you're

saying? I don't want to hear that kind of talk.'

'You may not want to hear it, but it's true. I'm certain that the rocket control failure was deliberate. Sabotage.'

'No!'

'Yes.' Robinson felt his resolve begin to slip. Perhaps he had been too hasty, too impetuous. But, deep down, he knew he was right. All the signals were there. They were too obvious to ignore. He took a deep breath. There was an eerie silence from the other end of the phone. Robinson could hear the amplified sound of his own breathing.

'Do you have any idea of who or why?' Ferrera finally asked.

'No. No ideas.' Robinson knew that he had to come up with something convincing to get Ferrera to accept the idea of sabotage even as a remote possibility. 'That sort of tampering would be too complex for most technicians. Whoever did it has a great deal of electronic knowledge. They also must have had unrestricted access to the lower electronics compartment while that ship was in Phoenix, possibly to the quality control tests also. It would take some time – a few hours, I'd imagine – to install a new device or make alterations to the existing components. The lower compartment beneath the cockpit is where the rocket control circuits are located.'

'If it were sabotage – and I'm not implying that I believe it was – why couldn't it have occurred at the airline facility? Where's Consolidated's maintenance hangar? New York? I'm sure that ship's been through New York often enough during the last four weeks.'

'Yes. I guess so.' Robinson wiped a drop of perspiration off his forehead. 'It's possible that the sabotage could've occurred in New York.' But Robinson didn't believe it. The overwhelming coincidence – that Ship N35CA had spent fourteen days in Phoenix the month before – was too strong. The malfunction itself was too complex to have been rigged by some itinerant mechanic in an airline hangar. Whoever did it understood not only how the circuits worked, but also how they were built and how they were tested. At least Robinson thought it seemed that way. But maybe he was wrong; maybe he had jumped the gun. Perhaps he was looking for any excuse to defend the integrity of the airplane. *His* airplane. Perhaps he was looking for an excuse so he could be involved with his airplane again.

'Okay, Ben. I understand what you've told me. Your theory doesn't seem very likely, but I'll admit that it's possible. For that reason, I want you to keep an eye out for any sort of conclusive evidence that will substantiate what you've said. But I caution you that, until you come up with something firm, you must keep your suspicions strictly confidential. If this idea of sabotage leaks out, we might be in even more of an awkward legal position. For that reason I'm going to insist – and I'm serious about this – that under no circumstances are you to discuss this sabotage theory with anyone other than myself and Ray Lee. Do I make myself clear on that point?'

'Yes.'

'Good. Now, let's get back to the problem at hand. Lee agreed with my suggestion that we get as many of our technical specialists as possible on the scene – both for practical reasons and for the legal implications that are bound to follow. There's no sense sending people from the factory – they wouldn't arrive until after it was long over. From what I can determine, we've currently got only one group of technicians in the East.'

Robinson was thankful for whatever help Ferrera would send. The more company people, the better. 'Who are they?'

'The three team leaders from electronic engineering – Becker, McBride and Krause. They're meeting with the Martin representatives in Baltimore. I'll get through to them as soon as possible and send them down to meet you at Goddard.'

'Okay. Fine.' Robinson was pleased with the three names he had just heard. *Becker. McBride. Krause.* Those three understood more about the electronic components inside the *Star Streak* than anyone else at United Aerospace.

'I tried to catch them at their hotel, but they had already left. I don't expect to locate them until they show up for the Martin meeting. It's scheduled for eleven-thirty, your time. Another hour and a half.'

'That'll be okay. In the meanwhile, I'll need a complete readout of the history of that airplane. Log books, special data – the works. I'll need technical manuals.'

'I'll send the data direct to the Goddard computer center. You can have access to it through their display system. I've already made arrangements for a complete set of the technical manuals from Consolidated's office in New York. I knew you'd need them. Consolidated is chartering a small airplane to bring them down to you – they'll be at Goddard shortly after you arrive.'

'Good. I'll call you from Goddard when I get there.'

'Yes. I'll want you to set up a direct line, so we can stay in close communication. We want the factory to be able to assist you in whatever way we can. Any request you send us will take absolute priority. You have complete authority to represent the company,' Ferrera said as he slowed his words down to add emphasis, 'with one exception. The area that you and I discussed a short while ago – the sabotage theory – is strictly off limits.'

'I understand.'

'Fine. Good luck.'

'Thank you.' Robinson hung up the phone and turned to Lee. 'What's the best way to get ourselves to Goddard?'

'Not me – just you. Ferrera wants me to stay here and deal with these imbeciles from Astrex. You and I can stay in telephone contact throughout the day. We can get together tonight to go over details. By that time, the situation will already have been resolved – one way or the other.'

'Yes. One way or the other.' Robinson was annoyed at how everyone – including himself – had become mentally prepared for a total disaster.

Lee shrugged. 'Getting back to our first problem, we still need to get you transportation to Goddard. We could borrow a car, but then we'd have to explain what happened.'

'Not good.'

'No. The press will spread the word soon enough, but there's no need to air our own dirty linen earlier than necessary. Our friends here at Astrex will use our dilemma for leverage. I'll try to wrap up these negotiations without you, before they find out.'

'Yes. Take whatever deal you can get.'

'Okay.' Lee stared blankly across the room for several seconds, then turned back to Robinson. 'As far as getting you to Goddard,

41

I guess you should take a taxi. It'll be a long ride – do you have enough cash to cover it?'

'Yes.' Robinson strummed his fingers on the hardwood table. 'Can you come up with an explanation for these people?' He pointed a finger toward the door. 'We have to give them a reason for why I needed to walk out on the scheduled meeting. Be as vague as possible.'

'There's no need to tell an attorney to be vague. I'll give them an explanation that'll cover everything from stomach cramps to bankruptcy.'

'Good.' Robinson thought about his own explanation – his hunch, really – for what could have happened to the Consolidated flight. He had no idea where to start his search for proof of the sabotage, but he felt he would find it, somewhere. The thought of someone purposely tampering with the rocket controls of a *Star Streak* sliced into him as painfully as if it were a sliver of steel rammed deep into his skin.

Lee watched the expression on Robinson's face. He could guess what was going on in his friend's mind. 'Don't put aside the lesson of the *Titanic*,' Lee said in a neutral voice as he scooped his papers off the desk and shoved them into his briefcase.

'What?'

'The *Titanic*. The unsinkable ship that sank on its maiden voyage.'

'I'm familiar with the story,' Robinson said sardonically. He waved his hand to indicate that he had other, more pressing thought on his mind.

'The first time I heard it,' Lee continued, ignoring the rebuff, 'I thought it was a nickel novel, some bad writer's idea of a good story. But it's really a *prima facie* example of how the truth can be stranger than fiction.'

Robinson looked at Lee. He frowned. 'So I've been told. Repeatedly. I assume your point is that just because we specifically designed against a rocket-engine runaway is no reason to think it couldn't happen.'

'Precisely.'

'Horseshit.' Robinson began to move toward the door. 'But I will keep what you say in mind.'

'That's all I ask.' Lee paused. 'Except for one additional thing.'

'What?'

Lee walked up to Robinson and put his hand on his friend's shoulder. 'I know how much the loss of your pilot's license has hurt you,' Lee said softly. 'I realize that it's caused considerable friction between you and your wife. Don't allow that wound to surface as a fantasy about sabotage, about the evils that have been done to both you and your airplane. That's all I've got to say on the subject, at least for the moment.'

Without another word, Robinson stepped out of the conference room and into the empty corridor. *Sabotage*. No matter what Lee and Ferrera said, he was absolutely convinced that somehow, and for some unknown reason, a murderous act had been intentionally committed on Consolidated Flight 14.

Chapter Three

'OH, GOD! What happened?' Chris Diederich sobbed. She opened her eyes, but the spinning, tumbling sensation was, if anything, worse. She closed them again, tightly. 'Paul, I'm going to vomit.' She found her husband's hand and clasped it so tenaciously that her nails dug deep into the flesh and drew blood. Neither of them noticed.

'Don't touch your seat belt. Keep it on,' Paul Diederich forced himself to say through his own dizziness and nausea. 'We'll be okay. Keep your head still.' He, too, was on the verge of vomiting. There was nothing to do but wait, like trapped animals. He finally managed to pry his eyes open. His senses had told him that the airliner continued to tumble end-over-end, yet his eyes told him that it did not. He turned toward the window.

The Earth was far away. The corners of the horizon fell off symmetrically. It appeared rounded and huge, like a giant beach ball held at arm's length. The images on the Earth's surface – clouds, oceans, land masses in every conceivable size, shape and color – spun slowly and lazily. Incredibly, the Earth was *above* the tip of the wing. The airliner was evidently lying on its side, slightly upside down. It was suspended in a bank that was slightly more than vertical.

Paul Diederich could not get his bearings. The weird angle made his dizziness worse. He allowed his eyes to close and he fought back the impulse to gag. After several long seconds, he turned his head the other way and forced his eyes open again.

The view in the cabin was horrifying. Hundreds of items, large and small, floated in midair. A large cluster of debris – books, clothing, pieces of torn Fiberglas trim, blankets, shoes – hovered in a tight knot around the forward galley, less than a dozen feet from where Diederich sat. It looked as if those inanimate objects had acquired a sense of free will as they whirled around.

Diederich spotted something startling. It was a woman's cashmere coat, suspended in space as if it were a fancy Fifth Avenue window display, held by thin, invisible wires. But there were no wires, and this was no immobile display. The coat drifted eerily toward them, its arms flailed out as if it were possessed by spirits. The spirits of hell. Paul could hardly believe what he saw. 'God. Look,' he said in amazement.

'I can't.' Chris kept her hands pressed against her head and her eyes tightly shut. She knew that if she moved a fraction of an inch, she would lose control over her nausea.

Paul Diederich watched the coat in horrid fascination. It seemed to skim along on a river of air. As it came closer, he put his hand up and pushed it away. To his surprise the coat remained rigid, yet it changed its course without apparent effort. It began to float toward the other side of the cabin. It was rigid, yet weightless. *Weightless*. Diederich visualized that solitary word, etched in bold-faced print in the high school science textbook that he taught from. Beneath the word was a photo of the three Skylab astronauts poised in midair inside their capsule. The image hit Diederich like a shotgun blast. 'Jesus.'

'Paul, I'm scared.' Chris had opened her eyes, but she kept her head back against the cushioned seat. She, too, had fixed her stare on the debris that floated in the aisle and near the galley.

'Wait. Be quiet.' Diederich listened. The passengers were relatively silent. A few moans, and the scattered sounds of crying and sobbing. It was too calm. He remembered moments like this, after the battles he'd been part of in Vietnam. The worst battles always ended that way. Dead calm. 'Are you alright?' he asked his wife.

'Yes. I think so.'

'I don't know what to do.' Diederich reached for his seat belt. His arms felt strangely light, buoyant. His legs felt as if they had fallen asleep. He ignored the mild sensations. He wanted to do something, anything, to return their world to normal.

In the cockpit, Captain Donald Collins carefully worked his way rearward. He maneuvered across the cockpit hand-over-hand, as he grabbed fast to places that were safe to touch. He was afraid that he might inadvertently drift into one of the flight controls. Touching anything in the cockpit might upset whatever delicate balance had been established, whatever fine thread held them in this precarious equilibrium. 'Be careful,' Collins said out loud, although he had spoken mostly to himself. In the background, he could hear Briscoe repeating their distress message over and over.

'Mayday! Mayday! Consolidated Flight fourteen calling Mayday! Does anyone read? Flight fourteen is trapped in orbit. Our rocket engines locked on at full power. We're out of fuel. Answer our Mayday, goddammit!' Briscoe slammed his hand into his audio panel, selected another radio, then another frequency. 'Mayday,' he began again as he repeated the frantic message.

'No answer?'

'No. Nothing. Not a goddamn thing on any VHF frequency, not since that short answer we got on the first call.'

'Try the HF band.' The first reply had been too garbled to be sure that the ground station had understood their message. The deadened silence from the radios had become even more frightening than the weightlessness. The floating in zero gravity had made Collins' trip from the captain's seat to the cockpit door – a distance of only ten and a half feet – a slow, arduous process.

Briscoe flipped off the radio he had been using, selected a new one and began to transmit again.

Collins turned toward the door and opened it slowly and carefully. 'God Almighty.'

'What is it?' Briscoe laid down the microphone. His shirt was soaked with sweat. A pencil floated past his face at eye level. He knocked it away with his hand. 'For chrissake, what's happening in the cabin?'

Collins hovered in midair. He kept one hand on the side of a circuit-breaker panel to keep himself from floating away. 'Junk. Garbage. It's everywhere. I can't see more than a few feet.' He turned toward the flight engineer. 'Call the galley on the interphone again. Call both galleys.'

Katie looked up at him. Her face was a stark, pale white. Her lips were slightly parted and the expression on her face was drawn down and hollowed by pure fear. 'I'm trying. There's no answer in either the forward or rear galleys.'

'Damn.' Collins held the cockpit door open a few inches. The forward end of the cabin was in shambles. He closed the door. In the cockpit, a few unsecured items – flashlights, pencils, maps – floated haphazardly out of their cases and seat pockets. 'Grab that crap. Strap it down. Put it into something. Don't let it float around.' Any amount of order was preferable to the utter chaos of their small world.

'What's happening in the cabin?' Briscoe repeated.

'Grab that crap *now!*' Collins shouted. His loud, quivering voice reverberated around the small enclosed area of the cockpit. 'Don't let it drift into the circuits. It could cause a hell of a problem.'

'We've already got a hell of a problem,' Briscoe said defiantly. But he began to gather up the scattered debris and stow it. Katie Graham did the same.

Briscoe suddenly leaned forward in his flight chair. He pressed his headphones firmly against his ears, as if that would squeeze out the last drop of sound from them. 'Wait. I hear something.'

'What?'

'They're calling us! God Almighty, yes!' Briscoe turned, a big grin on his face. 'They *did* hear us before. They know what happened.'

'Yes. I hear them, too.' Katie said, her voice excited, agitated, as she pressed her own headphones against her ears. 'Something about NASA. It's very garbled, but I can make out some of it.'

'Quiet, for chrissake.' Briscoe lowered his head and cupped

47

both hands over his ears. 'They're breaking up badly. Some military station, I didn't get the name.'

'Answer them. Quickly.'

'Right.' Briscoe waited a few more seconds, then picked up the microphone and transmitted a short reply. He pressed hard against his headphones again as he waited for their answer. He frowned. He pressed the microphone button and spoke again, longer this time.

Collins could not hear what Briscoe said, but he could tell from his expression that there was some problem. 'Katie, what's happening?' She too, was frowning.

'They had heard our first message. But they don't hear us now.'

'Damn.' Collins shook his head. If they could at least establish a channel of communications with the outside world, that would be the first step. *First step? To what?* He pushed aside that disquieting thought. 'Try again.'

Briscoe was already into his next transmission. The results were, if anything, even less satisfactory. 'It's no use,' Briscoe said. 'Not right now. We've lost them. But they did mention NASA. They also said that we should expect to lose communications for a portion of every ninety minutes.'

'Ninety minutes?'

'Are you kidding me?' Briscoe saw no need to disguise his annoyance at Collins. The only thing that remained constant throughout their nightmare was that Collins was still an asshole.

'What are you talking about?' None of it made sense to Collins, not the radio problems, not Briscoe. 'I don't understand.'

'We're in orbit, right?'

'Yes, but . . . '

'Then for part of the time we're going to be on the wrong side of the globe for their pattern of antennas.' Briscoe made an exaggerated turning motion with one hand while he held the other hand stationary. 'It takes ninety minutes for an object to orbit the Earth – or didn't you know that, either?' The building pressure of Briscoe's fear and anger had forced more of it to vent. 'Where the fuck have you been for the last twenty years?'

'It's ninety-four minutes,' Katie interrupted. She wanted Briscoe to stop. 'That's the number I remember,' she said calmly, as unemotionally as she could. 'It takes ninety-four minutes for each orbital pass.'

'Yes. Thank you.' Briscoe nodded toward her, then looked back at Collins. 'Ninety-four minutes. It's as simple as that,' he said as if he were lecturing a ten-year-old. 'We can't talk through their satellites because they don't use aviation frequencies, and our sets don't have their channels.'

'Yes. Of course. You're right. Jesus Christ.' Collins wiped the sweat off his forehead.

'We should stay on this frequency. I'm sure they'll keep transmitting until we hear them.'

'Okay.' Collins tried to force a smile, to display at least a small measure of satisfaction that they had successfully made their problem known to the rest of the world. He was not able to. Collins looked around the flight deck. A torn section of a map floated in a far corner. The madness was all around them, everywhere. He wondered for an instant what kind of hell he would find in the main section of the cabin. He realized that at least part of his concern about the radios was his reluctance to go back to the passengers. He had already put that off for too long. 'Okay. We're in radio contact, or we will be shortly. Great.'

'Yes. We're in radio contact, for all the goddamn good it'll do.' Briscoe's voice dripped with contempt.

Collins ignored Briscoe's comment. 'You work the radio. Katie, monitor the auxiliary power units and the oxygen supply. I'm going to the cabin.'

'Yessir,' Katie said.

Briscoe said nothing.

Collins pulled the door open a few inches. 'Gayle,' he shouted. He still could not see through the mass of floating debris. Of the four flight attendants on the aircraft, the only one Collins knew to any extent was Gayle VanCroft. She had always been pleasant to him, friendly. 'Gayle. Can you hear me? Are you okay?' There was no response. Collins looked over his shoulder. 'Keep trying the galleys on the interphone,' he ordered.

'I'm trying. Still no answer,' Katie replied.

'I'm going back.' But Collins made no move to open the door further. He racked his brain for some reason – some acceptable reason – for the flight attendants not answering. The interphone was not dead, he could hear its buzzer not more than ten feet away. *They've left the galley. They've gone to the cabin.* Of course. That would explain it. Collins refused to consider any other explanation. 'Make sure the door closes behind me. Don't let this crap float into the cockpit.' Collins' voice sounded barely in control, even to himself. He could see that his hands had begun to shake. Collins took a deep breath, as if he were about to dive into a pool of water, then pushed himself out quickly and into the forward end of the cabin.

The mass of debris swirled all around him. A playing card – a jack of hearts – floated by at eye level. Collins suspected that he was inside the densest part of the debris, yet he was afraid to move further. He kept one hand clasped firmly to the door handle to keep himself from floating away. In the distance, he could hear sobs, cries and a loud mixture of voices. One voice – a man's – seemed distracted and high-pitched, as if he was talking in his sleep. 'Can anyone hear me?' Collins shouted above the noise from the cabin.

'Yes! Is that the pilot? Help us!'

'Stay in your seats. I'm coming back.' Collins hovered in midair inside the whirling pile of debris, unable to see far enough to make out anything in the cabin. An assortment of items – books, magazines, shoes, galley supplies, pillows and blankets – brushed into Collins' face. He kept one hand near his eyes, to keep the debris away. The arm of a coat wrapped around his leg like a snake. He shuddered. 'Don't move,' he shouted. 'Tell the flight attendants I'm coming back.'

'Hurry. Help us.'

Collins suddenly realized that he had completely forgotten about the public address system. 'Damn.' He should have used it first, to calm the passengers. To reassure them that the ship was still under control – or, more accurately, that conditions were stable. He considered going back to the cockpit for the P.A., but decided against it. It was too late. He wondered how many other logical steps he had neglected. Collins cursed his own stupidity,

50

then tried to force himself to ignore his fears. *Calm down, for chrissake.* He knew that he had to start thinking clearly, to start to plan out his actions.

The forward galley has a P.A. microphone. Even though he couldn't see it, Collins knew that the galley was only seven or eight feet to his left. He would find that microphone, make a brief announcement, then proceed to the cabin.

As he pushed aside some of the floating debris, Collins caught a momentary glimpse of something that took him back. Long strands of blond hair. They floated haphazardly in all directions, just inside the galley – just at the spot where the flight attendant seats were located. 'Oh, my God.' His entire body trembled. He moved forward in jerky, hesitant motions, his sweaty hand repeatedly slipping off the few protuberances he could find on the wall to hang on to.

'Captain? Is that you?'

Collins stopped. He turned toward the cabin. Through the debris he could make out fleeting glimpses of a man's green sport jacket. Whoever it was hovered no more than ten feet from Collins, at the outer edge of the floating debris. 'Get back. Sit down,' Collins said.

'Captain, it's Paul Diederich.'

'Who?' An expensive lady's pocketbook coasted into the side of Collins' head. He pushed it away too violently, and the motion of his arm stirred the hovering debris as if it were a pile of leaves caught in a windstorm.

'Diederich. Paul Diederich.'

Collins vaguely recalled the name, but didn't remember why. He didn't care who it was. The last thing he needed now was interference from a passenger. 'Get back, for chrissake. Stay in your goddamn seat,' Collins shouted. He dropped the man's name from his thoughts and concentrated on getting to Gayle.

When Collins edged forward several more inches, he saw the male flight attendant. 'God Almighty.' Now he could see why they had not answered the interphone. The young man was still strapped in the seat beside Gayle, his head slumped forward, his arms dangled marionette fashion. Collins tried to think of his name, but couldn't. More debris brushed into Collins' face as he crept forward. It was like walking through an old barn filled with cobwebs.

'Gayle. Can you hear me?' An area of whirling dust and shards of Fiberglas hovered in front of him. Collins closed his eyes and kept one hand over his nose and mouth to prevent himself from inhaling them as he pushed forward. After he had edged ahead several inches, he felt his shins bump into the side of the flight attendant's seat. He opened his eyes.

As close as he was, he still could not see the two flight attendants clearly. Hundreds of sheets of newspaper floated around his head. Collins used one hand to push the debris away from his face, and kept the other hand planted firmly on the sidewall rail he had found to steady himself with. When the debris had finally been shoved away, he inched down as carefully as if he were on the catwalk of a boat that pitched in a storm, even though the aircraft did not exhibit the slightest trace of turbulence.

'Gayle. Can you hear me?' Collins pushed a shredded magazine off her lap. He saw a welt on the side of her head, with a small trickle of dried, caked blood around it. Countless bottles and dinner trays floated around them; any one of them could have caused the wound. Collins reached up and grabbed her shoulder. 'Gayle.'

She slowly opened her eyes. She raised her head and looked at Collins, more bewildered than frightened. She shook her head to clear it. 'What happened?'

'Are you okay?' Collins' heart pounded.

'I don't know.' She felt as if she'd been in a drugged sleep. 'I think so.' She rubbed her forehead. 'Ouch. Damn it.' In addition to the welt, there were a number of scratches on her face. One of them – a long, deep line of pink that ran from near her left eye to beneath her chin – had begun to hurt. She pressed the palm of her hand against it. 'Am I cut?'

'Yes. But not badly.'

'Did we crash? Are we on the ground?' She kept her eyes fixed on Collins, as if anything more would be too much to comprehend.

'No.' Collins couldn't bring himself to tell the truth.

'Then what happened?' Her memory triggered suddenly, and it

52

all came back to her in a flood of hideous images. 'God. No.' The wild ride with the *Star Streak*'s nose pointed straight up. The overwhelming forces that drained the blood out of her. The sickening sensation of tumbling, just before she blacked out. 'Did it happen during the climb? Did we have a midair collision? Are we still flying?' Her words poured out, all of them packed together, one on top of the next, as fast as she could formulate them. She grabbed his arm and leaned forward. She pressed her face into his chest and began to cry.

'No collision. We're still flying.' Collins gently stroked the back of her long blond hair as he listened to her whimpering sobs. He wondered how long he would continue to give cryptic answers. He wondered why he tried to protect her from the truth. Maybe to protect himself. He thought about the instrument panel in the cockpit. Every indication on it was useless, except for the clock. They were flying so fast that there was no way to measure speed. So high that measurements of altitude were beyond the scale of the gauges, and were meaningless anyway. Collins didn't have the stomach to give her a complete explanation. Not yet.

Gayle pushed herself back and, for the first time, noticed the things in front of her. She pushed aside several sheets of newspapers that had floated down around her. The papers moved as if they were being blown in the wind, yet she could feel no wind. 'Where are they coming from? What happened?' Then she noticed the rigid objects that floated by. Her mouth dropped open, her eyes grew wide, and she began to sob convulsively as the first waves of inexpressible, haunting fear flooded over her.

'Stop. Stay calm. Help me get him out of here.' Collins pointed to the male flight attendant.

'Who?' Gayle turned and saw Carl Tyson in the seat next to her. 'Carl!' He was slumped forward, unconscious. She had forgotten about him, but now she remembered everything. She began to sob again, louder, in breathless gasps. She was on the verge of hysteria.

'Stop, damn it!' Collins shouted. He grabbed her shoulder and shook her violently. 'Get hold of yourself.' Collins could feel his own self-control begin to slip.

'Carl. God, no.' She looked at Tyson. That was exactly how

53

she had last seen him, his arms stretched out, his head down. It was only seconds before she blacked out herself. 'Everything started to fly at us.' Her words were choked, almost incomprehensible. 'It was awful. I raised my hands to protect myself.'

'Yes. Stay calm. Let's get him out of his seat belt.'

Gayle rubbed the tears out of her eyes, then turned. 'Carl? Are you okay? Can you hear me?' She pulled his inert body backward against the seat.

'Be careful,' Collins said, a fleeting moment before he saw the knife.

'God! Oh, no!' Gayle had also seen it. A basic, primitive scream rose up from deep inside her throat. She released her grip on Tyson's body.

'Christ Almighty.' Collins couldn't believe his eyes. Tyson's body dropped forward, but only slightly. In the zero-gravity condition, his weight meant nothing. He hovered in a hunched-over position, his arms still extended, his head bobbing up and down as if he were listening to a conversation. The silver-bladed galley knife stuck out from the center of his chest.

Collins looked behind him, at the metal drawers on the far side of the galley. Many of them were open, their latches busted off. He could easily imagine how the violence from the climb into orbit had thrown the knife out of a galley drawer and across the short distance. He looked back at the knife's wooden handle. It was covered with large droplets of blood that adhered to it like condensation on the outside of a cold glass.

Gayle could not take her eyes off Tyson.

'He's dead.' Collins saw the unmistakable signs. Tyson's face was pasty-white. The knife was in the proper position to penetrate the heart. That explained why there wasn't much blood. He had died nearly instantly. Collins ran his tongue across his dry, parched lips. He could no longer hide from the facts. His decision to pitch up the *Star Streak* had killed Carl Tyson. That much was for certain. 'Unfasten your seat belt. Get up.'

Gayle sat motionless. She continued to stare at Tyson, as if she expected him to stand up and return to his duties in the galley. Fragmented thoughts whirled through her brain. She could hear his words, picture his face. 'I didn't ask him to sit there,' she blurted out. 'Carl wanted that seat.'

'Get up,' Collins said loudly. *'Now.'*

Gayle obediently released her seat belt. She took Collins' hand and allowed herself to be tugged upright. 'What's happening? God! Stop!' The sense of weightlessness, which she hadn't particularly noticed while strapped to her seat, now overwhelmed her. She grabbed for Collins as if she were drowning.

'Weightlessness. No gravity. Stay calm, it won't hurt you.' They moved together to the other side of the galley, where there was less debris. 'We've flown too high.'

'What?'

'We're in orbit around the Earth.'

'Orbit?'

Collins tried to avoid her eyes. 'Yes.'

Gayle nodded, as if the captain had explained nothing more unusual than the need for them to fly around bad weather, or go to an alternate airport. 'When will we come down?'

Collins ignored the question. He motioned for her to be quiet. 'Listen.' There were loud sobbing cries in the cabin, and, far away, he could hear what sounded like shouts or screams. 'Something's happening in the back.'

'Yes.' Gayle looked around the galley. 'Call the rear galley on the interphone.' She pointed to the black plastic handset mounted on the galley wall.

'Right.' He reached for the interphone. He buzzed the rear galley.

Stewardess Adrienne Brown had already tried to unfasten her shoulder harness and seat belt, but even that minimal effort had drained her. She sat back in her rear galley seat for a few more seconds to gather her strength. She was bruised and battered from the pounding they had taken when the stack of dinner trays had broken loose. Adrienne wondered for a moment where all the trays were. Except for a scattering of plates, a few bottles and utensils, the rear galley seemed empty.

As Adrienne closed her eyes, a woman's shrill screams suddenly filled the rear half of the airliner. 'God. What's that?' Adrienne could hear loud voices in the cabin, and the sound of continuous crying. She turned to the stewardess beside her, who had finally opened her eyes. 'Nancy, are you okay?'

Nancy Oehlbeck sat in the adjacent flight attendant seat in the rear galley. She did not respond. Five feet ahead of her, a miniature bottle of liquor climbed lazily along the vertical wall of the stainless-steel galley as if it had sprouted legs. Nancy watched it with rapt, grim attention as it crept upward. 'What happened to us?' she asked tearfully.

'Nancy?'

Nancy turned and looked at her friend. She stared at her blankly. Finally, she nodded. 'Yes, I'm alright. I think so,' she answered in a quivering voice. 'My arm hurts. My shoulder, too.' She was near tears again. When she touched her shoulder, she could tell that it was bruised. 'I don't know what happened,' she sobbed.

Before either of the stewardesses could say anything else, the interphone buzzed. Adrienne reached for it. As she picked it up she realized how light it felt, how effortlessly it had sprung out of its cradle. 'Hello?'

'Who is this?' a sharp male voice answered.

'Adrienne. In the rear galley. What happened?' She had recognized the voice as the captain's.

'What's the situation back there?' he asked abruptly. He ignored her question.

'I don't know.' Adrienne looked up the aisle. 'Things are floating through the cabin. There's this strange sensation. Lightness. Levitation.'

'Yes. Weightlessness. Don't worry, it's temporary.'

Adrienne glanced at Nancy, who continued to stare straight ahead. 'Both of us must have blacked out. I hear loud voices, and one woman is crying.'

'Is there any damange to the aircraft?'

'I can't tell.' Adrienne looked toward a batch of Fiberglas slivers that hovered near the ceiling like a swarm of insects. 'There are pieces floating everywhere. but it doesn't look like there's any broken windows. The cabin lights are on. I think the air conditioning is working. I can't tell for sure.'

'Okay. Calm everyone down. Keep them in their seats. I'll come back as soon as I can.' He hung up the interphone before she could answer.

Adrienne had no idea of what to do next. 'That was the captain. He said the weightlessness is temporary.'

'Weightlessness?' To Nancy, the idea was senseless, imponderable.

'Yes. Don't worry.' Adrienne touched her friend's arm. 'He just wants everyone to stay in their seats.' She mentally flipped through the pages of her manual, but nothing seemed to apply. Finally, she decided to use the standard P.A. procedure. She pressed the button on the handset and began to speak. 'Please. Stay in your seats,' she announced in a voice that was surprisingly relaxed, almost casual. 'For your own safety, keep your seat belts fastened.'

But her announcement had just the opposite effect. The loud electronic words that came out of the overhead speakers had aroused a number of passengers from their emotional stupor. Several of them had not understood the stewardess's words. Others had chosen to ignore them. All through the cabin, numerous people had begun to wake up and unfasten their seat belts.

'Nancy. Look!'

Directly across from the rear galley, in seat number 28B, Peter Martinez rose up from his seat as if he were a toy balloon. The first motions caught him by surprise. Before he could twist himself around, he had risen out of reach of the seat back. 'God Almighty. Becky. Grab me,' he called to his wife.

'Here.' Becky Martinez reached out as far as she could, but her seat belt kept her too far from her husband. 'I can't!' She was too afraid to unbuckle her own seat belt to help him.

Martinez drifted slowly upward until he approached the overhead luggage rack. His body was at an awkward angle to the cabin floor. He had begun to drift slightly backward. His arms and shoulders rubbed against the ceiling, but he did not have the presence of mind to use the roof to push himself down.

'Stop me!' Martinez bellowed. One segment of his mind attempted to convince him that there was no apparent danger.

There was no physical pain involved, and no obvious threat. That message was overwhelmed by a basic, more primitive reaction. What lay ahead was unpredictable. Unknown. Martinez felt utterly defenseless and helpless.

Several of the seated passengers began to shout to Martinez and the others. For a few seconds it appeared as if the hovering passengers were drowning in a sea of air. They kicked their legs and flung their arms in wild desperation.

But then it ended nearly as quickly as it had begun. Everywhere in the cabin, those who were still seated reached up and grabbed those who weren't. They pulled them down to the safety of their seats.

In the forward galley, Collins heard the commotion finally subside. 'The cabin sounds like it's under control. Thank God.' An empty plastic cup drifted into his shoulder, and he brushed it aside as if it were a bothersome insect. Collins wanted badly to go back to the cockpit, to stay out of the next circle of hell that he was certain to find in the cabin. But he knew that it was his responsibility to inspect the cabin. It was his responsibility to deal with the passengers.

'Yes. They're calming down.' Gayle looked at Collins. She had calmed down enough to think clearly, to analyze the situation in front of her. The captain's eyes were glazed over with fear, and his hands shook. It was a normal response in this incredible, hellish situation. She imagined that she looked as nervous as he did, if not more. But her response was not important, Collins' was. She knew that the captain would have to stay firmly in control of himself if he were going to get them out of this madness. Gayle didn't understand a great deal about technical problems – and especially about what had happened to them – but she realized how deeply in trouble they were. 'Is the aircraft damaged?'

'No. There's no indication of damage. We've flown too high, and run out of rocket fuel. That's all.'

'Do we have enough oxygen onboard?'

'Yes.' *For a few more hours.* 'Don't worry.'

Gayle nodded. His pandering answer had told her that oxygen would be one of their major concerns. Orbit. Weightlessness. No rocket fuel. Oxygen. She shuddered when she thought about what other probems might still be ahead of them.

'Conditions are stable,' Collins volunteered unconvincingly.

'Yes.' She realized that if she had begun to think morbidly, perhaps the passengers had also. 'Maybe you should say something.' Gayle pointed to the public address microphone.

'Christ, yes.' Collins had forgotten again. He bit into his lower lip. 'I was going to, before.'

'Do it now.' Gayle's gently spoken words made it into more of a command, not less.

'Yes. Okay.' Collins had no idea of what to say. Snatches of sentences flowed through his head. They seemed like parodies of in-flight announcements. He had never been very good at it anyway, and the prospect of reassuring a cabin filled with intelligent, sensible people that the situation was not hopeless seemed beyond him. An impossible task.

'Hurry. Before they start a commotion again.' The cabin was relatively quiet, but Gayle knew that it wouldn't last.

'Right.' Collins hoped that the passengers would believe whatever he said. He had seen it happen before. Anyone in a snappy uniform or with an official-sounding title could tell passengers anything, and they would swallow it. Gladly. Collins decided to jump into the announcement fast, like a dive into cold water. He picked up the microphone and pressed the switch.

'This is the captain.' He paused. He thought about what the passengers could see outside their cabin windows. On the left side, the Earth spun lazily beneath them at an outrageous angle; the sun reflecting off the tops of clouds hundreds ot thousands of feet below, the deep blue of the ocean, the hues of brown and green from the land. Outside the right windows were hundreds of bright stars, even in the broad daylight. The sky itself was crystal clear, bright – and yet black. Collins shuddered.

'Keep the announcement going,' Gayle whispered.

Collins nodded. Beads of perspiration were scattered along his forehead. A pillow, a shoe, bits of food floated between him and Gayle. He ignored them. 'This is the captain,' he said again. He could hear the metallic echo of his own voice as it carried out through the cabin speakers. *God Almighty, help us.* He swallowed

59

hard, then continued. 'There is nothing to worry about. Our situation is unusual, but not critical. We have temporarily flown beyond the fringes of the atmosphere, and are, for the moment, orbiting the Earth. But conditions are stable. The safest course of action is for us not to rush our recovery. I will inform you before we begin any maneuvers. We are experiencing a lack of gravity at the moment and it is essential that you remain seated with your seat belts fastened. I assure you, there is nothing to worry about. Please stay calm.'

Collins hung the microphone up, closed his eyes and steadied himself against the bulkhead. *Conditions are stable.* He would have laughed, except that the truth was so frightening. Conditions were *permanently* stable. They were trapped in orbit with no fuel to get themselves out, and with a six-hour supply of oxygen.

'Very nicely done,' Gayle said. She wondered for an instant if any of it could possibly be true. She decided not to ask. Instead, she turned. 'I'm going to the cabin.'

'Okay.'

Gayle began to maneuver past the debris and out of the galley. As she did, she spotted a bundle that hovered in the corner. It seemed different from the rest. It drifted towards them. She watched it closely.

'What is it?' Collins asked as he saw the puzzled look in her eyes. As Gayle's facial expression changed to amazement, Collins whirled around. He saw a blue blanket, its top corner draped down. Beneath the folds was an infant. 'Christ.' He let go of the galley shelf and pushed himself toward it. He used his forearm to knock aside small pieces of debris between him and the baby. 'I've got it.' The baby's eyes were closed. He could see no signs of life, although Collins didn't know what to look for. He held the infant awkwardly. He could feel the warm wetness of the child's diaper as it soaked through his shirtsleeve.

'Is the baby okay?'

'I can't tell.' Collins gently pulled the tiny child to his chest. With the debris that floated around, he wanted to get out of the galley area. He inched himself along the row of storage bins. The outstretched arm of a gray topcoat swirled through the air in front of him like a groping tentacle. Collins pushed it aside. He maneuvered into the unobstructed cabin area aft of the galley at the same time that Gayle did.

The man in the green jacket moved up toward them. 'Do you need help?'

'I told you to stay in your seat.' Collins looked at him angrily for a few seconds, until he realized who he was. Paul Diederich. He was the husband of that ex-stewardess. Collins had been introduced to him before the flight. Collins remembered from their brief conversation that Diederich had known a great deal about airplanes. He might be helpful.

'Let me give you a hand,' Diederich said as he ignored the captain's first remark. He looked down at the bundle in Collins's arms. A baby, hardly more than two months old. 'Son of a bitch. Was the baby in there?' Diederich asked as he pointed to the mass of hovering debris.

'Yes.'

'Is he alive?'

'I don't know.'

'What can we do?'

Collins shook his head. He was accustomed to machines, not people. Even in the best of times, he was not comfortable with the problems of human beings – medical or emotional. The methods of dealing with human problems were too speculative. The results were too unpredictable.

'Give me the baby.'

Collins turned. A short, heavy man with a round cherub face stood in the aisle, his hands braced on the rows of seats to either side of him. There was a gash across his forehead, and he seemed pale.

'I'm a doctor. Give me the baby. Hold me so I don't drift away.'

'Are you alright?' Collins asked.

'Certainly.' The doctor glanced at the epaulets on Collins' shirt, then touched the deep gash on his head. 'I always like to do this sort of thing to myself, Captain. It eliminates in-flight boredom.'

'I only meant . . .'

'Give me the baby.' The doctor looked at Collins with

unmasked annoyance. 'Let *me* play the doctor today, okay? You can play the pilot.'

'Here.' Collins was glad to hand the infant over.

Paul Diederich grabbed the doctor's belt.

The doctor yanked away the baby's blue covering, then picked him up and held the infant's chest against his ear as if he were listening to the ticking of a watch. After a few seconds he lowered the baby, then announced in a flat, almost indifferent voice. 'A heartbeat. Faint, but regular. The baby is still alive.'

'Any broken bones?'

'How the hell would I know?' The doctor looked accusingly at Collins before he turned back to the child. He unwrapped the blue blanket further and continued his examination. 'You think I've got X-ray fingers?' he mumbled, loud enough for all of them to hear. 'You expect me to conduct an examination in the middle of an airplane while I'm floating through space? My goddamn head hurts.'

'Wait a minute, doctor.' Collins felt the need to defend himself. Everyone was listening. He could feel their eyes on him. 'I don't want to be here either.'

'Then, for the love of God, get us down.' The doctor looked back at the unconscious baby before Collins could respond. The child's round face was framed with wisps of fuzzy brown curls. A blissful, sleeping infant – except that this one had been knocked unconscious and might be near death. 'The child may have green-stick fractures. His legs. See? That's what it looks like. He may have a concussion, too, although I don't see any physical damage to the skull. After I wrap him in the blanket, there's nothing else we can do but keep him warm. Not until we get to a proper facility. He's too young for most medications. Too young for most anything. He'll either live, or he won't. Someone change this diaper. Where's the mother?'

'I don't know.' Gayle wondered why he hadn't thought of that himself. 'Gayle, do you know?'

'Yes. I think so. I remember when she boarded. A young woman, she's sitting in the back somewhere.' Gayle wondered why the mother hadn't searched for her child.

'Okay. Go back to her.' Collins paused, then leaned forward, closer to the doctor. 'What should we tell her?' he whispered.

The doctor scowled. 'Tell her I'm examining the baby. Nothing more than that. Tell her I'll bring the baby back shortly.'

'Okay. Do what he says.' Collins didn't want to deal with the doctor any longer than he had to. He looked down the aisle. He could see a lot of movement in the rear of the cabin. Near the aft galley he could make out the black flight attendant, Adrienne, as she moved around cautiously. 'Call me if you need assistance. Let me know if you see any structural damage.'

'Yessir.' Gayle began to move carefully down the aisle, her hand gripped to the overhead rack tightly as she propelled herself toward the back of the airplane. 'Stay in your seats. Stay calm. Everything is under control,' she kept saying over and over, partially to reassure those passengers who had fully regained consciousness, and partially to stop anyone from asking questions that she couldn't answer. She knew that if she kept talking and kept moving, she could pretend that there was nothing to worry about. Gayle was amazed at how well everyone in the cabin had held up to the stress. Many were still groggy and dazed and several passengers appeared to need medical treatment, but on the whole, they had fared well. Better than she would have guessed.

'Miss. We need more airsick bags.'

'Yessir. I'll get some.' She forced a smile, then continued to move toward the rear. Gayle's grip on the overhead rack was so rigid that the muscles in her hands had begun to ache. She had to get more airsickness bags to the passengers or the globules of vomit that occasionally floated by would multiply. She thought about Carl Tyson's bizarre death. It had been a fifty-fifty chance. It could just as easily have been her. Carl had finished his pre-flight duties first, so he had been the one to take the inside seat. A progressive shiver ran up through her spine, and it almost caused Gayle to lose her grip on the overhead rack.

'Stewardess. My wife has a cut on her arm. We need a bandage.'

'We have a doctor on the airplane. He'll be here in a moment.'

'Thank you.'

Gayle nodded. The passengers seemed remarkably calm. Almost passive. They seemed to have emotionally accepted the captain's explanation. Most of them looked out the windows. Some talked quietly amongst themselves. A few sobbed or openly cried. But there were no longer any loud voices. No panicked screams. Gayle wondered how long their blind compliance would last.

'Miss. Please. Stop.'

A man in his mid-twenties tugged on her skirt. Reluctantly, Gayle turned toward him.

'This man,' he whispered across the short distance. 'I think he's dead.' He pointed to an elderly man in a three-piece suit who sat by the window.

Gayle could see that his skin was the same pale tone that Carl Tyson's had been. His facial expression was frozen in a grimace of pain. She reached across and touched his wrist to feel for a pulse. Nothing. His flesh was cold and clammy. This time, she felt no trembling horror, no massive fright. She was too numb to feel anything. 'Yes,' she whispered, you're right. We have a doctor on the airplane. I'll tell him. Please keep this to yourself.'

'Of course.'

She continued down the cabin, nodding, smiling, and using the same useless, senseless appeal that had worked so well. 'Stay in your seats. Stay calm. Everything is under control.' But inside, she was anything but calm herself – and she suspected that nothing was under control. She was so tense that her stomach seemed like an oversized hollow pit. Her voice seemed not her own. So far, there were two dead, plus the potentially critical injuries to the infant. As she passed the lavatories in the center of the cabin, she spotted the young woman who had boarded with the baby. She was seated further back, on the right side. She appeared to be unconscious, her head propped uncomfortably against the wall. That explained why she hadn't searched for her baby. Gayle rushed to her.

As Gayle touched the woman's shoulder, she opened her eyes and looked around.

'My baby,' Linda Lewis said in a choked, exhausted voice.

'He's alright. He's up front, with the doctor.'

'Doctor?' Linda managed a small vacuous smile. The vivid memories of the hospital, not two months old, had come back and mingled with the memories of the flight. The faraway voices were the doctors and nurses. There were bright lights above her. Everyone who walked past wore white coats and white masks. 'Doctor, how is the baby?'

'Fine,' Gayle lied. She began to examine the woman.

'Did you count his fingers?' Linda rambled. Her voice had begun to fade out incoherently. 'Isn't he beautiful?'

'Yes.' The woman had two large blotches of black-and-blue on her face, and a piece of skin dangled off the side of her chin. Gayle tore a section of cushion from the empty seat beside her. 'Hold this against your head. Like this.' She pressed the cloth against the raw, open cut.

'Has Andy seen the baby yet?' Linda slurred most of the words. She tried to raise her head off the seat back. She moved a few inches, but soon fell back again. 'Let me see my baby.'

'Very soon.' Gayle could see that she had lost a lot of blood. Incredibly, most of the blood was beside her, gathered together in a red sphere the size of a baseball. It floated in the empty space between the woman's seat and the row in front of her. 'Hold the cloth against your face. I'll be right back.' Gayle intended to get the doctor. She knew that bleeding had to be dealt with first. Dealt with quickly. She pushed herself out of the row and turned around. As she did, she saw that several people had rushed toward the front of the cabin.

'Hurry! She's choking!'

Chris Diederich was in the center of the aisle, her hands clawing at her neck, her mouth wide open. Even from where Gayle was, she could see that the Diederich woman's eyes had bulged out in terror.

'She's inhaled something! Damn it!' The doctor handed the bundled infant to one of the passengers, then began to move forward to the suffocating woman as quickly as he could.

Paul Diederich was the first to reach his wife. Her color had already turned. Her face was distinctly, unmistakably blue. 'Oh, my God.'

She looked at him in agony. She pressed as hard as she could against the front of her throat, in a futile attempt to dislodge whatever was trapped there. None of her meager efforts were successful. She could feel the object, raw, oversized, twisted, as it remained lodged in her windpipe. She knew she was dying.

Paul did not know what to do. He grabbed Chris's arm and twisted her around, then slapped her on the back as hard as he could. That motion caused him to be propelled backward in the weightlessnes, away from her. He could see that she still continued to choke. 'Help her. Someone. Please!' As he drifted across the width of the cabin, Paul reached out toward the opposite wall so he could use it to push himself back.

Chris drifted forward, into an empty row of seats. Her lungs were drawing down hard, but they were unable to get any air past the obstacle. The middle of her body screamed for air. Blood drained from her face. It seemed as if her throat and chest were ready to explode.

'Here!' The doctor yanked her out of the row, turned her around and positioned himself behind her. 'For chrissake, someone keep us steady,' he shouted as the two of them drifted together, the doctor holding firmly to Chris, toward the center of the aisle.

Collins had gotten close enough to grab the back of the doctor's shirt. 'Go ahead. I've got hold.' He latched on to the overhead rack with his free hand.

'She's fainted.'

Chris's head bobbed loosely up and down and her arms drifted aimlessly in front of her.

'Hurry.' To Collins, she looked just like Carl Tyson had when they had first found him in the galley. A lifeless marionette.

The doctor wrapped his arms around Chris's midsection. He made a fist with one hand and grabbed it with the other. He then pressed into her abdomen with a quick, upward thrust. The Heimlich maneuver. He had applied pressure to her diaphragm. The doctor knew that, most often, the air displaced from the victim's lungs was sufficient to pop the obstacle out of their windpipe.

The foreign object lodged in Chris's windpipe budged slightly. But it was too large, too irregularly shaped to come out. Chris Diederich continued to choke.

The doctor tried the Heimlich maneuver three more times.

66

Finally he gave up. 'We've got to do this fast.' He twisted Chris around and pushed her into an empty seat. He fumbled in his pocket and pulled out a small pocketknife. 'Hold her. Keep her head up.'

'Okay.' Collins grabbed Chris's head and pulled it back against the seat. Her face had grown a harsh, dark blue. Collins sweated profusely. 'Christ. Hurry.'

'Keep quiet.' The doctor opened his pocketknife and aimed it at Chris's throat. 'Raise her chin.'

'What the hell are you doing? My wife!' Paul Diederich lunged toward the doctor's arm.

'Get back, dammit!' The doctor turned aside to get out of Deiderich's reach. 'Someone get the husband away from me! Goddammit, get him away!'

Two passengers grabbed Diederich from behind and held him.

The doctor moved toward Chris again. 'Hold her chin. Hold it steady, for chrissake.'

'Yes. I'm trying.' Collins' hand shook. He wedged his legs into the adjacent row to give himself more leverage. 'Okay. Go ahead.'

The doctor ran his fingers along the base of Chris's throat. He quickly found the soft spot and, just above it, the cricothyroid cartilage. Using two fingers, he spread the tissue as flat as possible. He raised the pocketknife. 'Steady.' Without hesitating, he cased the knife expertly into her flesh.

A small splattering of blood flew out, the drops floating off into space like a scattering of buckshot. 'God.' Collins turned his eyes away as his own blood rushed to his stomach. He felt as if he might faint.

'Keep holding. Keep it steady.' The doctor maneuvered the knife around to create an incision in the woman's trachea large enough for air to move freely through. 'There.' He felt the first surge of her breath as it moved past his fingers. 'We've got it. She's breathing.' He let out a deep breath himself. 'Now we've got some time.' The doctor looked up, satisfied. 'Get me a tweezer. Something. I'll extract the object.'

Within a few seconds the doctor had been handed a pair of long tweezers. He began to work again. 'Open her mouth. Yes. That's

67

right.' He pulled her tongue out of the way. 'Yes, I see it. Just another minute. Here. I've got it. Wait. Yes, it's out.'

The doctor pulled the object out of Chris's throat. He held it up as if it were a trophy. It was a broken, jagged piece of red plastic the size of a quarter. 'Here it is,' he announced.

There were scattered murmurs of applause.

The doctor smiled. 'Thank you. But don't tell my malpractice carrier.' He turned to Paul Diederich, who had moved beside his wife. 'Once we patch up that little hole I made, she'll be good as new. She should regain consciousness shortly. There might be some pain, but not a great deal. I've got a sedative I can give her.'

Paul Diederich opened his mouth, but found that he could not speak. Big drops of tears began to streak across his face. 'Thank you,' he finally said in a soft, deferential voice. 'Thank you, doctor.'

'Okay, let's finish.' The doctor leaned over Chris and became engrossed in his work again as he checked her over and began to bandage her up.

'Can I let her chin go?' Collins asked nervously.

'Yes. Of course.' The doctor did not look up.

'I'm going back to the cockpit.' Collins pushed himself away gently, maneuvered around the crowd, and toward Gayle.

'Incredible,' Gayle said. 'I've read about tracheotomies in first aid, but I never could have done one.'

Collins did not answer. He looked around the cabin. Some order had been restored to the chaos, but not very much. Their real problems were still in front of them, still to be dealt with. 'Tell everyone to be careful about inhaling things,' he said. 'Have the cabin cleaned up. Use the passengers to help. Get the loose objects into bags. Stow them in the galley bins.'

'Yessir. There are two dead passengers in the cabin.'

'Two?' Collins looked toward the rear. Adrienne was trying to comfort an elderly woman. An old man was slumped down in the seat next to her.

'That woman's husband,' Gayle said as she followed Collins' eyes. 'Another elderly man, too. He was evidently traveling alone. What should we do with them?'

Collins felt as if his head were in a vise, as if his entire body were trapped in a tiny, dark tunnel that was caving in around him. 'Christ, I don't know,' he said, a little too loudly. Several people turned toward him. 'Let the doctor decide. Whatever he wants to do with the three bodies. It's a medical problem.' Collins grabbed the overhead rack and began to move himself forward.

'Wait.' Gayle looked at him. 'Are you okay?'

'Yes.' Collins kept his back to her as he continued to move off briskly, toward the front of the cabin. Without hesitating, he pushed himself into the swirl of debris around the galley, one hand over his nose and mouth. Instead of going into the cockpit, he turned to his right and went into the galley. He moved quickly past Tyson's body. He brushed lightly into the dead flight attendant's outstretched arms, but did not notice.

Collins opened a latched galley drawer. With fumbling hands he took out an airsickness bag. He pried it open quickly and stuck it against his mouth. He began to vomit repeatedly. The bile from his stomach burned his tongue. When he had finally finished, Collins sealed the bag and placed it in one of the bins.

Out of the corner of his eye, he saw something that he wanted. Something that he needed. Collins snatched it out of midair as it floated past him on the inside edge of the hovering debris. He looked at it. A miniature bottle of Seagram's whiskey, its colorful label filling his field of vision. Collins had never, in his 25 years of flying, taken a drink during a flight. But this was not a flight. This was a cruel nightmare.

Collins unscrewed the cap, put the bottle to his lips and drained it quickly. He could feel the warmth as it traveled down the middle of his body and dumped into his empty, knotted stomach. He flung the empty Seagram's bottle toward the back of the galley, into the mass of debris. Then he closed his eyes, pressed his hands against his head, and allowed himself to drift along slowly, his back and shoulders rubbing against the galley wall. Donald Collins doubted if he could take one more minute of this madness.

Chapter Four

DR. RALPH Kennerdale stood on the rear steps of the Capitol Building and looked toward the parking lot. A group of Girl Scouts strode past him in double file on their way up the marble staircase. A cluster of Japanese tourists stood to his left, and in unison they pointed their cameras at the building's dome. 'Excuse me,' Kennerdale mumbled as he maneuvered around them. Fragments of their singsong conversation floated around him as he methodically scanned the half-empty parking lot.

'Dr. Kennerdale. Over here.'

Kennerdale turned. Gilbert Novak waved at him from the driver's seat of the NASA staff car parked 50 feet away. Kennerdale continued down the steps. With the summer tourist season over, there wouldn't be much noonday traffic to contend with on the way to Goddard. From what Novak had said on the phone, time would be a crucial factor. It always was.

Kennerdale approached the car on the driver's side. 'Who else knows?' he asked, as soon as he was close enough to speak in a normal tone. Lately, Novak's owlish-looking facial expressions made his skin crawl, and he often regretted that he had taken on the young man as his personal aide. Next time, he would pick someone lighter on intelligence and stronger on obedience.

'No one. I took the first call.'

'Good.' Kennerdale hesitated a moment, then stepped toward the rear door. 'I'll sit back here,' he said as he slid into the Cadillac's back seat. He wanted a few quiet moments to think things over. He still had enough time left to change his mind and play it by the book. If his plan didn't work out, Kennerdale knew that his career would be over, to say the least.

'Furgeson leaves on the ten-fifteen flight,' Novak said as he wheeled the car out of the parking lot. He glanced in the rearview mirror, but all he saw was a flash of Kennerdale's silver-gray hair as the assistant administrator moved to the far corner of the back seat.

'From Dulles?'

'Yes. It's a nonstop.'

Kennerdale nodded, then glanced at his wristwatch. Nine fifty-five. For the next twenty minutes, they would be violating one of the space agency's procedures by not notifying the most senior official in the chain of command. Irwin Lynch, the director of NASA, was on the China trip and Deputy Director Les Furgeson was next in line. 'Did you say anything to Furgeson's secretary?'

'No. I made it sound routine. I verified the times for both his departure and return.'

'Fine.' Kennerdale removed his wire-rimmed glasses and rubbed the bridge of his nose. He had disliked both Lynch and Furgeson from the very first and, as far as he was concerned, his hunch had proven correct. The director and deputy director had both come to NASA when the new administration had taken over, and both men had shown themselves to be nothing but budget-cutters. 'What kind of information did you leave at headquarters?'

'Only that I was picking you up, and we would be at Goddard.'

'Good thinking.' Novak's star was on the rise. Maybe, Kennerdale thought, his young assistant would become an asset after all.

'Thank you.'

Kennerdale sat back in his seat and thought about what he was about to do, and why. Even more than Lynch, Les Furgeson had become NASA's official equivocator. Furgeson would never give the go-ahead for anything remotely risky. An attempted rescue mission on that stranded airliner, no matter how beneficial it might be for the agency, would be outside the province of his pedestrian thinking. Once Furgeson was onboard that flight to Los Angeles, the rescue mission could be played strictly by the rules. Dr. Ralph Kennerdale, the most senior of the old-line NASA headquarters people, was the next in the chain of command. 'Have you heard any more on the airliner?' Kennerdale asked as he leaned forward.

'Yes.' Novak always waited for Kennerdale to ask for what he wanted. Volunteering information was the quickest way to piss him off. 'What I told you on the phone has been confirmed,' Novak said as he steered the Cadillac onto Constitution Avenue, then began to weave carefully around the sparse traffic. 'Consolidated Flight fourteen, en route from New York to Melbourne, is trapped in a low, circular orbit. The rocket engines somehow locked on. The first estimates peg their orbit at approximately a hundred and ten miles.'

'How the hell could something like that happen?'

'Damned if I know,' Novak answered.

Kennerdale nodded. He had seen machines do too many impossible things. The *Apollo 13* in-flight emergency had caused him months of aggravation. At least that potential disaster had turned out okay. But the major incident before that, the fire in the cockpit of the first *Apollo* test vehicle, had nearly spelled the end of the program. Astronauts Grissom, White and Chaffee were inside the capsule when a fire – another impossibility, according to the engineers – had broken out. The three astronauts had burned to death. During the investigation that followed, it appeared as if the entire *Apollo* program would be killed as quickly as the astronauts had. The never-ending congressional inquiries, the second-guesses from industry and the *mea culpas* from the NASA people had nearly been too much to weather. Luckily, Kennerdale and a few of the others managed to influence enough of the proper people to save the program. 'Anything is possible,' Kennerdale said, as he began to think about the airliner again.

'I guess.'

'Did we get any estimate of their decay time?' Even though he was basically an administrator, Kennerdale had learned enough in his many years with the space agency to understand the elementary concepts of space travel. At 110 miles, the airliner had not gone high and fast enough to totally escape the effects of the Earth's gravity. After a certain period of time in a low orbit, it would be dragged down to Earth again. It would be as graphic as Newton's apples.

'I discussed the decay time with the people at Goddard. Thirty hours is their current guess. Maybe more.'

'Oxgyen?'

'Six or seven hours remaining. The airline is working up an exact figure.'

'Shit.' Kennerdale strummed his fingers on the velour seat. 'We've got less time than I thought.'

'Yes. It seems that way.' From the very first when the emergency phone call had been routed to his office, Gilbert Novak had realized their good fortune. It didn't take him long to convince Kennerdale. Novak knew that if they successfully pulled off a rescue, everyone – including himself – would get a share of the credit. If the rescue flopped, it would be Kennerdale's ass. 'How did the budget hearings go this morning?' he asked solicitously.

'Not well.' Kennerdale thought about the infuriating morning he had spent on the Hill. The space telescope was a dead issue, and so was the second-generation Shuttle program. The way things stood now, there'd be no Jupiter shots and no funding for a Mars landing. Fucking politicians. They'd hock their mothers' pacemakers for votes.

'Which group was it?'

'The education coalition. Bastards. They want more audio-visual programs for grade-school children, or some such crap. The little morons can't read, so they're going to show them pictures instead. The assholes from Health and Welfare are backing that fiasco to the hilt.' As far as Kennerdale was concerned, the lobby groups in Washington were willing to swap the future of America – the future of the world, really – for another batch of do-nothing programs. All it ever meant was more paperwork, and more staff to administer it. Kennerdale needed a way to get the congressional mood swung back to being pro-space and pro-NASA, the way it was in the early sixties. A dramatic rescue by NASA's Space Shuttle would be just the ticket. 'Have you mentioned that Shuttle-rescue idea to anyone?'

'No. All I've said so far is that NASA can provide communications and technical advice. That's what they're billing as our contribution to the rescue.'

'Good. Sit tight on that Shuttle idea. I need to check it out. If anyone suggests it to you, I want you to dismiss it out-of-hand. Tell them it's impossible.'

'Right.'

'How are the survivors on that airliner doing?'

'They're still alive, or at least they were a while ago. Now we're not sure.'

'Why?'

'Radio problems.' Novak frowned. He hated technical things. He had gone to Harvard Business School, not Cal Tech, and he had no desire to spend time chatting about radio failures and reception distances. 'We lost radio contact a short time after their first distress message. But it could be anything. The Goddard technician figured it was probably positioning.'

'Probably.' Kennerdale reached into his pocket for a cigarette. The technician had a point. Radio problems with orbital vehicles were often caused by the flight's position in relation to the Earth-based antennas. On the other hand, if none of the people onboard Flight 14 were alive, that would account for it also. Kennerdale was deep in thought when the phone in the car buzzed. He laid his unlit cigarette down and snatched up the phone. 'Yes?'

'Hello, Ralph? It's John Sample.'

Kennerdale groaned. The administrator of the Federal Aviation Agency was not the man he most wanted to talk to. Not now, not ever. 'Hello, John,' he said, without enthusiasm. Kennerdale had never gotten along with him, and he knew that Sample and Lynch often played tennis together.

'You don't sound happy to hear from me,' Sample said tauntingly. He had no great love for Kennerdale. His friend Irwin Lynch had told him repeatedly that Ralph Kennerdale was a pain in the ass. A pompous, holier-than-thou bureaucrat who acted as

74

if he were beyond the jurisdiction of elected and appointed officials.

'Don't be silly, John. What can I do for you?'

'I understand you'll be in charge of coordinating the rescue on the Consolidated flight?'

'Maybe. If there is one.' Kennerdale wondered how Sample had found out so soon. From the airline, probably. 'It's too early to say for certain.'

'Of course.' Sample paused. 'I know that Irwin Lynch is in China. Where's Les Furgeson?'

'En route to Los Angeles. He left this morning,' Kennerdale lied. He glanced at his watch. Ten-o-five. Kennerdale squirmed in his seat. For all he knew, Les Furgeson could be stepping into an airport phone booth at that very moment with a fistful of dimes.

'Then I won't keep you. I realize you're busy. I assume you'll set up a command post at the Goddard Center?'

'Yes.' Kennerdale looked out the window. The Robert F. Kennedy Stadium was behind them, and they were about to cross the East Capitol Street Bridge. From there it was no more than ten miles to Goddard, a straight shot up the Baltimore-Washington Parkway. 'I'll be at the Center in fifteen minutes. I'll keep you posted.'

'There's no need, although I appreciate the offer. I'll assign a technical representative from the FAA. He'll contact you at Goddard and you can establish a communications liaison with him to our appropriate offices.'

'Wait, John.' Kennerdale could think of no way to phrase it cautiously. He ran his hand nervously along the window molding. 'Why don't we do it an easier way,' he finally said. 'I'll call you directly, if we need help.' Kennerdale listened to dead silence from the other end of the telephone for several seconds.

'Don't be ridiculous.' Sample laughed, then his voice grew cold and firm. 'You know damn well that the FAA has legal jurisdiction. I won't press the point, but I'm not going to be brushed off, either. It's still an airliner, so we've got our own interests to cover. Don't waste any time with that don't-call-us routine. My man will contact you shortly after you get to Goddard. And Ralph, one more thing.'

'Yes?'

'I'd like to make a suggestion.'

'What is it?'

'I think it would be wise on your part if you made damn sure that the Federal Aviation Administration is used properly during this attempted rescue.'

Before Kennerdale could respond, the phone clicked off. 'Son of a bitch,' he said.

'What?'

'Never mind.' Kennerdale waved his hand distractedly at his aide, then turned and looked out the window. With the FAA involved, NASA would have to share a portion of the credit for a successful rescue. Kennerdale didn't want to share any of it. Certainly not with any of the *them*. They were all spineless paper shufflers. Leeches. Kennerdale had half a mind to fix those bastards by not taking charge of the rescue. They sure as hell wouldn't. They'd do something typical, like initiate a feasibility study. It would drag on for longer than the survivors could hold out – if there were any survivors. If it wasn't for the enormous potential for good public relations for NASA, Kennerdale knew that he would drop the idea of a rescue. 'Gilbert, I need a match,' he said after he picked up his cigarette.

'I thought you gave it up.'

'No. I never said that. You suggested that I should, but I never answered.'

'Right.' Novak smiled. One of the benefits of being the boss was that your memory could be as selective as you cared to make it.

Kennerdale reached out and grabbed the book of matches. He lit his cigarette, then inhaled deeply. As he blew out a long swirl of smoke, the car phone buzzed again. Kennerdale took another puff before he picked up the handset. 'Kennerdale,' he said tersely.

'Hello, Ralph. This is Stuart Goldman. I hear we've got quite a problem on our hands.'

'Yes.' Kennerdale's mind whirled. Goldman was the President's personal advisor. He had spoken to him a few times, but only briefly and always at official functions.

'I'll get right to the point,' Goldman said. 'Any attempted rescue of the passengers and crew of that trapped airliner is something we feel has great potential. Candidly, it's political dynamite. I'm going to be contacting you periodically, so I can keep the President close to the situation. I wanted to let you know how important the President feels this rescue might become.'

'Thank you.' Kennerdale shook his head. His plan was being turned into a circus. 'But I'm a little concerned that we might spread ourselves too thin. What I mean,' he said hesitantly, 'is that my people at Goddard are going to be damned busy. The FAA has also requested to be kept informed. The staff at Goddard is not our largest, and I'm beginning to think . . .'

'Don't worry,' Goldman interrupted. 'I only intend to speak with one person. You. I'm sure,' he continued dryly, 'that you'll be able to find a spare moment to talk to me.'

'Yes. Certainly.' Kennerdale ignored the barb. He knew he had no choice but to come running to the damn phone every time Goldman called. But there was no need for him to make it too easy, to be too cooperative, to volunteer too much. 'All we can provide is coordination. I don't see how we're going to come up with a workable plan to save those people. I pray that we can,' Kennerdale said, even though he already had firm ideas on how he intended to rescue them.

'Of course. We all do.' After they exchanged a few perfunctory remarks, Goldman hung up.

Kennerdale sank back into the deeply cushioned seat. He could see that they were nearly at the Parkway's Goddard exit. From there, it would only be a few more miles until they reached the NASA Center. Kennerdale glanced out the rear window and up at the sky. Through the broken deck of clouds he could see patches of blue. He wondered for a moment where in its orbit the airliner might be.

'It's ten-fifteen,' Novak announced solemnly.

Kennerdale nodded. It was now official. He was in charge. For the first time since the talk of the rescue mission had begun less than an hour before, Ralph Kennerdale felt that he had stuck his neck out too far. The attempted rescue would be a risky affair. Worse, he had given John Sample and Stuart Goldman ammunition to use against him, although Kennerdale imagined that it would be easy enough to get around the problem of what time Furgeson's flight had actually left for Los Angeles. Novak would be the obvious fall guy for that if it ever came to it. The real crime of the whole mess was that it was probably all for naught. Kennerdale had a feeling that, more than likely, everyone onboard that airliner was already dead.

Ben Robinson sat rigidly in the back seat of the yellow cab as it weaved around the Washington traffic. The cab's meter ticked away, cold air leaked around the rattling doors, and drops of water splashed against the windows as they sped through the puddles that remained from the overnight rain. Robinson watched the young driver as he reached to tune the portable radio that lay on the dashboard. The scratchy, irritating sounds of rock music mixed with the continuous road noises and filtered across to the back seat. 'Driver,' Robinson said in a loud voice. He leaned forward. 'How much longer to Goddard?'

'Not much traffic. Thirty, thirty-five minutes.'

'Thank you.' Robinson sat back and watched the passing rows of government buildings. The dome of the Capital was visible in the distance. He fidgeted in his seat, then kicked inattentively at a small clump of dirt on the floor of the dirty taxi.

Sabotage. As he waited for the cab, he had spent those idle minutes in front of the Astrex office trying, halfheartedly, to convince himself that his theory was wrong, that Lee's cautions were correct. But the more he thought about it, the more he knew that it was the only explanation. Otherwise, there were too many impossibilities and coincidences to be explained away, too many dangling, nagging questions that could only be answered if the premise of sabotage was accepted as fact.

Okay. Keep backtracking. Find the next logical step. Find a motive. Robinson rubbed his eyes, then glanced out the window at a row of dismal houses packed tightly along a side street. His mind began to click off the possibilities.

Revenge? It was possible, but not very likely. The sabotage scheme seemed too complex, too elaborate to have been nothing but a madman's idea of retribution. There were too many easy ways to cause problems for United Aerospace and Consolidated Airways. A psycho would've done something quick, like planting a homemade bomb or trying to murder key personnel. He wouldn't have spent countless hours in the design and construction of what was essentially a one-shot weapon.

Adverse publicity? Financial instability? The publicity from a tragic accident would be bad, and there would unquestionably be costs involved. But it was all calculable. The public had a short memory, and the financial stability of either the manufacturer or the airline would not be in jeopardy. Insurance would pay the greatest portion of it anyway. From a strictly business point of view, the sabotage of one *Star Streak* would have little long-range effect. Robinson could rule out bizarre financial schemes or corporate conspiracies.

Money. Robinson sat upright. *Ransom.* He clinched his fists. *Hostages. Kidnapping.* Suddenly, it all fit. A plan as complex as this one would tie it all together. Nearly one hundred passengers were aboard that aircraft. They were now trapped beyond reach. It was the ultimate kidnapping.

Robinson shook his head. He could see how futile the NASA involvement was going to be. The saboteur had been far too thorough to leave any obvious way to get that ship out of orbit before its onboard oxygen ran out. The Space Agency's involvement – the use of its communications and tracking network – would actually help the saboteur's plans. The kidnap victims would be provided with the most sophisticated method available to send their pleas for help. But there was nothing that could be done for them. They had become the perfect bargaining pawns. There was no question about what would happen next if the ransom demands weren't met.

Two devices. Of course! Two separate devices were planted on that *Star Streak* – one to get them trapped into orbit, and another to get them down again! Without that second device – or at least the assurance of a second device – the first one would be useless.

Robinson took a notepad out of his jacket pocket and jotted down a few key words. The engineering involved in getting the *Star Streak* out of orbit seemed less complex than what had

79

already been displayed in getting it up. Robinson knew that any one of a dozen possibilities -- an extra tank of rocket fuel or some exotic propellant stuck away in an inaccessible spot and actuated by a coded electronic signal – would work. It would get the airliner started out of its orbit and back into the atmosphere. Then the *Star Streak*'s normal jet engines could be restarted to bring it home. It would be the location and operation of that second device that would be exchanged for the ransom. The usual bargain would be struck: lives for money. Robinson put his notepad away.

In spite of the drafty breeze in the back seat of the cab, Robinson was drenched with sweat. He took out a handkerchief and used it to wipe the perspiration off his forehead. If his theory was correct, then the saboteur would soon make contact. The offer for the exchange would have to be made quickly, to give the airline a chance to deliver the money. The first contact would come very soon.

But who could it be? It seemed incredible that anyone outside United Aerospace could have designed and installed the sabotage device, then somehow managed to get it safely past the quality-control computer checks. There were not more than half a dozen people in the world who had the knowledge and ability to meet those requirements.

Becker. McBride. Krause. Robinson's handkerchief fell to the floor. His mouth hung slack-jawed as scattered, fragmented thoughts finally came together. He knew that the three electronic engineers from United Aerospace had each volunteered for this month's trip to Baltimore. The three of them were now conveniently – coincidentally – within a short distance of being at the proper place. It was almost the proper time.

Becker. McBride. Krause. Each of them had unlimited access to that *Star Streak* while it was in Phoenix the month before, and unlimited access to the engineering drawings and computer quality-control data. They each had enough personal knowledge of the *Star Streak* to design and construct an electronic system that could've done precisely what had happened to Consolidated Flight 14 – something almost no one else could have done. Robinson looked down at his hand. It was shaking. He leaned

80

forward. 'Driver. Can you go faster? I've got to get to Goddard as soon as possible. It's urgent.'

'I'm going the limit now.'

Robinson fumbled in his pocket. He pulled out a wad of bills. 'Here's twenty if you step on it.'

'I've already got two points on my license.'

'Here's twenty more.' Robinson held another bill in his hand. 'It's yours. But only if you get me to Goddard within fifteen minutes.'

The driver eyed the bills in the rearview mirror. 'Sure thing, Mac.'

As the taxi wheeled into the left lane and shot ahead of the other traffic, Robinson sat back in his seat. He knew that Ferrera's telephone call to intercept the United Aerospace people at the Martin plant would have been the expected first step. It was the beginning of a long and complex chain of events that had been carefully planned. Unless Lee was right and the entire sabotage theory was no more than a fantasy born out of Robinson's personal anguish and despair, the saboteur of Consolidated Flight 14 was one of the three United Aerospace engineers now in Baltimore.

With the pilot's manual strapped to the engineer's desk in front of her, Katie Graham finished the last of the items she had been asked to verify. 'Captain. The cruise-profile checklist is complete. Is there anything else you'd like me to do?'

'No.' Collins had answered without turning around in his flight chair. He continued to work with the series of monitoring lights on his side console. 'Not yet. Maybe soon.'

'Fine.' Katie sat forward and allowed herself to look closely at the profile of Ernie Briscoe. He was a handsome, rugged man. He was young and full of energy. Sometimes he spoke a little too quickly, but that wasn't too much of a fault. At least he wasn't a hypocrite. Ernie had simply never learned how to overlook incompetence, and that was good – especially today. Katie was glad that he had been onboard, glad that the outcome of Flight 14 didn't depend solely on Donald Collins.

'Finished,' Briscoe announced, a degree of annoyance in his

voice. He slid his flight chair backward and looked at Collins. 'Is there anything else you want me to do? Do you have any other vital projects in mind?'

Collins looked at the copilot for several long seconds, as if he might respond to the hostile tone of Briscoe's voice. 'No,' Collins finally answered without emphasis. 'I'll let you know when.' The captain turned back to his side console.

'Fine with me,' Briscoe turned half around to face Katie. He looked at her directly, nodded toward Collins, then shrugged in disgust.

Katie smiled and nodded sympathetically. She agreed that Collins had done nothing but find countless ways to waste their time with nonsensical checklists, although she hadn't come up with any other ideas about what to do while they waited. 'Did everything on the cruise profiles check within limits?' she asked Briscoe. The captain's attention remained focused on the panel to his left. Katie picked up her hand, reached across the short space between her and Briscoe and rested her hand on his shoulder.

'On the button.' Briscoe laid his own hand on top of hers. Her fingers were smooth and delicate, and the warmth of her skin felt incredibly sensual. He let his eyes roam across the tight lines of her body, the soft swells that marked her breasts. 'When we get down, I'm taking you for for the biggest afterflight drink you've ever had.'

'Make it two drinks.'

'How about three?'

'Sure thing.' Katie smiled, slid her hand on top of Briscoe's and squeezed it. She knew how ironic it was that she had made romantic plans for a time that might never arrive. But perhaps it wasn't so ironic after all, perhaps it was only natural that one basic urge – the fear of death – would be balanced by another. That was what her college psychology professor had said. He also would have pointed out that it was nothing to be embarrassed over. Natural, human urges. That was a good way to put it. It was a good concept to understand. When they finally got the *Star Streak* out of orbit, Katie intended to climb into bed with Ernie Briscoe, and she didn't intend to climb out until she was thoroughly satisfied.

*   *   *

The cabin of the airliner had regained a semblance of order. A few clusters of dirt and dust hovered in midair, but the greatest mass of debris had already been gathered up and stowed in the galley and overhead bins. The broken sections of Fiberglas, the pillows, coats, magazines and bits of food that had floated everywhere were gone. At least that part of the problem was behind them. 'Are the bodies strapped down?' Gayle VanCroft asked. Her face was covered with perspiration.

'Yes.'

'Good. Thank you.'

'It's still dark,' Adrienne said nervously as she peered out the small window in the forward galley. The moon had risen a few minutes before and it hovered low in the sky, a big sphere of white laced with blotches of gray and black. Its glow provided a measure of illumination for the dark sky, but not enough to light up the ground beneath them. The earth remained engulfed in an ominous and impenetrable black. 'We might be over an ocean. That might be why we can't see any ground lights.'

Gayle watched Adrienne's eyes. They were glassy. She seemed perilously close to losing control of herself. Gayle knew that if another member of the crew went into hysterics – as Nancy Oehlbeck had – that would be the end of the precarious order that had been restored to the cabin. 'Are you okay?' she asked. She gently touched her arm.

Adrienne shivered involuntarily. 'Yes,' she said without conviction. Adrienne pushed herself away from the galley window, but as she floated backward she carefully kept herself turned from the rear of the cabin where the three blanketed figures lay strapped across a row of seats. 'Believe it or not,' Adrienne admitted nervously, 'I never touched a dead person before. It's a horrible feeling. One had his eyes open. I didn't know what to do.'

'You did fine,' Gayle assured her. She, too, had been afraid to reach down and close the dead man's eyes. She had wanted the doctor to do it, but he was too busy. Instead, no one had. She could picture the old man's face beneath the blanket, his hideous stare locked straight ahead. Thank God that two of the men in the cabin had taken care of wrapping the blankets around Carl

Tyson's body. Gayle shuddered. It seemed ironic that she had lived for 36 years and had been so totally insulated from death.

'Did the doctor say what could've killed the passengers?' Adrienne asked in a hushed voice.

'No.' The doctor hadn't offered a verdict, and Gayle had seen no reason to ask for one. She had guessed that the two elderly men who died during the violent climb into orbit had suffered strokes or heart attacks. If it were something else that killed them – something that might eventually affect each of them – Gayle preferred not to know. She would find out soon enough. 'Did you get the doctor's name?' she asked as she looked around the cabin for him. She spotted him strapped in a seat in the aft end of the cabin, bandaging a woman's arm. 'I didn't get a chance to ask him.'

'Akins. He's an eye surgeon.'

'He's good with a knife.' Both flight attendants looked to where Chris Diederich sat quietly, her eyes open, her head back against the seat cushion. There was a large white bandage around her neck. Akins had already given her a sedative.

The woman in seat 6B suddenly let out a piercing, hysterical scream. Her husband looked at her with a mixture of concern and embarrassment, then grabbed her arms and held them forcibly down. The woman was transfixed by a book that had suddenly appeared out of nowhere. It floated a few feet in front of her. She remained oblivious to her husband and the others who turned to watch.

'See if you can stop her. She'll get the whole cabin going again.'

Adrienne frowned. 'I don't know what I can do. She's scared out of her mind.'

'So am I. Do what you can.'

'Okay.'

Gayle watched as Adrienne moved slowly and carefully, her motion something of a cross between the strokes of a swimmer and the crawl of a baby. She stayed near the overhead luggage rack so she could use it as a hand hold. That was the best way to get around. Zero gravity was a frightening experience because if you allowed yourself to drift too far from the cabin wall, you would be stranded in midair. Then nothing – not flailing your arms nor kicking your legs – would have the slightest effect on your motion. Eventually, like a rowboat drifting toward a dock, you would sail close enough to something to throw an arm or a leg out to anchor yourself. Until then, the feeling of utter helplessness was overpowering. 'Adrienne,' Gayle called out. 'A cabinet is open. To your left.' One of the overhead bins had jarred open, which accounted for where the first book had come from. Two additional books and a handful of magazines slid out while Gayle spoke.

'I'll get them.'

Gayle watched the hovering books as Adrienne moved toward them. In relation to the rest of the cabin, the books and magazines had begun to tumble. If you watched the books closely, it appeared as if they were the stationary objects and the airplane was in motion around them. It made Gayle think of the prints of M.C. Escher paintings that her boyfriend had given her. The weird, surrealistic disorientations. The stairways that melted from vertical to horizontal. The characters that could move simultaneously in all directions. Those Escher paintings were like the airliner they rode in. Nothing had a proper up or down. Every angle was just as correct – or just as wrong. That lack of reference was what had gotten Nancy Oehlbeck to go into raving hysterics, and it was probably part of the panic the woman in 6B felt. Gayle rubbed her eyes. She tried to get her thoughts back to more practical matters.

'Miss?'

Gayle turned. It was the doctor. 'Yes?'

He moved closer. 'I've got more sedative with me that I didn't tell you about. An additional bottle of Vistaril,' he whispered as he held up the small vial. 'I didn't want to mention it with the others around. It's partially empty and it's not enough for more than three or four more people. I wanted to keep it in reserve. But that woman,' he said as he glanced over his shoulder toward the passenger in 6B, 'is bad enough to warrant a dose.'

'How much have you given out?'

'Too much.' Akins frowned. He gestured toward the woman in seat 22C. 'I gave that old woman the most. She's in shock from her husband's death. Clinical hysteria. There was no other way to

85

deal with her. The Diederich woman got a fair amount. I used what was left in the first bottle for seven or eight smaller doses.' Akins waved his hand toward the cabin. Everyone wanted a sedative. They seemed to think that a poke from his needle would solve their problems. Better living through fucking chemistry.

'It's your decision, doctor. Use the sedative as you see fit.' Gayle saw no reason to get involved in an area she could delegate to someone else.

'I just wanted you to know.' Akins touched the bandage he had put on his forehead. The deep gash beneath it had begun to throb.

'How long is the sedative effective?'

'Depends on the dose. Four hours. Maybe longer.'

Gayle glanced at Christ Diederich. The sedative the doctor had given her had obviously worked well. Thank God. Four extra hours of this madness was too much to ask from her. Too much to ask from any of them. 'Save some for me.'

'Sure.'

Gayle turned and watched Adrienne. She had gathered up the loose books, closed the cabinet, and had begun to talk to the woman in 6B. Her hysterical screams were replaced by a sobbing cry. As Adrienne continued to talk, the woman seemed to regain more of her composure. 'It sounds like she's getting better.'

'No,' the doctor said emphatically. 'She sure as hell is not. You'll see in a few minutes.' Akins resented the need to explain his diagnosis. He was a craftsman, and his patients, to him, were no more than overly animated objects who existed solely to allow him to display his surgical and medical skills. He had already made up his mind about the patient in 6B. 'The slightest provocation will set her off again. I'm certain you realize that hysteria is contagious.'

'Yes.' Gayle remembered what had happened to Nancy Oehlbeck. It was a scene of utter insanity. When Nancy inadvertently floated upside down, she began to scream hysterically. After only a few seconds, half the cabin was in a frenzy. If one of the men in the cabin hadn't grabbed Nancy and calmed her down, there might have been no way to stop the panic from spreading. 'Let's do whatever you think is best.'

Dr. Akins nodded. That was clearly the reply he had expected.

Gayle looked down the aisle at Nancy Oehlbeck, who was still strapped to the seat she had been left in. The young stewardess appeared to be in a lethargic stupor. Her face was streaked with tears. 'Doctor, did you give that flight attendant a sedative?'

'I gave her some. I might give her more.' Dr. Akins turned abruptly and began to work his way slowly toward the sobbing woman in 6B, his hand clasped tightly to the protruding edge of the overhead luggage rack.

Gayle took a deep breath to steady herself, then glanced out the window. The moon was higher in the night sky, and the horizon seemed to glow faintly from underneath. She pushed herself nearer to the window in the galley wall. As her eyes adjusted to the darkness outside, Gayle saw hundreds of tiny pulsations of light far out ahead of them. It took her a few moments to realize that what she observed were the lightning flashes from a large area of thunderstorms.

Several of the pinpoints of lightning would go off at once, and they, in turn, would trigger dozens of other flashes across the wide area. The pyrotechnics would last for several seconds and then the area would go black. After a four- or five-second pause, the lightning sequence would begin again. Sometimes that entire section of the sky would light up, but not long enough for her to identify any of the features on the ground.

The lightning phenomenon was, in a strange way, reassuring. It was the first evidence of normality. Gayle swung her body into position for a better view. As her legs moved across the galley, her foot inadvertently hit the top of the large coffee jug in the rack. The toe of her shoe kicked the restraining clip that held down its lid. Gayle felt the slight motion but ignored it.

Unnoticed by Gayle, and unfettered by the normal restrains of gravity, the boiling hot coffee began to edge up to the top of the jug. The inherent surface tension of the liquid, which was an insignificant factor when normal gravity was present, became the mass's dominant influence. The black liquid formed itself into a perfect sphere – the shape and color of a dark and forbidding planet – and then floated out of the jug and into the galleyway. It hovered unnoticed a few feet behind Gayle.

Finished with the view out the window, Gayle pushed herself

away and turned toward the window on the other side of the galley. As her body came around, she was face-to-face with the spherical globe of boiling hot liquid. She moved slowly but intractably toward the floating sphere of coffee. 'Help! Help me!' She screamed. She turned back to the galley wall, but was already too far away to reach anything to hold on to. She continued to drift helplessly toward the liquid.

'Help me! Someone help!' She could hear a bevy of excited voices from the cabin. They were coming. But the distance between her and the hot liquid was less than 24 inches. 'Hurry!' she shouted. She kicked her legs frantically, but it had no effect on her slow, drifting path. The liquid hovered nearer. Eighteen inches. Twelve inches. Six inches.

Gayle ducked her head in an attempt to stay under the floating glob of coffee, and she managed to get her forehead several inches beneath the hot liquid. The radiant heat simmered off its surface. Gayle saw that the coffee would pass over her harmlessly, as long as she kept her head down a few seconds longer. She stayed rigid, her chin tucked as close to her chest as she could manage.

But Gayle did not see the trail that her long blond hair made. It hung above and behind her, unable to fall naturally because of the weightlessness. The sphere of coffee drifted into the strands of hair. It had found a suitable path and traveled quickly down it. The hot, boiling liquid poured against the back of Gayle's head, then enshrouded her face like a giant jellyfish intent on its prey. The liquid covered her eyes, nostrils and mouth. It clung tenaciously to her skin and burned and blistered every inch of it, in spite of her wild, hysterical clawing to push it away.

Dr. Akins was the first to arrive in the galley, with Paul Diederich behind him. 'Quick! A blanket.'

'Where?'

'Over there.' Akins pointed toward a red airline blanket stuffed into a nearby compartment. Akins grabbed the blanket from Diederich and flung it against the burning coffee. The liquid splattered out in all directions, like hot grease from a skillet, and he could feel the blistering impact as drops of it touched his skin. After a few attempts, he managed to get the coffee off the unconscious stewardess. He pulled Gayle into the cabin. 'Stay here with the blanket,' Akins said, out of breath. 'Keep the liquid contained in that area until it cools.'

'Okay.' Paul Diederich held the blanket in front of him as a shield. He braced himself against the coat closet opposite the galley entrance. The coffee had broken up into hundreds of smaller globules and most of it had floated harmlessly against the far galley wall.

Akins moved to an empty seat in the third row and placed Gayle in it. He pulled out the seat belt and strapped her in.

'How is she?'

Akins didn't bother to look up. 'Not good.' He concentrated on examining the stewardess's face. A beautiful face. To the untrained eye it appeared as if she had nothing beyond a bad sunburn. But Akins knew that the skin had been ruined. Boiled like a lobster. The trauma had been severe. She would be hideously scarred, and if she didn't get proper medical treatment soon, she might die. Severe burns were nasty, difficult problems to deal with. Akins had always disliked burns because, no matter how talented the doctor was, there was always some evidence afterward that his work hadn't been perfect. It was a blemish on the physician's skill. Akins reached into his pocket, pulled out the half-empty vial of Vistaril, and filled his syringe. He injected the unconscious stewardess with a double dose.

'Christ. What happened?'

Akins glanced up at the new voice. It came from a man who wore uniform epaulets, each with three gold stripes. The copilot. Akins had seen him earlier, when he had come back from the cockpit to speak briefly with the stewardess. 'Burns. From hot coffee. Do we have any ice onboard?'

'Here's ice,' Paul Diedcrich said as he pulled himself over to the row of seats where the unconscious stewardess had been strapped. 'I figured that's what you'd want.' He handed Akins a covered bucket.

'What I need is a hospital burn unit,' the doctor said with annoyance. He grabbed the ice bucket from Diederich. As he took the cover off, several ice cubes floated away in different directions. 'The hell with them. Let them go. They'll evaporate.'

Akins grabbed for more ice. He began to apply the cold, wet cubes against Gayle's skin.

'Adrienne. Go to the cockpit and get the first-aid kit from there,' Briscoe ordered. 'I think it might have a bottle of burn ointment in it.' He pointedly resisted the compulsion to stare down at the unconscious stewardess. She was too attractive to deserve having her face badly disfigured. 'Don't forget to tell the captain what happened,' Briscoe said. The stewardess clung tremulously to the overhead rail as she moved past Briscoe and toward the cockpit door.

'Thank you,' Akins said sincerely. He was glad that someone onboard still knew how to exercise authority.

'I'll shut off the galley power,' Briscoe added. 'We don't want a repeat performance. Is there anything else I can do?'

'Yes. You can get us on the ground.' Akins allowed silence to intervene for a moment before he asked the next question, the one that was in everyone's thoughts. 'How much longer before we get down?' he said, phrasing it as if it were no more than an idle query about when cocktails and lunch would be served.

Briscoe scanned the dozens of faces who waited for his reply. A few of the passengers had decided to brave the weightlessness, and they floated in midair near Briscoe. 'We don't have a firm estimate. Not yet.' He felt like an ass giving such an evasive, stupid answer.

'What the hell does that mean?' one of the passengers shouted. A chorus of angry, frightened voices filled the cabin.

'Hold on,' Akins interjected. He wanted to head off any outbursts that might lead to a general panic. The doctor pushed himself away from his patient and allowed his body to rise up to where Briscoe was. 'Is what the captain told us earlier still true? That's it's best if we don't rush the recovery maneuver?'

'Yes. Absolutely.' Briscoe knew that it was as true now as it had been then – which was to say, not at all. He thought back to the words of Collins' first announcement, which he had monitored in the cockpit. *Conditions are stable. Our situation is unusual, but not critical. There is nothing to worry about.* Briscoe had to give the bastard credit. The speech had been a masterpiece of vagueness and reassurance. It was sugar-coated bullshit.

'Then our best course of action,' Akins said in a voice loud enough for half the cabin to hear, 'is for us to continue to wait until conditions are perfect for recovery?'

'Yes. There's no question about it. Right now we're waiting for the ground stations to reply to our last request.' Briscoe was careful to omit the additional fact that they waited for a reply because the *Star Streak*'s radio had gone dead. They might wait forever.

'You expect a reply shortly?'

'Very soon,' he lied. As things stood, they were trapped in orbit without the slightest means of communicating with anyone on the ground, and with a dwindling oxygen supply. 'Everything is going well,' Briscoe announced to the assembly of passengers. He could feel the insides of his stomach tie into knots. 'I've got to get back to the cockpit. I'll let you know as soon as I hear.'

'I'll go with you,' Dr. Akins said. 'I want that first-aid kit.' He turned to a woman passenger and pointed to the ice bucket. 'Keep applying the ice against her face. Don't leave the cover off the bucket, or you'll chase the ice around the damn cabin.'

'Yes, doctor. I understand.'

Akins grabbed onto the overhead rail and began to work his way forward with the copilot. He could see that they had all gotten better at maneuvering in the zero-gravity condition. Once a person got the hang of it, it didn't seem so bad. Effortless, actually. It was amazing, Akins thought, how quickly human beings could accommodate themselves to the strangest situations.

'I'll get the first-aid kit for you, doctor,' Briscoe said. 'I don't know what the hell could be keeping the stewardess.'

'Wait a minute,' Akins said in a low, gruff voice. They were safely out of range of the others. 'What kind of crap are you handing out? Those idiots may be scared enough to buy it, but I'm not.'

'What?'

'Cut the shit. What are you covering up?'

Briscoe shrugged. For some reason, he was glad that at least one of the passengers in the cabin had seen through his charade. 'You want the truth?'

'Of course.'

Briscoe felt comfortable with the doctor. He seemed to be a strict realist. There was no need to find a back door to the hard facts. 'Things are bad. We were able to communicate with the ground for only a few minutes, right after we got ourselves locked into this fucked-up orbit. Since then, we can't through to anyone.'

'Radio failure?'

'I don't know.' Briscoe shrugged his shoulders. 'Could be anything. We're not operating in our normal element.'

'How did we get up here?'

'The rocket engines locked on. An impossible failure. If we ever get out of this, I'm going to kick the shit out of the first aeronautical engineer I get my hands on.'

Akins couldn't help but smile. He liked the copilot. He was a no-nonsense guy, just like himself. A man who saw straight through to the core of the problem, a man who saw no need for sentimental drivel and hollow pleasantries. It was a trait that invariably brought results. 'Is there a plan for our rescue?'

'I think so. NASA is involved.'

'In what way?'

'Who knows? Our radios quit working before we got to that part. That's why we haven't told anyone,' Briscoe said as he gestured toward the cabin with his free hand. He used his other hand to keep himself anchored to the cabin bulkhead. 'We didn't want to admit that we were out of radio contact. If we brought up the NASA business, the passengers would've had a million questions we wouldn't be able to answer.'

'That was smart.'

'It was my idea.'

'How is the captain holding up?' Akins rubbed his chin nervously. He already had his doubts about the man, from the time they had spent together in the cabin.

'Ask him yourself.'

'You tell me.'

Briscoe thought over his possible responses. 'He's an asshole,' he finally said. 'After the rocket engines locked on, the captain was the one who got us deeper into this. He pulled the nose straight up. I told him not to.' Briscoe wondered what would have

92

happened to them if Collins had followed his advice. He pushed that thought out of his mind.

'Then it's the captain's fault?'

'More or less.' Briscoe wondered if he had said too much. He could always deny it later.

But Akins was not interested in placing blame. His concerns were more immediate. He understood enough medical school psychiatry to know that because the accident was the captain's fault, perhaps that's why he seemed almost paralyzed with fear. With guilt. He might try something outlandish to save them. Something heroic, to save face. Akins had always had a deep suspicion of heroes and do-gooders. Guilt was a socially contrived pattern of behavior that invariably lessened an individual's odds of survival. Individual survival was always the first order of business. 'What's the captain's plan? Is it reasonable?'

'Damned if I know. He keeps changing his mind. Nothing he says makes much sense.'

'Shit.' Akins shook his head, then moved closer to Briscoe. 'This captain of yours . . . '

'Ours,' Briscoe interrupted.

'Yes,' the doctor nodded. He and the co-pilot shared the same point of view. Akins felt a sense of welcomed relief as he talked to him. 'This captain of ours is under one hell of an emotional strain. I've seen it in him already. I have my doubts that he can hold up.'

'Me, too.'

'I'm going to give it to you straight.' Akins said. He felt that he needed an ally among the crew if he were going to eventually get an inside track in this race to stay alive. The copilot seemed to fit that bill. 'The captain's liable to try something off the deep end. If you feel that he's lost control of himself and intends to do something to endanger us, we can deal with it.'

'How?'

Akins took out the vial of Vistaril from his pocket. As he did, two dimes, a few pennies and a key chain floated out with it. 'This damn no-gravity is a pain in the ass,' Akins said as he snatched his key chain out of midair and shoved it deep into his pocket. He let the coins drift away.

'It sure is.' Briscoe watched the coins float lazily into the galley.

'This,' the doctor said to get back to the point. He held up the small vial. 'This is a sedative. I've only got two doses left. If anyone in the cabin asks, I'll say I've used it all. That way, you and I will have enough left to deal with the captain if he gets irrational.'

'Good.' For the first time since the ordeal began, things had taken a turn for the better. 'Look,' Briscoe said as he pointed to the window. 'I figured it would happen soon.

'What is it?'

'The sunrise. We've finally come back into daylight.'

Briscoe and Akins crowded together to look out the window. An arc of an aurora extended far above the horizon. It blended with a faint glow from above. A dark-blue line streaked across the rounded curve of the Earth and was capped by an orange-and-gold band. The band grew bigger and brighter as the sun poked nearer to the horizon. A thin sliver of the yellowish-white fireball finally stuck itself above the black curve of the Earth. The deep hues of red, orange and blue began to wash out. In another minute or two, the colors would be gone, replaced by the stark brilliance of the unrelenting sun.

'That's a hell of a sight,' Akins said as he shoved himself away from the window.

Briscoe nodded absently. The view didn't interest him. What did was the fact that he and the doctor had come up with a way to keep Donald Collins from screwing up even more. 'Things might work out,' Briscoe said, mostly to himself. If NASA could help them. If their oxygen held up. If there was no structural damage to the *Star Streak*. If a thousand other details went in their favor.

'Keep a close eye on the captain.'

'I will. How's your head?' Briscoe asked as he pointed to the bandage on Akins' forehead.

'I'll live.'

'Good.' When he thought about it, Briscoe had to admit that they were one hell of a long way from being home. He glanced at his watch. Ten forty-five. They had been in orbit for over an hour, and they only had enough oxygen left for another five. 'I'm going back to the cockpit,' he said.

'Keep me informed.'

'Sure.' The copilot pushed over to the cockpit door. Before he opened it, he glanced out the window again. The sun had risen completely above the horizon, and it shone too brightly to be looked at directly. The sky was crystal clear. Briscoe could make out the form of a large land mass to their left. He sighed, then allowed his thoughts to drift along as effortlessly as his body. Ernie Briscoe wondered how many more sunrises he would get to see.

Chapter Five

DR. RALPH Kennerdale strode into the upper level of the operational control center at NASA Goddard as if he, rather than the United States Government, owned the facility. At one of the front electronic consoles he spotted the senior technician on duty, Kurt Reiman. He marched directly toward him. 'Everything taken care of?'

Reiman spun around in his seat. 'Yessir. Just like you asked on the phone, I've given the orders to get this place up to full staff.' What Reiman had omitted were a few of the details. He had given the appropriate orders, but he knew that finding each of his technicians might take some time. They were scattered across Goddard's 1200 acres, in any of 21 buildings. Reiman knew that telling Kennerdale of a delay, even a short one, was not the sort of answer the assistant administrator would tolerate.

'Good. Fine work.' Kennerdale glanced through the glass enclosure of the balcony, toward the floor beneath him. Many of the technicians' consoles were staffed. There were a few men and women standing near the large, blank video screens at the front of the room. But to Kennerdale's surprise, there seemed to be far more empty consoles than there were standing personnel. He conducted a quick head count. 'Wait a minute, Reiman.'

'Yes?' Reiman knew what Kennerdale wanted. He kept his eyes fixed on the sheets of checklists in front of him, his fingers running along the pages. This, he could tell, would have been the day to be elsewhere. Reiman had come to work that morning with a headache, and he cursed himself for not following his wife's advice and calling in sick. He knew he would have a migraine before the day was over.

'What the hell is going on?' Kennerdale said. He laid down his paperwork, then stood silently. He had no intention of speaking until he had the man's full attention.

Reiman reluctantly pushed aside the checklist sheets and turned.

Kennerdale gestured toward the lower level. He frowned. 'I expected every one of those consoles to be manned by the time I got here. There are too many empty positions down there. Where are those people?'

'I've called for them. They're coming.' Reiman shrugged, as if the absence of his technicians was just as much a mystery to him. He glanced up at the clock. 'But it's only been a little over fifteen minutes since you called. I promise you they'll be here in time.' He had promised himself that whichever of his people weren't at their positions in five more minutes, he would put their asses in a sling. Probably the same sling that Kennerdale would put *his* ass on.

'I hope so, Kurt. There are lives at stake here.' Kennerdale knew that the best way to get absolute deference from the staff was to insist on it, come on strong. He made a point to always back off a little later – just enough to appear reasonable, without looking weak. The only important criteria were whether or not the job got done. 'We'll begin a prelaunch sequence in fifteen minutes,' he said, knowing perfectly well that he really intended to begin in half an hour. He still needed time to make one more telephone call – a call that was too critical for him to have made from the back seat of his car.

'Yessir. Fifteen minutes.'

Kennerdale reached down and scooped up his papers.

'Dr. Kennerdale?' Novak put down a phone at a rear console and walked toward him.

'What is it, Gilbert?' Kennerdale looked at his assistant with annoyance. He hoped to hell this didn't mean that another problem had sprung up.

'I've finished that job you gave me. A Mr. Ferrera at United Aerospace has assured me of their complete cooperation. He intercepted one of their vice-presidents at a meeting in Washington and he'll be here shortly. A Mr. Robinson. He has full authority to represent the manufacturer.'

'Good.'

'They're also trying to locate three of their technical personnel who are at meetings in the East. They were part of the original design team on the *Star Streak,* so they'll be able to supply us with whatever technical data we need.'

'Fine. I expect we can contact the factory if we need any additional information?'

'Yes. It's already arranged. We'll have a direct line to their Phoenix facility available. I've made arrangements for the United Aerospace people to use one of the empty communication rooms on the first floor.'

Kennerdale arched an eyebrow. 'Is that necessary?' Having a large audience to watch as he orchestrated the rescue might not be a bad idea. 'Can't they work in here?' He gestured toward the empty consoles on the upper levels of the OPSCON.

'They could. If you prefer.' Novak tugged at his shirt collar. Even when Kennerdale spoke mildly, his voice still retained an abrasive edge. 'But we don't know how many technicians might eventually show up. Even though the airline hasn't said so yet, they might also be sending people. I thought that this area would be better utilized if we did it differently.'

'You did? Why?'

Novak knew that he needed to watch what he said. He fumbled for the proper word. 'Allocations. We should allocate these key command consoles only to the people involved – directly involved – in the actual rescue. The NASA staff, mostly, although the manufacturer's representative could utilize one of them.'

Kennerdale smiled. Novak had indeed caught on. There was no sense in muddying the waters when it came down to which organization played the major role in the rescue. 'Good idea,

Gilbert. Reserve one console for United Aerospace, and hold another console open in case a representative of the airline shows up. I doubt that the airline will send anyone, since they've already said they'll do their coordinating from New York. I'm sure they're burrowing in to keep their exposure to a minimum.'

'What good will that do?'

'The fewer times Consolidated Airways' name is mentioned the sooner the public will forget.'

'I see.'

'The manufacturer is not so fortunate. Everyone remembers the DC-10 crashes, but it's the rare bird who can name the airlines involved.' Kennerdale took several steps away from Novak and toward the command console in the center of the balcony area. 'If you'll excuse me,' he said, his back still turned, 'I've got an important call to make.'

'Certainly.'

Kennerdale waited until he heard Novak's footsteps fade away down the empty corridor, then he sat down at the command console to look it over. A blank video screen the size of a small TV occupied the center portion of its raised metal cabinet. Clusters of buttons and several groupings of dials surrounded the screen. Kennerdale's eyes ran across those parts of the panel rapidly, since most of it meant absolutely nothing to him. But there was one section that he knew how to operate.

Kennerdale reached for the telephone handset. He lifted it from its cradle. He leaned forward and began to carefully study the labels above the long row of switches at the head of the console. After he had located the switch that he wanted, he hesitated several seconds before he finally pushed the button. He was reluctant to begin the closed-circuit telephone call that would answer the one question that still hung over the operation. In a few minutes Kennerdale would know for certain if there was any chance of rescuing the trapped airliner.

The yellow cab jerked to a stop in front of the metal barrier that hung from the side of the security building. 'Here it is, Mac. Goddard. This is as far as I can go.'

Robinson peeled off several bills and dropped them on the

cab's front seat. He got out and walked into the security building entrance.

'Can I help you?'

Robinson stepped up to the young man in the uniform shirt who stood at the front desk, a holstered pistol strapped to his side. 'Yes. I'm Robinson. From United Aerospace. I'm supposed to go to . . . ' He fumbled for his notepad. 'The OPSCON.' He disliked talking in acronyms. 'Did I get it right?'

'Yessir. The Operational Control Center.' The guard glanced down at a clipboard on the counter, then back at Robinson. 'You've been pre-cleared. Do you have any identification?'

'Certainly.' Robinson showed his United Aerospace identity card.

'Fine. Thank you. Please step through the metal detector.'

Robinson walked past the device, which remained silent.

Satisfied, the guard handed over a visitor's pass. 'First building on the right. It's faster to walk.' He went on to explain where to enter the building and how to get up to the OPSCON.

Robinson stepped out the rear door, got his bearings, then began to walk rapidly down the sidewalk that paralleled the high metal fence. As the sidewalk turned, Building 12 lay directly in front of him.

Robinson had never been to the NASA Goddard Center before. It was nothing like he had expected. Except for a few antennas stuck on the rooftops, the large microwave tower in front of him and the elaborate security that ringed the facility, it more resembled a tranquil college campus than a hub of scientific activity. Even as he approached the front door of Building 12, it still looked more like an administration complex than a structure that housed some of the world's most sophisticated electronics.

Robinson opened the door and stepped inside. Following the guard's instructions, he hurried down a long corridor, past several crowded control rooms, and through a small lobby. He rode up in the elevator, then followed the sound of loud voices. They came from a dimly lit room across the narrow corridor at the far end.

'Kurt, I'm not interested in your problems,' Ralph Kennerdale said in a booming voice that drowned out the man's feeble objections.

'No sir, they're not problems, Dr. Kennerdale. I just felt that . . . '

Kennerdale cut the man off with a wave of his hand. He looked up in time to see a balding, middle-aged man as he entered the room. He frowned. One of the entrance gate guards had called with an accurate-enough description: a stocky, powerful man wearing a blue jacket and tan pants. To Kennerdale, he looked more like a foreman in a steel mill than the vice-president of a major aerospace corporation. Kennerdale sighed. He was now burdened with the prospect of having to deal with yet another distraction, another useless drain on his time and attention. He was rapidly running out of what little patience he had left. Kennerdale turned back to the NASA technician in front of him. 'I'm going to say it one more time, Kurt. Are you listening?'

'Yessir,' the technician answered meekly.

'Good. I expect then that I won't have to repeat it a third time. Each position in the control room,' he said as he swept his hand expansively in front of him, 'will be manned within the next few minutes with qualified personnel. No trainees. No one who isn't totally qualified and up to speed. I don't care what other projects you've got to shut down. This mission takes absolute priority. Declare a four-zero security status if you have to. Just be certain that everyone is at their station. Do I make myself clear?'

'Yessir.'

'Wonderful.' Kennerdale kept his intense stare fixed on the man for several seconds longer than was necessary. Finally, he turned.

The man scurried away.

'Dr. Kennerdale? I'm Ben Robinson, from United Aerospace.' He stuck out his hand.

'You've arrived sooner than we expected,' Kennerdale said. He took the man's extended hand and shook it briefly. 'We haven't had time to prepare for your arrival.' Kennerdale allowed the dour expression to remain on his face. He saw no need to make Robinson feel completely welcome. That would only invite more challenges to his authority.

'I wasn't far from here when my office called.'

'Have you been to Goddard before?'

101

'No.'

'I'm sorry we don't have time for a tour.' Kennerdale's voice was indistinct, neutral. He stepped over to an adjacent console and leafed through a pile of papers.

'I'm not expecting one.' Robinson looked around the upper and lower levels of the OPSCON anxiously. He scanned the faces of the people he could see. He tried to spot an overt sign, a clue as to whether his prediction of a ransom demand had come true yet. Everyone appeared too calm, too matter-of-fact. 'Have there been any developments? Any new messages?'

'Messages? For you?'

Robinson nodded. 'Yes.' From Kennerdale's response, he could see that the saboteur had not yet issued any demands. Until he did, Robinson knew there was very little he could say. Very little any of them could do.

'No messages. None that I've heard.' Kennerdale glanced into the lower level of the OPSCON. As he watched, several more NASA technicians filed in. He could see that nearly all the positions had been manned. That was good. They could, very shortly, begin the countdown sequence – except that Kennerdale had yet to complete that one critical telephone call. He bit into his lower lip. That goddamn Ty Bellman hadn't been in his office. The people at the Cape had promised to locate him immediately and have him call back. That was nearly ten minutes ago. Until Bellman returned his call, Kennerdale wouldn't know if any of their preparations meant a damn. It might be nothing more than a drill, a colossal waste of time. He turned back to Robinson. 'I've been quite busy,' Kennerdale said distractedly.

'I can imagine.'

'Sit down. Observe. I'll be back in a few minutes to brief you. In the meantime, if you have any questions ask my aide Gilbert Novak.' Kennerdale gestured toward his assistant, who sat quietly at the back of the room.

'Wait. Just tell me the airliner's status.'

'No change. There's still no radio contact.' As much as he had tried to hide it, Kennerdale had begun to look haggard, beleaguered. The lack of communications was another open question that would soon need to be dealt with. He glanced at the

102

wall clock above the darkened display screens in the lower center of the front wall. 'But we expect to resume communications shortly, as soon as they've gone further along in their orbit and back into a favorable antenna position.' *Maybe*.

'How soon?'

'Very soon. Momentarily.' Kennerdale waved his hand in a gesture of dismissal. 'Now, if you'll excuse me,' he said as he began to walk out without waiting for a reply.

'Certainly.' Once Kennerdale had turned the corner, Robinson glanced around the room to take in the details. He stood in a glass-enclosed balcony at the rear of a large two-story structure. Three rows of electronic consoles, controls panels and video screens were lined up in front of him. Beyond that, extending down to the level beneath them, was a full wall of special displays. Five unlit screens sat in the center. Above the screens was a large and colorful map of the world, ringed with time-zone clocks. It filled the remaining space. Bright red letters proclaiming *The Goddard Network* capped the display. It was straight out of Hollywood. 'Very impressive,' he said as he walked to the rear of the room and sat down next to Novak. He wondered how much of this had been built as razzle-dazzle for TV coverage.

'The technicians are on the level beneath us,' Novak volunteered. 'This is the command post. From here, we have instant access to every NASA facility in the world.'

'Really?' He wasn't in the least bit interested in public relations drivel. Novak looked the sort of aide who had a mouth stuffed with official bullshit. Robinson looked behind them and noticed a small, windowless conference room off the corridor. A few men stood in there, sipping coffee and speaking to each other in low voices.

'Most civilians think that the Kennedy Space Center in Florida is the major NASA facility, but that isn't true,' Novak droned on. 'All the Kennedy Center does is light the launching fires.' He paused and waited for him to say something.

Robinson sat quietly.

'We have thirteen major facilities around the country. Each has an important mission.'

'Is that so?' Robinson smiled politely. He could tell that Novak

103

had made this speech a thousand times before. Robinson allowed his eyes to wander around the room again. Through the glass that enclosed the balcony, he could see down to the floor of the lower level. Most of the technicians who sat at the rows of consoles seemed indifferent, almost bored. 'Do those people normally work in this room?'

'Only during launches. That's the only time the OPSCON is used. We've never attempted a launch with so little advance notice. If it wasn't for the importance of the mission, we'd never attempt it.'

'Launches?' It had taken a moment for that word to make an impact on Robinson. 'What do you mean?' He sat upright. 'What do you intend to launch?'

Novak squirmed. Clearly, he had said too much too soon. Kennerdale would be furious. 'This is confidential,' he murmured in an attempt to recoup.

'Of course.' Robinson leaned forward to indicate that he expected to hear more. He dropped his voice to a near whisper. 'What do you intend to launch?' he asked again. He was willing to play Novak's game, as long as it got him the information he wanted.

Novak could see that there was no way out. If he didn't answer, the man would simply confront Kennerdale with questions about a launch. That possibility was even worse. Novak cursed his own impetuous stupidity. He'd have to learn to keep his mouth shut. 'The Space Shuttle. It will rendezvous with the airliner. It can supply it with fuel and oxygen.'

'Christ.' Robinson's thoughts raced ahead. The Space Shuttle. NASA wasn't simply coordinating communications, they were going to attempt an actual rescue – as if the orbiting airliner were no more than a floundering ship at sea. *The Titanic. The unsinkable ship that sank on its maiden voyage.* Ray Lee's words flashed through Robinson's mind. Truth could indeed be stranger than fiction. He allowed the words to fade.

'Without the Space Shuttle, it doesn't seem as if those people stand a chance.'

'I agree.' At least NASA was going to try something overt and positive – something that perhaps the saboteur hadn't thought of either. It was their only chance to get those stranded people down without having to deal with a psycho. *Becker. McBride. Krause.* 'Can the Space Shuttle do it? Can it be launched in time? The airliner's only got a few hours of oxygen left.'.

'I know. It's too early to tell.' Novak looked nervously down the empty corridor. He expected to see Kennerdale reappear at any moment. 'It depends on a great many factors. We'll do our best.'

Ty Bellman sat at his desk in the Kennedy Space Center, his feet up on the console in front of him, his swivel chair tilted backward almost far enough for him to fall over. To any observer he would have looked relaxed and at leisure. But he held the telephone in his hand with a death grip. His lips were pressed together tightly. He could hardly believe what he had heard. 'Ralph, don't be an ass. It's out of the question. Absolutely impossible.'

'Nothing's impossible,' Kennerdale answered quickly. It had taken over ten minutes to locate Bellman and a few additional minutes to get the two of them connected. Bellman's syrupy Southern drawl had been Kennerdale's first irritation since the call began, and now the phone line had an annoying hum in the background. 'Can you hear me okay?'

'Yes. Of course.'

'Must be only on my end,' Kennerdale snapped. It never failed to amaze him how the god-almighty NASA communications network could accomplish the miracles of crystal-clear communications when they spanned distances measured in light-years, but a simple static-free phone hookup to Florida was too much to ask. 'Ty, we've got to see it through. The request came straight from the top. The President himself spoke to me not ten minutes ago,' Kennerdale exaggerated. He thought back to his brief conversation with Goldman. That was close enough to the political stratosphere to give him a little license with the truth.

'I don't give a fuck if Henry the Eighth called you, there's no goddamn way I can get the Shuttle launched in the next few hours.' Bellman spun around in his seat and glanced out the over-sized windows of Launch Control Room Number Two. Out in the distance, across several hundred yards of Florida scrubgrass, sand and gravel stood the gleaming white Space Shuttle. It rode on top of the crawler, the monstrous diesel-powered flatbed that carried the enormous orbiter to Pad 39A. 'You might have forgotten, Ralph, but the goddamn crawler goes less than one mile an hour. It'll take . . . ' Bellman glanced up at the wall clock.

'I haven't forgotten,' Kennerdale said as he jumped quickly into the lull, 'but we've got that much time. There's at least six hours of . . . '

'It'll take two more hours for the crawler to reach the pad,' Bellman began, as if Kennerdale hadn't said a word. 'Three days, Ralph, that's how long the prelaunch checks will take. Maybe I can get it down to two days, if we bust our ass. You going to authorize the overtime?'

'Fuck the overtime!' Kennerdale shouted into the phone. It was a ludicrous remark from him, and he knew it. He had always been a stickler about project costs, especially the way the technicians always insisted on doing every conceivable time-delaying, cost-inducing test. He had gone round and round with Bellman over the very issue of staff overtime not two months before. 'What is the exact status of the Space Shuttle?' he asked to change the subject.

Bellman rocked forward in his chair and reached for a clipboard on the side of the console. 'Ship zero-two is the one on the crawler. It's scheduled to launch in three days for a weather satellite repair mission, and orbital placement of classified cargo for the Department of Defense. We've got the prelaunch check up to date, and everything looks good so far.'

'Then, as far as you know, the ship is perfectly capable of an immediate launch?'

'No.' Bellman gritted his teeth. The administrators up north were experts in space technology, except that they didn't know one end of a rocket from another. 'It's not that simple. You've got to be reasonable. That Space Shuttle is one goddamned elaborate piece of hardware.'

'I'm aware of that.'

'Then don't ask me to be part of some asshole stunt!' Bellman saw that a dozen of the technicians in the room had turned toward him. He pulled the phone closer and swiveled the chair away from them.

'What's the status of the other ship?' Kennerdale's words were calm, casual, matter-of-fact.

'Ship zero-one is due to be moved from orbiter processing to the vehicle assembly building tomorrow.' Bellman looked out toward the huge building to his left. The giant steel doors, over 450 feet in height, had been opened just enough for him to see the dark emptiness inside. Soon, the gleaming white fuselage of Space Shuttle zero-one would be in there. 'It landed day before yesterday. They've still got some off-loading to do from the previous flight.'

'Then zero-two is the only chance we've got?' Kennerdale was pointedly attempting to trap Bellman into admitting that there was a chance. A slight chance, perhaps, but one that Kennerdale felt they should take. The Space Shuttle was almost on the launch pad. If they could get it off earlier than scheduled, it could carry fuel and oxygen up to the airliner trapped in orbit. It could bring passengers down.

'How many passengers on that airliner?' Bellman asked.

Kennerdale was glad to see that Bellman was finally cooperating. He didn't want to use a direct order unless it was the only way. He wanted enthusiasm for his rescue plan from some of the old-line NASA people at the Cape. 'Nearly one hundred, plus the crew.'

'And how do you expect to get them all onboard the Shuttle? The cabin will only carry a dozen, at most.'

'We'll use the Shuttle to bring up oxygen, and to carry back a few of the passengers. If we can get them enough life-support equipment to hold out, the Goddard staff has calculated that the airliner will come down of its own accord in approximately thirty hours.'

'They've calculated the decay time? Marvelous,' Bellman said sarcastically, his South Carolina accent adding an additional dimension to the words. 'Did they come up with a guess as to how quickly those people will have their brains fried on the way down?'

'What?'

'Reentry temperatures, or haven't you heard of the phenomenon?' Bellman could hear the background sound of a

107

pencil scribbling on paper. He could picture Kennerdale taking notes. It almost made him laugh.

'Then the airliner will burn up on reentry?' Kennerdale asked. 'Are you sure?'

'No. I'm not clairvoyant.' Bellman leaned forward and touched the video screen in front of him. It was, at that very instant, monitoring the condition of Space Shuttle zero-two as it sat on top of the crawler transport. Row after row of green numbers were printed on the screen. Bellman pressed a button and the display changed to a different readout. But most of the numbers remained green. There was a scattering of amber-colored lines, but that was routine. Expected. He wished that one of the lines – something unquestionably critical – would turn up red. That would terminate this incredible, moronic conversation. 'That's my point, Ralph. All I can do is guess. Your idea doesn't give us enough time to check things out. I'm sorry, but that's the way it is. If I had to lay odds, I'd say that the airliner – it's one of those United Aerospace *Star Streaks?*'

'Yes.'

'I'd have to bet heavily that it couldn't handle the reentry heat. I know that the airliner has ablative tiles on the bottom of its wings and fuselage. I also know that it has that new liquid-hydrogen cooling system on the leading edge of its wings and tail. That's the same type system we've been begging you to have evaluated for eventual use on the Space Shuttle.'

'Stick to the point. If the airliner has the type of liquid cooling you eventually want on the Shuttle, why would it burn up on reentry?'

'Because,' Bellman said, exasperated, 'the airliner is designed for less speed. Lower temperatures. Lower pressures. It's not supposed to be in outer space, for chrissake, only sub-space. That might not sound like much of a difference to you, but take my word for it – it's the difference between heaven and hell. I'll bet you a bottle of Jack Daniel's that the airliner's cooling system won't have the capacity to handle the extra heat. It's like asking a lawn-mower tractor to pull the same plows that a tandem diesel can.'

Kennerdale could see that he wasn't getting anywhere, although

108

he made a note to check into the reentry heat problem later. 'Okay, Ty. You've made your point. Your protest is duly noted. Now let me make mine.' Kennerdale paused and took a deep breath. In his mind's eye there was a flashing warning light, an internal signal that tried to tell him to back off. To listen to what Bellman said. Somewhere in his mind, he had weighed the variables and concluded that they were out-of-limits.

'Ralph. Please. This is insane,' Bellman pleaded.

'No. It's a calculated risk.' The total picture was too appealing. Too tempting. Kennerdale had prayed every day during the last few years for an opportunity like this one. With one bold gesture he could solve all his problems – all the Agency's problems. He was doing it more for NASA than for himself.

'The risks are too great. They're incalculable.'

'No.' Kennerdale had learned from experience that he could easily push men into doing more than they imagined. Men could be talked into things. Flattered. Threatened. 'I'm ordering you to proceed immediately with an emergency launch of Ship zero-two. For the sake of those people on the airliner, and for the sake of the Agency. I want that ship in the air within the next four hours.'

'Impossible. We can't finish one-tenth of the required safety checks in that little time. There's no way.'

'There *is* a way, and you sure as hell better find it,' Kennerdale answered in a cold, steely voice. In his sixteen years with NASA, Kennerdale had been able to understand the people he worked with, but not the machines. Machines seemed to either function or they didn't, and Kennerdale had no feel for why. He had learned to hate every last one of them, from the Space Shuttle down to his goddamned electric garage door opener. 'The space agency's reputation is on the line. Our funding for the next ten years might well hinge on this rescue. You always scream your damn head off for more money, but when you get a chance to do something about it you get cold feet.'

'But the safety checks . . .'

'As far as the safety checks,' Kennerdale added, his tone growing even more direct, 'forget them. Do all the safety checks you can fit in, and that will be the end of them. We'll just expect that expensive toy of yours to live up to its reputation. To live up

109

to the designed criteria that we paid so much goddamn money for.'

To his amazement, Ty Bellman heard the phone click off. 'Son of a bitch!' He slammed his hand into the console. The clipboard rattled and a communications headset fell off the side and onto the tiled floor. Bellman didn't notice. His eyes were locked on the crawler transport and Space Shuttle 02 as it continued to be moved, slowly but perceptibly, toward Pad 39A.

When Ralph Kennerdale came back to the OPSCON, he marched directly up to Ben Robinson. 'We're going to attempt an actual rescue.' There was a wry smile on his face. 'We'll use the Space Shuttle.'

'Yes. I know.'

Kennerdale shot an angry glance at Novak, then turned back to Robinson. 'Has your technical staff arrived yet?'

Robinson looked into the small back room behind the corridor, then glanced down to the lower level. The three engineers were nowhere in sight. 'I guess not.'

'We don't have time for guesswork, Mr. Robinson.'

Robinson frowned. He had already given Kennerdale too many free shots. He had taken all the verbal abuse he intended to tolerate. 'You know damn well what I meant.' He stared pointedly at the NASA chief, tension hanging in the air between them. Robinson had come to definite conclusions about the sort of man Kennerdale was, and he knew from past experience that taking a step backward to accommodate people like him would be the first movement of a full-galloped retreat. 'When my technicians get here, they won't hide in the closets. You'll see them as soon as I do. Maybe sooner.' *One of the technicians, especially. You'll hear from that person very soon.*

'Don't get upset. I'm looking to clarify things, that's all.'

'I'm not upset.' Robinson felt a slight ringing in his ears, and a hollowed churning in his stomach. It was the unmistakable first signs of another wave of the damned Ménière's disease. The doctors had warned him that emotional tension might trigger it. Robinson attempted to ignore his condition. 'I'll tell you as soon as I see my technicians,' he said calmly.

'Fine.' Kennerdale smiled congenially. Robinson would not be an easy man to push around. If it came down to a battle of wills, some other tactic would be necessary. 'We've made arrangements for your people to work in a separate communications room,' Kennerdale continued in a friendly tone. 'You, or the person of your choice, can occupy one of the consoles here on the command level.'

'Okay.'

'As far as a plan of action, Space Shuttle zero-two is being prepared for an emergency launch. It will rendezvous with the trapped airliner and supply it with enough food and oxygen to keep the passengers and crew alive and well. Approximately thirty hours from now the airliner will come out of its orbit of its own accord.' The problem of reentry heat flashed through Kennerdale's mind again. He would have to check it out shortly.

'Really?' The news came as a surprise to Robinson. As far as he knew, objects were either in orbit, or they were not. 'Why?'

'Because they're only orbiting at an altitude of a hundred miles. That's well within the range of the Earth's gravitational pull. A slight tug, you might say.' Kennerdale smiled. He always enjoyed being the dispenser of insider's information. 'The airliner will come down just the way our famous *Skylab* did.'

'I hope the *Star Streak* has a better fate than *Skylab*.'

'Don't worry. Once the airliner descends into the atmosphere, it can be steered by its pilots. *Skylab* had no wings, no flight controls and no crew, so it could not,' Kennerdale hoped to hell that he was right. He turned toward Novak and spoke directly to him for the first time since he had come back. 'What about the Department of Defense linkup?'

'The tie-in should be coming through any time now.' As if on cue, the large center screen with its map of the world went dark for several seconds, then popped back into view. 'There it is,' Novak said. He was happy that the conversation had been steered away from his premature Shuttle disclosure to Robinson.

A bright white dot appeared on the left side of the colorful map of the world. 'That white mark,' Kennerdale announced to Robinson in a voice louder than necessary, 'represents the position of the airliner in its orbit. As you can see, the airliner is currently over the southwestern edge of Alaska, near the Aleutians.'

'Is that a type of radar?'

'Not really. It's a computer plot from the Department of Defense, based on several electronic surveillances.' Kennerdale smiled. *White man's magic.* Even though Robinson obviously knew a great deal about the technical aspects involved, it never ceased to amaze Kennerdale how otherwise rational adults would accept any explanation that contained modern jargon. Radar. Computers. Electronics. To most people, none of it was more than a shadowy name – commonplace and yet mysterious. God had not died. He had simply enrolled in a graduate course in the sciences. That was a point worth remembering – and worth using. Much of NASA's political progress to date had been based on precisely that premise. 'The progress of that dot is the computer's opinion of where the airliner is at every moment during its orbit.'

'I see,' Robinson murmured.

Kennerdale walked over to the command console. He pressed the intercom button. 'Kurt,' he announced, his amplified voice echoing from the wall-mounted speakers scattered throughout both levels of the OPSCON. 'Put a thirty-minute projection line on it.'

'Yessir.'

Within a few seconds, a curved white line protruded from the dot on the screen. The line arced between and across the colored images of the Earth's land masses. 'We've now asked the computer to display the projected path for the next thirty minutes,' Kennerdale said for Robinson's benefit. He knew that a dose of NASA prowess would be good medicine. 'As you can see, this orbit will bring the airliner across the Central United States in a southeasterly direction within the next twenty minutes. From there, it will travel across the Caribbean and down the eastern side of South America.'

'How soon before communications can be established?' Robinson asked.

'Any moment.' Kennerdale glanced back at the wall map. According to the earlier estimates, the airliner should have been back in contact well before it reached the tip of the Aleutians. It

112

obviously was not. That meant that either one of their computer projections was slightly in error, or something had happened to the flight. There was nothing they could do but wait and see.

Novak edged closer to Kennerdale. He waited until Robinson had turned his attention to the map. 'I'd like to speak to you a moment,' he whispered. 'In private.'

Kennerdale nodded discreetly, then cleared his throat. Robinson turned. 'I've got a few things left to attend to,' Kennerdale announced. 'In the meanwhile, here are a stack of teletype messages we've received from Consolidated Airways. You might want to look at them.'

'Yes. Thank you.' Robinson took the papers from Kennerdale and walked to a seat at the rear of the room.

'I've had an idea,' Novak said, as soon as Robinson was out of range. 'But it might be risky.'

'Everything is risky. Let's hear it.' Kennerdale was certain that Novak knew him too well to waste his time. Maybe his aide had finally begun to earn his keep.

'How about trying to get an actual television picture? I don't know the logistics involved, but I do know that we've got several satellites in orbit with onboard video cameras. Perhaps we could alter the orbit of one of them and get it to rendezvous with the airliner – at least close enough to provide a reasonable picture. That way, we could monitor the approach of the Shuttle.'

Kennerdale looked toward the front wall, where three large television screens sat dark and unused beneath the wall map. They had often used those screens to monitor crucial operations. The space walks. The *Apollo-Soyuz* linkup. The moon landings. The hardware was already in place. The paths of the satellites could be controlled right from Goddard. It was a brilliant idea, and Kennerdale thought he knew how to arrange it. 'No. It won't work,' he said to Novak. 'Too complicated. Too risky. Forget it.'

Novak shrugged. 'Sorry.'

'That's okay.' Kennerdale turned. He began to walk hurriedly toward the corridor. 'If anyone looks for me, I'll be back in a few minutes.' He knew it wouldn't take long to get the proper person in the satellite control room started on a quick feasibility analysis of rendezvousing one of their television satellites with the crippled airliner. There was no need to give Novak credit because, of course, the implementation of the idea was where real genius was called for. On the other hand if the plan worked out poorly, the certain-to-follow official inquiry could be steered all the way back to Novak's original idea.

Novak watched, bewildered, as Kennerdale left the OPSCON. He stood awkwardly in the center of the room, nervously looking around, trying to make sense of Kennerdale's swings of mood. Nothing the man did was predictable. Novak began to walk slowly toward where Robinson was seated. 'Anything in that data from Consolidated you can use?' he asked, purely to make conversation.

'Nothing yet. It's routine data. I'm looking for something specific.' Robinson flipped to the next page. 'Wait.' His eyes scanned the documents quickly. 'Christ Almighty.'

'What is it?'

'The crew names.'

'Do you know them?'

Robinson had turned a pale, bloodless white. 'Yes. I know the captain.' He pushed the teletype papers aside. When Ferrera had first mentioned Consolidated Airways, Robinson had instantly thought of Collins – and almost as quickly had forced that possibility out of his mind. 'I know him very well. Donald Collins. We're friends. He was one of Consolidated's first pilots on the *Star Streak*. I trained him personally, back when I was doing most of our flight training. That was more than two years ago.'

'You were a pilot?'

'Yes. I was.' Robinson could picture Collins' face clearly, as if the man were standing in the room. Then he pictured the environment that the *Star Streak* was trapped in. Robinson shuddered.

'Is Collins a good pilot?'

'Yes. He flies the *Star Streak* well. But there's more to it than that.' For the moment, Robinson forgot that he was speaking to a total stranger. The emotional repercussions of seeing Collins' name had caused him to open up, to share personal thoughts that he normally never would have. 'Collins and I got along very well, right from the start. We stayed in touch. Visited back and forth

114

several times. He came out to commiserate with me when I lost my pilot's license because of medical problems. I always stop in to see him whenever I'm in New York.' Robinson paused. He shook his head slowly. 'The last time I saw Collins, I had made a special trip. It was only six months ago. To his wife's funeral.'

'Sorry to hear that,' Novak said automatically.

'So was I.' Robinson's head had begun to throb. He laid the teletype messages aside, closed his eyes and began to rub his temples. The situation for the passengers and crew on Flight 14 suddenly seemed hopeless. Kennerdale had made the Space Shuttle rescue sound strictly routine, but Robinson knew how complex and dangerous it would actually be.

'The prospects for a successful rescue seem quite good,' Novak said as he attempted to deal with his own negative thoughts.

'Yes,' Robinson answered, also unconvinced. With the *Star Streak* out of rocket fuel, there was no way it could get out of orbit on its own. What was left of their precious oxygen supply was dwindling rapidly. The aircraft was also, for some unknown reason, still out of radio contact. The three United Aerospace engineers – one of them more than likely a saboteur – had yet to arrive. The ransom demands had yet to be made. Robinson suspected that the real chances for a successful rescue were absolutely zero. Before the day was over, he would be making arrangements to attend the funeral of Captain Donald Collins.

Chapter Six

As THE rented tan-colored Buick with the three electronic engineers from United Aerospace came out of the tunnel on the north side of the Patapsco River, Ed McBride rubbed his eyes with his right hand while he steered with his left. Shafts of sunlight poked through the holes in the rapidly breaking overcast. He glanced at his wristwatch. Ten-fifty. 'It's clearing right on schedule,' he said cheerfully as he squinted into the sun.

'Yes. Right on schedule,' Alex Krause answered. He looked up at the sky. It was a picture-book October morning. The rain showers had moved through Baltimore, as predicted, leaving behind a brisk northwest wind and falling temperatures. Krause shifted his weight, then carefully adjusted the position of the stark-white plaster cast below his cut-off pants on the lower half of his left leg.

'Is that too much heat for you?' McBride asked. He had seen Krause's discomfort.

'No, I'm fine,' Krause said.

Bonnie Becker leaned forward from the rear seat. 'Keep the heater on. It's chilly back here.'

'Can't you have any consideration?' McBride glared into the

rearview mirror at the young woman. 'He's only been out of the hospital a few weeks.'

'Don't worry about me. I'm fine.'

'I don't want to get sick. That's how you catch pneumonia.' Bonnie had no intention of inconveniencing herself, even slightly, for Alex Krause or Ed McBride.

'Tell me if you're too warm,' McBride repeated to Krause as if the woman in the backseat hadn't said a word.

'I'm fine. Really.'

'Good.' McBride glanced over his left shoulder, swung the car into the left lane, then looked back at Krause. 'I just noticed that no one's signed your cast yet. Let me be the first.'

'Sure.' Krause smiled.

'Great. I'll write something lewd. You'll have to wear overalls.' McBride snickered as he scratched his bulging stomach. He was painfully aware that he had gained several more pounds over the summer, and had vowed once again to get back on his diet very soon. McBride looked at Krause's thin, muscular body. Weight-wise, Krause was no worse off for his three weeks of bed confinement. McBride knew that if it were him, he would have spent the entire time eating and watching the ball games on television. Then he would have gained 40 pounds and dropped another ten G's. He always made his worst bets when he wasn't feeling good, and if there was one thing McBride didn't need now, it was more debt on top of what he already owed. 'By the way,' McBride said as his thoughts brought the topic to mind. 'How's that foreman who was hurt with you? What's his name?'

'Gary Murphy. He's still in the hospital, but he's coming along okay. I've got to call him when we get back.' Krause thought about the man who had been injured with him and had shared the same hospital room. 'His shoulder isn't as bad as the doctors first thought. He'll be out in another week.'

'That's good.'

Krause had, during his three weeks in the hospital, repeatedly cursed his bad luck for being at that particular spot on the hangar floor when the overhead gantry crane came apart. Yet, in retrospect, both he and Murphy had been exceedingly lucky. With all those tons of steel falling around them, only one small piece managed to hit them. Other than his broken left leg, Krause had gotten away with nothing more than a few bad bruises on his buttocks and side. God had been with him that day. 'That's one hell of a paid vacation I had. All I did was eat, drink and sleep.'

'The company will probably bill you. Payroll deduction. A dollar a week.'

'Sure.' Krause laughed and McBride joined in. Krause noticed that Bonnie continued to ignore their conversation and had turned away. She pretended to watch the shipyards to their right. But Krause had long ago learned how to read women like her. That ever-present look of bored indifference etched across Becker's face was a thin disguise. Like most women Krause had met in his life, Becker was always thinking about something, *scheming* about something. She made Krause's skin crawl.

Her close-cropped, wind-blown red hair and the angular lines of her fashion-model face resembled one of Krause's ex-girl-friends. There were also other overriding similarities. Her arrogant smirk. Her double-dealing nature. The two of them were certainly twin sisters in spirit. One of the things wrong with United Aerospace was that they'd hire and promote a bitch like Bonnie Becker. Krause had never felt that she was as competent an engineer as everyone else had. Maybe the rumors were true, that they were going to fire her soon. Krause hoped so. That would add a certain ironic justice to it all.

'I'm lost around here,' Bonnie volunteered as she broke into the silence. 'I've never been to Baltimore before.'

'I'm surprised you'd admit it,' McBride answered in a teasing voice. He knew damn well what got her goat. Eccentric men were bad enough to work with, but having an eccentric woman as part of their group was more than he could tolerate. Especially today. 'Let's tell everyone how Bonnie deferred to the men on this trip.'

Krause did not answer.

'Don't be such an asshole,' Bonnie said. 'Don't forget the Equal Employment Opportunity Commission ruling on sexual harassment. I'm sure you've been reminded of it. If you keep this up, I'll file a complaint against you. Both of you.'

Krause turned slowly and looked at her, his expression a cross between astonishment and anger. 'Go to hell.'

'You have your goddamn nerve.' Bonnie glared at Kruase with undisguised hatred. He was a bastard. They were *all* bastards. They had, in more ways than one, attempted to turn her career to shit. They treated her as if she were no more than a curiosity, an oddball, a freak. She wasn't going to put up with it anymore. She didn't need any of them – not Krause, nor McBride, and not any of the people at United Aerospace. They would, very shortly, see for themselves.

They rode in silence for a few minutes.

'The Martin Airport is at the end of the Boulevard,' McBride said.

'How much further?'

'Seven or eight miles.'

Krause attempted to shift his position a few inches. As he did, a knifelike pain in his left hip sliced through the lower part of his body. He grimaced in pain.

'You okay?'

'Yes,' Krause answered, his eyes closed.

'You don't look good.' Krause's constant pains had made McBride apprehensive.

'No, he doesn't,' Bonnie said. She had managed to rein in her anger, to put a damper on her temper. No matter how repugnant it was, she realized that she should try to be cordial. Provoking a confrontation would be counterproductive. It would be over soon enough, and her actions would be the best display of how she had felt toward them. She leaned forward. 'Do you want us to stop?'

'It does hurt a little,' Krause said when he caught his breath. 'But I'm okay now. Don't stop.'

'Take it easy.'

'Sure.'

McBride hoped that Krause hadn't rushed his recovery. The consulting job with the Martin Corporation was Krause's first outing since his return to work. Ever since they landed in Baltimore the night before, McBride had kept an eye out for hospitals and police units. Sickness made him nervous.

'The doctors told me to expect this sort of thing,' Krause explained self-consciously. 'It'll go away. Eventually.' He decided to change the subject. 'Is there anything else left for us to review?'

'No. I think we've got it down pretty well. You came up with some nice touches last night.' Since he had been appointed a senior member of electronic engineering, McBride felt a need to meter out an endless quota of compliments. That was, he felt, the proper way to do business.

'Thank you. I'm glad I could help.'

'I'm not expecting any resistance from the Martin people,' McBride said as he shared the confidential management information that all three of them were already well aware of. 'I hear they're pretty much sold on the idea.'

'Yes.'

'All we've got to do is answer questions. With a little luck, they won't hit us with something we can't wrap up on the spot.'

'I'm sure we can do it.'

'We should stay away from discussing the subsystems.'

'Right.'

McBride swung the rented car into the left lane. 'Potholes,' he said. He pointed to the road crew working lackadaisically in the closed right lane. 'This country's going to hell. Even the roads are falling apart.' He slowed the car behind the packed traffic in the one lane that remained open.

'It sure it,' Krause agreed. He gestured toward a knot of men standing near the roadside, leaning on their shovels. 'The same thing happened in Rome.'

'Italy?'

'Ancient Rome. Everyone got greedy and lazy. That's what's wrong now. No one does a day's work. They're trying to live off other people's efforts.'

'It's a goddamn shame,' McBride agreed. 'Christ, it's backed up for miles.' They inched forward slowly, McBride staying uncomfortably close to the car in front of him. 'Isn't that typical?' he fumed. 'They've got four lazy bastards leaning on shovels, so they close half the damn road for miles.'

'Typical,' Krause agreed. 'Very typical.'

'By the way, did you work out the arrangements for your weekend in New York?' McBride asked. His own thoughts had drifted back to the personal arrangements he had made for his long-awaited trip to the East Coast. McBride had spent so many

120

months working out the details, he found it nearly impossible to believe that the time had nearly arrived.

'Yes. I called this morning.'

'A college friend, you said?'

'No. High school.' Krause laughed. 'When I said an old friend, I wasn't kidding. We've kept in touch, on and off, over all these years. I was best man at his wedding. I haven't seen him in a while. I'm looking forward to it.'

'Sounds like a good time.'

Bonnie opened her mouth to add something about her own personal plans for the weekend, just in case Krause – or anyone from United Aerospace, for that matter – ran into her. 'I'm going to New York for the weekend, also. To shop.'

'That so?' McBride coughed politely to cover his lack of interest in pursuing the conversation.

'Yes.' Bonnie sat back and looked out the window again.

'By the way, I forgot to tell you about lunch,' McBride said. 'Since we're working over the meal break, I've arranged for some sandwiches.' He grinned. 'We've got to keep up our strength during these tough technical sessions.'

'Right.'

'I told them to get roast beef and ham sandwiches, with some potato salad on the side. That okay?' The hell with the diet, McBride said to himself. He couldn't think straight if he was constantly hungry.

'Sure. Fine with me,' Krause answered.

'Just make certain that the roast beef is rare,' Bonnie said as she leaned forward to try to be more a part of the group. 'I can't tolerate well-done meat.'

McBride ignored her. 'I hope they send mustard and mayonnaise. Sandwiches aren't good without something on them.' McBride peered intently out ahead through the pack of cars. 'That's the end of the construction area. It's about time.' As soon as he could, he pounced on the accelerator and the car shot forward into the thinning traffic. 'I hope we're not going to be late. That's a bad start for any meeting.'

'We've got lots of time.'

They rode along in a predominance of silence for the next ten minutes, except for occasional comments from McBride as he pointed out sights he considered worthwhile, and an occasional complaint from Bonnie. Krause turned on the car radio, hunted the dial for a suitable station and, finding none, clicked it off. When they reached the entrance to the Martin Corporation's plant, they stopped at the security office to get their passes. A few minutes later they were back in the car. They drove further into the complex to the parking lot that served the Engineering Design building.

'Look. It's Ron Schneider.' McBride pointed to the man who stood at the curb.

'Who?'

'Schneider. He's the man we've come to see.' McBride rolled down his window. 'Hello, Ron,' he shouted as he drove closer. 'You the official welcoming committee?' Before Schneider could answer, McBride saw from the expression on his face that something was wrong. 'What's up?'

'A problem. For you guys.' Schneider put his hands on the windowsill and leaned forward. 'For you people,' he corrected himself when he saw the woman in the rear seat. 'We got a call from your office about an hour ago. They've been looking for you.'

'We stopped for a late breakfast.'

'There's been trouble with one of your *Star Streak* airliners. Consolidated Airways.'

'What happened?'

'You're not going to believe this,' Schneider began. 'I hope to hell it's not a practical joke.'

'For chrissake, Ron. What happened?' *One of your Star Streak airliners.* McBride fidgeted in his seat, then glanced over at Krause. Alex seemed not to be listening. He could feel Bonnie edge nearer to him. She was breathing down his neck. 'Well?'

'The airplane is stuck in orbit.'

'What? Are you out of your goddamn mind?'

'Listen,' Schneider said as his voice grew cold. 'This is the message from your office. You do whatever you want with it.' Schneider glanced back down at a paper in his hand. 'Consolidated Flight fourteen – ship number thirty-five – experienced a full-power lock-on of both rocket engines during climb. The aircraft was launched into a low-Earth orbit. The National Aeronautics and Space Administration will conduct an attempted rescue of the survivors shortly. It will be directed from a command post at the Goddard Center in Maryland. McBride, Krause and Becker are to go immediately to Goddard to provide technical assistance. Say nothing to the news media. Headquarters hopes to get additional technicians to Goddard as soon as possible.' Schneider looked up. 'The man I spoke to identified himself as Ferrera. He said that a Mr. Robinson will meet you at Goddard. He'll be in charge.'

'How far is Goddard?' McBride asked. His forehead was covered with sweat.

'Between Baltimore and Washington. A few miles east of the Parkway. You'll see signs. It shouldn't take more than forty-five minutes. Good luck.'

'Thanks.' McBride gave Schneider a halfhearted wave as he steered the car around and headed back for the boulevard. He searched his mind for something appropriate to say. 'Christ. I've never heard of anything so incredible. Is it possible?' McBride asked, more to break the tension than to get a response.

'Ship thirty-five was the one we worked on a month ago,' Becker said from the backseat. 'I don't see how it could've gotten through the computer checks if it was so screwed up.'

'I don't understand it either,' Krause added as he turned half around so he could see both of them. Krause's face showed that he had been visibly shaken by the news of what had happened to Ship thirty-five. 'The failure must have happened sometime after the ship left Phoenix,' he stammered. 'There's no question that the quality-control computer checks would've picked up any factory discrepancies.' Krause had been the engineer who had conceived of and then implemented the elaborate set of computer-analyzed checks that United Aerospace used whenever a *Star Streak* airliner went through the factory maintenance cycles. It was an ingenious and comprehensive program that had earned for Krause a small bonus and an immediate promotion to senior engineer.

'I'm sure you're right,' McBride said encouragingly. 'It

couldn't have happened at the factory.'

Krause looked directly at McBride. 'Even then, I don't see how it's possible,' he said as he began to mentally run the engineering drawings through his mind. 'Those rocket-engine control circuits seemed foolproof.'

'Evidently not.'

As the three of them sped across the Maryland countryside, they were each engrossed in their own personal thoughts.

Captain Donald Collins guided himself carefully past the entrance to the galley and toward the cockpit door. He thanked God that he had been able to calm himself down. He had begun to think clearly and rationally again – or at least his thoughts seemed rational. On the back of his tongue Collins could taste the lingering residue from that one ounce of liquir. It was a constant, disheartening remainder of how close he had come to completely losing his self-control.

Yet that one miniature bottle of liquor seemed to have done the trick. Shortly after he had taken that drink, he was able to get hold of himself and deal with the technical problems in the cockpit. A while after that, he had forced himself to go back into the cabin to talk with the doctor again, to check on Gayle's condition, to see Chris Diederich and to attend to other details. He had also gained enough presence of mind to sketch out a tentative plan to minimize unnecessary risks and to manage their dwindling resources.

Collins put his hand on the cockpit doorknob to steady himself in the weighless condition, then took one last look down the cabin aisle. All seemed in order, at least for the moment. The last remnants of the floating, drifting debris had been gathered up and stowed. Those passengers who had found the courage to try maneuvering through the weightlessness had, for the most part, lost interest. Most sat quietly in their seats, many with their eyes closed. If Collins had taken a photograph of the cabin, it would have looked no different than the en-route portion of any routine flight. It was only the view out the airliner's window that gave hint to the sort of threat they were subjected to.

The view out the left side was the surface of the earth. They were, at the moment, passing over the eastern edge of a vast ocean. The north Pacific, undoubtedly. Large parcels of land and the tops of flat, white clouds jutted toward them.

The view through the right-side windows was solely of the dazzling yellowish-white sun. It loomed larger than it did when viewed from Earth, and it continued to rise in the sky with marked, perceptible motion. At that instant, the sun sat only 15 or so degrees above the horizon line. Collins knew that it meant that it was approximately eight in the morning local time at that spot on Earth beneath their feet. Probably the northwest coast of Canada, near Alaska. Collins glanced at his wristwatch. Two minutes past eleven. At the rate they traveled, the sun would be directly overhead the aircraft in 15 minutes. It would be high noon in this insane, compressed span of a day that took barely 94 minutes to finish. Collins shoved open the cockpit door and pushed himself inside.

Katie was unbuckling herself from her flight chair as Collins entered the cockpit. When she saw him, she snapped the buckle of her seat belt together again. 'I was just coming back to get you. We've got them on the radio. Ernie's talking to them now.'

'Are they coming in clear?' They had received several short, garbled messages earlier, before Collins had left the cockpit.

'Yessir. Loud and clear.' Katie accented each of the words, happy to be reporting good news for a change.

'Very good.' Collins had expected as much. Briscoe's analysis of their radio problems had made sense, and from what they had deciphered from the garbled radio messages, the ground stations concurred. 'How long have they been transmitting?'

'Two minutes. Ernie is writing everything down.'

'Good.' Collins had determined from watching the sun, the stars and the sections of Earth he could identify, that their orbit was an elliptical one. They had, he guessed, departed from the northernmost extent of their elongated circle a short time before. Whenever they were too far north or south of the usual air routes, they would be out of radio contact. But during their journey across the middle latitudes of the globe, radio reception would become normal. The theory had proven itself correct. 'Which station is it?' Collins asked as he pushed himself forward. His body arched past the upper portion of the flight engineer's panel.

'The NASA communications station at Goddard, Maryland,' Katie answered. 'We're being patched through to them.'

Collins grabbed the back of his flight chair, pulled himself around carefully, then gently eased his legs down first. He fastened his seat belt to stop himself from floating upward, then glanced toward Briscoe. The copilot had his head down, his eyes fixed on the pad in his lap. He continued to scribble notes and listen intently to the radio message. Collins reached for his own headphones.

'We expect to launch the Space Shuttle from Cape Kennedy in approximately two hours,' the official-sounding voice continued as Collins flipped up the switch to listen in on the radio conversation. The man's hollow, metallic tones seemed vaguely familiar. 'The Shuttle will rendezvous with you twenty-three minutes after its launch. It will supply you with what you need.' The voice on the radio paused for a moment, then began again. 'Has the captain come back to the cockpit yet?'

'Yes. Standby.' Briscoe glanced up at Collins. 'They want you.'

Collins fumbled for the microphone by his side console. His hands were damp and slippery, his throat dry. He pressed the button. 'Go ahead, Goddard. This is the captain.'

'Donald. It's Ben. Ben Robinson.'

'Ben? Are you at Goddard?'

'Yes.'

'Good. Great.' Collins paused. The sound of his friend's voice had made him feel strange. Apprehensive. It was an uncomfortable, foreboding sensation, as if their risks had suddenly increased beyond calculable limits. Collins tried to shake the feeling by shifting his thoughts.

'Donald? Are you still there?'

'Yes.' Collins looked out his windshield. 'I read you loud and clear.' The clouds beneath them had abruptly ended, exposing an area of flat, sandy-colored terrain ringed by distant mountains. A desert, or a high, arid plateau. 'Go ahead with your transmission.'

'Roger.' Robinson took a deep breath. His speech to Collins was half-rehearsed. 'We've got the full cooperation of NASA, their facilities and staff, plus our own people to provide technical assistance.' *Do not discuss the sabotage theory with anyone.* Ferrera's words echoed through his thoughts. 'As I've already said, we intend to use the NASA Space Shuttle to provide you with what you'll need. Unfortunately, the Shuttle is not large enough to accommodate more than a few of your passengers at a time for the trip down, so they'll only bring down those people who are injured but can be safely moved. Your own ship will begin to descend, of its own accord, out of its orbit in approximately thirty-six hours.'

'Really? In thirty-six hours?'

'Yes.'

Collins didn't know what to make of that information. He would put it aside for the time being, since it would mean nothing unless more oxygen were brought up to them.

'How soon will the Shuttle arrive?' he asked.

Robinson hestitated. 'Shortly,' he finally answered, stumbling over the word. He knew that, deep down, he had doubts about how soon the Shuttle could get up to Collins, in spite of Kennerdale's reassurances. 'We expect to have oxygen, food, water and medical supplies up to you by two o'clock. We realize you've only got enough oxygen onboard to last until three forty-five. Incidentally, let's use only East Coast times from now on so there won't be any confusion.'

'Roger. What time do you have now?'

Robinson glanced up at the center clock on the front wall, beneath the electronic map of the Earth with its moving white dot to represent the stranded airliner. 'Eleven-o-eight and twenty seconds.'

'Eleven-o-eight, twenty,' Collins repeated as he checked his cockpit clock. It was, within a few seconds, indicating correctly.

'What's the rest of your situation?' Robinson continued as soon as the transmission channel was clear.

'We've had three deaths and three major injuries. A number of other people have been cut or bruised.'

'I know. The copilot already told me. What's the current condition of the three who were injured?'

'The stewardess is not well. The doctor says she needs immediate hospital treatment. The baby is in guarded condition,

127

although the doctor seems optimistic about him. The other woman – Chris Diederich – has gotten better. The object that blocked her windpipe had been removed and there should be no ill effects from the tracheotomy. She's weak and sedated, but otherwise, okay.' Collins was glad to be able to pass on a positive report, at least about Chris. If they could get out of orbit and down safely, Chris would be alright. He thanked God about that.

'Okay,' Robinson replied. 'And how's the equipment holding out?'

Collins glanced around the cockpit. 'Okay. Stable.' As he turned toward the flight engineer's console, Katie frowned and pointed to the temperature gauge that the two of them had discussed earlier. Collins nodded. 'The number-one auxiliary air-conditioning unit,' he said into the microphone, 'is still showing signs of overheating. We might have to shut it down.'

'That's great,' Briscoe volunteered. The copilot waved his hand toward the flight engineer's panel, then faced Collins. Other than relaying the message from the ground, it was the first time Briscoe had spoken directly to the captain during the last half-hour. 'What if the other spare system – the number-two auxiliary air conditioning – craps out? Then we get to die along with it? Is that what you want?'

Collins didn't answer immediately. He kept a blank, non-committal expression on his face. But he knew that Briscoe had come up with a valid point. Shutting down a system when it indicated a malfunction was normal procedure, but they had become too independent on what little equipment remained to voluntarily shut down any of it. Without the aircraft's engines running, they had very few backups left. They'd have to take chances, play percentages. None of their usual conservative flight procedures applied anymore.

'Your problem with the number-one auxiliary system might only be an indication,' Robinson said as he guessed correctly the trend of the pilot's thoughts. 'I'd advise you not to shut anything down. Not unless you're absolutely certain that it's critical.'

'Roger. Understand.' Collins felt the cold sweat break out on his forehead. His hand had begun to tremble again, and his breathing had become too rapid. *Calm down.* He tried to force himself to inhale slowly, regularly. Collins' carefully tended courage suddenly seemed as flat and lifeless as the ground they orbited hundreds of thousands of feet above. Talking to Robinson had made Collins feel more vulnerable, not less. 'Both auxiliary air-conditioning systems will be okay,' Collins announced suddenly. 'I intend to leave number one run.'

'Good. That's what I would do,' Robinson said, attempting to sound supportive.

'Everything else in the aircraft seems to be working okay,' Collins transmitted. He closed his eyes and rubbed his head. *Take command.* Those ironic, haughty, pompous words filtered into Collins' thoughts again, as they had earlier. Official words, official bullshit.

'I've already given the copilot a list of items in the lower bay I'd like to have checked,' Robinson continued. 'I need the serial numbers and a general opinion of the condition of those items, if that's okay with you.'

'Is that where the rocket-engine failure occurred?' Collins asked. The possible reasons for the initial failure had crossed his mind several times, but he had been too preoccupied to give it any real thought.

'Possibly. But I actually want the data to help with our rescue plan,' Robinson lied. Just as Ferrera had insisted, he had no intention of telling anyone – not even Collins – what his actual reasons and suspicions were. He had told Kennerdale and the NASA people that he would make the request for data from the lower bay simply to give the flight crew something to do, to give everyone the impression that a high level of activity was already underway. Kennerdale, in particular, seemed to buy that sort of explanation. 'Will you allow the flight engineer to get those serial numbers for me?'

'Yes. Certainly.' Collins nodded toward Katie, then watched as she released her seat belt, took the list from Briscoe and worked her way to the aft end of the cockpit. She released the latch that held the floor-mounted access door in place, lifted up on the door carefully and gingerly worked herself down into the lower bay. 'She's getting into the lower bay now.'

'Fine. The data you provide might be helpful in our technical analysis,' Robinson repeated. He hoped to deflect any further questions, at least for the moment. He was anxious to get to the aircraft manuals, which had just been delivered to Goddard. Perhaps there was something in the manuals that the saboteur had overlooked, some way that the *Star Streak* might be made to come out of its orbit. Robinson needed time to work out a few of the possibilities that his suspicions had provided him with. 'Unless you've got any more questions, I'll sign off for the moment and we'll go to standby until you can get that data to me.'

'No. Wait.' Collins felt a sudden need to keep talking, as if he could manufacture a solid, visible lifeline out of the electronic impulses that his radio transmitted. He didn't want to listen as much as he wanted to talk, to be heard, to be dealt with. 'I want to tell you a few things. They might be important.'

'Sure. Go ahead.'

Collins pressed the microphone button and began to transmit again, first about the facts surrounding their launch into orbit, and then about more general things. His words came out slow and rambling, each sentence making a statement in itself but none of them adding up to any sort of discernible message. Collins knew that he was supposed to stay loose, to evaluate and come to rational decisions. What was needed were unemotional responses that were unweighted by nonsensical considerations – the mental equivalent of their unweighted zero-gravity condition. But Collins realized that his brain was mired down, his ideas sluggish. He was stuck in mental concrete. *Take command.* The phrase again rattled around through his hollowed-out thoughts. The two words did not fit together because they implied a choice that Collins knew he did not actually have. Command was officially his, whether he cared to take it or not.

'Did I understand you correctly?' Robinson asked as soon as he could get a word in. He had focused on one of Collins's rambling statements. 'You're the pilot who brought N35CA – the same aircraft that you're in at the moment – to our Phoenix maintenance hangar a month ago? That's one hell of a coincidence.' *Coincidence.* That word had popped up again.

Collins thought about Robinson's statement for a moment before he answered. 'Not really. Consolidated's only got three

Star Streaks. We've only got nineteen pilots who are captain-qualified on the airplane. One in nineteen for normal odds. But then I stacked the deck.' Collins spoke nonchalantly, as if he were chatting across a small room and not across the depths of open, airless space. 'I volunteered for the ferry flight to Phoenix. It was a last-minute assignment, I had nothing else to do that day – both my boys were away – and I thought I'd get a chance to get together with you again.'

'Really? I don't remember you calling?'

'You were gone. Left for San Francisco an hour before I called. That's what your housekeeper said. Sally wasn't home either. I should've called before I left New York, but it was four in the morning, Phoenix time.' Collins paused but continued to hold the microphone button down. 'Wait. Katie's back. Here's the list you wanted. I'll turn the microphone over to her.'

'Fine. Thank you.' Something bothered Robinson as he picked up a pad and pencil. *Coincidence*. He sat down at the NASA console. *Gone to San Francisco*. He pushed the disquieting thoughts out of his mind as he began to copy the lists of numbers read by the flight engineer.

Collins glanced out the cockpit window as Katie continued to read the endless list of serial numbers into the microphone. They had already traversed most of the United States and were about to cross over the Florida peninsula. Collins moved slightly in his seat to get a better look at the ground below. Through the few scattered clouds he could easily make out Tampa Bay, Lake Okeechobee and the Everglades. To the left, on Florida's southwest coast, was the sharp indentation that represented Fort Myers. Even from their altitude of over a hundred miles, the topography appeared strikingly familiar and intimate. Collins could make out the individual beaches he had walked so many times during those idyllic vacations with Susan.

Susan. The sound of her name flowed through his thoughts and stopped him cold. Its effect was always the same on him. Her name seemed connected to more than just a human body and soul, more than to just her spirit and memory. Somehow, it was connected to life and time itself. *Susan*. He loved her dearly, tenderly, completely. Collins edged up in his seat, to the limits that his hinched-up seat belt would allow. He kept his eyes riveted to that forlorn, nostalgic spot on Earth as it passed beneath them. For a few moments he was aware of nothing beyond what he saw and what memories those sights evoked.

'Captain,' Katie announced, her voice breaking through Collins' mental fortress. 'Should I go ahead with the second list?'

'List?'

'Yes. The second list of serial numbers. Do you want to say anything more before I begin to transmit again? To add anything?' She held up the microphone and waited.

Collins coughed lightly to clear his throat. He could think of nothing further to say to Robinson – or to any of the other people on the ground, for that matter. It was too early to transmit a message for them to give to his sons. It was too early to even think about that sort of thing. Collins shook his head. 'No. Go ahead with the rest of the serial numbers.' As soon as she had begun to transmit again, he turned his attention back to the Florida coastline.

The mass of land had already vanished behind them, beyond the slight dip at the edges of the dark blue horizon. There was nothing below them but a few scattered islands – the Bahamas – and endless stretches of ocean speckled with several patches of billowy white clouds. *Cancer. I'm sorry. Your wife has cancer.* The doctor's familiar words played back again like an unwanted recording. Those dreaded words – as familiar as they had become – still sounded foreign, out of place. Cancer. The expression was too neat and compact to be loaded with so much misery and horror.

It seemed to Collins only a few days since he had last brushed his fingers against Susan's face and gently stroked her frail shoulders and arms. It seemed no more than hours since he watched her exhale a last shallow breath that marked her journey into that quiet isolation of death. It seemed only a few minutes ago that Collins had stepped into the hospital corridor on that sunny spring morning to tell his sons that their mother was gone forever. He knew damn well that his own insecurities the last twelve months had begun shortly after the diagnosis of Susan's illness. But no amount of rationally applied logic had made any difference. Collins couldn't stop his remorse, couldn't quell his fears no matter how hard he tried.

'Captain, I've finished with the list,' Katie said. She continued to hold the microphone in front of her. 'Should I mention the suggestion from the Diederich passenger? The idea about mixing fuels?'

Collins could not bring himself to answer our loud. With each passing minute and mile, their efforts seemed more meager, more pointless and futile. He kept his eyes averted from the other two in the cockpit and, with a barely perceptible motion, nodded briefly.

Katie pressed her microphone button again and began to relay the message.

Collins heard her transmitted words, and listened for Robinson's reply. To Collins' surprise, his friend sounded intrigued, enthusiastic. Diederich's suggestion might have merit after all. Attempting to mix some of their kerosene-based jet fuel with breathable oxygen in order to create a concoction that could be burned in the rocket engines was, in theory, possible. If they could do it, they'd have a way to propel themselves out of orbit. Collins hurriedly reached for his microphone and pressed the transmit button. 'Does the fuel mixing idea really seem possible?'

There was a pause on the other end before Robinson answered. 'Yes. I think so. But we'll need to experiment on this end first. I'll let you know. Don't try it on your own – it's too dangerous. The problem will be in coming up with the proper mixture. I'll get back to you.'

'Okay. Good.' But Collins knew that he felt anything but good about Robinson's reply. There was more of a message between Robinson's words than in them – and Collins suspected that he knew what the message really was. All of the messages from the ground – the encouragement about fuel mixing, the plans about the attempted rescue by the Space Shuttle – suddenly seemed to be nothing more than play-acting designed solely to keep the spirits of the victims buoyed up until that inevitable moment arrived. It was no more than a sham, a charade – like Susan's chemotherapy had been. 'I hope you're being straight with me,' Collins transmitted.

'Of course.' Robinson paused for a moment before he continued. 'You'll know everything I do. I'll keep you informed.' He knew that he had already, on Ferrera's direct orders, failed to mention the sabotage theory. Robinson wondered how many other points he might find it necessary to gloss over.

'Fine.'

Briscoe tapped Collins on the shoulder. 'Remind them that we've just completed one full orbit,' he said.

Collins shook his head slowly, then shrugged. 'What damn difference does it make? It's academic.' During the last 94 minutes they had flown completely around the circumference of the Earth. In a few more minutes they would enter into darkness again, as they flew over the back side of the Earth on their second orbit. Shortly after that they'd be out of range for radio contact, at least for a while. Those were straight facts, and no amount of talk could alter them.

'It doesn't hurt to remind them,' Briscoe argued. 'We don't know what sort of information they're working with down there. Besides,' he added, assuming a more taunting tone, 'it'll make it easier for them to keep score if we do the counting for them. One down and three to go.'

'What?' Katie held the microphone near to her mouth, but her finger remained off the transmit button. She looked at Briscoe, puzzled. 'I don't understand. What kind of score?'

'Three more orbits,' Collins answered quickly. He had gotten the words out before Briscoe could. He felt a sense of perverse joy at beating Briscoe to the inevitable, predictable punch line. Collins stared blankly out the front windshield and toward the dark horizon that marked the beginning of the nighttime sky. As much as he didn't like to admit it, he realized that he and Briscoe had, in spite of the bravado and hoopla, come to the same basic conclusions about their odds for survival. 'Three more orbits until we run out of oxygen,' Collins said as he learned forward and tapped his finger against his panel clock. 'Three more orbits until we die.'

Chapter Seven

BEN ROBINSON laid his pencil down. The yellow pad in front of him was filled with scribbled notes. They had been carefully worded so only he could decipher their actual meaning. It was another precaution – probably an unnecessary one – that he had taken to stay within the limitation imposed by Ferrera. *Say nothing about the sabotage theory.* Robinson fully intended to keep his promise, although he wondered – once again – if he had talked himself into believing something that was not true.

Robinson took a deep breath, then looked around the upper level of the OPSCON. He sat at a console against the right sidewall on the command level, two rows behind the front edge of the glassed-in balcony. From where he was, Robinson's view of the lower level was somewhat restricted – as Kennerdale had undoubtedly intended it to be. But Robinson was glad that Kennerdale had assigned him to that particular console. A distance of 15 feet between him and Kennerdale's front-and-center seat – where at that moment several NASA technicians were vying for Kennerdale's attention – was just enough. Robinson knew that from where he sat, he could get a better overview of the rescue operation and, better yet, be far enough away to keep people from intruding on the aspects he intended to keep private.

The TV monitor on Robinson's panel flashed on. A series of figures appeared. It was the electronic index that Novak had told him to expect. Robinson leaned forward to study the array. Each line of symbols indicated specific instructions on how to get more data from the machine. He selected a particular topic that he wanted to see, then pressed the coded number into his panel controls. The TV monitor went blank for an instant, then began to fill up with words and numbers as if someone were pouring them in from above. They were etched in tiny lines and figures created out of the grayish-white dots.

The figures were the current coordinates of the stranded airliner. Below them was the expected time for reestablishment of radio communications. Robinson looked over to the giant map in the center of the room to correlate the information that his screen had given him. He could see that it made sense. Satisfied that the airliner was just about where NASA had told him it would be, he selected another code on his console.

The screen filled up with new numbers, this time the flight path and projected orbital decay time. *Thirty-four hours, forty-six minutes.* That was, according to the space experts, how long the airliner would be trapped in orbit before it came down of its own accord. Robinson sat back and ran the key words through his mind. Decay time. Reentry. The phrases seemed more real than the actuality they were intended to portray. In spite of his years in aviation and his thousands of hours of test flying, the space flight concepts were outside his realm. He might as well be discussing submarines and the bottom of the sea. Robinson's thoughts were interrupted by a sharp buzz from his console telephone. He pressed a lighted button, then yanked up the receiver. 'Robinson.'

'Sir. Your people have arrived. Do you want them on the upper level?'

'Yes.'

'They're on the way.'

'Good.' Robinson hung up the phone, then made himself sit back again. *Relax. Don't show any emotion.* He knew he had to

136

be careful – very careful – if he wasn't going to give away his suspicions. Whichever of the three engineers was the saboteur, he or she would be primed to pick up the slightest hint that someone was wise to them. Robinson went back to his TV monitor and forced his eyes to scan the words, his mind to concentrate on the sentences and figures on the screen. He wanted to appear engrossed in technical details when the three engineers arrived. Robinson pressed a console button to return to the index display, then selected a different format and began to study it.

'Ben?'

Robinson wheeled around toward the source of the voice. The three electronic engineers stood ten feet from him, at the entrance to the balcony area of the OPSCON. Robinson felt his stomach churn as he forced himself to smile. 'Yes. Over here, Ed.' McBride was a few steps ahead of the other two. Krause hobbled along, his left leg set in a white plaster cast that extended from his foot to a few inches below his knee. Becker ambled behind. Robinson stood up to greet them. His seemingly casual glance at the newcomers was, in reality, a quick and cold calculation that took in the small details, from McBride's worn shoes to the circles under Bonnie Becker's hazel eyes.

'This is one hell of a thing,' McBride said. He reached out to shake hands with Robinson. 'We got Ferrera's message when we showed up at the Martin meeting. The guy who brought us upstairs filled us in on the airliner's current status and position. Is that information still accurate?'

'Unfortunately, yes. There's no change. The last time we heard from the airliner, conditions were stable. They're currently out of radio contact, but that was expected. We'll hear from them again shortly.' As he spoke, Robinson stepped around McBride, shook hands briefly with Krause and, finally, with Becker. He had hung back for an instant when Becker offered her hand, and Robinson hoped that she hadn't noticed. 'I'm glad as hell that the three of you were on the East Coast. So far, that's the only break I've had.'

'I hope we can help,' Krause said.

'I'm sure you can.' Of the three of them, Robinson had worked the most with Alex Krause, especially during the months the young engineer had set up the *Star Streak*'s quality-control program. Krause was quiet, extremely competent and technically one of the most qualified employees at United Aerospace. Robinson had, a few weeks before, telephoned Krause in the hospital to pass along his wishes for a speedy recovery. 'Good to see you back at work, Alex. How are you feeling?'

'Fine.' Krause smiled sheepishly, then glanced away.

'Good.' Robinson studied Krause's face. It was thin and hollow. He looked tired. Everyone knew that both he and the shop foreman had been very lucky when that gantry crane came apart. By all rights, they should both be dead. Robinson turned back to McBride. 'I think the best place to start is with the aircraft records. I've got a complete readout of the ship's history downstairs.'

'Downstairs?'

'Yes.' Robinson scanned their faces. He felt that if he could analyze every detail of each of their responses, then he'd be able to come up with some sort of a clue. That was the only way he had to discover which of them was the saboteur. 'NASA allotted us only one console here, but they gave us an entire room downstairs. Two rooms, actually. There's a main room with a console like this one,' he said as he patted the metal panel behind him, 'plus an inner office with another console. I'll use that inner office myself, when I'm not up here.' Krause nodded. McBride, seemed attentive. Becker appeared deep in thought, distracted, almost jittery.

'What are we supposed to look for?' Krause asked.

'Damned if I know.' *Which one of your bastards did this?* 'I guess we should first try to find an explanation for how this could've happened. That's a logical starting point.' Robinson watched the three of them. None of their faces displayed any emotion. 'We should try to come up with something positive, some backup action in case NASA's rescue plan fails. So far, it looks good – but you can never tell. Remember,' Robinson continued as he intentionally veered the conversation from its obvious conclusion, 'that the airliner only has enough oxygen to last them until three forty-five. That's our deadline.'

'What sort of rescue plan?' Krause asked. His eyes had

138

wandered to the large electronic map in the center of the OPSCON, its white tracking line moving slowly but perceptibly.

'The guy downstairs didn't say anything about a rescue plan,' McBride added.

Robinson held out a second longer than necessary before throwing out the biggest bait he had. The only bait he had. He knew that none of them would have been told about Kennerdale's plan since it was, officially, still a secret. 'The Space Shuttle,' Robinson said in a casual voice. 'NASA's going to launch it shortly. They'll rendezvous with the airliner. They'll supply it with fuel and oxygen.'

'The Space Shuttle? That's incredible. Can it launch in time?' Becker asked.

Her words had hit Robinson solidly – but so had the surprised expressions on the faces of McBride and Krause. They were – for one reason or another – all clearly stunned by the news. Robinson should have guessed as much. Anyone would have been surprised. A Space Shuttle rescue – it *was* incredible. 'Yes. That's what they say,' Robinson answered as he gestured toward Kennerdale and the cluster of technicians in the center of the room. He had thrown out a few leading lines and had naively expected that the saboteur would accommodate him by blurting out a full confession. He could see that his well-intentioned questions and statements were an idiotic waste of time. 'The NASA people tell me we'll get a firm launch estimate shortly.'

'Good,' McBride replied as he took a few steps toward the front of the balcony and peered through the glass enclosure.

Robinson looked at the three of them. There would be no easy way to distinguish between their surface reactions of legitimate concern and displays of personal fear or guilt. He'd need to come up with some other way to make his choice. 'I'll take you downstairs.'

Before Robinson could take a step toward the corridor, the phone on his console buzzed again. The particular lighted button told him that it was the line from Phoenix. Robinson reached for the handset and snatched it up. 'Yes?'

'Can you talk?' It was Ferrera.

'My three engineers are here now,' Robinson answered

without emphasis as he nodded toward them. 'I was just about to take them downstairs to begin a thorough briefing.'

'Okay. I understand. Get rid of them. Get them out of the area. I need to talk to you. Privately. I'll hold.'

'Certainly,' Robinson said, his voice still set at the same random tone it had been. 'Just give me a minute. I'll get right back with you.' He laid the telephone down and turned to Krause. 'It's the airline,' he said as he pointed to the handset. 'They've got some updates for me. I'll tell you where the downstairs office is and I'll meet you there shortly. You can start by reviewing the aircraft manuals and records – there's a complete set down there.'

'Sure.'

Robinson gave directions, then stood motionless as the three engineers left the OPSCON. He waited half a minute until he was certain that they had gone below, then he turned and picked up the telephone. 'Go ahead. They're gone.'

'Are you sure?'

'Yes.' Robinson glanced over his shoulder at the entrance to the corridor that lead to the upper level. It was still empty. He turned and looked around the balcony area. Only Kennerdale, Novak and one technician remained, and they were on the far side of the room. Robinson's heart pounded. 'For chrissake, yes,' he said in a hushed voice. 'Go ahead.'

'You were right.'

'How?'

'About the sabotage. There's no doubt.'

'What?'

'There's no doubt,' Ferrera repeated, his words slowed and carefully measured. 'The serial numbers you called me with – the components in the lower electronics compartment of that *Star Streak* – didn't match what's supposed to be in there.'

'God Almighty. Are you sure?' Even though it had originally been Robinson's idea, he still found it difficult to believe.

'Yes. The serial numbers on some of the components are fake, but the code numbers on the safety seals on the outside of those boxes are real.'

'Real?'

'Yes. The bogus components are wired in with real seals, from

140

the batch used during the period that aircraft was in Phoenix a month ago.'

'I see.' Robinson paused, his scattered thoughts swirling past nearly too fast to be focused on. 'But could someone have stolen . . . '

'Absolutely not,' Ferrera cut in, anticipating the question. 'None of our seals are missing, they've all been signed for. You were right. Something was put inside that ship – and it had to have been done at the factory. It could only have been done by someone who works – or worked – for United Aerospace.'

'I understand.' Robinson's imagination was far ahead of his words. *Someone who works for United Aerospace.* 'Yes. It makes sense. I've already had the same idea. I've narrowed it down. It can only be one of three people.'

'Three people?' Ferrera said incredulously. 'Who?'

Becker. McBride. Krause. Robinson began to explain the one additional aspect of his sabotage theory that Ferrera had yet to hear.

Alvin Kingsley stood atop the steel deck on the mobile launch platform, arms akimbo, head tilted back. He peered up at the gleaming white fuselage of Space Shuttle Ship 02. The midday Florida sun was almost directly overhead, and Kingsley felt its warmth on the back of his neck. He knew that if it wasn't for the strong ocean breeze, complete with its refreshing, antiseptic odors of salt and sand, the dark metal deckwork of the launch platform would have been uncomfortably, insufferably hot.

'Does it look good to you?'

Kingsley turned, then smiled at the technician. 'Sure does,' he shouted, loud enough for his voice to be heard over the throbbing, grinding whine of the two giant diesel engines that powered the enormous crawler transport beneath them. He glanced at the man's identification tag. DePhillips. Kingsley had seen him a number of times, but had only spoken to him once or twice before.

'Are you going up on this one?' DePhillips asked loudly as he pointed a finger toward the sky.

'Yes.' Kingsley couldn't help but allow his eyes to wander back

141

to the slick lines of the Shuttle. The approximate shape and dimensions of a medium-sized commercial jetliner, it was the heaviest, most elaborate piece of flyable machinery ever devised by man. With its solid-fuel rocket boosters and external liquid-fuel tank, the completed package weighed over four million pounds. Its enormous engines would consume almost 25,000 pounds of propellant every second during the initial phase of the launch. The cargo area inside the winged Shuttle orbiter was capable of carrying 33 tons of payload to an altitude of 175 miles. In just a short while, Alvin Kingsley would be the pilot in command of that incredible piece of hardware.

'Very good,' DePhillips said, his words mixed with the noises from the diesel engines and carried off by the incessant wind. He hesitated as if he intended to say more, but did not.

Kingsley began to walk slowly toward the edge of the mobile launcher. He gestured for DePhillips to follow him. By the time they reached the rail, the noise had lessened measurably. 'How much longer?' Kingsley asked as he pointed toward the large iron gantry tower that was a permanent part of Launch Pad 39A.

'Our platform tilt is perfect,' DePhillips said as he began to answer the question in a roundabout manner. He pointed toward the rear corner of the steel flatbed, where an intricate hydraulic leveling system had jacked up the hind end. The intricacies of the mobile launch platform were DePhillips' personal province. 'We don't want the baby to fall out of the crib,' he said, in standard launch-pad humor. He deflected his hand to duplicate the inclined angle of the road grade near the launching pad. 'Everything's worked perfectly so far.'

'How much longer?' Kingsley repeated, a hint of annoyance in his voice. He was always unhappy with the time it took his fellow NASA employees to answer even the simplest questions.

'Soon.' DePhillips glanced down at a clipboard in his hand.

'Could you give me a firm estimate? I'd appreciate it.' As the only black man in the astronaut corp, Alvin Kingsley felt a need to monitor his responses very carefully. He was intent on giving no one – from the top levels of NASA management down through the ranks of the security guards and the girls in the steno pool – any possible reason to want him out of the Shuttle program. 'An estimate in clock time, if you can,' Kingsley added as he tapped his watch. He knew that the supervisors at the pad would have the most up-to-date information.

'It's difficult to say.' DePhillips pushed back his yellow hard hat and rubbed his forehead. Beads of perspiration had formed on his upper lip. 'I don't have the authority to give an official estimate.'

'Then give me an unofficial estimate.' Beneath his smile, Kingsley seethed. He had spent his entire adult life – his college days at Michigan State, his two tours of duty in the Air Force – carefully on guard against any impetuous action that would hamper his career. As a newly designated Shuttle commander, he had almost arrived. His three previous Space Shuttle launches, all of them as copilot, had gone perfectly. He had no intention of fucking up now. Once he had gotten his first flight as commander behind him, Kingsley could then indulge himself by becoming as testy and difficult as most of the other senior-grade astronauts.

'Okay. An unofficial estimate.' DePhillips gazed out in the distance toward the large gray sound-suppression water tower and, behind it, to the spherically shaped liquid-hydrogen storage tank. The super-cooled fuel inside the metal bubble – at 420 degrees below zero, Fahrenheit – was so cold that there was a constant flow of condensation beneath it, wrung out of the humid Florida sky. DePhillips absently eyed the path the rivulets of water made through the scrubgrass as he mulled over the appropriate numbers in his mind.

'A ball-park figure. That's all,' Kingsley added as a prod.

'Okay. We'll be in launch position in thirty minutes. Hookups will take thirty more. We should be ready in approximately one hour.' DePhillips stopped. He looked directly at Kingsley. 'I understand they're going to eliminate most of the prelaunch tests.'

'Yes.' Since the first instant Kingsley had learned that his flight in the Space Shuttle would be three days earlier than originally scheduled because of the airliner trapped in orbit, he had refused to open his mind to speculation. 'The ship's reading in the green. I've seen the scopes myself. Everything's a definite go. There's no need for the secondary checks,' he said, repeating the official line he'd been given.

'That's what I've been told,' DePhillips said. He smiled again, this time out of sympathy. 'Have a nice flight. Good luck.'

'Thanks.' Kingsley turned and walked away. He stepped carefully over a pile of coiled cables, then maneuvered around a cluster of portable floodlights. As he passed alongside the white-painted tail of the Shuttle, he turned left and hurried directly toward the exit at the side of the deck.

'Wait!'

Kingsley spun around. Coming across the steel deck of the mobile launch system was Ty Bellman. He moved rapidly in a motion that was a cross between a run and a fast walk. Kingsley waved to indicate that he would wait, then watched the jerky movements of Bellman's tall and angular body. 'What's up?' Kingsley asked as soon as the launch director had come within a dozen feet of where he stood.

'I've got to talk to you,' Bellman gasped. He laid his hands on the chain barrier at the edge of the platform and took several deep breaths.

'You need more exercise,' Kingsley said in a friendly tone.

'Yes. I know.' Bellman continued to breathe deeply and rapidly. 'I've been looking for you,' he added when he had finally caught his breath.

'Here I am.' Kingsley had never been overly friendly with Bellman, even though the launch director had never done anything against him. It was, Kingsley suspected, nothing more than a latent reaction between his own black skin and Bellman's crew cut, pasty-white face and Southern twang. A bold-faced prejudice. 'What can I do for you?'

'We need to talk.'

'I'm all ears.' Kingsley leaned casually over the rail and looked down the three and a half miles of gravel roadbed that the Shuttle, strapped to its mobile launcher, had already traveled. At the far end of that special brown-gravel road he could make out, through the hazy sun-drenched sky, the huge vehicle assembly building. Alongside it was a small and squat structure that Kingsley knew was the launch-control center.

'I think this emergency launch idea stinks.'

Kingsley made no visible response.

'It's not my idea,' Bellman added hastily. 'I've advised them against it. I've been overruled by the big shots in Washington.'

Kingsley turned slowly. He glanced down at his wristwatch. 'I don't have much time. Randy's going to pick me up here in five minutes. We've still got to suit up. I want to review the flight profile once more.'

'Hull? Is he the copilot?'

'Yes.' Kingsley smiled to himself. In one hour from now when he would become the first black man to command a space vehicle, Randy Hull would be his assistant. Hull was the most photographed of the new astronauts. He was young, pretty-boy, whiter-than-white. The perfect photogenic model for the public relations brochures and TV specials.

'What does Hull think about the emergency launch?'

'He feels the way I do.' *He always does.* Kingsley knew how ironic it was that he got along better with Hull than any of the other new members of the astronaut team. When the final assignments were offered, Hull had made a special request to act as Kingsley's copilot. The two of them had become sincere friends. The profound differences in their backgrounds and expectations had allowed them to be friends without the usual distractions – competitiveness, jealousy – that most astronaut relationships were subject to. Hull was a pleasant, easy-going rich kid from the suburbs of Connecticut – and also the lowest test-score ranked member of their astronaut class. Kingsley was a hardworking city boy from a Detroit ghetto – and the highest scorer in their group.

Bellman could see that talking Kingsley out of the launch would not be easy. 'I think we should cancel,' he blurted out. Perhaps the most direct approach might work best. 'It's too dangerous. We need to do the preliminary checks.'

'Has anything showed up? Any negative areas?'

'No,' Bellman admitted.

'Any questionable scans? Any garbled readouts?'

Again Bellman shook his head. 'That's not the point,' he added quickly.

Kingsley stood up and looked at Bellman incredulously. 'Not the point?' Bellman had either turned stupid, or incredibly naive. 'It sure as hell is. What reason should we give for a delay or cancellation? A pressing engagement elsewhere? Cold feet?'

'Don't be an ass,' Bellman said too quickly. He could see from the change in Kingsley's expression that he had definitely said the wrong thing. 'What I mean is that we don't need a definable failure. You know the policy as well as I do.'

'Sure. It's your job to see that all the established parameters are met. It's my job to command the ship.'

'Exactly. You've got the authority to cancel. No questions asked.'

Kingsley shook his head slowly, then began to laugh. 'Is that the same speech you give to the Rotary Club? The same one you give to the high school kids? Let me understand this. You expect me . . . '

'Come on, now. Don't take it to the absurd,' Bellman interrupted.

'No,' Kingsley answered, his voice slightly raised. 'Don't *you* take it to the absurd. You expect me to exercise a command option to abort the mission simply because you have a bad feeling? You think something isn't up to snuff? Based on what? Tea leaves? Palm readings? A sixth sense?'

'Incomplete data. That's a good enough reason.'

'Incomplete data? How?'

'We haven't finished our prelaunch tests.'

'Christ.' Kingsley waved his hand in disbelief. 'That's stretching the definition of incomplete data, isn't it?'

'It'll work. I'll back you up.'

'Great. Then we'll both be out of a job.'

'I'll back you up,' Bellman repeated. 'It's that asshole Kennerdale who's pushing this. He's more concerned with the NASA public image than the safety of the mission.'

'And you suggest that we cancel?' Kingsley looked around in time to spot a gray government car as it drove into the security gate checkpost that led to Pad 39A. He glanced down at his watch, then turned back to Bellman. 'Let's get more specific. Why do you suspect we might have a problem?'

'For God's sake, we *always* have a problem!' As much as Bellman hated to admit it, problems were a fact of life in the space program. There was always something, somewhere that was out of limits.

'Not always,' Kingsley answered. 'Most of that crap is minor anyway. We both know that. Even if a few items do come up in the red, that shouldn't make a damned difference in the mission's outcome. We've got a great deal of redundant equipment onboard.'

'I strongly suggest that we stick to our original schedule,' Bellman said, exasperated. 'Do each of the normal checks. It's the only way to be certain. Otherwise, it's no more than Russian roulette – with your ass sitting on a couple million pounds of high explosives.'

'The only reason you've bothered talking to me about this is that you haven't found any negative indicators so you can cancel on your own. You don't want this launch to go, and you want me to stop it for you.'

Bellman knew that Kingsley had hit the nail on the head. He would certainly have canceled the launch itself – the hell with what Kennerdale and those assholes in administration thought – if he could find some way to do it. 'No,' he lied. 'I want you to be totally involved. I want you to agree that it's too risky.'

'And the people on that airliner?' The gray government car had left the security gate and had pulled up alongside the crawler transport. The car stopped. The door opened. Hull stepped out.

Bellman shrugged. 'I'm sorry, but there's nothing we can do. We're not magicians. We can't accomplish the impossible. We have no right to endanger a ten-billion-dollar program just to save a hundred people. It's not worth the risk. We can't endanger your life – and Hull's life – for the sake of a public relations stunt.'

Kingsley waved down at Hull. He gestured to indicate that he would be along shortly, then turned back to Bellman. He looked at the launch director with unmasked hatred in his eyes. 'Absolutely not. Until we've got firm evidence of a measurable problem, I'm not going to unilaterally cancel this flight. Don't call me unless you've found a definite – and serious – no-go condition.'

'Cancel it. Please. I'll stand behind you,' Bellman pleaded.

'Yeah. Sure. Until we get to the front door of Governor Maddox's restaurant.'

'What?'

'Never mind.' Kingsley began to walk away, but then stopped and turned. 'My father was in the ninety-ninth air wing in Africa in nineteen forty-four. He flew pieces of shit they called P-47's. No maintenance, no spare parts, no nothing. He flew them into combat. *Combat*, for chrissake. He didn't do a thousand motherfucking tests everytime he was scheduled for a mission.'

'That was different.'

'Bullshit, man.' Kingsley slapped his hand angrily down against the metal rail. 'I'm not going to let you do this to me, man. You've pissed on us long enough. You and your fucking friends.' Kingsley had begun to shout, but he no longer cared. 'I'm not going to be known as the chicken nigger who left all those nice white folks stuck in space. I'm not going to turn the Space Shuttle program into just another nigger joke. You can take your extra checks and your extra precautions and shove them up your ass. I intend to go. On schedule.'

Bellman watched in silence as Kingsley hurried down the metal stairway at the rear of the platform, stepped into the gray government car and sped toward the buildings in the distance.

Chapter Eight

'THEY SAY that it's possible.'

'Good. What's the chance for success?' Kennerdale asked as he looked down at the young NASA technician who sat at the console in the upper level of the OPSCON.

'Ninety, ninety-five percent.'

Kennerdale winced visibly. Another pet peeve of his was how, whenever you allowed them, the engineers would translate every reply into another set of meaningless numbers. 'I assume that you mean excellent, or something of that sort. Am I correct?'

'Yessir.' The young man's face had turned a deep red.

'Fine.' Kennerdale turned to Novak. 'That TV satellite idea we came up with seems feasible. I thought it might be.'

'So did I.' Novak knew that he was lucky to get even that much credit from Kennerdale for the satellite idea.

'Sir?' the technician interrupted. 'The satellite room is holding on the line. What should I tell them?'

Kennerdale took a step closer to the communications console. His body hovered over the technician who sat at the panel. 'Tell them that when it's steamboat time, it's time to steam,' he said, a pernicious smile on his lips.

The technician looked up, puzzled. 'I'm afraid I don't understand.'

Kennerdale's smile disappeared. 'Never mind,' he said tersely. Mark Twain was wasted on the educated elite who could speak only in the cryptic, disjointed grunts of science and engineering. If they understood nothing but cold and hard facts, Kennerdale would be happy to oblige them. 'Just tell them to immediately reposition that satellite. Have it rendezvous with the stranded airliner as soon as possible.'

'Okay.'

Before the technician could begin to relay the message, Kennerdale tapped the young man on the shoulder. He wanted the working staff to understand clearly the full scope of his intentions. He crouched down beside the technician. 'Also tell them,' he added in a hoarse whisper, his face only inches from the young man, his words slightly too loud for the shortened distance between them, 'that they should adjust that satellite's orbit very carefully. I don't want any foul-ups. None whatsoever. They should,' he continued, his words coming very slowly, 'plan to move that satellite as if their careers depended on it.'

The technician blinked in disbelief. Kennerdale seemed even worse than his reputation had indicated he would be. After several seconds of silence, the technician realized that the NASA chief expected a reply. 'Yessir,' he blurted out nervously. 'I understand completely. I'll pass that along.'

'Good.' Satisfied, Kennerdale stood up and turned around. He motioned for Novak to follow him as he began to walk toward his own console at the front of the room. 'We've still got a few additional items to deal with,' Kennerdale said as Novak scurried to keep up. Kennerdale plopped himself down heavily in his swivel chair. As he did, he noticed Ben Robinson on the other side of the room. The United Aerospace vice-president sat at the console Kennerdale had assigned to him, a telephone against his ear, his head down, his eyes averted. 'Has Robinson asked for anything?'

'No. Not since I showed him how to operate the communications network and the auto-dialer.'

'He will.' Kennerdale knew that Robinson would eventually be a damn thorn in his side. He was unquestionably the type. For the moment, however, Kennerdale had more pressing problems. He reached for his notepad. 'I want you to find Reiman. Get him to assign two of his best men to an immediate evaluation of this reentry temperatures business,' he said as he read over the notes taken during his conversation with Ty Bellman at the Cape. 'I want to know exactly what the prospects are for getting that airliner down safely once the deorbiting process begins.'

'Reentry temperatures,' Novak repeated as he jotted the words on his pad. 'Could that be a potential problem?'

Kennerdale shook his head. 'I'm not sure. Probably not.' He thought over Bellman's words. *Those people will have their brains fried on the way down.* More than likely, Bellman was simply exaggerating to keep his precious Shuttle enshrouded in its usual array of unnecessary prelaunch checks and bullshit. Still, the possibility of a reentry problem warranted a second opinion. 'By the way, there's one more thing,' Kennerdale added as he glanced back at his notes.

'Yes?'

'Fuel mixing.'

'Wasn't that Captain Collins' idea?'

'Exactly.' Kennerdale frowned. 'Fuel mixing seems unlikely to be successful – and it's probably dangerous.'

'Probably.'

'I'm glad you agree,' Kennerdale added sarcastically. He knew that Novak understood less about the technical factors than he did. The irritating part of the conversation was that both he and Novak knew damn well what they were really referring to. 'We sure as hell better convince a few more people.'

'Yes.' Since they had arrived at Goddard, Kennerdale had taken great liberties with NASA policies and procedures. If that airliner somehow found a way to get down on its own, Kennerdale wouldn't have a NASA rescue to explain away his actions. Lynch and Furgeson would have enough evidence to hang Kennerdale's ass – and they undoubtedly would. Novak would be out in the cold, too – and without any chance of landing another government job. 'We don't have too many choices.'

'We have no choices. None at all.' Kennerdale could see that it was too late to allow the possibility of a rescue without NASA. Right or wrong, they had made too many commitments.

'I think it was Abraham Lincoln who said that duty comes from self-interest,' Novak said self-consciously.

'That's a rough translation,' Kennerdale answered. 'Very rough.' But he couldn't help but smile. His young assistant, for all his faults, could at least be understood. The two of them spoke the same language. 'Lincoln also said that we should do our duty as we understand it.'

'Really?' Novak pretended to be interested in Kennerdale's continual references to Lincoln. Two months ago it was Thomas Jefferson – and Kipling before that. He was always quoting someone.

'Yes,' Kennerdale said. He paused, then took one long glance around into the lower level of the OPSCON before he turned back to Novak. 'We've got to find some way to kill that fuel-mixing idea.'

'That pilot sounded adamant. He's going to want an answer. He's going to want more than just our opinion.'

'I know.' Kennerdale leaned forward and scanned his notes. 'We've got to give them firm evidence against it.'

'That's not going to be easy.'

'Maybe.' As he went down his list a second time, Kennerdale found the answer that he needed. 'Here it is.'

'Where?'

Kennerdale grinned, then tapped his pencil against the notepad. 'That jerk at the FAA.'

'John Sample?'

'Yes. Call him back. Ask for his help. Ask him for FAA verification that attempts to blend kerosene with breathable oxygen might very well blow that airliner apart. Tell him that our preliminary evaluations showed fuel mixing to be too dangerous. Be certain that you phrase our request exactly as I've given it to you. Say nothing more, nothing less.'

Novak hastily jotted notes. 'I understand.' He nodded in agreement. 'It's a great idea. There's no way in hell that Sample will allow an FAA test group to take the rap. He's got to go along with our suspicion that it's too risky.'

'Of course.' Kennerdale sat back. He had, with one phone call, solved two of his major problems. John Sample and the Federal Aviation Administration would now have a face-saving assignment, which is all they really cared about anyway. Simultaneously, Kennerdale had guaranteed that another respected government agency – besides his own – would find fuel mixing as ill-advised. That outcome was as predictable as the bureaucratic mind. 'If I know Sample, he'll drag that testing out as long as possible. He'll turn it into a real sideshow.'

'We can ask him for an early preliminary report. From that point on, there will only be one option for rescuing people on the airliner. The Space Shuttle.'

'That's true.' Kennerdale felt a small flush of victory. The NASA plan – Kennerdale's plan – would soon be indispensable. His actions, no matter how unorthodox they might be, would be justified. Politically, he would be above reproach. Kennerdale fumbled in his pocket and pulled out his cigarettes. There was only one left. He took it out and lit it. He crumpled the empty pack and thew it on the floor. 'Okay. Let's get started.'

'Right.' Novak turned toward the corridor at the rear of the OPSCON.

'While you're downstairs,' Kennerdale called out across the room,' get me another pack of cigarettes.'

'Certainly.' Novak disappeared down the hallway.

Kennerdale swiveled his chair around and began to deal with the mounting pile of paperwork that lay on his console. He impatiently flipped through the stack for a few minutes before he realized that someone stood beside him. He looked up.

Justin Watts smiled down at Kennerdale. 'Hello, Ralph,' he said, his mellifluous baritone voice majestically bridging the gap between them. 'Nice to see you again.'

'How the hell did you get past security?' To Kennerdale, the outline of Watts' thick, sculptured hairstyle and billowy mustache were the punctuation marks for the irritating statement that his presence always created.

Watts gestured palm-up, then smiled again broadly. 'Lucky, I guess.'

'Maybe I should check with the guards. Find out which of those morons allowed you in.' Kennerdale pretended to reach for his telephone, knowing damn well that he had no intention of making the call.

'I've got my press credentials,' Watts answered automatically as he pointed to the television network identification card he wore on his lapel. He also knew that, in this particular instance at least, Kennerdale would be all sound and no fury. 'The relationship between NASA and the TV industry has always been quite cordial.'

'Bullshit. That badge of yours doesn't mean a damn thing around here. Not to me.' But Kennerdale knew how wrong he actually was. Big shots from the major TV networks had authorization to officially request cooperation whenever they wanted it. Unofficially, they had nearly unlimited access to any of the NASA facilities they cared to see.

'Don't get hostile. This is just a friendly visit.'

'I bet.' It was also no mystery about how Watts and his fellow media vultures could zero in on a new target as early as they did. 'If I ever find out which of our loyal NASA staff is on your payroll,' Kennerdale said as he glanced around the lower level of the OPSCON, 'I'll strap their balls to the first downrange vehicle we've got on the pad.'

'Don't be a sore loser. You've got your job to do. I've got mine. I can't run a TV news department by being shy.'

'Stop wasting my time. What do you want?'

Watts tugged at the corner of his brown bow tie. 'Nothing much. Just a little cooperation. Permission from you to plug into the live TV signal that you'll be getting shortly from that repositioned satellite.'

Kennerdale shook his head in disbelief, then looked back at the lower level. He wanted, badly, to catch someone glancing up toward them. He would get great satisfaction out of making a public display of whoever was Watts' stoolie. But whoever it was – even if he was inside the building – had the good sense not to look up. Kennerdale turned back to Watts. 'No,' he finally answered. 'This is a private government matter. I'm not going to turn it into a goddamn circus so the afternoon TV crowd can get vicarious kicks. Absolutely not.'

'That's not in line with the recent court decisions.'

'Don't give me "the public's right to know" crap. You and I know the real bottom line. You've got empty air time to fill. That's always your first priority. Screw the public and anyone else who gets in your way, just so you get your story.'

Watts shrugged. 'I don't make the rules. I work with what I've got.'

'Bullshit.'

Watts shifted his feet, then folded his arms casually. 'Normally I'd enjoy this tête-à-tête with you, Ralph. But not today. I've already got one hell of a headache, and it's only,' Watts peeked at his gold wristwatch, 'quarter after twelve. If we're going to hook into that satellite signal, I'm going to need a little lead time to get my equipment set up and operating. For that reason, I'm going to give it to you all at once. Straight from the shoulder.'

'Your pronouncements don't affect me.' Kennerdale picked up his paperwork and pretended to study it. He had, time and again, asked Lynch and Furgeson to stop treating the media with so much deference. Especially a bastard like Justin Watts. Kennerdale's pleas had always been dismissed as overreaction.

'Live TV coverage,' Watts began, his tone the familiar patter that the evening news had made him famous for, 'from that satellite will add another fine dimension to the excellent job you and NASA are doing during the attempted rescue of the stranded airliner. I can guarantee that we'll take time from our live satellite coverage – a substantial portion of time – to personally highlight the outstanding contributions that you've made to the rescue attempt.'

'I'm flattered,' Kennerdale said contemptuously.

Watts ignored the interruption. 'But the sad part is that if we don't have that live TV signal from the satellite, we'll have so much on-the-air time to fill that we'll probably need to analyze each move NASA has made. I'd bet a dinner at Sans Souci that it won't take long to uncover a few questionable areas. Perhaps a few outright errors in judgment.'

Kennerdale's mouth was slightly open, his eyes wide. He could hardly believe what he had heard and, at the same time, he had expected something just like it. 'Are you threatening me?'

'Just reporting the facts. It's nothing personal.'

The two of them stayed silent for nearly a minute. Kennerdale watched the white line on the large wall map as it inched along its preordained path. 'Okay,' he finally answered. 'You can hook into the signal. Work out arrangements with Novak or Reiman. They're downstairs.'

'Thanks. You won't regret this. It'll be good for both of us.'

'Maybe.' Kennerdale could find nothing wrong with the idea of the TV hookup. Actually, it seemed to meld nicely with his overall plan to enhance the NASA image and strengthen his personal position so that he could do more for the Agency. In any event, he seemed to have no choice. But in spite of the obvious advantages, a small but nagging doubt tugged at the back of his mind. Working with Justin Watts and the TV networks was against the grain of everything he stood for, everything he believed in. *A goddamn circus.*

As the ornate mantel clock on the polished teakwood credenza began to strike twelve, Stuart Goldman turned in his seat and glanced out the window of his office in the West Wing of the White House. Another shaft of sunlight had poked around the rapidly dissipating clouds and had bathed the area surrounding the Washington Monument in a warm and bright glow. Goldman ignored the view. 'Very nice. Very nice indeed,' Goldman said as he pressed the telephone receiver firmly against his ear. 'That does seem to be good news. Let's go over it one more time, so I can give the President an accurate report.'

'Certainly.' Kennerdale took a deep breath, then began to explain the details of his plan to maneuver the TV satellite.

'So – if I understand this correctly,' Goldman said, an edge of excitement in his voice, 'the TV networks have agreed to transmit this live signal during the actual rescue attempt?'

'Yes.'

'That's very good news.' Goldman checked himself before he said anything that might be inappropriate when considered in relation to the dire situation of those trapped aboard the airliner.

'All preparations on this end have gone well,' Kennerdale added as he took up a slack moment in the conversation. He was

156

glad to have taken the precaution to clue Goldman in on the involvement of the TV networks before it had become a *fait accompli*. Now, in spite of his initial dislike for the idea, he was convinced that it had been the best thing to do. 'I'm pleased that you agree with the idea of allowing the networks access to this TV signal,' he said, just to be certain there was no misunderstanding between the two of them.

'Of course. It's the public's right to be informed.'

'Naturally.'

'In any event, be certain to keep *me* informed. I'll pass this news directly to the President. He's quite anxious to see that every available resource of the government be used to bring about a successful rescue of the people onboard that airliner.'

'You can assure him that we intend to do our best. I'm expecting no difficulty.'

'Fine.' Goldman frowned. He thought he had heard a hint of doubt creep into Kennerdale's voice. Perhaps there would be a problem in getting the NASA Space Shuttle launched after all. If they were having difficulties, Goldman knew that Kennerdale would be the last to admit it. He added a few additional words of praise and encouragement, then ended the conversation. He hung up the phone, then stood up from his desk and walked to the window.

Goldman gazed blankly out across the White House lawn, deep in thought. The stranded airliner situation could be a terrific boon to the President – as long as NASA was able to launch a rescue attempt in time. If NASA failed or – worse – turned the rescue into a fiasco, the President would look bad. Goldman shuddered when he thought about the attempted rescue of the Iranian hostages a few years before. That monumental screw-up had been a major ingredient in bringing down the Carter administration. Goldman racked his brain for some way to minimize the downside risk, some way to make the President's involvement into a no-lose situation.

'Christ.' Goldman suddenly realized what unexplored option was still available to them. He stepped quickly back to his desk, picked up his telephone and pressed a special buzzer. 'Mr. President,' he said after a few seconds, 'I've got an updated report on the airliner trapped in orbit. But before I give it to you, I have one suggestion I'd like to make.' Goldman sat down at his desk, picked up a pencil and wrote down one word in bold letters across the yellow pad. He looked at the word for another moment before he spoke it aloud. 'Russians.' He paused to allow the implications to sink in. 'Call the Russians on the hot line. Ask them to help. That gives us two independent methods of rescue. That gives us a backup plan in case NASA fails. It reduces the potential for embarrassment to nearly zero.'

Goldman stopped and listened to the President's response. As he listened, he scribbled a few notes. 'Yes. Exactly,' he replied when the President had finished. 'If NASA fails and the Russians succeed, you still come out a winner. Your personal involvement will be heralded in the press as a great humanitarian effort that transcended the boundaries of nationalistic isolationism. It's got reelection potential written all over it. By the way, have I mentioned,' Goldman added, barely able to keep the glee out of his voice, 'that the entire orbital rescue attempt – no matter whether the actual work is accomplished by NASA or the Russians – will be televised live, via satellite camera, on national TV?'

Captain Donald Collins kept his eye on the area of clouds beneath them as he continued with his radio conversation. 'Then you expect us to be out of communications in seven minutes?'

'Roger, that's correct,' Robinson answered at his end of the radio link. 'Twelve forty-six to be precise. When you've reached the coast of Ecuador.'

'I understand.' Collins continued to visually follow the patterns of the clouds. 'There's one hell of a low-pressure area over the west side of the Gulf of Mexico. It looks like a textbook drawing.' The ever-tightening swirl of white clouds stood out dramatically against the deep blue of the water beneath it. The ridges showed some contour, but the overall impression was of a flat, one-dimensional disk. 'It looks like the photograph of a papier-mâchè model.'

'Roger.' Robinson had reconciled himself to the need to spend valuable time in vacuous chitchat. He could understand Collins' desire to talk. 'Our information shows that you are passing directly over Veracruz, on the east coast of Mexico. The projection line indicates that you'll depart the South American coastline near Rio de Janeiro at twelve fifty-seven. We don't expect to have you back in radio contact until one thirty-five.' Robinson had given Collins all the facts he had, all the information that was currently displayed on the NASA Circuits. Beyond that – and beyond the one additional request he had yet to make – Robinson had nothing left to say. As much as he tried, he found it increasingly difficult to be glib and reassuring.

'Okay.' Collins paused for a moment. He glanced around the cockpit. Briscoe continued to look out the other side, toward a cluster of dim yet distinctive stars. 'It's strange,' Collins transmitted, 'how we can see so many stars, even in broad daylight. Other than directly toward the sun, I can see stars in all directions.'

'Roger. Understand.' Robinson kept his microphone button keyed down, but said nothing for several seconds. 'Incidentally,' he finally added, 'I'd like you to have the engineer go to the lower compartment again. To check on several more items for me. Serial numbers, that sort of thing.'

'Sure.' Collins glanced at Katie, who picked up a pencil and nodded back. 'Go ahead with the request,' he transmitted. 'She's listening.'

Robinson began to read off a list of the new items he wanted checked. He had purposely waited until the last few minutes before radio contact would be lost so no one from NASA would be able to override his request or quiz him about its relevance. In another minute or two, no one would be able to sidetrack the flight crew by asking them to do something else instead. 'You'll be out of radio contact in another three minutes. Get the list items verified during the radio blackout. You can relay them to me at one-forty.'

'Roger. Will do,' Katie transmitted. She began to unbuckle her seat belt. 'Before I go,' she said to Collins, 'I was wondering if you wanted me to remove the electrical power from some of the other systems. The ones not in use.'

'Like what?'

'Fuel control, window heat, that sort of thing.'

Collins considered her idea for a moment. He looked down at the rocket fuel monitoring controls, which had become completely useless because of the empty liquid oxygen tank, then put his hand up against the warm glass of the cockpit side window. Collins glanced over his shoulder at the gray box against the window frame where the current for the heated glass was routed through. Both the rocket controls and the window heat were senseless to still have on, but there seemed to be no advantage in having them off. Either way, it didn't change their situation. 'No. As long as our situation is status quo, there's no sense screwing with those things.'

'That's the kind of talk I like to hear,' Briscoe announced.

Collins ignored him. 'Bring those serial numbers back as soon as you can.'

'Yessir.' With her list in hand, Katie moved carefully backward toward the floor-mounted access hatch at the rear of the cockpit. She activated the controls to open the electric hatch, then climbed down the vertical stairway.

Collins watched as she entered the netherworld below the cockpit floor. That was where the elaborate electronics were housed – electronics that had betrayed them and sent them soaring into this insanity. Shortly after Katie disappeared beneath the ledge of the rim, she activated the automatic door circuit from below. The airtight hatchway closed and locked. 'Any news on the Shuttle launch?' Collins asked as he returned to his flight panel.

'Still on schedule. Two-ten,' Robinson elaborated. 'That's still the expected rendezvous time. The launch is set for one forty-five – a few minutes after you come out of radio blackout.' He could say little more, since that was all that Kennerdale had told him.

'Okay. That's good.' The repeated declaration of the rescue timetable had a medicinal effect on Collins' spirit. Even though he had heard the schedule earlier, each time it was repeated it was a renewed excuse for optimism. 'One forty-five,' he said into the microphone as he stretched the tense muscles in his body and allowed himself to sit further upright. His tone was crisp and full, his eyes alert, his mind working diligently. He looked around at

160

his panel gauges. 'Oxygen usage is exactly what's been predicted,' Collins announced.

'That's excellent.'

'Yes. The three forty-five depletion time,' Collins added as he glimpsed the luminescent numbers of his clock, 'still seems quite accurate.'

'Our ground computations show the same depletion time.'

'Yes. Three forty-five.' As he listened to the sound of his own voice in his earphones, Collins felt a cold spasm of fear pass through him. He sat silently for several long moments, stunned by the sudden realization of how nonchalantly both he and Robinson had used that key word. *Depletion*. It was a discrete way of skirting the real issue. It was an official euphemism for suffocation, for death. *Three forty-five*.

'Three forty-five. That's fine. We've got no problem with that,' Robinson said as he tried to sound as reassuring as he could.

'There was static in your last transmission,' Collins answered. His thoughts had settled on a new problem, a more immediate concern. Even though he had been told repeatedly to expect as much, he was unable to disguise his disappointment. He was once again about to lose his link to Robinson, his lifeline. 'I think we're nearly out of contact.' He knew that maintaining radio contact meant very little at this stage of the rescue attempt. Somehow, to him, it still meant very much.

'Yes. Your transmissions are garbled on this end, also.'

Collins pressed down against his headphones. 'Your last words were nearly unreadable. Are we breaking up to you? Can you still hear us?'

There was no response.

'Goddard. Can you still hear us?' Collins repeated, the pitch of his voice slightly higher.

'Let it go.' Briscoe twisted around in his seat. 'Radio blackout. It's within sixty seconds of their prediction.' He motioned toward Collins' clock. 'We don't have much else to say to them anyway.' He shook his head in disgust. 'All this conversation doesn't amount to shit. Everything hinges on the Shuttle launch. They sure as hell better get their asses in gear down there.' Briscoe made a pointing motion toward the *Star Streak*'s floorboards. 'We don't have much time.'

Collins nodded absently. He made eye contact with Briscoe for a brief instant, then turned away abruptly. He looked out his side window. They had already passed the area of clouds and weather over the west side of the Gulf of Mexico. The clouds stood far behind them, silhouetted against the curved line of the horizon. They appeared tall and square, rather than the flattened shape they had been moments before. Sunlight played off the clouds at an oblique angle, and it caused them to transform from milky-white apparitions into creamy yellow structures that were possessed with definitive form and a malleable substance. The mound of clouds more resembled an overturned bowl of ice cream than an ethereal mass of swirling vapors. As Collins took in the new view, he realized – once again – how every passing moment of their orbit had caused everything to change radically. 'We've got to do something,' he said. 'We can't wait for them. We can't sit here and die.'

'God Almighty.' Briscoe tilted his head back and rolled his eyes. 'Not that line of crap again.'

Collins ignored Briscoe's mood. 'Yes.' He understood now, for the first time since the nightmare had begun, exactly what he had become so afraid for. The most frightening part of it all – just like the most frightening part of Susan's cancer – was the horror of waiting. The waiting to die. The waiting to see if life could be started over again. 'We've got to do something,' Collins announced adamantly. He began to unbuckle his seat belt.

'Where are you going?' Briscoe's words were a cross between a question and a command.

'I don't know.' Collins allowed his seat belt to fall away. He used one hand against the instrument panel glare shield and the other against his seat back to steady himself. 'I thought that . . . '

'Not more of that fuel-mixing crap.' Briscoe's jaw was set firmly, his eyes narrowed. He had no intention of allowing Collins – captain's authority or not – to blow the ship into a million pieces and scatter it into the far reaches of space. During the past two hours, Briscoe had put aside the memory of his own indecisions, his lack of a plan to save them, his inability to deal with their limited and dwindling options. 'It's absurd. Idiotic.' He waved his finger at Collins, who had become the personification of all the horror that had occurred to them. 'We're not going to do it unless NASA tells us it's a good idea. I doubt that they'll say that.'

'I'm not going to wait to die.' Collins flexed his arm and began to push himself out of his seat. 'But that's not what I intend . . . '

Briscoe grabbed for Collins' wrist. 'No. No fuel mixing,' he said before Collins had finished. 'I'm not going to allow it.'

'Let go of me, you son of a bitch.' Collins glared down at the copilot. A sensation of physical pain traveled up his arm, caused by Briscoe's abrasive grip. He could feel the cold and clammy sweat from Briscoe's hand.

'No.'

'Let go of me!' Collins had spoken louder than he intended to. He tried to yank his hand away, but the young copilot's hold was too strong. 'You bastard! Let go of me!' Collins knew that he had no intention of doing anything impetuous. He had only intended to discreetly talk with Diederich, Akins and a few of the other science-minded people in the cabin for new ideas on how they might deal with the situation.

'I'm not going to let you kill us. You're the one who got us into this insanity! It's your goddamn fault!' Briscoe's words tumbled out faster than he realized, faster than he could stop them. 'I shouldn't have let you pull us into orbit. I shouldn't have gotten into this airliner with you to start with.'

With his one free hand, Collins swung himself out of his seat and twisted his body around in an attempt to break Briscoe's grip.

'Stop. I'm not going to let you kill us.' Briscoe yanked hard on Collins' arm, more out of anger than any rational attempt to maneuver the man in a particular direction.

'Christ. Be careful!' Collins' body began to react to the forces Briscoe had imparted to it. His arm, held rigid at the wrist by Briscoe's locked fingers, acted as an anchor. In the zero-gravity condition, Collins' legs drifted upward and out. They moved with the current of free motion that the copilot had set into effect. In the confines of the narrow cockpit, Collins' legs quickly ran out of empty space. His feet hit against the roofline and bounced back, as if they were not more than a rubber ball flung against a concrete wall.

'Stop!' In obedience to the laws of motion that governed the weightless environment they were trapped in, Collins' body recoiled off the roofline and began to arch forward. He was thrust back toward where Briscoe pulled him.

'Get back!' Briscoe shouted. Out of sheet instinct, the copilot released his grip on Collins' wrist and threw his arm up to shield himself from the human projectile that Collins' body had become.

The contact between Briscoe's raised arm and Collins' body occurred directly over the copilot's seat and slightly at an angle to it. In the matter of an instant, Collins' body was again deflected by the new force. This time he had been pushed toward the right cockpit sidewall – and toward the unguarded flight engineer's panel.

'Stop me!' Collins yelled, as soon as he realized what direction he had begun to tumble in. His head was upside down in reference to the floor, and his feet dangled uselessly and dangerously ahead of him. His view of things was twisted and contorted by the weird orientations that his constant motion provided. Yet he could see, unmistakably, the direction he was moving in. 'The panel!' He kicked his legs and grabbed for a handhold along the ceiling. What few places he could reach were either too smooth or too slippery to provide any measure of grip.

'Here! My hand! Grab it!' Briscoe stretched as far backwards as he could in an attempt to snare Collins. He, too, had finally realized what would happen next. Briscoe repeatedly hit the buckle of his seat belt with his one free hand in an attempt to release himself, to give himself enough freedom to reach Collins. His hand kept missing the seat belt's catch.

The outstretched hands of the two pilots passed within inches of each other, their fingers groping to make contact. But Collins' trajectory was too angled. The captain continued to drift, unchecked, toward the flight engineer's panel.

Chapter Nine

BEN ROBINSON hurried through the brightly lit corridor in Building 12 of the Goddard Center. His shoes made a continuous squeaking noise against the waxed linoleum floor as he moved. His arms swung rhythmically at his sides, and his eyes darted from one doorway to the next. He searched down the high-ceilinged passageway for the auxiliary communications room that had been assigned to United Acrospace. The stenciled letters 11-10 loomed up on a wall column. Robinson stepped around the column, turned to his left and stopped.

Through the door's glass insert he saw Becker and McBride. The two of them stood near the far wall, adjacent to the electronic console.

McBride motioned forcefully and repeatedly with his hands, his gestures in apparent animation to his mumbled words, which were too indistinct to be heard through the closed door. His round, fleshy face bucked up and down in short, jerky motions. Bonnie Becker, who stood only a few feet in front of him, appeared equally intent. The corners of her mouth were turned down in an expression that was a cross between a pout and a scowl. When McBride finally stopped talking, Becker quickly

165

answered back. She narrowed her eyes and began to wave her finger at him. Robinson could not make out what either of them had said.

A dozen feet behind Becker and McBride stood Alex Krause. He seemed oblivious to what the other two were doing. His hands rested on an open sheaf of papers spread across a government-issue table, his leg with the cast stuck out at an awkward angle. As Robinson watched, Krause flipped through several pages of what appeared to be aircraft manuals.

Robinson took a few seconds to glance around the rest of the windowless room. It was exactly as Novak had described it. Long and narrow, with a small glass-enclosed private office at the rear. There were a few too many fluorescent lights in the ceiling and it caused the level of washed-out brightness to be nearly uncomfortable. Except for the metal-gray console and the electronic cabinets – one unit in the main section of the room and one in the private area – the facility looked more like a storage closet than a technical support area. Robinson took a deep breath, then opened the door.

McBride turned. When he saw Robinson, he smiled apologetically. 'You caught us in a disagreement,' he said. He nodded toward Becker, who continued to stand firmly, her body rigid, her face set in a deep frown.

'A disagreement?' Robinson forced himself to smile back. He wanted to appear unconcerned. 'What about?'

Becker broke her frozen stance. She shifted her weight, tugged at one of the legs of her linen suit, then took a step toward Robinson. 'This man,' she said, her thumb aimed toward McBride as if she were a mother pointing to her petulant child, 'is concerned only with the technical problems in that *Star Streak*. He wants us to spend our time analyzing the possible fault areas, nothing else. I feel we should concentrate on ways we can help, ways we might assist the rescue.'

Robinson ran his tongue across his dry lips. Becker was apparently not concerned about uncovering the reasons behind the catastrophic failure of the airliner's rocket controls. 'You want us to concentrate on other things?'

'Yes. On rescue-related ideas. Oxygen conservation, that

166

sort of thing. It would certainly seem more timely to me.'

'I see.' Was Becker trying to steer them away from areas that might uncover her own guilt? That was an obvious possibility. It might even be true. But it also seemed too convenient. Robinson knew damn well that his personal dislike for Bonnie Becker had begun to influence him too much. He needed to check himself, to keep himself objective and unemotional. Becker's resistance might be nothing beyond a difference of opinion, an alternate method for attacking the same problem. He ran his hand along his thinning hairline. 'It's difficult to say.'

'It's the only logical plan.'

'No,' McBride interrupted. 'The reason for the rocket failure is very important.' He sounded exasperated. 'Let's be practical. The failure data might come in handy during the rescue, but we're sure as hell going to need it later, when every damn *Star Streak* we've built is sitting on the ground because we can't explain what happened to Ship thirty-five.'

'That's true.' Robinson glanced at his wristwatch. Flight 14 had less than three hours of oxygen left. He was almost out of time. 'McBride's got a point. Maybe the failure can provide us with an idea we can use during the rescue.' Robinson decided to try to prod Becker into saying more. He fumbled for the appropriate words. 'You need to be more open-minded.'

'What?' She looked puzzled.

'Yes. Open-minded. More receptive to outside ideas. Unless you've got something positive and conclusive to add, I suggest that you listen carefully to McBride. He knows what he's doing.'

Becker's hazel eyes began to fill with a seething anger. 'You're the boss,' she answered curtly.

'McBride's the senior man of your group,' Robinson said as he rambled on. He had nearly run out of things to say.

'Fine with me.' Becker's jaw muscles were taut. She glared at Robinson before she turned away.

'Okay.' *Shit*. Robinson's heart sank. He had learned nothing. He had angered Becker without gaining the slightest bit of additional knowledge. Robinson avoided McBride's smile and instead looked back at Krause. The third United Aerospace engineer had shown no interest in joining the discussion. Robinson had seen Krause glance up at them several times, more out of obligation than purpose. For the moment, Krause's attentions were back on the aircraft manuals. Krause seemed to be the only one of them doing any actual work on the rescue. Robinson turned to face McBride, who still smiled broadly because of the trumped-up compliment that Robinson had paid him. 'Have you found everything you need? Has anyone shown you how to work the scope?'

'Yes. A NASA technician came down with us.'

'Good. Did they also tell you that the United Aerospace computer data has been fed into the Goddard network?'

'No. How do we get at it?'

'Use this prefix.' Robinson laid a sheet of paper on the console where he had written the code numbers Novak had given him. 'Once you've acquired access, you can use our standard formats to call up whatever company data you want.'

'Fine.'

Robinson nodded, then stood silently. He was now at another dead end. He sorely wanted to make his telephone call, but he also felt a need to stay in conversation with the three of them. Unless he figured out which of them was the saboteur, the rescue would be totally dependent on the success of NASA's Space Shuttle – a possibility that, in spite of Kennerdale's assurances, seemed chancy at best.

Robinson was certain that there was a second device onboard the airliner – a device that the saboteur intended to use to retrieve the aircraft after the ransom was paid. That was the only sabotage plan that made any sense, except for the possibility that there would be a promise of a second device without one actually existing. That kind of super-bluff seemed out of keeping with the careful planning of the rest of the sabotage and, besides, if it were true then none of this mattered anyway. He was convinced that one of the people standing in the room with him already knew how to bring the airliner down. 'Any other ideas?'

'I'm afraid not,' Becker answered coldly.

'We don't really know where to start,' McBride said.

Robinson rubbed his forehead. The nausea and lightheadedness from his Ménière's disease had increased. He had already taken two pills for controlling his faulty inner-ear mechanism, but so far they hadn't had any effect. 'I don't know where to start either,' Robinson admitted reluctantly. He looked back toward Krause. 'Anything in the books?'

'Nothing yet.' Krause stared at Robinson for several long seconds, then dropped his eyes to the aircraft manuals on the table. 'I'm having the same problem they are. I'm looking for a starting point. There's just too much to pick from. I'm sorry . . . ' His voice had trailed off to a pleading whisper.

'So am I. Keep trying.' Robinson touched Krause on the shoulder, then began to edge toward the inner office door. Right or wrong, he had already formed a distinct impression about each of the three engineers. Becker seemed the most likely candidate to be the saboteur, Krause unquestionably the least. He needed to talk to Ferrera. 'I've got a telephone call to make. Our legal department,' Robinson lied. 'I'll be tied up for the next few minutes.' Not waiting for a reply, Robinson stepped into the glass enclosure. He closed the door behind him, then walked over to the electronics console. He sat in the swivel chair and watched the three engineers as they huddled together and began to study the manuals. Finally, Robinson turned and faced the telephone controls on his console.

Just like the panel in the upper level of the OPSCON, the console in the private office had its telephone and auto-dialer controls across the top edge. Robinson leaned forward and punched several buttons, then began to dial in the numbers of Ferrera's private line in Phoenix. He planned to leave the number-one button on the console programmed as a direct link to Ferrera. As soon as he had a free minute, Robinson intended to program the Astrex Corporation's telephone number into position two, so he could quickly contact Ray Lee whenever it became necessary. That would leave position three open for any other calls. Robinson picked up the handset, selected position one and pressed the recall button. He could hear the series of rapid electronic beeps as the auto-dialer rapidly repeated the last programmed numbers. Within seconds, the call was routed through.

'Ferrera.' The senior vice-president had picked up his telephone before the second ring.

'Discover anything?' Robinson asked immediately.

'I sure have. I've got a rundown on each of them.'

'Go ahead.' Robinson pulled a pen out of his coat pocket and opened his notepad.

'From the hangar time cards I learned that McBride worked on that aircraft for two of the days it was in Phoenix. Bonnie Becker worked on it for three days.'

'What about Krause?' Robinson watched the tall, wiry engineer through the glass partition. With his leg in a cast, he stepped awkwardly around the desk as he reached for a stack of manuals on the far side.

'No chance. He was out sick. In the hospital. He was one of the employees injured in the gantry crane accident in the hangar.'

'I know. What were the exact dates?'

'From the afternoon of Saturday, August thirteenth.'

'August thirteenth,' Robinson repeated as he jotted it down. He may not have remembered the date of the accident, but he certainly remembered the experience of spending the entire week afterward on business directly related to it. When the biggest ceiling crane in United Aerospace's largest hangar fell apart, so did their normal routines and schedules. 'How long, exactly, was Krause in the hospital?'

The sound of shuffled papers filled Robinson's earpiece. 'I'm not sure what date he was released. I'll check that,' Ferrera said.

'While you're at it, ask them if there was any possible way for Krause to have sneaked out during the time he was supposed to be there.'

'Sure.' Ferrera paused. 'Do you think it's him?' he asked hesitantly, almost as if he didn't want to actually know. 'He's always been an excellent employee.'

'Yes.' Robinson's eyes followed Krause as he left the table and hobbled over to the electronics console. The engineer sat down in front of the TV screen, pressed several buttons, then began to read the updated display. 'I don't think it's Krause, but I want to be sure. I want to check every possibility.'

'It's fine to be thorough, but we don't have time to waste. I'd be inclined to dismiss Krause as a viable suspect based solely on his record. He's been enthusiastic and loyal since the day we hired him. Invaluable, too. He was the one who came up, single-handed, with the computer-generated quality-control program.'

'I know.'

'Putting Krause aside, which of the other two do you most suspect?'

'Becker.' Robinson had answered before he could stop himself. 'But I'm not certain,' he added quickly. 'Not by a long shot.' In spite of the prodding from Ferrera, Robinson was determined not to jump to hasty conclusions. The stakes were too high for that. Just like the test flights that he had conducted successfully for so many years, he intended to be careful, methodical, orderly. That was the only way to lessen the risk of making a wrong decision. Every one of them – including Alex Krause – would be equally suspect until the proper choice was unmistakable.

'If it's Becker, then why hasn't she issued the ransom demand yet?'

'I'm not sure.' Robinson yanked nervously at his tie. Ferrera had touched on the one aspect of his sabotage theory that was still a loose end. 'I think it's the Space Shuttle. The NASA attempt came as a complete surprise. Becker – or whoever it is – is waiting to see what happens.'

'That's possible,' Ferrera agreed. 'She won't make the ransom offer to provide the information on how to operate the second device – presupposing that the sabotage theory you mentioned earlier is correct – until the Space Shuttle is out of the picture.'

'Exactly.' Robinson coughed lightly to clear his throat. He hoped to God that he had been right about the sabotage having been too well planned to be nothing but an act of random violence, a senseless murder. 'We don't have to worry about any of them trying to sneak out. The saboteur wouldn't risk going anywhere until the Space Shuttle possibility has been resolved. They've got to stay here to see it through.'

'Don't let them out of your sight. Maybe you should alert the guards.'

'I've already done that. I called the Goddard security chief – a man named Frank Schaefer – a short while ago.'

'I hope you didn't say too much.' For all his apparent agreement, Ferrera still wasn't totally convinced that Robinson was correct about the sabotage. The last thing they needed now was a character defamation suit to add to their problems.

'No. I only told Schaefer that because of the possibility of adverse and premature publicity, we had to restrict the movements of our company people until a public announcement concerning the airline disaster could be made. I hinted that it had something to do with the trading of our corporate stock.'

'That's pretty farfetched.'

'He seemed to buy it. Schaefer assured me that no one from United Aerospace would get past the security gate. Not unless he got another call from me first.'

'Okay.' Without realizing it, Ferrera had begun to tap his finger against the telephone cradle while he gathered his scattered thoughts. A series of patterned beats resonated mildly through the circuit. 'Let's get back to your theory itself. What about the possibility of an accomplice? It seems improbable that anyone could pull this off alone. At the very least, they'll need help to issue the ransom demands and pick up the money.'

'There's probably a footman out there somewhere, waiting for word. We'll catch up to them later, once we've gotten this situation under control. But that part of their plan is nearly insignificant. The major ingredients in the sabotage – the initial idea, the design of the devices, the actual execution – had to come from one of these three.'

'You think so?'

'Yes. Absolutely.' Robinson resisted the impulse to turn and look at the engineers. Instead he focused his eyes on the console in front of him. 'By the way,' he said to change the subject, 'have you verified the aircraft's maintenance schedule?'

'Yes.' Ferrera rifled through his stack of paperwork. 'Ship thirty-five was put into the paint shop on Friday, August nineteenth. It was transferred to the electronics shop on Friday, August twenty-sixth.'

Robinson made a note of the dates. 'When did it go back to the airline?'

'September second.'

'Okay.' Robinson picked up his notepad and glanced at the figures. N35CA had been worked on in Phoenix from August nineteenth through September second. Slightly over two weeks. That was more than enough time for the saboteur to gain undetected access to the aircraft and the quality-control programs. 'Any other news?' Robinson asked as he rose from the chair. He stood next to the console, his hip laid against its flat metal side.

'I've reviewed their personnel files. Krause's record is literally packed with commendations. Becker's is filled with nothing but complaints. McBride's folder falls somewhere between the two.'

'That's what I would've guessed.'

'I've also learned a few additional things by poking around. Pure hearsay, but it might be valuable. I saved it for last.'

'Go ahead.' Robinson twisted his body away from the glass wall, so none of the three engineers could see his face. He had a feeling that this was the sort of information that would be the most useful.

'I've got a great many feelers out. Discreetly, of course.'

'Certainly.' Robinson tapped his foot impatiently.

'They tell me – all unverified – that McBride has money problems.'

'What kind?'

'Big ones. Gambling. He's compulsive. There's a rumor around that he owes a great deal to the wrong people. He's being pressed to come up with it.'

'Can you find out more?'

'I'll try.'

'Good.' Robinson felt a twinge of excitement in the pit of his stomach. McBride had a motive. 'What about Becker?'

'She seems to be number one on everyone's shit list. She's a difficult lady, to say the least.'

'Is that all?' Robinson was irritated. 'I'm not interested in her lack of charm. I need more to go on than that.' He peeked over his shoulder toward Becker. She hung back from McBride, her attentions focused not on the aircraft manuals that he pointed at but toward the wall clock instead.

'Give me a chance,' Ferrera shot back. 'I've got reports from

173

two reliable sources that she's made strong anti-company remarks lately. Within the last few weeks. That might mean something.'

'Yes.' That news fit well with what Robinson had already learned. Becker was quickly becoming the lead suspect again.

'But I've had another thought,' Ferrera interjected. 'I hate to sound like a broken record, but could all of this be a bigger conspiracy? Could two or even the three of the engineers be working together?'

'I don't think so,' Robinson said. 'There'd be no advantage in their being here together. It would only complicate things for them and make them more conspicuous, not less. There might be another United Aerospace employee involved, but probably no more than one of these three. Even if there is, by uncovering any one of them, that'll show us if they have partners. We should continue to proceed exactly as we're doing.'

'That makes sense,' Ferrera agreed. He went on to explain how he intended to verify and uncover more information. Robinson made a number of comments and suggestions. Their plans made, they both agreed on the time that Robinson would call back. 'By the way,' Ferrera added, 'how far ahead does your strategy extend?'

'What do you mean?' Robinson fidgeted. He ran his hand across a row of plastic switches on the side of the console. He knew damn well what Ferrera would ask next.

'If the Space Shuttle can't reach them, how are you going to get the saboteur to voluntarily bring down that airliner – assuming, of course, that it's actually possible?'

Robinson allowed a penetrating silence to fill the telephone line. It took several seconds before he could bring himself to speak. 'I don't know,' he said in a low, toneless voice, his eyes closed, his head tilted slightly back. The image of the *Star Streak* as it tumbled weightlessly through the chilled, black emptiness of space filled his mind, his own Ménière's-induced sensation of vertigo adding to the realism. 'I don't have the slightest idea.'

Katie Graham maneuvered carefully through the lower bay of the *Star Streak* airliner. When she had finished jotting down the numbers from the components in front of her, she twisted her body sideways to begin to hunt for the next group. The slight smell of ozone from the stacks of electronics filled her nostrils. She took several deep breaths. She was nervous, and she knew it.

Grow up. Don't be such a child. Katie pushed back her long auburn hair. She forced herself to look around. Since their launch into orbit, this was the second trip that she had made to the windowless lower compartment beneath the cockpit floor. She still had not gotten used to it. The compartment – six feet tall and nearly a dozen feet across – was crammed with electronic components, relay panels, wires and tubing. One small, yellowish bulb sat against the ceiling near the center of the room, and each of the four corners was filled with dark shadows. If it weren't for her flashlight, Katie knew that she would never have been able to read the serial numbers that the people on the ground had called for.

'Subsystem three-seven,' she said out loud. The sound of her own voice had become a welcomed companion. Katie aimed her flashlight across the compartment, its thin wand of brilliance slicing through the gloomy surroundings. 'Three-four. Three-five,' she said as she read the unit numbers in front of her, her high-pitched voice reverberating off the curved metal walls. 'Damn.' She had guessed wrong. She could see now that unit three-seven was part of the group against the far side. Holding her list in one hand and her flashlight in the other, Katie used her legs to push herself away from the wall where she was and toward the new spot across the compartment.

She was glad that she had at least gotten good at maneuvering in the zero gravity. The lower bay was a good place to practice since there were so many convenient handholds in every direction. To Katie's surprise, weightlessness had proven to be a pleasant, effortless way to get around – as long as the weird effects of disorientation didn't overwhelm you. The architecturally induced sense of what was right and wrong – local verticals, she remembered they were called – seemed to prevail regardless. Even though there was no physical reason for any one reference of up or down to have preference over another, Katie knew damn well that there still seemed to be a difference.

Daring herself, she tensed her muscles and allowed her body to drift upside down. She wanted to get another nibble of that feeling she had experienced the first time, that unusual, slightly horrifying sensation of vertigo without motion.

Katie's body turned completely over. Her feet touched lightly against the ceiling. Her fingers brushed against the metal grating on the floor. Being out of kilter was both exhilarating and intimidating. She was, she knew, simultaneously repelled and attracted by this strange experience.

The warm and mild glow from the single lightbulb in the center of the room came from a spot only inches from where Katie's feet were. The corrugated metal grating that normally comprised the compartment's floorboards took on the appearance of an exotic mosaic ceiling tile. She ran her finger along the intricate pattern of metal ridges that she had never before noticed, in spite of the hundreds of times that she had literally stepped all over them.

Katie slowly rotated her head. Her eyes saw everything as wrong, upside down, backward. To her left, a stack of electronic cabinets appeared to have grown down from above, like stalactites in a limestone cavern. Below it was a cluster of colored cables. The gangs of wires tumbled out in all directions like a nest of under-sea snakes. Some of the cables had fanned apart under the influence of their weightlessness, and they looked like the stems and petals in a large bouquet of flowers. The cables' vibrant colors – reds, greens, whites, browns, blues – added to the sense of unreality, the feeling that this was an unearthly, ungodly sight. Katie shivered. *Alice in Wonderland.* The Mad Hatter had nothing on this place. It was sheer craziness. Insanity.

Katie had seen enough. She began to turn herself rightside up, the way the room had been designed for. Using one hand and the slow and deliberate motions of her legs, she spun around in nearly the same spot she had started from.

Before Katie got all the way around, she heard noises from above. It was a scraping sound, followed by muffled voices. 'Ernie? Is that you?' she called out. 'Are you calling me?' She looked at the hatch that led to the cockpit. It was several feet from where she hovered in midair, her one hand clamped tightly to a nearby aluminium bracket, her legs dangling free. The hatch-way remained tightly closed.

Another noise came down from the cockpit, only inches above her head. This time it was more like a series of bangs, as if someone had deliberately kicked against the metal floor. That noise was mixed with the sound of louder voices, although the words were still indistinguishable. Something was definitely wrong. Katie was seized by fear. She wanted to get out of the lower compartment as quickly as she could.

Without realizing it, she released her grip on the pencil and notepad. They drifted lazily across the room, carried in the tiny currents of air produced by the compartment's self-contained pressurization system. 'I'm coming up,' she announced in a quivering, anxious voice, mostly for her own benefit. She leaned forward and grabbed for the ledge of the adjacent stack of electronic gear.

Out of the corner of her eye, Katie spotted something. A large warning light on the far wall of the compartment had blinked on. It flooded the lower bay with a harsh and ominous red glow.

The light was ten feet from her, adjacent to another hatchway. *Caution: Exterior Hatch Controls* read the label above the light. The door beside it was designed to allow access to the lower bay from outside. The appropriate page in the pilot's emergency handbook flashed through Katie's thoughts. *The lower-bay exterior electric hatch can be operated from either the controls adjacent to it, or from a switch on the flight engineer's panel. In case of an in-flight fire in the lower bay, the flight engineer should open the hatch to allow the pressurized air in the compartment to be dumped overboard. This action will smother the fire.*

'God, no!' Katie froze. She could hear a low-pitched whirling noise from the hatchway's internal mechanism. The door had begun to open. Even though she was several feet away, Katie could easily read the oversized label to the left of the warning light on the lower-bay door control panel. *Hatchway Emergency Override.*

'Ernie! No!' Katie had screamed out the copilot's name without even realizing it. Her conscious thoughts were now totally focused on the hatchway controls on the other side of the compartment. She pushed herself toward them.

Katie's arms clawed out ahead of her as she attempted to reach

177

the hatchway controls. She was still too far away. There was a space of at least 30 inches between her outstretched, trembling fingers and the plastic toggle switch she aimed for. Her body continued to float toward the hatchway controls.

Even before Katie could make out any change in the position of the door, she felt a rapid increase in the movement of the compartment's pressurized air. It had begun to rush toward the vacuum of outer space – a condition she knew that the ever-widening door slit would add to with every passing moment.

There was now less than 18 inches between Katie's hand and the hatchway override switch. Her legs kicked desperately. Her arms groped as far ahead as she could stretch.

With a sudden, audible noise, the exterior hatchway door popped open. It had parted enough to make the outside world visible through the slit.

Katie screamed again, her panic now complete. The sound that poured through her throat seemed not her own. The blues and greens and browns of the earth below, and the stark blackness of the horizon line, rotated at a distance that seemed only an arm's length away. Katie's hair swirled wildly around her face as the pressure of the air in the compartment gathered momentum in its rush to get out. She could feel her lungs being sucked empty by the insidious pull of outer space.

Her body's forward motion accelerated by the rush of outgoing air, the fingers of Katie's left hand slammed hard against the hatchway control panel. Carried in the invisible and powerful current that the immutable laws of physics had set into play, she continued to tumble toward the yawning hole of the opening hatch.

Katie attempted to grab at the plastic toggle alongside the red light. Its smooth, rounded surface slipped out of her grip. She was a helpless swimmer, caught in the riptide, her body tossed end-over-end, her arms and legs bounced repeatedly into the frame that surrounded the door.

Her body was finally propelled, feet first, through the opened hatch. Her hand slipped off the control panel. She screamed again. This time, there was no sound. She had entered the airless void of space.

Slowed by her collision with the door frame, Katie drifted only 30 feet away from the airliner's hatch that had spewed her out. To her horror, she remained totally conscious, her vision unimpaired. For the first few seconds, only the deafening roar of ultimate silence from her pressure-shattered eardrums and crushing, aching pain in her oxygen-starved chest remained as indicators of her inescapable fate.

Katie picked up her head and looked at the airliner. Its sleek lines hung motionless against a backdrop of brilliant stars. The angled rays of the slowly sinking sun had begun to dance luminously off the craft's silver wings.

She looked beneath her. A scattered array of clouds spread across an irregular pattern of land and sea. A coastline. A mountain range. Lit from one side because of the approach of darkness, the layers of cloud that surrounded the area appeared to be a majestic awning of gold leaf erected to shield the land below.

God help me. Katie felt as if her mind were a thousand miles away. Her body seemed to be accelerating backward at the speed of light, yet she could see that she was not in motion. *Pressure. Air. Help me.* Her rational thoughts had begun to evaporate as quickly as water tossed on top of a hot stove.

Without being aware of the depths of her suffocating pain, Katie's eyes closed. She had finally slipped into unconsciousness. The view of thousands of square miles of earth beneath her was the last sight she saw. Within seconds her body assumed a natural fetal stance, arms dangled in front, legs tucked slightly up and inclined to her chest.

Katie Graham slipped beyond the bonds of life. Her body continued to rotate in slow motion, the pressurized hull of the airliner she had once been a part of no more than 30 feet ahead. Particles of light danced off the winged airplane emblem pinned to her blouse, and off the tangled strands of her long and silky hair. Rays from the sun, from the billions of stars in the Milky Way, and from countless other galaxies through the universe mingled together to enshroud her body in an eerie, somber glow.

'How is she feeling?'

'Fine.' Paul Diederich looked up at the pudgy-faced doctor, smiled, then touched Chris's arm. 'She opens her eyes every once in a while. She doesn't say anything, but she doesn't seem to be in any pain.' He looked at the new bandage around his wife's throat. It was clean and dry – the bleeding had definitely stopped.

'I've got her pretty well sedated,' Akins answered. He patted the last vial of sedative in his pocket before he remembered that its existence was supposed to be a secret between him and the copilot. He was glad that Diederich hadn't noticed. 'She looks good,' Akins said as he complimented his own medical skills. 'It won't take her long to make a full recovery.'

'The captain has been back several times to check on her. He's very pleased with the job you've done.'

'That's wonderful,' Akins said dryly.

Diederich opened his mouth to add something, but nodded instead. He glanced down the aisle of the airliner. The doctor and one of the flight attendants were the only people not seated. Everyone was calm. There was a soft, continuous murmur of conversation in the background, all of it in hushed voices. It was as if the airliner's cabin had become a church. They were seated and waiting patiently for Sunday service to begin. But this was no lighthearted congregation. The unrelenting fear of imminent disaster was etched on the face of every man, woman and child. Diederich shivered. The hushed, sepulchral quiet made him more uncomfortable, not less.

'Christ'

Diederich spun around toward the doctor. The two of them locked eyes for an instant before Akins turned back toward the window. The doctor's mouth hung open as he gestured toward the Plexiglas.

'What is it?' Diederich's words were barely out before he saw the answer for himself.

Her long hair floated freely in all directions. Her slim, tanned body drifted at an inclined angle to their frame of reference, the deep blues of her pants and jacket and the dazzling white of her blouse standing out starkly against the dark, curved horizon. Diederich could hardly believe his eyes. 'God Almighty.' Behind him, a chorus of excited voices began to rise up as, one by one, the people on the cabin's left side spotted the body of the young flight engineer as she floated a few dozen feet outside the row of windows.

'That son of a bitch!' Akins turned and, with a powerful motion, pushed himself forward. He was headed toward the cockpit door, his one hand groping along the overhead rail, his other stuck deep into his pocket.

'Wait!' Diederich looked down at his wife. Her eyes were still closed, her parched lips slightly opened. She could, he knew, be safely left alone for the next few minutes. He released his seat belt and pushed himself up. Something told him that he had better stick close to Akins. 'Stop. Doctor. Wait for me.'

Dozens of people on the right side of the airliner had already come out of their seats. Many of them rushed toward the windows on the left, a few gathered in clusters and spoke in loud, excited voices. Diederich watched as Akins pushed himself past a few of them, his head down, his shoulders squared. He looked like a fullback battering his way through a defensive line. He seemed nearly irrational. There was a small and pointed object – a needle – clasped in his right hand. 'Doctor. Wait.' Diederich hurriedly maneuvered down the crowded aisle.

'He'll kill every one of us,' Akins shouted over his shoulder. As loud as his words had been, they were lost in the commotion and disarray that the cabin of Flight 14 had once again become.

Chapter Ten

RALPH KENNERDALE eased the telephone back into its cradle. He turned around in time to see two burly TV technicians hoist one of their cameras onto its pedestal. Kennerdale still wasn't sure that he had done the right thing by allowing Justin Watts to put live TV cameras inside the OPSCON, but that option was nearly moot. The networks were scheduled to begin transmitting their live coverage within the next quarter hour.

'Problems?'

Kennerdale turned and faced Watts. 'No. Just the opposite.'

'Really?'

'Yes. I've just received word that our satellite with the onboard TV camera is expected to rendezvous with the airliner in half an hour.' Kennerdale pointed through the glass enclosure around the balcony and toward the wall clock in the lower level of the OPSCON. 'At one twenty-nine, to be exact.' It was, he saw, already two minutes after one. He would need to call Bellman at the Cape shortly to verify that the Shuttle launch was still firmly on schedule.

'That's great.' Watts slapped Kennerdale on the shoulder and smiled effusively. 'If the signal from that satellite is half as good as what we're hoping for, it's going to be one hell of a shot in the arm for NASA.'

Kennerale ignored Watts' remark. 'Our computations show that the airliner will come back into daylight at one twenty-three. We expect radio communications to be reestablished by one thirty-five.'

'Excellent.' Watts brushed some imaginary lint off his brown pin-striped suit, then swept his hands out in front of him. 'For an opening camera shot, I intend to pan across the wall map. The white line representing the trapped airliner is a hell of a focus point. We'll angle the shot so we get a profile of your technicians in the foreground. It's very dramatic. It's better than a Hollywood set. By the way,' he continued, his voice solemn, 'do you think it's possible to have the taller technicians stand in the rear? In particular, that older man with the gray hair.' Watts pointed below. 'He'd be a perfect face to frame the shot around.'

'I'll see what I can do.' Kennerdale sighed. The more he talked to Watts, the more he regretted his decision to allow this troupe of clowns into NASA. Watts was a Neanderthal in a three-piece suit.

'Here comes your assistant.'

Kennerdale turned in time to see Gilbert Novak step out of the corridor at the rear of the OPSCON. The young assistant walked rapidly toward the two of them. 'Any news?' Kennerdale asked as Novak approached.

'All good. Everything's a go.' Even if he didn't care for the science behind it, Novak still enjoyed the jargon. 'Reiman tells me that there aren't any problems with the launch. None.'

'There better not be.'

'Right,' Novak fidgeted. 'But there is some bad news. Reentry temperatures.'

'Shit.'

'Calculations have verified that the heat developed on the airliner during reentry from orbit will be too much for the leading edge of the wings. That's where they've got the special liquid-hydrogen cooling system. The engineers say there's not enough flow to handle the job.'

183

'Wait a minute,' Watts interrupted. 'Doesn't the airliner have heat-resistant tiles on it, just like the Space Shuttle? I'm sure I heard that somewhere.'

'Ablative tiles. Yes. But only on the bottom. The front edges of the wings have super-cooled liquid hydrogen automatically pumped through them. It's a portion of their rocket fuel, actually.'

'Rocket fuel? But the airliner already ran out of rocket fuel. I heard you say that yourself.'

'For chrissake.' Kennerdale shook his head in disgust. 'We don't have time for a seminar in science. Why don't you do your own damned research?'

A broad grin spread across Watts' face. 'Patience was never your strong suit, Ralph. You should try to relax more. Go with the flow. Take up Zen. Enroll in est training.'

'Go to hell.'

Novak waited a moment, cleared his throat, then began to recite the explanation that he had received not more than ten minutes earlier. 'Rocket fuel is comprised of two basic components, liquid hydrogen and liquid oxygen. They're stored in separate tanks and mixed together inside the engine. What the airliner ran out of first was the liquid oxygen portion, that's why their rocket engines shut down. But they've still got a few thousand pounds of liquid hydrogen left aboard.'

'Very interesting.' Watts took out his pad and scribbled some notes.

'What's the bottom line?' Kennerdale asked. He fumbled in his pocket for a cigarette, took it out and lit it. 'Do we have to put everyone in the Shuttle? There's not enough room for that.' For a brief, horrible instant, Kennerdale envisioned the classic lifeboat scene. A hundred people trying to climb onto a raft only big enough for a dozen at most. Tallulah Bankhead and William Bendix transported to outer space. Kennerdale shivered at the thought. He would cancel the Shuttle rescue and let them die before he would put NASA – and himself – in such a no-win situation.

'The bottom line is favorable,' Novak answered. He was happy to have good news to balance out the bad. 'Reiman tells me that we can extend the airliner's orbit indefinitely by periodically linking it to the Space Shuttle.'

'How?'

'By having the Shuttle pull it. Like a tugboat.'

'A *space tug*! Christ Almighty! What a great story!'

Novak ignored Watts' interruption. 'By hooking the two crafts together with a steel cable, the Shuttle's engines could provide enough thrust to keep both of them in orbit.' He watched as Kennerdale nodded his approval, then went on with the rest of his report. 'Our technicians are, at this moment, on the telephone with key people at United Aerospace's design headquarters in Los Angeles. They're investigating the feasibility of modifying the wing-cooling system enough to eventually get the airliner safely down.'

'Fine. Keep me informed.'

'Certainly.' Novak paused. 'By the way, there's one additional idea I'd also like to discuss. With the both of you.'

'What?' Kennerdale looked at Novak skeptically. He was leery of any request that started out with vagueness and innocence.

'It involves the TV networks. They'll need filler material.'

'Filler material?' Watts took half a step closer. 'What for?'

'When the airliner and the satellite go around the Earth and back into darkness, the live TV signal isn't going to be worth a damn.'

'Christ. I never thought of that.'

'That's half the time spent in each orbit – forty-five out of each ninety minutes.'

'Damn.' Watts stroked his fingers lightly against his bushy mustache.

'I knew you'd need something else, even though that character profile you intend to do on Dr. Kennerdale will take up most of the free time.'

'Naturally.' Watts smiled congenially. Kennerdale did not respond. 'You can also explain, on the air, the stuff about the airliner's ablative tiles and the liquid hydrogen cooling its wings.'

'Wonderful,' Kennerdale answered dryly.

'There's still bound to be a few minutes left over,' Novak continued. He peeked toward his boss to see how he was taking it.

Kennerdale remained expressionless. 'I've come up with something. Something to show. Something graphic.' Novak knew damn well that Kennerdale would see through the bullshit and realize what the suggestion really was – a hollow excuse for Novak to get his face on national TV. But it was worth the gamble. That exposure, more than any other possibility, would be his best insurance for a long and successful government career.

'What's your proposal?' Kennerdale asked.

'A display of the historical similarities.' Novak studied the faces of the two men. He had gained their complete attention. 'As you know,' he said, understanding full well that Kennerdale probably didn't, 'the orbital profile of the trapped airliner is almost an exact duplicate of one of our most famous space launches.'

'Which one?' Watts asked.

'The John Glenn flight. MA-Six, launched on February twentieth, nineteen sixty-two.'

'*Friendship Seven*? The first orbital flight?'

'Yes.'

Kennerdale nodded his agreement but remained silent. He could see that Novak had done his homework. If there was any flight that would jog the public's memory, *Friendship 7* was it.

'Holy shit. That's fascinating as hell.' Watts gestured enthusiastically. 'What's your plan?'

'I figured I could make a comparison chart to show how the three orbits of Glenn's mission twenty years ago have been duplicated by the airliner trapped in orbit. That would be an interesting way to fill open TV time.'

'Interesting, hell. It's *incredible*.' Watts smiled broadly at Novak, then turned to Kennerdale. 'That's a great idea. A real grabber. You don't have any objections, do you?'

'No.' Kennerdale shook his head briefly, more in reaction to being upstaged by his assistant than for any other reason. Still, the idea of comparing the airliner to Glenn's flight was intriguing. It would make the entire rescue more understandable, more interesting – and that would help the bottom line. 'It's a direct duplicate?'

'Very close. The altitude and course are quite similar. The

biggest differences are with decay time and oxygen. Glenn's capsule would have come down of its own accord in eighteen hours, and he had taken twenty-eight hours of oxygen up with him.'

'That's a nice touch,' Watts said. 'Very nice. We'll play that angle.' One of the TV technicians waved toward him, and Watts nodded back to indicate that he would come over shortly. He turned back to Novak. 'You say you'll have charts and graphs? Something we can put on-camera?'

'Yes.'

'Great. Then let's do it.' Watts patted Novak on the shoulder, then walked away to huddle with the cameramen.

'It's certainly a good idea,' Kennerdale said after Watts had left.

'Thank you.' Novak stood his ground and waited for more. He knew, instinctively, that Kennerdale had not finished with him yet.

'I'm sure you'll do a fine job with the project. Use whatever materials you need to make the display appear professional. Nothing slipshod.' Kennerdale reached for a handbook on his console. 'But let's not forget what our prime purpose is.'

'Sir?'

Kennerdale stepped closer to Novak. Their faces were only inches apart. 'Our purpose is to convince the fucking politicians that the space program is worthwhile, that NASA should get a bigger slice of the budget,' he said, his voice too low for anyone other than Novak to hear. 'Years from now, people will thank us. We'll be praised for our farsighted planning, for our managerial skills, for our ability to keep such an important project alive in spite of the self-serving pedestrian whims of the general public.'

'I'm sure we will be. It's unquestionably the right thing to do.'

'But until then,' Kennerdale continued as if Novak had said nothing, 'we've got to play their game. Public relations. Media tie-ins. Promises. Exaggerations. Ass-kissing. As much as I'd like not to think so, all of that has become necessary. If we want man to reach the stars, it seems that we've got to first spend some time in the mud.'

'Yessir.' Novak wasn't sure what Kennerdale's point was, but he had the good sense not to ask. 'I understand,' he lied.

Kennerdale stood ominously silent. His eyes were trained on Novak, but the man's thoughts were thousands of miles away. Light-years away. It seemed incredible to him that the vast, awesome mysteries of outer space could be relegated to second position. It was not the science or the engineering that Kennerdale gave a damn about, like so many of the fools who worked for NASA. Those people had their priorities ass-backward. Space, to them, was an excuse to build expensive toys.

Kennerdale realized full well that he despised technology. But that was not an inconsistency. To him, the potential of NASA was nothing less than the glory and lure of exploration. To fly out of the galaxy. To eventually go beyond the limitations of time and space. To hurtle toward a rendezvous with a destiny that could not yet even be dreamed of. These were – or should be – the cosmic concerns of the infinite future. Kennerdale blinked, then cleared his throat. 'If you're really part of this team – and there are damned few of us – then as far as I'm concerned you can do whatever you need to in order to accomplish our goal.'

'Yessir. Thank you.'

'Fine.' Kennerdale paused for several seconds. An awkward silence hung between the two of them. 'But I warn you,' he added, his eyes narrowed as he stared intently through the lenses of his wire-rimmed glasses. 'If you do anything that gets in the way of making NASA into the agency that it should be – the institution that, for the sake of mankind, it must become – then,' he said, as he pointed his finger dogmatically at Novak, 'you'll sorely regret it. That much I can promise you.'

Vladislav Zholobov stood at the window of his residence at the Baikonur Space Center in Kazakhstan Province. The early winter snowstorm that had swept across southern Russia had nearly ended, and Zholobov spotted a slice of the white-faced moon through a break in the clouds. 'The snow has stopped. Their prediction is nearly correct, for a change.'

'Did Moscow mention if they had also gotten snow?' Oleg Nikolayev asked as he stretched his legs.

'No.' Zholobov looked down at the black telephone. 'No

mention of snow, one way or the other.' The Moscow weather had been the last thing on Zholobov's mind during his brief, terse conversation with the Kremlin moments before. He had taken their request as an insult not only because of the inanity of it, but also because it had interrupted his off-duty time. Idle moments spent with sincere friends were too valuable to throw away on craziness. As deputy technical commander of a launch section, Zholobov had done precisely that too many times in the past.

Nikolayev looked up at the older man. 'What did you tell them?'

'That I'd get back to them shortly.'

'Always a good answer.'

'Yes.' The two men smiled at each other. If Zholobov had taught the young scientist anything, it was how to deflect an official inquiry until the time for an answer was more suitable. That was an essential requirement of Soviet life – particularly for anyone involved in the space program. Zholobov eyed the mound of snowflakes that lay on the windowsill. 'We have time,' he mumbled. His words drifted casually across the cozy, overheated room. He turned back to the young scientist. 'It seems incredible that the Americans could have been so stupid.'

'It was an airliner?'

'Yes. Their rocket-powered airliner.' Zholobov glanced up at the night sky. The moon was now three-quarters visible. Bands of dark clouds were mounded above and below it. 'How could that airliner have launched itself into orbit? It seems impossible.'

'Accidents happen. We've had our share, too.'

'I hadn't noticed.' Zholobov waited a moment before he unleashed his booming laugh. It filled the small parlor. 'Their error is not in having accidents. Only in admitting to them.'

'Of course. The American propensity for self-humiliation.' Nikolayev rose from his chair and laid his playing cards facedown on the table. 'What do you intend to do?' he asked bluntly. Even though it didn't involve him, Nikolayev had been the commander's personal friend long enough to ask such a question.

'I don't know.' Zholobov took a few steps across the room, toward where the chilled bottle of vodka sat in a bucket of ice. 'More for you?' he asked as he poured himself a drink.

'Certainly.'

As he strolled across the room with the two brimming glasses in his hands, Zholobov caught a glimpse of himself in the mirror. His round, puffy face and the thinning strands of his pushed-back hair – now as white as a field of Siberian snow – told him more than he cared to acknowledge about his many years. He had worked too hard for too long. He was scheduled to retire at the end of the summer. He would get a bachelor's villa on the Black Sea. It was nothing too plush, but not bad either. Vodka, caviar and sunshine. He would be invited to Moscow for celebrations. Then he would have an excuse to pin his medals and ribbons to his chest and stand on a platform with dignitaries. He would be a minor member of *nachalstvo,* the elite. But none of that sat too well with him. 'The big shots get the credit if things work out. Otherwise, the underlings get the blame.'

'How is that?' Nikolayev took his glass from the older man. He took a long drink, then settled himself at the table. He knew that his friend would not allow it to end there.

'If I authorize a rocket launch to rescue the Americans and it fails, I will spend many days inside one of those windowless rooms in the Kremlin.'

'Or at Dzerzhinsky Square.'

'True.' The mere mention of KGB headquarters caused Zholobov to shudder. The Stalin era was over, but the sight of that gray seven-story building in Moscow was still enough to make any man feel fear. 'I have reason and common sense for my defense, but I wonder if that would be enough.'

'How soon do they request that the rescue attempt be made?'

'Within hours. They want us to supply food and oxygen. Enough for one hundred people for thirty-six hours. They have only enough oxygen to last until sometime after midnight, our time.'

'Midnight?' Nikolayev peeked at his wristwatch, then shook his head. 'Only two more hours?'

'More or less.' Zholobov waved his hand in disgust. 'But none of it is anything but numbers. The idiots in the Kremlin couldn't care less about our problems.'

'Keep your voice down.' Nikolayev smiled, but he was only

partially joking. 'There are *stukachi* everywhere.'

'To hell with the informers,' Zholobov answered angrily. But he had also taken the precaution to lower his voice. 'No one in this room is on the KGB payroll.'

'But what of the next room?' Nikolayev pointed out the window. The adjacent row of apartment buildings could be easily seen. The warm glow from their rows of windows cast an interlocking pattern of rectangular shapes on the new coat of freshly fallen snow. 'We all know that Kirlenko would turn on his own children if the price were right.'

'The man is pure scum,' Zholobov said. He pretended to spit on the floor.

'But what about the rocket? Is it possible to launch a rescue mission? Two hours is no time at all.'

'We do have one rocket in position. It might be possible.' Zholobov pulled out his chair and sat down. He looked at the young man. 'Let me take a few minutes to think it over,' he said as the possibilities whirled through his mind.

'Consider it carefully. It sounds like a great risk.'

'It is.' Zholobov took one more drink from his glass, then looked down at the scattered playing cards strewn across the table. 'Let us talk more while we play. The cards are relaxing. Your questions and opinions will help me decide.'

'Whatever you prefer.'

Zholobov scooped up the deck of cards and handed them to Nikolayev. 'It's your turn to deal,' he said distractedly. His thoughts were already on the American airliner trapped in orbit.

Ben Robinson sat back in his swivel chair, the telephone pressed against his ear. He forced himself to look out the glass enclosure of the private office in the basement of the Goddard Center and into the adjoining private room. His eyes locked with McBride's for a brief instant and Robinson nodded absently. Through sheer willpower he had been able to prevent the voice on the telephone from visibly affecting him.

'I went all the way back in Krause's file,' Ferrera continued. 'I even looked through the corroborating records. Everything was squeaky clean, except for one terse memo from Elliot Nichols.'

'Nichols?' Robinson couldn't place the name.

'Legal department. He handles our patents and licenses. He got into a minor disagreement with Krause over how the company should apply for the patent on the quality-control program that Krause had designed. I understand that's been resolved.'

'Good. What about the other two?'

'McBride's the friendly sort, although he's not particularly dependable. He calls in sick quite often – and many of those times he's been seen around town or at the airport. I seriously doubt that he was on his way to the Mayo Clinic.' Ferrera paused as he shuffled through his papers. 'Becker is cold and aloof. Not the sort to show up at the company picnic. She also seems to have a talent for finding problems where none exist.'

'Yes. I'd agree.' Robinson looked through the glass and watched as Krause waited patiently for Bonnie Becker to stop talking. 'She's always on the offensive, always looking for a fight.'

'That's what the personnel manager told me.'

'We're finally getting somewhere. The important news is that Krause has been definitely ruled out.'

'His alibi is firm. He didn't get out of the hospital until September eleventh.'

'And there's no chance he could've snuck out – and back in – before that?' Robinson's natural conservatism made him ask the question one more time so he could complete his mental checklist.

'The doctor laughed when I asked. Krause's leg had been badly broken. It required being set in one of those traction things. On September second – that's the day that Ship thirty-five went back to the airline – he was still firmly strapped to his bed. I can't imagine he did much traveling in that condition.'

'Okay. Then it's either Becker or McBride.' Robinson felt a deep sense of relief. He had asked a great many penetrating questions about Alex Krause just to be certain, but all along he had felt that Krause was the least likely of the suspects. Now he would have another ally to work with. 'I'm going to clue Krause in and let him know the situation. He might be of help.'

'Use your own judgment.' Ferrera thanked God that Ben Robinson was the man on the scene. If anyone could handle this enormous, insane catastrophe, Robinson could. 'By the way, the initial feasibility study on modifying the *Star Streak*'s wing-cooling system is going well. It'll take a week or more to complete the automatic cooling-control redesign but it looks as if we'll be able to get that airplane down. I think the insurance company is willing to foot some of the modification bill.'

'Great.' Robinson quizzed Ferrera on several more items, then hung up. He sat quietly for a moment, thankful that the symptoms of his Ménière's disease had subsided enough to be tolerable. Finally, he rose from his chair, stepped out of the private office and into the adjoining room. A mild hum from the electronics console was the only noise that broke into the incessant silence. The three engineers waited expectantly. 'How's it going?' Robinson asked.

'Slow.' McBride shook his head, frowned, then pointed to the opened manuals spread across the table. 'Every time we find a lead, we come up with ten reasons why that couldn't be the answer.'

'It's got to be a multiple problem,' Krause said as he stepped forward. 'No simple failure could possibly have done it.'

'I hate to be the one to bring this idea up, but could it possibly be a design fault?' McBride asked sheepishly. 'I don't see how anything else fits.'

'That's a good point,' Krause chimed in. 'A design fault.'

'Do you agree?' Robinson asked Becker.

'There's not enough data. We're guessing.' She nodded toward a pile of papers, but volunteered no more.

Robinson looked around the room. The red sweep-second hand on the wall clock traveled smoothly across a fifth of its arc. He cleared his throat. 'We're not getting anywhere. Let's try something different. You two work on the design fault concept,' he said as he pointed toward Becker and McBride. 'I'll have Krause start backtracking through the quality-control computer checks, since he knows that system better than anyone.'

'That's a good idea,' Krause answered as he followed Robinson.

'Have there been any alterations to the quality-control program in the last few months?' Robinson asked as the two men stepped into the private room.

193

'No. Not any. The program hasn't been modified since early last winter.'

'Good.' Robinson closed the door and locked it behind them. He turned and gestured for the young engineer to stand where he was. 'Face me. Don't turn around. I've got to tell you something. I don't want them to see your reaction.'

'Who?'

'Those two.'

'I understand. Go ahead.'

'Ship thirty-five was sabotaged. It was done by either Becker or McBride.'

Krause stood rigidly silent. He blinked several times. 'Are you absolutely sure?'

'Yes. You and I both know that there's no way that those rocket controls could have failed.'

'That's what I've been thinking.' Krause shifted his weight. He rubbed his hand against his left hip.

'Of course. A failure like that isn't possible. It had to be deliberate. There's not more than five or six people in the country – in the world, for God's sake – who understand the design of that airliner well enough to accomplish that sort of alteration. All of those people are employees of United Aerospace. Only a few of them could have had access to that particular ship, and to the factory seals and coded tags, while it was in Phoenix.' He went on to explain the remainder of his sabotage theory to Krause, careful not to make any movements or gestures that might alarm the two engineers on the other side of the glass.

'I see what you mean. I hadn't thought it out that far. But I agree. It's too complex to be an accident. Too complex for anyone outside the company. Too unlikely to anyone outside the Phoenix facility. That narrows it down considerably. Strictly to our department.'

'I know it couldn't be you,' Robinson said. It was time to deal with the open question that hung between the two of them. 'Besides your reputation, it's your accident. You're the only one of the three supervisors in electronic engineering who has a firm alibi.'

'What dates were involved?'

194

'They're on my notepad.' Robinson handed it over and watched Krause as he scanned it.

'Right.' Krause handed the notepad back. 'What's the next step?'

'Do you have any ideas?'

'If you mean suspicions, yes. I think it's Becker.'

'Why?'

'She's a rotten bitch. She also told me something this morning. When I mentioned that I was going to New York City after our Martin negotiations to visit an old high school buddy, she said that she was also going to New York. It was a little too quick, too phony – as if she were trying to convince me. There was no reason to have mentioned it. Maybe she needs a cover story. I know it's not much.'

'It's better than nothing.'

'I'm sure it's Becker. It's a feeling I've got.'

Robinson fidgeted. He had also gotten an odd feeling during the last few moments, but his feeling didn't make sense. He pushed it out of his mind. 'We need proof. Something substantial.'

Krause shrugged, then stood silently.

'I was supposed to give you something to do.' Robinson looked around the private room. 'Sit down. Pretend to be busy.'

Krause took a step toward where Robinson had pointed. 'Here?'

'Yes. Sit at the console. You're supposed to be working.' Robinson glanced out at Becker and McBride. The two of them had their faces averted from Robinson's view, evidently in conversation. 'I need time to think.'

'What should I do?' Krause cautiously moved his bulky cast underneath the desk of the console as he sat in the chair. He was obviously uncomfortable.

'Christ, I don't care. Anything. Use the telephone. Make a call. Call your high school friend. Tell him that you won't be able to come to New York this weekend. That much I can guarantee. Do you know his number?'

'He's at home. He's a freelance commercial artist. He lives on the East Side of Manhattan.'

'The New York area code is two-one-two.' Robinson pointed toward the telephone controls along the top edge of the gray panel. 'Use the button on the end.'

'Okay.' Krause picked up the black handset and leaned forward. 'The switch on the end?' he asked again as he pointed toward the first square plastic button in the line.

'On the end,' Robinson repeated. His eyes were riveted on Bonnie Becker as she strolled around the edge of the table in the far room. Her back was turned.

'The area code for New York is two-one-two?'

'Yes.' Robinson watched Krause push those numbers on the telephone dialer, then he turned to watch Becker as she replaced the technical manual that he had seen her pick up only a few minutes before. He knew there was no way she could've done more than just superficially scan the handbook in that little time. She was obviously play-acting – going through no more than the barest of motions in her search for a reason behind the rocket failure in the *Star Streak*. That gave Robinson an idea.

'Hello, George? This is Alex. I'm afraid I've got bad news.'

'Stay on the phone,' Robinson said as he wheeled around before Becker had turned back toward him. 'Keep talking.' He reached for the paperwork that was stacked on the top of the console. Robinson realized that Becker would be sensitive to any investigation into the area of the second sabotage device, the device designed to retrieve the airliner once the ransom had been paid. If he could manipulate her properly, Becker's reactions might provide a clue as to where that device was located. With that much to go on, Krause might then be able to figure out what the device was and how it worked.

'I can't make it to New York this weekend.' Krause looked up at Robinson while he spoke. 'Problems at work. I'll be tied up.'

'Don't hang up yet,' Robinson whispered. 'I need more time.' Without waiting for Krause's reply, Robinson walked past the corner of the gray cabinet, took out his pen and began to jot down notes on the papers he held in his hand.

'Wait, George. I've got a few minutes.' Krause leaned back in the swivel chair and ran his hand nervously up and down the telephone cord. He tried to keep his eyes away from Robinson, but every few seconds he found himself glancing toward the man. 'How about if we try to come up with another date?' Krause said after a short silence. 'Something near the end of the month. That would work out well for me.'

Krause's idle words buzzed through the back of Robinson's thoughts like a swarm of annoying insects. He attempted to ignore the distraction so he could concentrate totally on the list he had written, a list of six of the *Star Streak*'s subsystems. They were, he imagined, the only possible locations where a rescue device might be located. 'Okay. Hang up. I'm ready to review this with you.' Robinson knew that if he could correctly guess which subsystem contained the second sabotage device, he might be able to sandbag Bonnie Becker.

Chapter Eleven

'STANDBY. WE should be getting a picture shortly.' Ralph Kennerdale put his hands against the console and leaned forward. Through the glass balcony he peered down at the center screen beneath Goddard's electronic map of the world. The TV screen remained a gray blank. 'Soon,' Kennerdale said to no one in particular. He hoped to hell that nothing had gone wrong with the satellite linkup.

'A few more seconds,' Novak whispered as he put down the console's interphone.

'We're ready,' Justin Watts added, his voice also hushed. He glanced over his shoulder at the senior TV technician, who frowned back at him. Watts attempted to smile, but found that he couldn't. He had violated the most sacred creed of TV broadcasting by purposely switching to an unusable signal. He had decided that a few seconds of blank screen would add dramatic impact to the satellite's live picture of the airliner – but not more than a few seconds. Watts pressed a headset against one ear and listened to the audio monitor from the studio. The commentator was attempting to explain the gray, fuzzy screen to the TV audience, and he had nearly run out of things to say. Watts knew

198

that he couldn't let it go on much longer. 'Shit. If that satellite picture doesn't come up right away, we'll need to fade back to the OPSCON shot,' he announced to the people who stood around him. No one responded.

'Here it comes.' Novak pointed toward the center screen, even though no one's attention had left it. The square patch of indistinct gray began to fill with a rapid series of alternating black and white horizontal lines. A hint of what seemed like a picture flashed for a brief moment, then faded, then flashed again. 'There. Yes. That's it.'

'Where?' Watts' heart sank. The picture on the screen was hardly more than a mass of irresolute shadows, an indistinct curved line across the lower middle, a darker patch above. Watts could imagine the millions of angry TV viewers at home as they rose from their chairs and began to walk across the room to shut off their television sets. 'It's not clear. It's no good, damn it! We'll need to change to the OPSCON shot again.' Watts could feel the stinging burn of acid as it poured into his stomach. 'Camera two, get ready,' he shouted at the technicians.

'God Almighty.'

Watts spun around. To his amazement, the picture on the center screen had cleared magnificently. The sleek silver lines of the hypersonic airliner had suddenly emerged out of the blackened background as if someone had turned the klieg lights on center stage.

The stranded airliner filled three-quarters of the screen, its streamlined nose pointed down several degrees in reference to the dark horizon, its flat and angled wings showing enough substance to give a true feeling for the craft's immense size. 'My God. This is unbelievable,' Watts whispered hoarsely. The shot was better than anything he had hoped and prayed for. The airliner gave the appearance of a model hung by invisible wires in a hobby shop, yet it simultaneously looked frighteningly authentic. Glints of sparkling sunlight danced off the rounded metal walls that formed the cabin. Symmetrical spots of yellowish-white light poured through each of the cabin windows on the aircraft's port side.

'What's that?'

'Where?'

'Below the nose.' Novak pointed to a drab spot in space a short distance beneath the glow from the cockpit windshield. 'There.'

'I can't make it out. Not yet. The sun's still too low.' Kennerdale adjusted his eyeglasses and strained to bring that dark spot into focus, but he wasn't able to. 'A few more seconds.'

As the blazing white sun rose above the curved horizon, the remainder of the shadows on the TV screen were instantly washed away. Suddenly bathed in direct and unrelenting sunlight, the drab object that floated a short distance beneath the nose of the orbiting airliner took on its true shape and form.

'Oh my God!' Novak's voice was only slightly louder than the sudden burst of startled gasps and excited sounds that had exploded from the throats of everyone in the room.

The human body that floated in space tumbled in continuous slow motion, end-over-end. It was the body of a young woman. Her lifeless arms drifted out in front of her, her legs were tucked up toward her chest, and her long hair danced in eerie swirls around her face and neck. The two gold stripes on each sleeve of her uniform jacket had caught enough of the direct sunlight to glimmer noticeably.

'A stewardess.'

'No. A pilot.'

'Yes. One of the pilots.'

Kennerdale fumbled for his paperwork. When he found the crew list that the airline had sent, he scanned the column. 'Here,' he announced loudly, to quell the continuous flow of muddled voices from behind and below him. 'Katie Graham. The flight engineer. It's got to be her.'

'Yes. God help her.' Watts stepped closer to the edge of the balcony. The quality of the TV picture was superb, the focus excellent, the framing and composition perfect. Watts wondered for an instant if the changing angle of the sun might adversely affect the picture's balance. He turned to Kennerdale. 'Can the TV satellite be moved again?'

'What?'

'Can the satellite be maneuvered up and down? To different angles?'

'Possibly. It depends.' Kennerdale looked puzzled. He had no idea what Watts' intentions were. 'Why?'

'Is it risky? Could we lose the signal entirely if we try to reposition that satellite?'

'For chrissake,' Kennerdale snapped back, his voice choked with anger. He took a quick glance at the TV screen before he looked back at Watts. 'What the hell are you talking about?'

'Never mind.' Watts waved his hand in dismissal. He had decided to wait and see how the movement of the sun would actually affect the quality of the picture. His concern was premature. 'Tell me how it could have happened,' he said as he pointed to the young woman's body as it hovered in the lower left of the large screen. His mind had already raced ahead to the voice-over he intended, very soon, to do personally. He planned to interrupt the studio commentator with some on-sight observations of his own. An opinion from Dr. Kennerdale would be a perfect addition to his narrative.

'I don't know.'

'Take a guess.'

'No.' Kennerdale swiped at a growing line of perspiration on his forehead, then looked up at the wall clock. 'We'll know for sure in another three minutes. That's when the airliner is due back into radio communication.'

'Yes. Three minutes.' Novak glanced around the room and then down into the lower level of the OPSCON. Most of the technicians were still standing, their eyes fixed to the television screen. But the bevy of excited voices had dwindled away and the entire OPSCON had fallen into discomfited silence. One by one, each of the people in the room had realized what the flight engineer's death implied. Novak was the first to say it out loud. 'Three more minutes might not mean anything. There might not be anyone left alive in that airliner to answer us.'

'Let me get past,' Ben Robinson said to McBride as he tried to move himself away from the electronics console that the four of them had been huddled around. 'I've got to call Phoenix.'

McBride stepped aside, but did not remove his eyes from the image of the dead body that floated in the lower left corner of the TV monitor.

'Let me pass,' Robinson mumbled as he nudged against Bonnie Becker, then stepped past Krause. He strode rapidly across the room, toward the glass-enclosed area on the far side. He stepped inside, locked the door behind him and sat down at the room's private console.

Robinson swung around in his chair, yanked the telephone handset off its cradle and poised his finger along the row of three auto-dial buttons. He had nearly pressed the number-one button to call Phoenix before he changed his mind and moved his finger to the number-two button. *Calm down, for chrissake.* Robinson's hand trembled as he pressed the number-two button and listened to the rapid sequence of clicks. Ferrera could wait, he needed to talk once more with Ray Lee.

The auto-dialer quickly dialed the private number inside the Astrex Corporation that Robinson had programmed into the machine a short while before. Within seconds the telephone rang, and Lee picked it up.

'I'm watching it, too,' Lee said, his voice strained. 'But all they could find for me is a damn six-inch TV with a portable antenna. It's fuzzy as hell and I can't make out much of anything. There's no signs of damage on the ship? Just the one body?'

'Yes.' Robinson leaned forward, pressed the monitor switch on his private console and studied the image of the airliner as it floated in space. 'I'm looking at the TV picture right now. Except for the one body, everything appears normal. The ship appears to be intact.'

'What could that mean?'

'I don't know.' Robinson flipped off his monitor switch and jumped up from his swivel chair. 'I can't even guess.'

'Neither can I.'

'We'll know soon enough, one way or the other. They'll be back in radio contact in just a few minutes.'

'Right. That's what the TV announcer just said.'

Robinson cleared his throat. 'There's something else I wanted your opinion on,' he added as he got to the actual reason behind his call. 'It's Krause. He isn't acting right.' Robinson turned and peeked out at the three engineers. Becker and McBride had stepped a few more paces back from the console. Krause stood at the same spot he had been before, his face still fixed in that contorted expression of thinly disguised terror. Somehow, it seemed inappropriate. Excessive. Robinson passed on that observation to Lee, and also a few other observations about Krause. 'He looks as if he's horrified but afraid to show it.'

'A great many men are like that. It's not macho to display real feelings.'

'That's not what I mean.'

'Then I don't follow you,' Lee said puzzled. 'Inappropriate? Excessive? What, precisely, do you mean?'

'It's hard to put into words.'

'It seems to be.' Lee mulled over Robinson's statements for several more seconds before he responded again. 'Why are you suddenly after Krause?'

'Don't play lawyer with me. I realize that none of this qualifies as courtroom material. It's just a feeling.'

'Not good enough.'

'Did you every interrogate a pilot after a crash?' Robinson asked, getting the conversation back on more familiar terms.

'Of course not.'

'I have. Too many times. Whenever I did, I tried to determine whether the pilot was aware of the actual pre-crash situation.'

'Like what?'

'Bad weather. Low fuel. Equipment problems. Stretching safety margins too thin, that sort of thing. The point was to find out whether the pilot was actually caught by surprise, or whether he was attempting to cover up an outright mistake.'

'And Alex Krause was not surprised when you mentioned sabotage?'

'Exactly. He took it too well.'

'Is that all you've got?'

'Yes.' Robinson watched as Krause sat down in the electronics console. The other two engineers continued to stand a few feet behind him. 'He's not acting strange.' Robinson mentally toyed with the next sentence before he decided to use it. 'He's acting guilty.'

'Bullshit.' The usual soft tone of Lee's voice had taken on a hard edge. 'You don't want me to play lawyer, but then you try to do exactly the kind of thing that lawyers are supposed to prevent.'

'Stop right there. Let's not get into a discussion on lawyers,' Robinson snapped. In spite of their close friendship, he and Lee had quarreled several times over Robinson's opinion that unscrupulous attorneys and technicalities in the law stood in the way of justice more often than not.

'I agree with you on one point – that we shouldn't discuss it.' Lee paused to gather his thoughts. 'All the other facts aside – Krause's loyalty, his reputation, his lack of motive – the bottom line is that the man had no opportunity. You've proven that yourself. There's no evidence so you're guessing, pure and simple. I suspect it's because you still don't have anything firm on Becker and McBride. For some reason, Krause had become an easy target.'

'I tried to get something on Becker just a little while ago. I set her up by pretending to be interested in only those areas where the second sabotage device would be.'

'Did she bite?'

'Not a goddamn nibble.' Robinson could feel the pulses of his growing headache as they traveled in irregular spasms across the front of his skull. He pressed the palm of his hand against his head. 'She acted like she didn't give a damn.'

'Maybe you picked the wrong areas. Maybe she's a damn good actress. Maybe there is no second device.'

'Maybe.' Robinson scratched his head. His certainty about Krause's guilt had disappeared as rapidly as it had developed. Lee was right, he had made too much of his feelings and intuition. Becker was still the most logical choice. Robinson looked at the wall clock. One thirty-two. 'Do you have any idea why the saboteur hasn't issued the ransom demand yet?' Only two hours and thirteen minutes of oxygen remained in that airliner. *Where is the missing piece? There has to be something I'm overlooking.*

'It's got to be the NASA involvement, the plans for the Shuttle rescue. They've frightened the saboteur off. It's become too much of a risk when weighed against the potential for zero gain. If the saboteur makes the ransom demand – which, as we all realize, might somehow be traced back to them – and the Shuttle rescue succeeds, then they've stuck their necks out for nothing.'

'Don't bank on the Shuttle.' Robinson thought about Kennerdale, Novak and the rest of the people he had met in the OPSCON. Something in their manner had told Robinson that all was not well with the Shuttle, something in their manner had told him that they were not to be trusted. Robinson was scheduled to go upstairs in a few moments to get an update.

'From what I can tell, NASA has a good shot at succeeding.'

'An outside chance, nothing more. Trying to launch a Piper Cub in less than two hours can sometimes be a nightmare, for chrissake. Who the hell does Kennerdale think he's kidding?'

'It's still a chance,' Lee answered. 'NASA must feel that there's a high probability of success or they wouldn't try it.'

'I don't believe it, but I hope so.' Robinson exchanged a few more ideas with Lee about what their next step should be. Finished, the two of them hung up.

Robinson decided not to call Phoenix since he had too many other things to do. But he did allow himself to sit quietly for a moment. He closed his eyes, pressed both his hands against his forehead and tilted his head back. Between the grating pulses of his headache, the slight ringing in his ears and the churning nausea, a series of frantic thoughts continued to filter through his mind. Within a few seconds, a definite trend had developed. *Inappropriate.* Once again, Robinson could smell the whiff of coincidence. *Krause isn't acting right.* Coincidence was the single element that Ben Robinson distrusted the most. *Krause is acting guilty. Where is the missing piece?*

'Christ, I need a cigarette.'

'Me, too,' Paul Diederich answered, even though he didn't smoke. If it weren't for the use of pure oxygen and the strictly enforced ban on smoking, he might have lit one up himself. 'I wish I could,' he said as he pointed to the illuminated no-smoking sign at the head of the cabin.

'I understand.' The middle-aged man across the aisle from him shrugged, then turned away. The young boy at his side continued to stare across the aisle toward Diederich for several more seconds before he, too, turned.

Diederich glanced down the length of the cabin. In compliance with the captain's rule about unnecessary movement, everyone sat rigidly in their seats. The aisle itself was as deserted as a dusty road at high noon. Even the level of conversation among the passengers, which had not been forbidden, had also dried up. No more than three or four whispered voices floated across to Diederich. Everyone sat stoically. It was as if there was nothing left to say.

'Paul?'

Diederich turned toward his wife.

'I can't read the letters,' Chris said, her words barely distinguishable, her voice weak and thin. 'What does it say?'

Diederich leaned forward and peered out the cabin window. The television satellite that flew in formation with them had drifted close enough to the airliner to make the painted letters on its ribbed metal sides easily visible. 'United States. That's all it says. No America. No flag.' Diederich turned to his wife and forced a smile. He tried not to stare at the large stains of dried blood that had soaked through her white blouse. 'Stay quiet,' he said as he looked out the window.

Fifty feet below the windowline floated the body of the young flight engineer. A hundred feet beyond that, and slightly above it, was the TV satellite. Behind them, in the background, was a sea of white clouds. Patches of blue water were visible beneath the long stretches of unbroken white. On the horizon, masses of land in varying shades – light and dark browns, flat greens – were scattered haphazardly. 'Go back to sleep, honey.' Diederich knew that his wife was no more than half-conscious, but there was no need to upset her further with more of that inane view outside the window. He reached up and lowered the plastic windowshade. He had no idea if Chris had heard him, since she had already closed her eyes. Satisfied that she was well enough to be left alone again, Diederich unbuckled his seat belt, pushed himself upright and began to maneuver away from the row of seats.

The sickly-sweet smell of medicine and bandages, and the sour smell of vomit mingled with other odors in the stagnant air. Diederich could tell that, just as the captain had announced, the air-conditioning airflow had been cut down to its absolute minimum for the sake of oxygen conservation. The results were already evident. Many of the passengers – particularly the elder ones – sat in a catatonic stupor, their bodies drugged by the minimal amounts of oxygen they were able to get. Diederich noticed that he had also begun to feel sluggish and lightheaded.

'Are you going up to the cockpit?'

Diederich gripped the overhead rail and turned himself around toward the voice. The black stewardess hovered in midair across the aisle, her left hand wrapped tightly around the edge of the overhead rail, her feet dangling several inches above the floor. She had come out of the forward galley. 'Yes. The captain knows I'm coming up.'

'He told me.' Adrienne Brown tugged at the makeshift strap she wore around her hips in order to keep the skirt of her stewardess uniform from billowing up over her head in the zero gravity. 'You've been authorized unlimited access to the cockpit. You and Dr. Akins.'

Diederich nodded. Uniforms. Authorizations to enter the cockpit. Even during the worst moments of this disaster, authority and decorum continued to flourish. To Diederich's surprise, no one had yet to breach the rules, violate the code. The passengers were content to take orders.

It was, Diederich realized, a display of the passengers' individual social status, their business positions, their personal wealth. Each of them knew what the chain of command was for any given situation, and they accepted the need to stay within it. Corporate presidents, board chairmen, society ladies. They had spent their lives within the narrow bounds of rules, written and unwritten. They were content to live – and even to die – that way. 'How are they holding out?' Diederich whispered as he gestured toward the cabin.

'Okay for now. I'll ask the captain to make another P.A. announcement shortly. That should keep them satisfied.'

'Right.' Diederich nodded politely, then began to move himself forward. He felt out of place in the cabin. Even though he knew very little about the actual tasks involved in being a pilot, at least up in the cockpit he was familiar with the basic science that made it possible. Pragmatic, practical science – that was the language he spoke. That was the only language he understood. Diederich inched his hand along the overhead rail until he reached the galley, then he pushed himself across the open expanse.

As Diederich reached the cockpit door, he turned and looked down the aisle again. The faces of those few passengers who glanced up at him were etched in despair. A sense of hopelessness permeated the cabin. It had become their only emotion.

The death of the young flight engineer was the trauma that swept away the fragile sense of hope they had, for a while, managed to cling to. The arrival of the TV satellite buoyed their spirits for a few minutes, but that optimism soon gave way to reality. The TV satellite, they had all soon enough realized, would be utterly useless to their rescue. It hovered no more than a few hundred feet away across the airless void of space.

The TV satellite was a mocking gesture, a grotesque joke. Its hideous lens protruded out of the satellite's nose, and it pointed unrelentingly toward them. Pictures of their suffering were being broadcast on worldwide TV. Their agony and their death would be the media event of the month. Each of their sons and daughters would be able to watch. Diederich thought about his own daughter, Kim, as he pictured her at home in front of the TV. He shivered, then pushed open the cockpit door and went inside.

'Let me understand this,' Collins said into his microphone as Diederich maneuvered himself carefully toward the front of the cockpit. The captain glanced over his shoulder to see who had entered the flight deck and, satisfied, he turned back to his radio conversation. 'Fuel mixing won't work because the proportions are too volatile? Is that what you're saying?'

Diederich could see that Collins was busy. So was Briscoe. The copilot sat strapped in his flight chair, a copy of the aircraft manual in his outstretched hands as he held it up for Collins to look at. Diederich pulled himself down into the space behind the captain's seat and turned to Akins, who had strapped himself into the empty flight engineer's seat. 'How's it going?'

'How the hell should I know? These guys talk in some kind of code.' Akins motioned toward the two pilots. 'I don't understand one-tenth of the crap they're saying. But at least they've agreed to lay off each other until we're back on the ground.'

'Good.'

'Then they can kick the shit out of each other for all I give a damn,' Akins added, just a little too loud.

Diederich wondered if Collins and Briscoe had really argued over the fuel-mixing concept as they had said. He couldn't shake the feeling that Briscoe had something to do with the opening of the lower-bay door while Katie Graham was below. While he waited for the pilots to finish, Diederich considered saying something else to Akins about the syringe. He was certain he had seen one in the doctor's hand when the two of them had rushed to the cockpit after the flight engineer's death – but the doctor had vehemently denied it. Diederich decided not to bring it up again, at least for the moment. It was probably the last vial of sedative the doctor had, and he didn't want anyone to badger him for it. Akins was unquestionably headstrong anyway. He wouldn't tolerate too many questions about any subject, particularly medical ones.

'Okay. I understand,' Collins transmitted. 'Fuel mixing is definitely out.' He laid down his microphone and turned to Briscoe. 'The FAA has tested it. Out of four dozen attempts, they say they blew up their test batch forty-eight times.'

'Not good odds,' Briscoe answered. There was a faint smile at the corners of his mouth.

'Right.' Collins glanced around the cockpit, rubbed his hand nervously along the bridge of his nose, then looked back at Briscoe. 'I don't know if we should believe them. It sounds full of shit to me.'

Briscoe blinked in amazement. 'Why do you say that?' He looked toward Akins, then back toward the captain. Collins *had* lost his mind – he had begun to distrust even the scientists on the ground.

'Because forty-eight failures is pure bullshit. Fuel mixing is theoretically possible, so it's only a matter of the proper proportions. If they failed forty-eight times, it's because they weren't really trying.'

'That doesn't make a damn bit of sense.' Akins frowned, then pointed his thumb toward the floorboards. 'That's *your* friend down there, not mine. Work it out with him.'

209

'I will.' Collins looked at the panel clock. It was one fifty-five – which meant that the Shuttle was already ten minutes behind schedule. Yet every time Collins asked anyone about it, all he got were platitudes and evasions. They were all – including Ben Robinson – hiding something.

'You're not giving any of them a chance,' Akins said.

'I'm giving them too many chances.' Collins shook his head in disgust. Robinson might have once been a friend of his, but the United Aerospace vice-president would get his future paychecks from the same company that had produced the hypersonic piece of garbage they were trapped in. Bastard. Collins yanked his microphone out of the restraining clip on his side console, held it up to his lips and pressed the transmit button. 'Robinson. Get those people to put their asses into gear. Get that Shuttle up here. Fast.' Without waiting for a reply, he flung the microphone down against the console. The hardened plastic smacked audibly against the Fiberglas bulkhead before it ricocheted away to the limits its cord allowed. The microphone and its cord drifted lazily over the forward glare shield, like a fishing line cast across a serene lake.

'Just wait,' Briscoe said after a suitable silence. 'The Shuttle will be up shortly.'

'And what if they're not?'

All three men turned to Diederich. 'What's your point?' Akins asked abruptly.

Diederich pushed himself upright, hooked his left foot beneath the back of the captain's seat and laid one hand against the protruding frame of the cockpit window to stabilize himself. 'We should cover ourselves. At least we should try.' Being civilized was one thing, laying down to die was quite another.

'Christ,' Briscoe mumbled. 'Not that line of shit again.'

'Wait. Let's hear him out.' Collins twisted around in his seat and faced Diederich directly. He, too, had heard enough of the promises from the ground. 'Do you have any ideas?'

Diederich shook his head. 'Not yet.'

'I didn't think so,' Akins said with acerbity.

'But we're sure as hell not going to come up with any if we don't try.'

'I can agree with that.' Collins let his eyes wander around the *Star Streak*'s cockpit. From active airline pilot, he had somehow become the chief curator at an aviation museum. The gray instrument panel in front of him, with its neat rows of switches and gauges, had become a useless array. None of it meant a damn – no more than the cockpit controls in those aircraft on exhibit at the National Air and Space Museum in Washington. That was the place he had taken his sons to see a few months before, their first outing together since Susan's death. Collins felt like he was back inside that chopped-off nose section of the museum's relic DC-7, not inside a real hypersonic jet. He almost expected to be able to turn around, walk down a short set of wooden steps and back into the main exhibit floor.

'Our situation is static,' Briscoe argued as he repeated the same phrase Collins had used hours before on the public address system. 'Playing games can only screw us up.'

But Collins knew that the copilot was wrong. 'No,' he said as he pointed to the only two gauges on his panel that were still functional, still capable of delivering accurate information. As he looked, the numbers on the digital clock flashed to indicate that another minute had passed. It was one fifty-six. They had less than two hours left. The tiny white needle on the oxygen quantity indicator sat perceptibly lower than it had been a while ago. 'Time and oxygen aren't static,' he said. It was also obvious from the gauges that the oxygen conservation measures he had set into effect had accomplished very little.

'If you start running around looking for ways to do the impossible, all you'll do is use up oxygen at a faster rate. You'd do everyone a great service if you'd just go back to your seat and keep real quiet.' Briscoe glanced at his side panel where one of the three portable bottles of extra crew oxygen were stored. There was, he knew, a green-colored portable bottle alongside each of the three crew seats in the cockpit. Collins had already said that he intended to open all of them at 3:40, shortly before they had exhausted their normal onboard supply. That would add three or four minutes of breathable air for all aboard the ship. Briscoe had calculated that if he wasn't forced to share his bottle with anyone, he'd have an extra two hours beyond the ship's supply. Two

211

hours of extra insurance, in case the Space Shuttle was late.

'There's no damn need to throw oxygen away,' Akins said without being asked. He turned to Diederich and scowled. He was defying the man to bring up the subject again.

Diederich faced Collins. 'How much oxygen am I going to use if I look around for some way to help our situation? How much of a difference?'

'Five, six minutes. At the most.' Collins tapped his finger on the oxygen gauge. 'That estimate should be accurate, based on what our rate of consumption has been the last half hour.'

'Then it's worth the risk. There's no question in my mind. I promise not to hyperventilate.'

'Don't volunteer to shorten my life, for chrissake.' Akins waved his finger at Diederich. 'This isn't a kid's game. Every time we touch something, it's a potential danger. Look out the goddamn window if you don't believe me.'

As much as he tried to resist, Collins turned his head and glanced out the port side of the cockpit window. Katie Graham's body was no more than 50 feet away. It was at a right angle to them, her long hair still trailed behind her but her legs had dangled apart. She moved in slow motion, her body tumbling continuously, like a gymnast filmed at quarter-speed. Collins closed his eyes.

Briscoe. In spite of what he had told Akins, Diederich and the passengers – that the accident had been caused by the girl's own carelessness – Collins knew damn well whose fault it was. It had been Collins' body that had pressed against that switch on the flight engineer's panel, but it was Briscoe's stupidity, his impulsiveness that had led to the young woman's death. If they ever got out of here alive, Collins vowed to see that the copilot would be held accountable. All he could offer to the memory of Katie Graham was the promise of justice.

'I'd like to know why you think you're a space expert?' Akins asked Diederich caustically.

'I've been involved with science my whole life. I've been a physics teacher for eighteen years.'

'Where?'

'A private high school in . . .'

'High school!' If it wasn't for his fastened seat belt, Akins would have jumped out of his seat. His hands had begun to tremble, his face had turned bright red. 'You're a fucking madman, that's what you are! You teach kids, and you think you know more than NASA!'

'Calm down,' Collins ordered. 'Your hysterics are using more than your share of oxygen.' He kept his eyes riveted on the doctor. He had no intention of tolerating any more irrational outbursts.

Akins shrugged. 'But there's no need . . . '

'Wrong. There is a need.' Collins took a long, measured breath. Somewhere deep within him, an old resolution from his early days of flying began to stir. *Take command. Don't tolerate bad trends.* 'Our situation tells me that we've got one hell of a need.'

'Your argument doesn't hold water,' Akins said.

Collins raised his hand. 'That's enough. I've listened to each of you, now I'm going to make my decision.' Collins laid his hand on top of the control column. The wheel rocked uselessly beneath his fingers. 'I've put this decision off for too long.' Collins realized that, up to a few seconds ago, the ship had no real captain. Now it did. The mental haze that had covered his thoughts for longer than he could remember had suddenly lifted. Like a morning fog burnt away by the hot sun, the course ahead had become clear. 'Diederich is the most qualified general science person onboard. That makes him, with the exception of the medical area, our resident expert. If there's even a small chance that he might come up with something . . . '

'There's not,' Briscoe muttered in the background.

'Then we'll accept the penalty,' Collins continued without interruption. 'A few minutes less oxygen is a small price to pay for a chance – any chance – that might lead to something positive.' The memory of his dead wife filled Collins' thoughts. He allowed it to linger a few seconds before he gently nudged it aside. For the first time Collins realized that, as difficult as it was, he needed to accept reality. Perhaps it was because he now saw the need to accept the very real possibility of his own death. He turned to Diederich. 'You have my authorization to conduct any investigation you like. See if the fuel-mixing idea seems feasible to you. You might find some lines in the lower bay that we can tap into. Don't make any changes without consulting me first.'

'Certainly, Captain,' Diederich answered formally. 'I'll get started right now. I'll let you know if I need any help.'

'Right.'

'You do that,' Akins added tersely. He pressed his hand inconspicuously against the side of his coat pocket where he had stuck the vial of sedative. He was glad that he had put the syringe away before Collins had seen it, and glad that he had denied its existence to Diederich. 'Captain. Don't forget to keep me posted,' Akins said as he released his seat belt, his tone now affable.

'Of course.'

Akins pushed himself away from the flight engineer's panel. If Diederich came up with some harebrained scheme and Collins went for it, Akins knew that he had enough sedative left to split the remaining dose between the two of them. In any event, he would use the sedative on Collins before the 3:40 deadline Briscoe had given him. If it came down to it, Akins had no intention of allowing Collins to go through with the grand, futile gesture of dumping the contents of the three portable oxygen bottles into the ship's supply and diluting it to nearly nothing. As the copilot had so tactfully pointed out, access to three bottles of extra oxygen would do wonders for the chances of at least one or two people to live through this nightmare.

214

Chapter Twelve

THE TWO men rode up in the small elevator in silence, the loud whirling noises from the elevator's motor and cables drowning out whatever outside noises might otherwise have reached them. Beads of perspiration glistened noticeably on the dark-brown skin of Alvin Kingsley's forehead.

'Ladies lingerie,' Randy Hull said as the elevator stopped and the door jerked open. He stepped out on the 147 level of Pad 39A's fixed launching platform and waited for Kingsley to step outside with him. 'One thing I like about launch day is that you have to have this place to yourself,' Hull said as he made reference to the NASA rule that forbid anyone other than the flight crew and a few select technicians from being near the Shuttle within 45 minutes of launch time. Hull swept his free hand out in front of him in a broad circular motion as he smiled, a panoramic view of the Cape's launch areas surrounding him.

'Right,' Kingsley said. 'We'll be alone until the shit hits the fan. Then we get to share this place with two million pounds of burning hydrogen.' He laid his portable air-conditioning pack on the steel deck and carefully straightened out the hose between it and his space suit.

'Have any discrepancies shown?' Hull asked as he placed his own air-conditioning pack alongside Kingsley's. His smile had disappeared.

'No. Everything's been perfect.' Kingsley had told the truth, but he wondered why he couldn't get himself to believe it. *Something always goes wrong. We always have a problem.* The memory of Bellman's words was an irritation that Kingsley hadn't been able to put aside. As much of an exaggeration as the launch director's warning had been, it had also been true. Problems. Complications. They were as much a part of life in NASA as the chinch bugs and thousand-leggers that outnumbered the people in the State of Florida by a trillion to one. Kingsley turned toward the rear of the structure and looked at the emergency slidewire.

'Thinking of taking a ride?' Hull asked, when he saw what Kingsley's attention was on.

'Sure. Nice day for it. I can work on my tan.'

'Good idea.' Hull laughed. He turned and looked at the emergency slidewire. He had spent dozens of hours in practice with that unwieldy emergency evacuation system during his years of astronaut training, and it had proven to be another of those things he had experienced trouble with. The ten heat-resistant baskets – two suspended from each of the five steel-wire cables that were strung from the rear of the fixed launching platform to the bunkers buried in the earth 1200 feet away – were capable of carrying two people apiece. 'I hear they tried to test the slidewire the other day, but the baskets would only go halfway down. Some poor jerk spent six hours rocking in the breeze until they figured out how to retrieve him.'

'The damn thing is more of a pain in the ass than it's worth.' Everyone knew that the slidewire didn't offer much protection. Supposedly, 20 souls could escape rapidly from this level of the launch platform and be shielded from the effects of explosion or fire in the earth-covered concrete bunkers at the base of the wires. But it took a minute or more to get into the baskets, and another 35 seconds to ride down. 'If the silo goes, we won't get a chance to use their fancy slidewire,' Kingsley volunteered.

'That's true,' Hull answered. He looked carefully at Kingsley in an attempt to figure out what the man's point was.

'Forget it,' Kingsley said. He found that he couldn't look Hull in the eye. He pretended to fiddle with the hose that dangled out of the right side of his space suit. 'I'm edgy, that's all. Nothing's wrong.' Kingsley thought about the stories his father had told him, stories about his own pre-mission jitters. His father had admitted to nearly crapping in his pants more than once before the 99th went out on those air strikes during the winter of '44.

'That's okay. I understand,' Hull nodded. 'I think it's these damned suits.' He tugged at the plastic and nylon collar around the top of his bulky orange pressure garment. 'It's hot as hell in this thing. They must've bought my air-conditioning pack army-surplus, it's not worth shit. I'm glad they at least carried our helmets out to the ship.'

'Me, too.' Kingsley picked up his portable air-conditioning pack and began to walk slowly toward the end of the platform that led to the Space Shuttle. Like all the astronauts, both he and Hull hated the full-length pressure suits. Part of the attraction of the Shuttle program was that the pilots were allowed to work onboard in a shirt-sleeve environment, even during the launch. Once you worked without them, putting on a space suit was like voluntarily stepping into a straitjacket.

'I guess wearing the suits during launch is worth it. I'd hate to ask those people on the airliner to hold their breath because I couldn't get my zipper up.'

'Good point.' Kingsley had agreed to have them wear the suits for this entire mission so that no time would be lost in putting them on after rendezvous. They would fasten on their helmets, then quickly leave the Shuttle and maneuver to the stranded airliner. Since it would take time to carry over the dozens of portable oxygen bottles they had brought along, there was no need to build in an additional delay. Kingsley glanced at his wristwatch. Two o'clock. It was 31 minutes before the rescheduled launch time. 'That first launch estimate of one forty-five was totally unrealistic.'

'The mission sure as hell would've launched without us,' Hull said as he glanced at his wristwatch.

'Right. Let's get this road show moving.' Kingsley picked up his own pace, his motions awkward and unstable because of the bulk of his suit.

Through the maze of ironwork, scaffolding, pipes and grates, several sections of the gleaming white structure of the Space Shuttle were visible. With every passing step, more and more of the giant spacecraft's frame began to emerge from behind the spider-like metal webbing of the launch tower.

As they turned the corner and entered the narrow catwalk that led to the Shuttle cockpit, the huge white center tank – the silo – dominated the view. Nearly half again as tall as the ship itself, this tremendous fuel tank looked as if it should be sitting in a farmer's field and stuffed with corn and oats rather than strapped to a launch pad with nearly two million pounds of super-cooled liquid hydrogen and oxygen inside. Kingsley could see the continuous stream of icy vapors as they poured out of the vent holes that were scattered around the perimeter of the tank.

Kingsley stopped walking, and Hull stopped alongside him. 'Looks like a goddamn loading dock,' the Shuttle commander said as he pointed to the shoulder-high pack of iron cylinders in front of them. He put down his portable air-conditioning pack and leaned against the platform's rail. 'Might as well wait. No sense trying to climb over that crap. We've got time.' With weekly launchings on the schedule, space travel had become so common-place that the pomp and ceremony had been cut out. To some extent that had been an advantage, but Kingsley still ached for those days years before when an astronaut never waited for anyone or anything.

'They'll be done soon.' Hull watched as three men in white NASA jumpsuits struggled to load each of the green cylinders carefully through the orbiter's small hatchway. The older of the three men groaned loudly as he wrestled with the next tank from the top of the stack. 'The hernia brigade,' Hull said. 'I'd give them a hand, but that's not in my job description.'

Kingsley didn't respond. His attention was focused on the pile of cylinders that remained on the platform. The stenciled words *Pure Oxygen* were on the sides of each of the tanks the men picked up. 'Eight to go. That's half. I said we'd carry fifteen in the cockpit with us. The other hundred and sixty-five should already be in the cargo bay.' He pointed at the thin, dark seam along the top of the orbiter's white fuselage where the two halves of the 60-foot cargo door met. The big electrically operated doors were already tightly shut.

'Fine.' Hull glanced out in the distance toward the gray hydrogen storage tanks and, beyond that, at the Cape's coastline. Tall stands of palmetto grass were bent over at nearly a 90-degree angle in the incessant breeze that blew off the ocean. The heavy smell of salt air seemed nearly thick enough to cut with a knife. Hull looked back at the Shuttle. His only previous trip into space – also as copilot – had been in Ship 04 seven months before. He had no idea when, if ever, he'd get his own command. Probably never, if the rumors were correct. Severe cutbacks in the program had been repeatedly hinted at. Hull sighed, then looked at Kingsley. 'The port SRB's been up twice already,' he mentioned.

'That's what they tell me.' Kingsley shot a glance at the closest of the two crayon-shaped missiles mounted on the sides of the center fuel tank. 'The one on the right is brand-new.'

'One new, one retread. Just like my Chevy.'

'Right.' The two solid rocket boosters, each 150 feet high, were reusable components in the Shuttle array. They would, together with the orbiter's three main engines, provide the initial seven million pounds of thrust to lift the Space Shuttle off Pad 39A – power equivalent to over one hundred Hoover Dams. Once the Shuttle had attained an altitude of 27 miles – less than three minutes into the mission – the two solid fuel boosters would jettison and would be parachuted back to Earth. They were targeted to splash down 160 miles off the coast of Florida, where they would be retrieved and used again. The SRB closest to where they stood had already gone through that cycle twice.

Kingsley's eyes traveled back to the silo tank, which was the only Shuttle part that was destined to oblivion. When it separated from the orbiter just prior to reaching orbital velocity, it would tumble back to Earth and disintegrate on its way down because of the intense reentry heat. The winged orbiter itself, with its crew of two pilots and six or seven of the injured passengers from the stranded airliner, would be spared the same reentry fate because of the thousands of ablative tiles along the ship's front and bottom. 'I hear the top office has commissioned another reentry temperature study,' Kingsley said. 'Problems with the ablative tiles again. The new super-glue isn't holding.'

'I could've predicted that.' Hull leaned back against the rail.

'Really? Why?'

'Glue won't keep tiles up in a *bathroom,* for chrissake.' Hull had a smirk on his face. 'The only thing super about NASA glue is its price.'

'I think we'll eventually go back to the original design concept,' Kingsley added in an attempt to keep the conversation serious. 'A liquid cooling system. Hydrogen, probably. It'll add weight, but it'll be dependable.' Without waiting for an answer, he picked up his portable air-conditioning pack and took several steps closer to the stack of oxygen tanks. Friend or not, he was getting tired of Hull's vaudeville routine, tired of every sentence being transformed into nothing more than a straight line for another of his inane jokes. Randy Hull was reputed to be the coolest guy under fire since John Paul Jones, but he was also a juvenile. 'What the hell happened to the safety rail?' Kingsley shouted above the wind noise as he strode toward where the older technician hovered over another oxygen bottle. The sides of the last ten feet of the catwalk between him and the cockpit hatchway were bare.

'Repairs,' the older man shouted without standing up, the green metal cylinder wrapped tightly in his arms. 'Temporary. Fixed tomorrow.' The creaking noises from the cold-soaked silo tank, the clanking from the oxygen tanks and the Florida sea breeze overpowered his words.

'What? I can't hear you.' Kingsley took another step closer to the pile of metal tanks between him and the old man.

'Chrissake, be careful!' The old man let the top oxygen bottle fall back on the stack as he stood bolt-upright. He had realized too late what would happen next.

Kingsley's boot caught an angle of iron at the base of the dismantled rail. The weight and bulk from his pressure suit made it impossible for him to keep his balance. He stumbled, then fell forward. Both Hull and the old man lunged out for Kingsley, but both missed.

Kingsley fell heavily onto the deck's metal grating, and his body came perilously close to the edge of the unprotected catwalk. At the last instant he grabbed onto a short stub of rail and stopped himself from going over the edge.

'Christ! Look out!' Hull's sudden movement toward Kingsley had accidentally kicked out the restraining wedge from beneath the wheel of the cart that carried the stack of oxygen bottles. The cart, unbalanced by the unequal distribution of the weighted bottles, quickly rolled the few remaining inches to the other side of the open catwalk.

'Grab it!'

The cart hesitated a brief moment at the ledge of the metal deck, looking as if it were one side of a perfectly balanced seesaw. Then, prodded by the wind and the movements of the people toward it, the cart was jolted out of its static position. It tumbled over. The eight heavy cylinders plummeted rapidly toward the deck of the launch platform.

Before any of the three men on the catwalk could say a word, the heavy cart and bottles crashed noisily into the fairings around the base of the Shuttle. A sickening sound of crunching, twisting metal reverberating loudly around the launch tower.

'Oh, shit.'

One of the NASA ground crew stuck his head out of the opened cockpit hatch. 'What the hell was that?'

'Damn.' The old man rolled his eyes, then pointed below. 'We sure as hell broke something.'

'Son of a bitch. You let the cart go over? Christ Almighty.' The younger technician looked at the faces of the three men on the catwalk before he spoke again. 'You guys better get your stories straight. I'll call Launch Control.'

'Wait.' Kingsley rose to his feet. There was a small scrape on the side of his face, but that was all. 'Are you in charge of the ground crew?' he asked the younger man.

The man nodded silently, not happy with the new focus on his responsibilities.

'Let's look at the damage. You and me. There might be nothing to report. Nothing worth delaying the launch for.'

'Are you kidding me?' The young technician crawled out of the Shuttle's hatchway and walked up to Kingsley. 'That cart and those bottles must've weighed over a thousand pounds. It's a hundred and fifty feet straight down from here.' He glanced over the side of the open catwalk, then back at the astronaut. 'I could tell from the noise that something down there . . . '

'No.' Kingsley's stare was unrelenting, his voice firm. 'There might be no damage. Not enough to report.' He spoke each of the words slowly, carefully, forcefully. 'Just you and me. We'll go down to look. Your men can finish securing the cargo already in the cockpit. The copilot can begin the checklist. We've got no time to waste. Everything might be okay.'

'You can't be serious.'

'I sure as hell am.' Kingsley picked up his portable air-conditioning pack and began to retrace his steps toward the elevator. Halfway down the catwalk, he shouted over his shoulder. 'For chrissake, man. Let's go.'

The technician stood his ground. He glanced at his two men, then toward the copilot. All three of them remained expressionless. 'Shit,' he muttered. 'It's not my ass.' He scurried quickly after the black Shuttle commander. The two of them reached the elevator just as the doors opened. They both stepped inside and the door shut.

'You got more oxygen?' Kingsley asked as he pressed the ground level button on the elevator control panel.

'You mean extra bottles? Yeah. On the truck. Three more, I think.'

'Good. That's enough. How long will it take to get them in the cockpit?'

'Ten minutes.'

'Fine. Plan on it.' Kingsley tried to twist the knob on his portable air-conditioning pack but found that he had already put it in full-cold. As the elevator crept slowly down, the image of a young black army air corps pilot climbing into the cockpit of an ancient P-47 filled Kingsley's thoughts. *Combat, for chrissake.* By the time the elevator doors opened, Kingsley's muscles were rigid with tension, his face and neck bathed in pools of sweat. He tapped the technician on the shoulder. 'You get those extra oxygen bottles. I'll look at the damage myself.'

* * *

Ben Robinson hurried down the deserted basement corridor of the Goddard Center. He glanced up at the wall clock as he passed it. Ten minutes after two. From what Kennerdale had said a few moments earlier, Presidential Aide Stuart Goldman would be on the air by now, conducting a live news conference. Robinson could tell from Kennerdale's tone that Goldman's backup plan to use the Russians had come as an aggravating, unwanted surprise. To Robinson, the news was neither good nor bad. He doubted that the Russians could get up to the airliner in time if the Shuttle didn't launch as scheduled in 20 more minutes. All they'd be able to do would be to retrieve the bodies.

Robinson opened the door to room H-10 and stepped inside. With the electronics console shut down after they had left for the OPSCON, the room had become deadly quiet. Robinson walked across the white linoleum floor and over to the door to the private inner office. He unlocked it, stepped inside, then moved to the front of the electronics console.

The console in the private room had inadvertently been left on. A man in a dark suit, standing in a formal-looking room and reading from a sheet of paper in his hand, was on the TV monitor. It was Stuart Goldman, more than likely. His tinny, petulant voice poured out of the console's three-inch speaker.

'The President has been in direct contact with the Russian space authorities. We continue to make every effort to back up our own NASA Space Shuttle rescue attempt. The Soviet Union is currently evaluating the level of assistance they could feasibly provide. We expect to hear word from them shortly . . . '

Robinson reached up and flipped off the switch that controlled the television monitor. He wasn't interested in Goldman's made-for-TV news. Except for the standby hum of electronics, the room had once again become reverently quiet.

Robinson sat back in his chair and stared at the ceiling. Even though everything seemed to be going as well as expected – the Shuttle was poised for takeoff, the Russians were actively involved – Robinson felt less confident now than he had anytime since he had learned about the *Star Streak*'s flight into orbit. He took a deep breath, rocked forward in his chair, then reached for a stack of papers on the console. He held the papers in his hand for a moment, but then changed his mind. He laid the papers back down.

Robinson swiveled to his left, picked up the telephone and reached for the auto-dial controls. Although he wasn't sure of what he would say, he felt that it was time that he talked to Phoenix again.

Robinson pressed the first button in the row, the one he had programmed with Ferrera's number. He leaned back in his chair as the series of rapid electronic clicks filled the earpiece. The phone rang once before it was picked up.

'At two o'clock, the temperature in Central Park was forty-six degrees under partly cloudy skies. The New York Metropolitan area forecast for this afternoon and this evening calls for decreasing clouds, falling temperatures and brisk winds. Currently in midtown . . . '

What the hell is this? Robinson sat upright. He looked at the auto-dial controls along the top row of the console. Clearly, he had used the proper button to call Phoenix. *Damn electronic crap.* He hung up the telephone, reached for his notepad and flipped through several of its pages.

After he found the correct number, he disconnected the auto-dial controls and began to manually dial his call to Phoenix. *The New York City weather report. Christ.* Robinson shook his head in disgust. Although he had never felt that way before, he had begun to think that modern high-tech crap wasn't worth a damn. Just like the rocket controls in the *Star Streak,* the telephone auto-dialer had seemed to develop a mind of its own.

Garbage in, garbage out. The phrase passed through Robinson's thoughts. It was a technician's smug bromide for explaining away equipment foul-ups. Human error, that's what they would always say. When we put crap into the machines, we get crap out. It made sense, and Robinson had seen that concept apply more times than he cared to remember.

But not this time. Robinson hung up his telephone before it had begun to ring. Something was wrong. He was dead certain that he had programmed Ferrera's number properly. Hell, he knew damn well he had. He had used the auto-dialer to Phoenix twice already. No one else had been inside the locked private room to screw it up.

Sit down at the console. Pretend to be busy. 'Jesus Christ!' Robinson jumped up and sent his swivel chair sailing backward across the small room. Someone else *had* been inside the private room. Krause. He had sat at the console not 45 minutes before, at Robinson's insistence. *Call your friend in New York. Use the button on the end.*

'God Almighty.' Krause had lied. He had not called any friend in New York. While Robinson stood beside him, Krause had apparently dialed the only New York number he could think of. But in doing it, Krause had pressed the wrong button on the telephone control panel. *Hello, George? This is Alex. I'm afraid I've got bad news.* Krause had carried on a long-winded fictitious conversation while the New York weather played over and over in his ear. Why?

Robinson realized that there could be any number of possible explanations. Perhaps Krause hadn't wanted, for some personal reason, to call his friend in New York but didn't want to argue with Robinson over it. Perhaps there was no answer or the number was busy and Krause felt a need to carry on a fictitious conversation simply to appear occupied – as Robinson had ordered.

But perhaps it was something else entirely. *Perhaps there was no friend In New York to begin with.* 'Damn.' *Too many coincidences. Play the probabilities. Look for firm evidence and positive correlations.* The guidelines that Robinson had used so successfully for so many years as a test pilot ran through his mind and he decided to use them again. The decision he was about to make could mean the difference between life and death for those onboard the *Star Streak*. Robinson almost felt as if he were back in the pilot's seat again, back in control. He knew that he needed to remain alert and objective if he were to make the proper decision.

Robinson had already chalked up one strike against Krause simply because the young engineer had acted guilty. Appearances weren't everything, but they certainly had to be counted. Strike two was the bogus telephone call to New York – also not conclusive, but enough to warrant a closer look. What Robinson needed was another piece of evidence that Krause had lied about something pertinent during the last few hours.

Robinson retrieved his swivel chair, pushed it back toward the computer console and sat down, deep in thought. *Bonnie Becker said she was going to New York this weekend.* Robinson frowned, there was no way for him to test the validity of Krause's earlier statement without giving away too much to Becker. Robinson had to avoid being impetuous – Becker was, for the time being at least, still the prime suspect.

I'm having the same problem they are. I can't find a starting point. But there was nothing in that statement of Krause's that Robinson could use, no way for him to pry it apart to discover whether Krause had been telling the truth or not. Robinson racked his brain for another of Krause's statements, one that he might more easily use to test Krause's honesty.

The quality-control program hasn't been modified since early last winter. Robinson nodded. That would be an easy enough place to start. In order to modify a computer program, a technician had to sign himself and his secret code number into the machine before any alterations would be accepted. But all of those entries were automatically sorted and compiled. Robinson picked up the paper on which the NASA people had written the applicable instructions, then hunched over the computer keyboard and began to program the Goddard screen to pull up the appropriate information out of its tie-in with the United Aerospace computer. Within a few seconds a table of contents filled the screen. Robinson selected the category he wanted, then hit the proper keystrokes.

'Son of a bitch!' Robinson's eyes traveled no further down than the very top entry. Since the log of revisions page was kept in descending numerical order, beginning with the current year, the date on the top would be the most recent input.

AUGUST 5/MISCELLANEOUS MODIFICATIONS/KRAUSE

Krause! The young engineer had modified the quality-control programming only two weeks before the work on Ship 35 was done, even though he had told Robinson that no one had touched the system since early last winter! There was now no doubt why the after-service computer checks on Ship 35 hadn't discovered the sabotage device – the computer had been specifically programmed to ignore it! *Krause was the saboteur.*

Robinson slammed his hand hard against the console. Several of the papers fell off the cabinet. They drifted lazily to the floor. Strike three, Krause was out. All the facts fit – all the facts except that Krause had no opportunity. Robinson bent over and scooped up the scattered sheets off the floor. *I'm overlooking something. A missing piece.*

Robinson began to carefully go over his notes. He reviewed each of them once, twice, then three times. Nothing. He pored over them again. Finally, he glanced up at the clock. Eight minutes had gone by since he had entered the private room.

He was nearly out of time. Robinson now knew that Krause was the saboteur, but without conclusive and unarguable proof against him, Krause would undoubtedly deny his involvement. He would stall. Then it would be too late for the people onboard Flight 14, too late for Donald Collins.

Robinson closed his eyes and rubbed his fingers against his throbbing temples. The people onboard the airlier would suffocate in 90 minutes. Collins was as good as dead. There was nothing Robinson could do.

I'm sorry I missed you. Collins' words echoed in Robinson's thoughts. *You left for San Francisco an hour before.* Among his other regrets, Robinson also regretted that he had missed seeing Collins for that last time. He was sorry that he had left Phoenix for that one weekend in August, the only weekend he had left town the entire summer. He should have spent that weekend home with Sally, rather than going to San Francisco with Ray Lee.

Weekend? Robinsons eyes opened wide. In the back of his mind he felt the abrasive friction between two conflicting thoughts. *Weekend in San Francisco?* Something was wrong with that idea, something was out of keeping with the rest of the facts Robinson had seen. He tore back into his paperwork, hurriedly flipping through dozens of documents, notes and messages.

227

'Damn it!' Robinson couldn't believe the two papers he held in his hand. It had been there all along, buried in a ream of data about schedules, delays and cost overruns triggered by an earlier problem in the hangar. Robinson could see from the paperwork that the airliner had arrived in Phoenix on Saturday, August 13th, but *had not been put into the hangar until Friday, August 19th.* In their haste and excitement, he, Ferrera, Lee – all of them – had missed that slight variation in the company's normal routine.

'Christ!' The facts in front of Robinson showed that, in reality, *Star Streak* N35CA had not arrived in Phoenix one day before it was first put in the hangar – even though that was the customary method for scheduling maintenance on the ninety-eight-million-dollar hypersonic airliners. Because of the gantry crane accident in the United Aerospace hangar, N35CA had sat outside on the ramp for six full days – beginning the very weekend that Robinson had gone to San Francisco. *Beginning the very day that Krause had been injured at the airport when the gantry crane came apart.*

There was something else, too. Krause's accident in the hangar had taken place on a Saturday, but his department *never worked on weekends.* No one had thought to ask Krause why he was in the hangar that Saturday afternoon. Robinson cursed his own stupidity, then reached for the telephone to pass on the facts to Phoenix.

Before he dialed, Robinson looked up at the clock. 'Damn.' There was no time for any more calls, he would need to make this decision on his own. A command decision. He put down the telephone. There was no real choice. Robinson had to immediately find Krause and get the saboteur to cooperate.

He gathered up his paperwork and moved quickly out of the room. The only way to get Krause to cooperate would be to show him that he had no other option, that he would be caught regardless. Convicted regardless. Robinson intended to try to convince Krause that, if he cooperated and voluntarily brought that airliner down, the severity of his crime would be lessened. The penalty would be lessened. Except for a Space Shuttle rescue – which Robinson found that he had already discounted no matter how hard he tried to believe in its chance for success – finding Krause was the only hope they had.

Robinson ran down the long corridor that led to the OPSCON. He would confront Krause with the make-believe telephone call to New York, the quality-control modifications, then the remainder of the facts. That, plus the actual sabotage equipment installed in Ship 35, was enough evidence to prove that Krause had planted the electronic device in that airliner soon after it had arrived in Phoenix, sometime between the hours of ten in the morning and three in the afternoon on Saturday, August 13th. That was only a short while before his accident in the hangar had put him into the hospital. Krause was definitely the saboteur.

Chapter Thirteen

THE BRIGHT moonlight reflected off the unbroken expanses of freshly fallen snow. It provided enough light for Vladislav Zholobov to easily read the large billboard across the square.

SLAVA TRUDU! SLAVA KPSS! The big letters were painted in bright red against the brown background of the building's wall. 'Glory to labor! Glory to the Communist Party! What a hideous joke,' Zholobov said as he turned away from the view out the window.

'So?' Oleg Nikolayev leaned back in the couch and stretched his legs. 'They prefer to give us glory in place of consumer goods. It is less expensive to produce glory than shoes and automobiles.'

Zholobov did not answer. He took a few steps closer to the black telephone, but still did not reach for it.

'You must make up your mind quickly,' Nikolayev said as he uncoiled his body from its reclined position and rose to stand near his friend. 'You have waited too long already. If they call back before you have decided, your problems will multiply.'

'That is true.' Zholobov took the remaining steps toward the table, then laid his hand on the telephone. He did not pick the receiver up.

'There is not much choice,' the younger man said as he attempted to prod his friend. 'Listen to your own words. Then your decision will be made.'

'Possibly.' Zholobov blinked, then wiped the dampness away from his eyes. The vodka, the late hour, the counsel of his cherished friend had hollowed him out. He ached inside. Zholobov had been through too much misery, seen too much horror. After living through the seige of Leningrad as a young man, after the tours of duty in forced labor camps during the fifties, after the endless bouts with corruption and indifference for all of those years that followed, he had no strength left. *'Defitsitny* affects not only our consumer goods. It also affects our courage.'

'Short supply,' Nikolayev nodded. 'A good choice of words. But . . . ' The young scientist shrugged in the gesture that was understood across every inch of Mother Russia. 'We are, one by one, too small. Too insignificant. Nothing will change the sadness.'

'We make our own sadness.' Without hesitation, Zholobov picked up the telephone and spoke a harsh command to the operator. He stood with his eyes shut for the entire time it took for the connection to Moscow to be made. He worked at keeping the vision of his Black Sea villa and not the stranded, orbiting American airliner in his thoughts. 'Comrade, the situation here is impossible,' he said after the call had gone through and the introductions had been made. 'We cannot help the Americans.'

'The die is cast,' Nikolayev whispered with obvious relief. He had prayed against any foolish or impetuous commitments from Zholobov. 'There is no turning back now.'

The old man wearily nodded in agreement, while he continued to listen to the response on the telephone. While he waited for the Moscow official to finish, he ran his hand nervously through his thick strands of white hair. 'Yes. Of course. There is no question that, with more time, our Soviet technology would easily be capable of accommodating their request. It is only a matter of notice, of timing. What they ask is simply not possible within the next few hours.'

After another minute of additional exchange – while Zholobov was once again forced to repeat his statements for someone new at the Moscow end of the line – he was finally able to hang up. For several seconds after he had put down the receiver, he continued to firmly press it against its cradle – as if that effort could somehow prevent the telephone from ringing, Moscow from calling back.

'Through with them? Will they want more?' Nikolayev asked as he watched Zholobov.

The old man removed his trembling hand from the telephone. 'Finished,' he said. 'Completely. The matter is closed.' Zholobov stepped to the card table and reached for his glass of vodka. The clear, odorless liquid was the only antidote that could neutralize the lies that his lips had been forced to speak. He knew, too well, that the rocket on their launch pad might well have been able to reach the airliner in time to supply it with oxygen. But that would have meant an unmistakable risk – and the possibility of a failure. Zholobov took a long, deep drink, then turned back to his young friend. 'I told them no more than what they wanted to hear.'

'Good sense.'

'They encourage no involvement, no concern,' Zholobov said angrily. 'So that is all they get.'

'It seems fair,' Nikolayev answered. For the first time since the original call from Moscow had come nearly an hour before, he allowed himself to smile. He sat down on the couch again.

'No, my friend,' Zholobov said as he smiled back wanly, then shook his head. 'It is now *your* choice of words that is wrong.' Zholobov put down his glass and walked over to the window. The moon was hidden by a thin veil of cloud. Slowly, like an unraveling blanket, the clouds began to peel themselves away to expose the bright moon beneath. 'Fairness is not the question,' he said sadly, 'so it can never be part of the answer. The people onboard that American airliner are caught between forces – human forces – that they have no knowledge of. Yet those forces are so real and powerful that it will cost them their lives.'

Alvin Kingsley moved his eyes down from the thick, black-rimmed glass of the Space Shuttle's windshield. He sat in the quiet, motionless cockpit of the orbiter with his back at a 90-degree angle to the ground, his face pointed straight up at the blue

Florida sky. Without moving his head, Kingsley glanced at the section of gray panel that held the luminescent clock. It was 2:37 – six minutes past the rescheduled launch time. Yet the Space Shuttle was still firmly anchored to Launch Pad 39A.

'We should unionize,' Randy Hull said from the copilot's seat. He turned his head slightly toward Kingsley, his chin rubbing along the circular plastic collar that his pressure helmet would later clip to. 'This flat salary stuff is for the birds. The astronauts should go on strike. Pay by the hour, that's what we need. Then the delays wouldn't be bad.' Hull laughed nervously.

'Right.'

The two astronauts lapsed back into silence. Hull rubbed an irritated spot on the left side of his neck. No matter how calm and cool he tried to be, he knew that nothing was worse than the waiting. With their cockpit checklists completed, the enforced idleness of the endless countdown holds and delays caused endless thoughts about how any of the ship's thousands of crucial parts might break down, how millions of pounds of flammable explosives were not more than a dozen feet beneath their feet. This was the only time that Randy Hull worried about his self-control. He knew that if they didn't get something to occupy his hands and his thoughts very soon, he might well find himself climbing out of his seat, opening the hatch and getting out of the Shuttle. 'Do you want to review the rendezvous checklist once more?'

Kingsley did not reply. Instead, he pressed the thumb switch on the angular, stubby steering stick that was mounted between his legs. 'Launch? Are we ready to resume the countdown?'

'Standby.'

'Bastards,' Kingsley muttered, his thumb sliding off the transmitting button an instant before his voice would've been carried out of the Space Shuttle on the open radio channel between him and Launch Control.

'Bastards,' Hull repeated. He tried to think of something else to add, but found that he couldn't. He tried to force the smile back on his face, but found that he couldn't do that either. Instead, he took his hand and wiped away the puddle of perspiration that had collected at the base of his neck. He turned back toward Kingsley. 'Are you sure about the damage?' he asked abruptly. Hull knew that something was wrong with Kingsley, but he couldn't figure out what it was. He prayed to God that it didn't have anything to do with the dropping of the oxygen bottles a half hour before, but he had a suspicion that perhaps it did.

Kingsley didn't respond for several seconds. He kept his eyes focused on the black gyro horizon in the center of his flight panel, the instrument he would use to monitor their liftoff and to maintain precise attitude control of the orbiter during reentry. A dozen different answers raced through his mind before he turned to Hull. 'Yes,' he said, settling on the only reply that was still open to him. 'Like I told you before, there's nothing to worry about.'

'Explain it to me again,' Hull said without the slightest hint of humor in his voice. 'I'd like to hear again exactly what you found when you went below.'

'The bottles missed the Shuttle completely,' Kingsley answered petulantly. 'They impacted around the base of the SRB launch deck.'

'All of them? All eight? Even the cart?'

'Yes.' *No.* 'They landed within a fifteen-foot radius of the number-two SRB restraining clip.' *All but one. That motherfucker hit square on the number-two clip. Right on its dome. The dome is dented. It might be cracked. I can't tell.* 'Everything's fine,' Kingsley lied. 'I moved the bottles to the far end of the gantry. They won't be in the way.' Kingsley paused. He strummed his fingers along the edge of the center console between the two pilot seats. 'We were lucky,' he added for effect.

'Okay,' Hull nodded. He would have been satisfied, except for the look in Kingsley's eyes. Hull knew that Kingsley was the sort of guy who took everything super-seriously, and that was good. But today he looked more frightened than worried. That was unusual. Something was not right. Still, this was Kingsley's first flight as Shuttle commander. There might be any one of a thousand different things on his mind. 'Are you concerned about the rendezvous and the EVA?' Hull asked.

'No.' In the strictest sense, the Space Shuttle commander had told the truth. Kingsley knew that maneuvering the Shuttle up alongside the airliner would be a piece of cake. Putting on their pressure suits and beginning the Extra-Vehicular Activity out of the Shuttle and over to the airliner would be a little more complicated – but it was nothing that they hadn't practiced in principle a hundred times before. 'It's only the waiting. It's got me edgy as hell. That's all.'

'Me, too.'

Kingsley turned to his side panel and pretended to examine the rows of plastic switches. The training diagram of the eight SRB restraining clips flashed through his mind. Four of the five-foot-high conical supports were located under each of the two solid rocket boosters. When the Shuttle's main engines were ignited four seconds before the actual launch, the restraining clips would hold the Shuttle from lifting off the pad prematurely. Once full power had been attained, the clips would release simultaneously and the Shuttle would be free.

'Shuttle, this is Launch Control,' the radio crackled. 'The anomaly in hydrogen pressure has been corrected. We will resume countdown from T minus five minutes, forty-two seconds at my mark.'

'Roger,' Kingsley transmitted tersely, then moved his finger off the button. He closed his eyes. *Clip number two is dented. It might be cracked.* Kingsley knew that if one of the restraining clips released early, the Shuttle would lift off at an odd angle. Cockeyed. How much? There was no way to tell, since it depended on too many factors. If the clip didn't release at all, the Shuttle would topple over on the pad. The silo tank would explode. He and Hull would never know what hit them.

Kingsley opened his eyes and looked out ahead at the warm, blue sky. The restraining clip might also be perfectly fine. It might be dented only on its dome, or, even if there was some damage inside, only enough to cause a slight variation in the Shuttle's liftoff angle – one that could easily be controlled by the Shuttle's rocket steering system.

'Mark. T minus five minutes, forty-two seconds.'

'Mark,' Kingsley answered as he again pressed his finger against the transmit button. He glanced over at Hull, who nodded back and gave a thumbs-up gesture. 'All systems are a go from this end,' Kingsley said crisply into his microphone. *Maybe.* Because the damage to the number-two restraining clip was purely physical, Kingsley knew that none of it would show up on the monitor boards in Launch Control. All they could check was the electrical continuity of the circuits, which were still normal. There was no sure way to tell the extent of the damage without tearing the restraining clip completely apart and running a thorough test. That would add hours, maybe days, to the mission. It would eliminate any attempt at saving the people on the stranded airliner.

'Hydro-pressure is green. Circulating pump is off. TK valves are open,' Hull transmitted as he picked up his part of the cockpit checklist. A renewed smile formed on the corners of his lips as his hands ran across the center and side consoles to activate the appropriate switches.

'On my mark, T minus four minutes.' The tinny voice from the radio paused a few seconds, then added, 'Mark.'

'Roger,' Kingsley answered on cue. 'Vent valves are closed. We are configured for liftoff.' Kingsley knew that he could call a delay and ask for a thorough check. But if nothing out of limits were found, he would never be able to live down that decision. *Nigger leaves white folks stranded in space.* Kingsley shuddered, then balled his hand tightly into a fist. The decision had been made. There had been no choice, really. Taking the Shuttle as is was no more than a calculated risk. It was, Kingsley guessed, no more of a risk than flying an old P-47 into combat over the North African desert.

Ben Robinson stood in the upper level of the OPSCON with his face six inches from Bonnie Becker's. His expression was contorted with tension and anger, his forehead and scalp glistened with sweat. 'I don't have time for these goddamn games of yours,' he said in a low, menacing voice. 'I'm going to ask you once more. I want a straight answer.'

'Don't you try to intimidate *me*,' Becker answered flippantly. But she knew that Robinson had done precisely that. While she didn't feel that anyone had a God-given right to pry into her private affairs, there was no doubt in her mind that this particular man was not the one to make that point with. 'I don't understand how my private life affects *you*. My plans for the weekend have nothing to do with United Aerospace.'

'I can't explain it to you. Not now,' Robinson pleaded. He couldn't take the chance that she might – intentionally or unintentionally – say something to Krause.

'If you won't tell me why you want to know, then I won't answer.'

'You goddamn self-centered bitch. Did it ever occur to you that there's more out there than your personal problems?' He turned away from her briefly as he glanced quickly around the OPSCON. Krause was nowhere in sight, and neither were Kennerdale, Novak and the man from the TV network. According to McBride, the four of them had left the OPSCON together a few minutes before Robinson had gotten there.

'Shut up and leave me alone!'

'Go to hell.' Robinson was thankful that, except for one TV technician in the far corner, the upper level of the OPSCON was for the moment empty. 'Where were you going this weekend? Why were you going to New York?' he asked again. He needed to verify his suspicion that Krause had acted alone in the sabotage, just to be absolutely certain that he was about to do the right thing. If he didn't get a satisfactory answer from Becker soon, he didn't know what he would do. Have her arrested, maybe. But that might lead to a public commotion and might jeopardize his position with Krause.

'Why are you picking on me?' Becker said, nearly in tears. 'Why do you always pick on the women? Did you ask the two men that same question?'

Robinson could see the bewilderment in her hazel eyes. That alone told him nearly all he needed to know. But he still felt that he needed to hear her explanation before he committed himself to the plan. 'I sure as hell did. McBride was going to Atlantic City.' Robinson thought back over McBride's words. *I've got a new system. I want to try it in the East, where they don't know me. I can beat the blackjack tables.* It was too much of an absurd statement to be fabricated.

'How about Krause?' Becker said.

'I can't find him. He's with Kennerdale. I'll ask him as soon as he gets back.' *If he gets back*. Robinson prayed that Krause had not caught on yet. If he had, then Krause would already be long gone from Goddard. 'For the last time, tell me where you intended to go for this weekend.'

'Okay.' Becker pushed her hand through her clipped red hair. 'It's a business deal. I'm leaving United Aerospace. There are a group of backers in New York who'll put up front money so I can open my own electronics design firm.'

'Christ. Why didn't you tell me?' Robinson took a step backward. He could see, plainly, that she had told the truth.

'Because I was afraid.' She moved her hand to her face to wipe away the one tear that had run down her cheek. 'If the company found out, I thought they might fire me. Then my backers might pull out. I had to keep it all a secret.' Becker took a step toward Robinson and touched his shoulder. 'Please promise me that you won't use that information against me. Please. Don't screw up my big chance.'

'Don't worry,' Robinson said absently as he backed away. He turned and stepped quickly toward the door at the rear of the OPSCON, his thoughts and plans whirling through his brain. Everything was now in place. The rest of them had alibis. The only thing that was missing was Alex Krause. Robinson had no idea where the saboteur might have gone.

'T minus sixty seconds and counting.'

Alvin Kingsley did not reply to the radio message from Launch Control. Procedurally, no report from him was required since everything was preprogrammed. The rocket engines would ignite in sequence – first the orbiter's main engines, then a few seconds after that the two solid rocket boosters strapped to the sides of the silo tank. Everything was set to happen automatically, unless someone in the Shuttle cockpit or in Launch Control purposely intervened.

Kingsley glanced over his left shoulder and out the Shuttle's side window. Far in the distance, beyond the gantry crossbeams that lay along the edge of his view, were several hazy, indistinct shapes. It was, Kingsley knew, the Vehicle Assembly Building and, to its left, the squat structure that housed the Launch

Control Center. Their presence loomed over his shoulder like a lurking, scolding father. 'Fucking Bellman,' he mumbled.

'What?'

'Never mind,' Kingsley answered sharply. He turned to Hull and pointed at the copilot's instrument panel. 'How's the hydrogen pressure holding up?'

'Dead-center. Everything's perfect.'

'Great.' Kingsley nodded, then frowned. He glanced down at his own panel. Pressures, temperatures, quantities – all were in the green. *The dome is dented. Might be cracked.* For the first time since he had become an astronaut, Kingsley found himself silently praying that something in the ship would show up as being out of tolerance.

'T minus thirty seconds and counting. All systems are go.'

'Roger,' Hull replied. He leaned forward and pressed another switch on his side panel. 'The camera is on.'

Kingsley's eyes traveled to the stubby wide-angle camera lens aimed down at them from the ceiling above. Every scene in the Shuttle's cockpit was being transmitted to Launch Control and recorded on film. A permanent record was being made of every action they took, of everything that happened to them. Kingsley shivered at the thought of what that film might show in just a handful of seconds.

'T minus fifteen. We have a go for launch.'

'Here we go,' Hull said to no one in particular. He squirmed slightly in his flight chair, then glanced at Kingsley. 'Ready?'

'Ready.' *No.* Kingsley's heart pounded. His jaw and neck muscles ached. The saliva in his mouth tasted foul and bitter. He held the arm of his chair with a locked grip, the fingers of his hands turned bloodlessly pale. *The number-two SRB restraining clip is cracked.*

'Ten, nine, eight, seven . . . '

Kingsley felt the familiar dull thud beneath him. The orbiter's three main engines had ignited. They had begun to spool up from idle power.

'Six, five, four . . . '

The thrust from the ship's main engines began to increase rapidly. A white cloud of super-heated hydrogen billowed up

239

outside the Shuttle. It enveloped the pad, the gantry and everything in the launch area in an obscuring blanket of dense, steamy fog. *Damaged. Cracked. We'll topple over. Explode.*

'Three, two, one . . . '

Kingsley thrust his arm out toward the center console. Without hardly registering a conscious thought, Kingsley's finger had flipped aside the cover that guarded the Shuttle engine ignition switches and, with that same motion, had pressed down hard on the center button.

Before any definitive thoughts had formed in Kingsley's brain, the computer connected to the Space Shuttle had sensed and evaluated the new switch position. The override switch for rocket engine number two had been engaged, which meant that its engine had been manually shut down.

The electronic monitors took heed of that abnormality. Within another microsecond, the out-of-sequence condition triggered a computer alarm. A metered flow of voltage was sent throughout the entire electronic launch linkup.

'Abort!' the radio voice from Launch Control shouted. 'We have an auto-abort!'

Before Kingsley had removed his finger from the plastic console switch, the computers in Launch Control that monitored Space Shuttle 02 had automatically shut down the ship's engines and aborted its launch.

'You sure as hell better be telling the truth,' Ralph Kennerdale said. 'I hope, for your sake, that this isn't some trumped-up line of shit.'

'Absolutely not,' Ty Bellman answered quickly, his smooth Southern drawl filling the telephone earpiece. 'Kingsley aborted the launch five minutes ago, on the suspicion of a cracked SRB restraining clip.'

Kennerdale could picture the mounting clips beneath the Shuttle's solid rocket boosters, and vaguely remembered their purpose and importance. 'Those things should have been checked.'

'They were,' Bellman answered curtly.

Kennerdale listened to silence from the other end of the telephone. The launch director had obviously decided not to volunteer more than he had to. Kennerdale glanced at the three men who shared the small conference room with him. Justin Watts stood with his back against the wall, his arms folded, his expression blank. Gilbert Novak sat on the edge of a government-issue chair, his neck craned forward, his mouth slightly ajar, his fingers moving continuously. Alex Krause sat in the chair to Novak's immediate left, the cast of his left leg stuck out across the aisle in front of him. Krause appeared calm, but his eyes darted around the room in a constant, distracted motion. Kennerdale returned his attention to the telephone. 'How the hell did Kingsley know that the clip was damaged?' he said. 'Did you tell him? Did you send someone out to the pad with a sledgehammer?' With one ring of the telephone the rescue situation had gone from promising to hopeless.

'I understand that it was a loading accident,' Bellman answered. He purposely avoided being provoked by Kennerdale's mocking questions. 'Kingsley had evidently seen it happen, but had decided that there was insufficient damage to report it.'

'He should have stuck with his first decision.'

'No. He guessed right. We just did a quick restraining clip test. The number-two clip is frozen solid. The Shuttle would've toppled over on the pad.'

'I sure as hell hope you're not bullshitting. I intend to investigate this thoroughly.'

'Be my guest.'

Kennerdale slammed down the telephone. He looked up at the wall clock, then toward the three men across the small conference room. 'No Shuttle. Not for twenty-four hours.'

'Shit.' Justin Watts unfolded his arms, then rubbed his hand along his mustache. 'We sure blew that one. That's a lot of potential we've missed.'

'Not necessarily.' Novak had already given the prospect of a Shuttle delay some thought. All eyes turned toward him as he stood up, straightened his jacket, then walked slowly across the room. 'If the Shuttle can be ready in twenty-four hours . . . '

'That's what they say,' Kennerdale answered cautiously.

'Then the basic plan we discussed earlier is still operative.'

Novak tugged at the collar of his starched white skirt as he turned to look at Watts, then at the fourth man in the room, Alex Krause. 'The airliner will be leaving the communication area in nine more minutes, and will be out of communications for the next half hour.'

'Yes, but how . . . '

'We should announce that the Space Shuttle has been delayed only slightly. Nothing more than that,' Novak said emphatically. 'Five minutes. Something minor. We can tack another five minutes on after that.'

'So the airliner crew will still believe that the Shuttle is on its way?' Krause asked as he moved his leg slowly, pulled himself upright and stepped toward the center of the room. Krause had begun to understand Novak's reasoning and instantly realized how well Novak's idea would fit in with his own plan.

'Exactly.'

'But what good will that do?' Kennerdale looked at the wall clock. 'The airliner will be back in radio contact at three twenty-five. We'll certainly have to tell them the truth by then. They're scheduled to run out of oxygen approximately twenty minutes later.'

Novak saw that there was no way to sugarcoat what he was about to suggest, no way to pussyfoot around it. But they had gone too far to back down now. Everything – the future of NASA funding, Kennerdale's personal exposure, his own career – pointed to only one solution. He coughed to clear his throat, then began. 'We had agreed to call Mr. Krause,' Novak began as a preamble as he pointed to the United Aerospace engineer, 'to assist us with technical questions about the stranded aircraft.' Novak ignored the fact that, of the four united Aerospace people at Goddard, only Krause had seemed cooperative and approachable – the young engineer had actually volunteered his services before Kennerdale had asked for them.

'I'm glad to help,' Krause offered self-consciously. He shifted his weight, then laid one hand on the corner of the conference table. His face was ashen-white, his forehead covered with sweat.

'We also agreed,' Novak continued, 'that Captain Collins' renewed threat to begin some sort of desperate reentry attempt –

possible fuel mixing, or something along those lines – would be detrimental to the overall Shuttle rescue attempt.'

'Fuel mixing is too dangerous,' Kennerdale said, although he omitted any mention that the greatest danger might well be to his own career. If Collins managed to somehow mix the fuel without first blowing up the airliner, NASA would look like a bunch of assholes outsmarted by an amatuer. Worse, any investigation of the initial NASA fuel-mixing tests would prove them to be nothing more than pure fiction. Kennerdale had already, on live TV, publicly alluded to those tests. That combination would pop the lid off the can.

'It was Dr. Kennerdale's idea,' Novak continued, 'to have Mr. Krause come up with a way to prevent the airline crew from doing anything rash. That idea is even more important now.' Novak smiled meekly at Kennerdale, then looked back at Krause. 'We've got to be realistic. Without help from the Russians and without the Shuttle, it has become physically impossible to save the lives of those onboard that airliner. We must convince that pilot to do nothing that will physically endanger his ship. If we can, then most of the benefits of the rescue are still available to us.'

'You've lost me,' Watts looked puzzled.

Novak had hoped that nothing more explicit would be necessary. He took a deep breath, then reluctantly pointed to the wall clock. 'In forty minutes everyone on that airliner will suffocate.'

'That's true, but . . .'

'Twenty-four hours from now – once the Shuttle has been fixed – we can send it up to bring down the bodies. It will take two or three days to load the bodies into the Shuttle cargo bay. That'll give us nearly a week of continual media exposure.'

'Just like the *Columbia* launch,' Kennerdale eagerly agreed. That first flight of the Space Shuttle – complete with its dramatically canceled countdown two days earlier and the ad nauseum coverage over the few nonessential tiles that had come off during the launch – had held the public's attention for nearly a full week. There had been a lot of pro-NASA clamor right after that first *Columbia* mission, but Kennerdale also had seen too many times how short the public's memory was. NASA desperately needed another week-long shot of publicity to loosen the congressional purse strings during the upcoming budget debate. 'Like Plutarch said, "Forgetfulness changes everything into a nonoccurrence."'

Novak rolled his eyes, forced an insipid smile, then began to pace up and down in front of the three men. 'The best part,' he continued, 'is the potential for a State funeral for the victims. The President can attend. We can moan about the unforeseen delays that made us just miss our chance to rescue them. It's almost as good as getting them down alive.'

'Yes. It'll prove to everyone that NASA could have done the job, if only we had more time – and more funding.'

'I see your point,' Watts agreed.

'It's to everyone's benefit,' Kennerdale continued, his words coming out rapid-fire. 'Not only NASA.' He turned to Krause. 'United Aerospace will have one hell of a time discovering what the problem with that aircraft was if Captain Collins destroys it in some half-ass reentry attempt.'

'Of course.'

'And don't think that your cooperation won't be rewarded,' Kennerdale added as he saw that the time was right to bring Krause firmly into the plan. 'I can promise you that NASA will recognize your contributions. We'll name you as the United Aerospace technician to go up with the Shuttle when it launches tomorrow.'

'What about my leg?'

'In a weightless condition, your cast won't make any difference. It won't hamper you. You'll be able to investigate the airliner while the crew loads the bodies. Bring back whatever parts you feel might aid your accident analysis.'

'Thank you. I'd appreciate that opportunity,' Krause said. He could hardly believe his good fortune. He had volunteered to assist Kennerdale simply to be close to the inside information, to see how close he could play it. With Robinson so damned near to the truth, he needed to know for sure what the chances of recovery and detection were. Now, it seemed, he'd be the one who'd get into the *Star Streak*'s lower bay first. He could destroy the two sabotage devices before anyone else had gotten to see them, before Robinson had somehow realized that it was he, not Becker or McBride, who had planted them.

The four men in the room stood silently for several seconds. Finally, one by one, each of them nodded in agreement.

'Okay.' Kennerdale reached for the telephone and dialed the OPSCON. 'Kurt,' he said after the chief technician had come on the telephone line. 'I want you to transmit the following statement to the airliner. The Shuttle launch has been delayed five minutes by a minor servicing requirement. Prognosis for launch and rescue remains excellent.'

'But I've just received word that the Cape has experienced an auto-abort.'

'Have you told the airliner that yet?'

'No.'

'Tell them nothing beyond what I've just told you. I'll be upstairs shortly to explain.' Kennerdale hung up before the technician could respond. 'It'll be a simple case of mistaken data,' he said as he turned to the other three. 'That's how I'll cover my ass on the "short delay" bullshit.'

'Great. That'll give us the time we need.' Novak turned to Krause. 'I hope you can come up with some way to stop that pilot from destroying the airliner. None of the three of us have enough technical knowledge to do it.'

'I'm sure I can do it,' Krause lied. He could see that none of them knew a damned thing about technology or they'd understand that there was no way to stop Collins from doing anything he wanted to. But none of that was Krause's concern. If the airliner destroyed itself on the way down that was, as much as Krause hated to admit it to himself, the best thing that could happen. That would be the fastest, cleanest way out of the situation. If the airliner stayed in orbit and the Shuttle eventually reached them, then Krause was scheduled to be the first person to investigate the *Star Streak*'s lower bay. Investigate his own crime. Krause would be able to make that arrangement work out very well. 'I'll need some time to think,' Krause said to Kennerdale. 'Without any interruptions. Especially from Ben Robinson. If he locates me, he'll put me on some other project.' Krause felt a shiver travel down his spine as he thought about Robinson, thought about all the things that had happened in the short span of just a few hours. If it wasn't for the potential of getting away scot-free, he would have bolted immediately.

'No problem. Stay here. I'll tell Robinson that I've sent you out on assignment. To another building.'

'Fine. By the time the airliner is back in communications, I'll have a way to stop Captain Collins.'

Chapter Fourteen

PAUL DIEDERICH took his hand off his wife's lap and reached up to rub his eyes. Because of the increased foulness of the cabin air and the minimal airflow, his eyes had begun to water incessantly. The stale odors had become nearly overpowering. As the percentage of breathable oxygen lessened, each of the people onboard had become more groggy and listless. Many of them had already lapsed into a deep and dream-filled sleep. Diederich felt half-asleep himself.

Chris slowly opened her eyes, blinked several times, then turned to her husband. 'Stay?' she said in a faint voice. She attempted to raise her head off the pillow behind her.

'Yes.' Diederich gently touched his wife's cheek, then pressed her head back toward the pillow when he saw that even her little movements had caused her obvious pain. 'Don't move.'

Chris opened her mouth to protest, but no words came out. Instead, she obediently laid her head back and allowed her eyes to close again.

Diederich found himself studying the contours of her face, as he had done so many times during the 14 years of their marriage. Right from the beginning, he had been intrigued by the soft puffiness of her cheeks, the way the top of her neck curved inward so sensuously. Diederich sighed, then turned away.

Since he had come up with no way to get the airliner down from orbit, Diederich had decided that he would stay in the cabin with Chris. There was no sense leaving her alone when nothing of value would come of it. Collins' vow to attempt fuel mixing as a last resort had come too late. Diederich had investigated that possibility and reported to the captain that it would take two or three hours to accomplish the necessary plumbing changes – if they could be done at all. If the Space Shuttle didn't arrive in the next 30 minutes, they would all die. It was as simple as that.

Diederich shook his head in an attempt to clear it, then looked around the cabin. A few of the passengers sat with their eyes open, several sobbed gently, one or two openly cried. Most appeared to be asleep. Hardly anyone spoke. They all prayed for the arrival of the Shuttle, although each of them had also made their separate peace as best they could.

Diederich looked further down the cabin aisle, toward the rear of the aircraft. Doctor Akins was the only one out of his seat. He worked his way slowly forward, with great apparent effort, his short, stubby body preposterously hovered midway between the floor and the ceiling, his hands groping along the edge of the overhead rack. From what the doctor had said earlier, Diederich guessed that he was headed back to the cockpit. Diederich knew that Collins expected him also, but there was no sense to it. There was nothing left for him to do.

Diederich peeked out the cabin window at the blackness outside. The Earth below was totally invisible, which meant that they were either over a large ocean or above a deep and solid cover of clouds. Either way, it would make no difference. Unless the Shuttle arrived very soon, this would be their last orbit. What existed only a hundred miles below them might as well have been as far away as the Andromeda Galaxy for all that it mattered.

Diederich coughed several times, then looked back at the night sky. Somewhere outside, in very close formation to them, were both the TV satellite and Katie Graham's body. Both were obscured by the veil of black. That was just as well. The less they saw of that sort of thing, the easier it would be for all of them. He reached across and pulled down the windowshade.

Diederich sat back and closed his eyes. After a few seconds he felt Akins brush past him on the way to the cockpit. Diederich resisted the temptation to look up at the doctor. Instead, he concentrated on the nonsensical suggestion Chris had made a short while before.

Anchor. Drop one into the atmosphere. Pull us down. When she had first said it, Diederich hadn't been able to determine if she was serious or not, hallucinating or not. Still, as obviously ludicrous as it had been, there was something intriguing about the idea. *Anchor. Atmosphere.* He took a deep breath, forced himself to relax, then allowed his thoughts free rein.

Anchor. Boat. Wind. The disjointed words flashed through his mind like the flipping pages of a dictionary. *Wind. Force. Forced air. Anchor.* For some reason, he kept coming back to Chris's first word. He decided to try that word again.

Anchor. Diederich allowed his thoughts to unfocus, as if they were a beam of light diffused through an opaque glass. *Anchor.* His fingers unwound their tense grip on the armrests, the muscles in his neck relaxed. *Anchor. Brake. Wheel.* Nothing. A dead end. He tracked back to the beginning. *Anchor. Brakes. Wheels. Tires. Wheels. Tires. Landing.* Diederich opened his eyes. *Landing. Landing gear.* He sat upright. *Landing gear.* 'Christ Almighty.'

'What?' Chris had also opened her eyes. 'I didn't . . .'

'Wait.' Diederich fumbled with his seat belt, released it, then began to rapidly push himself upright. Before he moved too far, he leaned toward his wife. 'I think I can get us down,' he said, his voice an odd blend between a whisper and a shout. His face was covered with cold sweat as his body trembled.

'What?' She sat up as much as she could. 'I don't . . .'

'Don't say anything. Not yet. I'll be back in a minute.' Without waiting for an answer, Diederich turned away from his wife and hurried rapidly toward the cockpit. *Landing gear.* There was no doubt in his mind, he could picture it clearly, distinctly. The forces involved would unquestionably be enough. If the Shuttle didn't arrive in time, Diederich had finally found a way to get the stranded airliner out of orbit.

When Donald Collins heard the first sound behind him, he assumed that it was Briscoe carrying out his orders to check the circuit breakers in the rear of the cockpit. Collins had no idea that anything else was about to happen until Briscoe's arm locked around his neck.

'Let go!' Collins shouted, his words choked off by the intense pressure of Briscoe's arm against his windpipe.

'I've got him! Now!' Briscoe reached over the captain's shoulder with his free hand, unbuckled the man's seat belt, then dragged Collins backward over the top of his flight chair. 'I'll turn him around.'

'Are the oxygen bottles still full?' Akins asked quickly.

'Yes.'

Collins felt his body being spun forcibly backward and to his right. He caught glimpses of the side of Briscoe's face as his head was yanked back and forth. Collins gasped for air. Behind Briscoe he spotted Akins, the doctor's one arm gripped to a ledge in the rear of the cockpit, his other arm out in front of him, a syringe held in his extended hand.

'Move this way. Put his arm against the window.'

'Okay.' As powerful as Briscoe was, the weightlessness and Collins' response had nearly proven too much for him. Once, then twice, Collins nearly slipped out of the copilot's grip before he found a position with enough leverage to keep him in tow.

'Hurry up, for chrissake. I can't hold him much longer.'

Collins twisted his body and kicked his legs frantically, but could not get free. He tried to shout, but Briscoe's grip on his throat was too tight. He could barely breathe. Every time there was the slightest relaxation of pressure, Collins sucked in a deep breath – only to find that Briscoe had immediately been able to tighten his grip again.

'Hold him.'

'Make it quick.'

Akins pushed himself forward. He used his free hand to grab the windowsill beside Collins, then concentrated on aiming the long silver needle filled with sedative. 'I'll go through his shirt.'

'Hurry.'

With Briscoe above and behind him, Collins was pinned hopelessly against the cockpit side window, his face and shoulder jammed against the warm glass. All Collins could see were the plastic wall panels, the black frame that surrounded the glass, the switches with their placarded numbers and letters below. On the side of the frame was the squared-off gray box that housed the contact points for the window heating elements.

'He's squirming. Quick.'

'I'm going as fast as I can, you asshole. Hold him steady.' Akins took his left hand off the side panel and grabbed Collins' arm to steady it. His right hand, with the syringe in it, moved quickly toward the spot he aimed for. 'One more second. Hold him steady.'

Collins wrestled one arm free enough to move it a few inches – enough to reach the small gray box against the window frame. Without hesitating, he jammed his finger past the cover guard and against the metal contacts.

The voltage in the window heat circuitry arced painfully into Collins' finger and instantly burned away a small circle of flesh. The voltage traveled along the lines formed by the muscles and tissues of Collins' arm until it reached the point where Akins had placed his sweaty hand.

Henry Akins had hooked his right foot to the metal clamps underneath the bottom of the observer's Fiberglas covered flight chair to keep himself steady. As the voltage from the window contact sensed no clear route to complete the circuit along its original course – a path of least resistance – it took readily to the newly discovered route. As if that were its original intention, the flow of voltage jumped into Akins' arm, then across the middle of his chest, then down his right leg. It exited his body at the point where his ankle lay against the metal frame of the flight chair, the current charring a blackened spot on his flesh just above his sock where his skin rubbed against the metal tubing.

Akins fell forward. The syringe tumbled out of his opened hand and floated toward the cockpit ceiling.

Briscoe had involuntarily relaxed his grip when he felt the

current, and Collins wrestled free. The captain sucked in a gulp of air, spun himself around, then threw his body against the copilot's.

'Bastard!' Collins tried to lift his right arm, but found that because of the damage done by the electrical shock, he couldn't. The two men's faces were bare inches apart. Briscoe's hot and sour breath poured over Collins.

Briscoe took the first swing, but Collins deflected it with his left shoulder. Briscoe's punch landed hard against the Fiberglas ceiling panel.

With what little strength he had left, Collins swung his left arm. His clenched fist caught Briscoe squarely on the jaw as the copilot continued, off balance, to float backward in the weightlessness. Collins felt Briscoe's jaw break as he drove the copilot's face up into a section of the ceiling only inches from the overhead panel. As Briscoe rebounded off the roofline, his body went limp.

'Christ!'

'Collins spun around. Diederich had entered the cockpit.

'What happened?' As bewildered as he was, Diederich had the presence of mind to close the cockpit door behind him so no one in the cabin could see what had happened. The last thing he wanted was a full-scale panic from the passengers.

'Portable oxygen,' Collins stammered, hardly catching his breath enough to speak. He leaned forward, closed his eyes and inhaled as deeply as he could.

Diederich looked around the cockpit. Slowly, he realized what had taken place. Briscoe, the copilot, and Akins, the physician – the man who had saved Chris's life – had tried to keep the extra oxygen for themselves. Diederich turned to Collins. 'Are you okay?'

'Yes. I think so.' Collins grabbed his seat back with his left hand to steady himself. His right arm hung uselessly, still numbed from the electric shock, although he now felt a series of continuous pains through it as if a dozen long slivers of metal had been shoved into the muscles.

'Don't move.' Diederich went across to Collins and helped maneuver him into a more comfortable position behind the captain's chair. He looked down at Collins' hand – the tip of the right index finger was burned black. 'What happened to your hand?'

'Grabbed the window heat contacts.'

'That was one hell of a gamble.'

'No choice.'

Diederich nodded silently, then turned and maneuvered forward to retrieve Akins' body. He pushed it forcibly into the observer's seat and buckled the seat belt. He took Akins' pulse, then listened for his heartbeat. 'He's dead.' Diederich could see from the marks on the doctor's arm and the burnt spot above his ankle which way the current had flowed. By traveling from his left arm to his right leg, it had crossed the center of his chest. Crossed over his heart. That direct jolt was what had killed him. Diederich turned back to Collins. 'You took one hell of a chance,' he repeated, 'If your body had shifted a few inches and had touched against any piece of the metal airframe, then you would've been the one electrocuted.'

Collins didn't answer. He took another deep breath, shook his head slowly from side to side, then maneuvered himself upright. He pushed himself across to where Briscoe's unconscious body floated against the ceiling, grabbed Briscoe's dangling arm, then steered him toward the observer's chair and strapped him in with Akins.

'What's that?'

Collins saw what Diederich had pointed at. He reached across the cockpit glare shield and grabbed the floating syringe. 'Sedative.'

Diederich nodded. 'I saw it before. I should have realized.'

'They saved it for me. They wanted the portable oxygen bottles for themselves.'

'Incredible.' Diederich shook his head, then glanced at the two men, one dead, one unconscious. When he thought about it, it wasn't so incredible after all. Raw, basic survival. Diederich marveled at how the other hundred people in the airplane had kept themselves above that sort of thing – or was it simply because they hadn't known about the three portable oxygen bottles? He was glad that he would never know for sure. Diederich looked over at Briscoe. The copilot had a large discolored mark at the base of his chin, but he was obviously still breathing. 'Bastard.'

'Do you know how to use this?' Collins asked as he handed the syringe to Diederich.

'Yes.'

'Give some to Briscoe. I don't want him in our way when the Shuttle gets here.'

'Right.' Diederich took the syringe and moved toward the copilot. 'But I was coming up to tell you . . . '

'Wait.' Collins attempted to move his right arm. He grimaced in pain, but found that he was able to lift it several inches. The damage had evidently not been permanent. He pushed himself forward to where the three portable oxygen bottles were strapped and pulled each of them out. One by one, he twisted open their valves. The pressurized oxygen rushed audibly out of each bottle as the contents were dumped into the cabin. 'That's five extra minutes.'

'Might need it.' Diederich looked out the cockpit window. It was still pitch-dark outside, although there was a hint of light on the horizon. They would be back in daylight in a few minutes. 'Where the hell is the Shuttle?'

'I don't know.'

Diederich turned back to the copilot and stuck the needle filled with sedative into his arm. He gave Briscoe only half of the remaining dose, just to be certain that it wasn't too much. 'But what I wanted to tell you . . . '

'Flight fourteen, do you read Goddard?' the radio speakers suddenly blared. 'If you read, acknowledge.'

Collins dove for the microphone on the copilot's console, snatched it up and pressed the button. 'Yes, Goddard. Go ahead. We read you loud and clear.' Collins could feel every single beat of his heart, the motion of every ounce of his blood as it poured through his veins and down into his stomach. He looked at the panel clock. Three twenty-five. Communications had been re-established precisely on schedule.

'I'm sorry,' the voice began plaintively after several additional seconds of silence. It was unmistakably the NASA official

254

identified as Kennerdale. 'The Shuttle has aborted its launch. We are unable to get to you in time.'

'Yes. I agree,' Ben Robinson said. He held the plastic microphone tightly as he leaned over Kennerdale's console in the upper level of the OPSCON and peered below. *Where the hell is Krause?* Robinson shot a quick glance over his shoulder, then down to the lower level again. No Krause, even though Kennerdale had said that Krause would return by the time the airliner had come back into communications. They had resumed radio contact nearly five minutes before, yet Krause had not appeared.

'I'll drop the landing gear shortly,' Collins answered, his voice booming through the radio speaker in the center of the console.

'Wait.' Robinson released the transmit button, wiped the perspiration off his forehead, then looked toward Kennerdale and Novak. Watts stood behind the two of them, his back turned, as he gestured toward the TV technicians in the far corner of the room where a camera was being repositioned.

'What? What the hell should I wait for?' Collins replied. The anger in his voice was tempered by his difficulty in breathing. He coughed several times on the opened microphone before he could regain control. 'You people want another feasibility study? When would you like me to find the time to do it? If Diederich hadn't come up with his idea, the delays on fuel mixing would've done us in.'

'No studies. Your plan checks out.' Robinson glanced at the pad of figures he had just been handed. There was very little doubt that the idea to drop the landing gear – which would released the air pressure trapped inside each of the *Star Streak*'s enormous pressurized wheel bays – would create enough force to get them moving down, moving out of orbit. The blast of pressurized air – air that they couldn't have gotten to for breathing in any event – was such a simple and foolproof idea that Robinson couldn't imagine why he or no one else at United Aerospace or NASA hadn't thought of it. Forest for the trees, probably. Everyone on the ground had concentrated on the obvious solution of rocket engines and rocket thrust.

255

'At least we'll be able to get out of orbit, no thanks to your people,' Collins transmitted.

'But reentry temperatures are still too severe.' As much as he didn't want to say it, Robinson knew that the facts were unmistakable. He wrestled with the idea of not saying anything, but then decided that Collins should be told the truth. 'The forward edges of the wings will burn up. That's what our calculations show.'

'I'm banking that your people can't calculate worth a damn.' Collins still wasn't sure how to feel about Robinson, but he had already made up his mind about the rest of the people who worked for United Aerospace. 'They sure as hell don't build much of an airplane.' Collins stopped transmitting as he allowed himself to mentally shift gears. 'It's a chance we'll have to take,' he said, his tone more benign. 'There's no other choice.'

Maybe. Robinson pressed the transmit button and held the microphone to his lips. His mouth opened as if to speak, but he said nothing. *Where the hell is Krause? He knows how to get you down. I'm sure of it.* Robinson allowed his finger to slide off the button without having said a word. Telling Collins the truth was one thing, needlessly tormenting him with a promise that was impossible to keep was something else. The transmitter clicked off.

'We are in the process of securing everything in the cabin. We're getting everyone ready,' Collins answered when the radio channel had finally cleared. 'Three more minutes. Then I'll drop the landing gear.'

'Roger. Understand. Three minutes. Good luck.' Even though the large TV screen contained live satellite coverage of the airliner in orbit, Robinson kept his eyes fixed to the grillwork that covered the console speaker. It was as if he expected, along with the voice, to see Collins' face appear directly in front of him. After several seconds Robinson laid the microphone down, glanced at the TV image of the airliner on the front screen, then turned around.

Alex Krause stood in the rear of the OPSCON. His arms were folded casually across his chest. His body leaned back against the rear wall. Krause's attention was focused on the large TV screen beyond the edge of the balcony as he watched the progress of the stranded airliner.

It took Robinson a moment to react to Krause's presence. He had already written off any hope that the saboteur might return. The papers in Robinson's hands tumbled out of his opened fingers and scattered haphazardly across the floor. 'Christ.' Robinson rushed forward to where the young engineer stood.

'What's the situation?' Krause asked nervously as Robinson came up to him.

Robinson forcibly grabbed Krause's arm. His head swarmed with a hundred statements, a thousand accusations. 'You bastard,' he finally said in as low and controlled a voice as he could manage. 'I know it's you.'

'What?' Krause reeled slightly backward. The plaster cast on his leg smacked noisily against the rear wall. 'What the hell are you talking about?' Krause's eyes darted around the room and he quickly saw that no one was listening to them.

Robinson held firmly on Krause's arm. 'I can prove it,' he said in a snarled whisper. He turned his body to block the view of Krause from everyone else in the OPSCON. If there was any chance of getting the saboteur to cooperate, he had to be approached privately, to be made a deal with. 'The telephone call to New York was a phony. You modified the quality-control programming on August fifth so it wouldn't pick up what you intended to do. You planted that sabotage device during the morning of August thirteenth. Just before your accident in the hangar.'

'You're crazy.' Krause tried to move toward his left, but Robinson's grip, plus the off-balance stance caused by his cast, prevented him. 'Let go of me.'

'No. Tell me what the second device is. I know there's one. You're caught. I've got the proof. If you help me get them down, it'll go easier on you.' Robinson hoped that Krause didn't question him too closely on what sort of proof he had, since he really had very little. Without the actual sabotage devices from inside Ship 35, the evidence he had acquired so far might not hold up in court. It was nothing beyond a few uncovered lies, an apparent opportunity, and Robinson's own convictions and speculations.

'Easier on me?' Krause pretended not to understand Robinson's last statement as he quickly analyzed the altered situation. Robinson was even smarter than he had guessed. The man had figured out too much already. The best thing for Krause to do would be to agree with anything Robinson said. Krause knew that he needed to buy time. Robinson obviously had a plan in mind – something about a second device – or otherwise the OPSCON would've been packed with police. Finding out what Robinson's plan was and playing along with it was the only chance that Krause seemed to have.

'I'll say that you came to me voluntarily. The court would take that into consideration. They'd go easier on you.'

'No one would believe it.' Krause had begun to get an idea of where Robinson might be leading. With a little more information, he'd know for sure.

'You can write a confession. I'll put the date and time on it. That'll be the proof that you came to me on your own.' Robinson knew that his offer of proof wasn't much, but it was all that he could come up with. He hoped that Krause was as desperate as he had become. In another fifteen minutes the airliner's oxygen tanks would be empty. A few minutes after that, once their residual oxygen had been used up, everyone onboard would suffocate.

'A voluntary confession. I see.' Krause ran his tongue across his dry lips, then nervously patted his hand against his plaster cast. *Second device. Help me get them down.* That was the part that still made no sense.

'Hurry up. Make up your mind. It's your only chance. There's not much time left.' Robinson prayed that he hadn't pressed Krause too hard or too quickly. 'They'll be on their way out of orbit in another minute. They're using the landing-gear-bay trapped pressure.'

'The air pressure in the landing-gear bays?' Krause had heard a vague comment to that effect when he first stepped into the OPSCON a few minutes before. Until now, he didn't realize the implication.

'Don't play-act, goddammit. Isn't that part of your retrieval plan?'

Krause waited a moment, then shook his head slowly as if he had just come to decision. 'Yes.' He eyed the TV image on the front screen. The airliner sat in apparent motionlessness, sharp angles of reflected sunlight bouncing off its polished metal surfaces. From what he could see, the landing-gear doors were still tightly closed.

'I know you've got a plan to get around the reentry heat. You've got to tell me what it is.' In the background, Robinson could hear Kennerdale as he spoke on the radio to Collins. From what he could make out, the NASA chief was trying, in a round-about way, to persuade Collins to lay down and die, not to attempt any sort of reentry. Even from this far away, picking up only bits and pieces of the conversation, Kennerdale's agonized, convoluted reasoning sounded absurd. Robinson had suspected for some time that Kennerdale, Novak and Watts were up to no good, but now he was certain of it.

'Alex,' Novak shouted from across the OPSCON when he finally caught a glimpse of Krause. Novak took a step away from where both he and Watts huddled beside Kennerdale. 'Do you have anything for us? Anything to tell the pilot?' he asked.

'I'm not sure,' Krause answered cryptically. He alternated his glances between Novak and Robinson.

'Anything's worth a try.' Novak motioned for Krause to come over, then turned toward the front console again.

Robinson looked at the three men across the room, then at Krause. 'What the hell does he mean? What's he talking about?'

Krause could see that there was a slim chance to escape still left open to him. It would be a desperate gamble, but he had no other choice. The first steps of an overall plan had already begun to jell in his mind. He had to admit to the sabotage. *Voluntary confession. Retrieval plan. Reentry heat.* 'Those men are more adept at this sort of thing than I am.' He pointed at the three of them across the room.

'Them?' Kennerdale and his two friends had, as he suspected, definitely been up to something. Robinson cursed himself for not realizing it sooner.

'They've lied about a great many things, right from the beginning. Most of the rescue attempt was nothing but an act.' If he were going to admit to it, Krause saw an advantage in taking Kennerdale, Novak and Watts down with him. At the very least, that would strengthen his credibility.

'We don't have time for that now.' Robinson wasn't interested in anything that didn't directly affect the survival of the people on the airliner, at least not at the moment. He looked at his wristwatch. 'Do you have a way to get the airliner safely past the reentry heat? Give me a straight answer.' It was only great personal effort that prevented Robinson from grabbing Krause by the throat.

Krause glanced at the TV screen. His thoughts and his plan were already a few sentences ahead. 'I never wanted to hurt anyone.'

Robinson nodded, but said nothing.

'It's just like you guessed. Opening the landing-gear bays was the first step.'

'But the reentry heat . . . '

Krause held his hand up. 'Like you've said, I've already planted the second device. You've even guessed, in a roundabout way, what it does. It modifies the preset instructions to the wing-cooling pumps. That's what you told me the company intended to do in a few weeks to get the ship down.' Krause said as he repeated what he had been told an hour earlier.

'Yes.' According to the United Aerospace preliminary analysis, increasing the liquid hydrogen flow into the wings should do the job. But that would take time to accomplish. 'How long . . . '

'The circuits are already onboard.' There was a hint of pride in Krause's voice. 'My device gets the pumps to run at triple their normal capacity. It'll only take a moment to set them in motion. It's all automatic.'

'Triple capacity? Can the wing pipes and valves take that much pressure?'

'Certainly.' Krause nodded enthusiastically. 'I did a thorough analysis of all the components.' Krause glanced around the room, then back at Robinson. 'Most of the material I used came out of my work on the quality-control program. You know how careful I was on that.' Krause allowed his eyes to drop toward the floor for a moment before he looked at Robinson. 'I thought I knew exactly what I was doing,' he said in nearly a whisper. 'I never intended to hurt anyone.'

'I believe you.' Robinson stared at Krause. He had no idea whether he believed him or not, but there was no time to think about that sort of thing now.

'Give me a pen,' Krause said suddenly. 'I'll write a confession.' He knew that the written confession, more than any verbal assurances he could give, was necessary. It would make everything seem right.

'Quick.' With trembling fingers, Robinson yanked a pen out of his pocket. He handed it to Krause. 'Make it short.'

'I'll also put in something about Kennerdale, Novak and Watts,' Krause said as he peeked up at the three men in the center of the room. They were, in his mind, the ones who should be caught, the ones who had no reason for doing what they did. Not like him. They hadn't been swindled, like he had been. 'I'll write down the things those three asked me to do.' Krause leaned against a nearby console, lowered his head and began to write quickly. The scribbled words soon filled the page.

'That's enough.' Robinson ripped the paper away just as Krause signed his name, then spun around in time to see Kennerdale lay the console microphone down. The NASA chief shook his head in disgust.

'Don't bother me with that crap!' Collins voice exploded loudly out of the speakers in the OPSCON and filled every corner of the suddenly hushed room. 'I've had enough from you people – every damned last one of you.' Collins coughed several times, then began to speak in a lower voice. 'It's three thirty-four. Including the three extra bottles I've just discharged into the cabin, we've got a lousy sixteen minutes of oxygen left. I've already lowered the landing gear. The three bay doors have opened. We're on the way down. God help us.'

Chapter Fifteen

'WE'RE NOT moving,' Paul Diederich said. From where he sat in the flight engineer's chair, he had a clear view through both the captain and copilot's windshield. The Earth's horizon curved symmetrically in front of him, the rounded edges dropped off into an indistinct mass of haziness at the far corners. 'How much time?'

'It's been forty seconds.' Collins pointed at the panel clock. The green digital numbers continued to tick off methodically.

Diederich leaned forward as far as his fastened seat belt would allow and peered out at the Earth below. Irregular patterns of clouds covered most of the area under them. A quiltwork of deep-blue ocean water and the browns and greens of land jutted out beneath several bare spots in the cloud cover. Diederich still could not make out any apparent change in their motion. 'Maybe I was wrong. Maybe the landing gear won't work,' he said nervously.

'Wait.' Collins turned to his side window and looked out. In the distance was the TV satellite. Collins concentrated on sighting against it as if it were no more than a space-age marking post. 'Look.'

'Where?' Diederich followed Collins' gesture.

But Collins hadn't pointed to the TV satellite. Instead, he had pointed to something closer. To Katie Graham's body. Her left arm had floated up to a position above and behind her head, but otherwise she continued to tumble slowly end-over-end exactly as she had for the last hour. Above and behind Katie was the satellite. 'Watch the relative positions.'

Diederich leaned closer to the side window. After a few seconds he also saw the change in relative position between the two objects. The change was visual proof of the airliner's own downward movement. 'Yes, dammit, yes! We're on the way down!'

'Right. Great work.' Collins tried to sound enthusiastic, but found that he couldn't. No matter how he tried to cover it up, there was still an ominous, foreboding tone in his voice. His thoughts were focused too far ahead to find any joy in this particular moment. Collins picked up the microphone and reported the news of their verified descent to Goddard.

'I guess they've seen it also.' Diederich gestured rearward. Muffled shouts of joy drifted through the closed cockpit door as the passengers quickly realized that the ship's downward motion had actually begun.

'They should sit quietly. They're using up oxygen.'

'It won't make a difference.'

'Probably not.' Collins shifted his body too quickly, and that triggered an intense pain in his right arm. 'Son of a bitch,' he moaned as he closed his eyes.

'You okay?' Diederich knew full well what the answer was, but also knew that it didn't matter. It couldn't. Without Collins, no matter what his condition, their chances went to absolute zero.

'I'll be alright,' Collins answered softly, his eyes still closed, his head tilted back. He hoped that, when the time came, he'd be able to make his right hand respond enough to accurately operate the flight controls. 'What were we saying?' he asked as he opened his eyes and turned carefully toward Diederich. He knew that he had to keep his mind off the throbbing, slicing pains in his hand and on the task in front of him.

'Oxygen. What they use won't make a difference.'

'You're right.' Diederich was correct, that they had more than

263

enough oxygen remaining to complete the reentry. The battle with the oxygen supply had been won by default. One way or the other – either intact or in a million pieces – the flight would be back in the breathable atmosphere before the oxygen tanks were totally empty. The five extra minutes in the three portable tanks had made the difference.

'We're really moving down now,' Diederich said as he looked out the side window again. The TV satellite was barely visible in the distance; Katie's body was too small to be seen.

'Right.' There was no stopping their descent, even if they wanted to. Collins wiped the perspiration off his forehead. The heat, the odors, the stuffiness in the cabin had grown insufferable. 'Okay,' he said as he cleared his throat and began a review of the aircraft configuration. 'The landing gear is back in the wells. The flaps are up. We're trimmed for high speed.' *High speed.* They would shortly be traveling at 25 times the speed of sound – three or four times what the airplane had been designed for. That alone was a hideous-enough joke. Collins had to put that out of his mind and concentrate instead on the last crucial task that still remained to be done. 'Are you ready with the wing-cooling checklist?'

'I'm ready.' Diederich fumbled with the printed card in his hand, then glanced over the rows of switches on the flight engineer's panel. After running through the procedure twice with Collins, he felt he understood his role well enough not to make any errors. At least he hoped so. 'I've got it down okay.'

'Just follow my commands.'

'I will.' Diederich glanced down at the printed card. 'Here we go.'

'Go ahead. I'm monitoring the pressure.' Collins watched the twin needles on his panel as Diederich activated the switches to start the wing-cooling valves and pumps into operation. Once begun, the system was totally automatic. According to NASA, it was also totally inadequate for the amount of reentry heat they were about to face, that the flow rate of the liquid hydrogen into the wings was too low. It would be like trying to put out a house fire with a tray of icecubes.

'Valves indicate open.'

Collins saw the needles creep off the bottom of their scale. They still had a long way to go before they indicated normal pressure. 'Continue with the procedure. Exactly as written.'

'Here it goes.' Diederich flipped two switches, then one more. He held his breath. If the liquid-hydrogen cooling system operated normally, they stood a slight chance of a successful reentry. Without it, there was no chance at all.

'Fifty pounds,' Collins reported in a low, flat voice as he stared at the white needles mounted on the lower edge of his flight panel. 'Fifty-five pounds.' The needle moved up slowly, ponderously.

'Keep going, baby.' Diederich tried to look over Collins' shoulder, but couldn't see a thing. The gauge was mounted too low on the captain's panel. 'Keep going.' Every pound of additional wing cooling gave them more insurance. It put them one step closer to home.

'Sixty-five.'

'God. Please.' Diederich whispered. 'Keep it going.' He sat as close to the edge of his flight chair as his seat belt would allow.

'Seventy.'

'Keep pumping. Don't stop.'

'Eighty pounds.' Collins turned to Diederich. There was, for the first time, the hint of a smile on his face. 'It's reached mid-scale. Normal.'

'Can we get any more out of it.'

'No. It's automatic. Preset. But at least we've got that much.'

'Thank God.' Diederich let out a long sigh, then sat back. His insides were churned up and he tried to calm them by breathing in slowly and deeply. The foul, stale air made him cough.

'Take it easy.'

'Right.' While Collins busied himself at his console, Diederich glanced around the cockpit. He wondered what would happen next in this never-ending madness. Orbit. Weightlessness. Chris's injury. Attempted murder by Briscoe and Akins. Briscoe, the ship's second in command, drugged unconscious. Akins, the man who had saved Chris's life a few hours before, dead. Diederich reluctantly looked to his left, toward the observer's flight chair where he had strapped Briscoe and Akins together a short while before. 'Look.'

'What is it?'

'Over there.' Diederich pointed across the cockpit. Briscoe's arm had come loose from underneath the shoulder strap and it bobbed eerily up and down in front of him. 'His arm is out. Should I strap it back down?'

Collins turned but couldn't quite see Briscoe's face. 'Is he conscious?'

'No.'

'Then the hell with it. Forget it. We don't have time.' Collins didn't want any additional distractions from this point on. According to the figures NASA had given Collins a few moments before, it would take only 11 minutes from the beginning of their downward motion until they descended to an altitude of 50,000 feet – the altitude at which their jet engines could be restarted and the normal air-conditioning pumps turned on. That would occur at 3:45 on the panel clock. If they could get themselves down that far without breaking up, then a safe landing would be assured. 'What did you tell the passengers when you went back?'

'Exactly what you said. Less than fifteen minutes to deorbit. To stay in their seats, in the brace position, until you made an announcement.'

'Fine.' *Assume the brace position. Bend over and kiss your ass good-bye.* Collins was glad that he had been too busy with cockpit duties to go back to the passengers. 'You didn't say anything about the reentry heat, did you?'

'Of course not.'

'Good.' Collins knew that Diederich wouldn't have said a word about that to anyone – he seemed hardly able to acknowledge the fact himself.

'Everyone in the cabin is ready,' Diederich said as he made conversation to fill time. 'Chris is awake – she looks better. That stewardess with the burns doesn't seem as bad as she did, either. That ice saved her face; I don't think she'll be disfigured. Some infant is crying his head off in the back.'

'There's only one baby onboard.'

'I guess that's also a good sign.'

'I guess.' Collins nodded absently, then looked around his flight panel. 'Six more minutes until maximum dynamic pressure, according to the NASA data,' Collins said as he tapped his finger against the digital clock. 'At three forty-three. If we can get through that point of maximum pressure, we're home-free.'

'We'll make it.'

'Sure.' Perhaps Diederich was right. They should put the reentry problems out of their mind. Dropping back into the Earth's atmosphere from an altitude of over one hundred miles should be considered as routine as any other landing approach. They already had done all they could and, besides, the scientists and technicians at Goddard might very well be wrong about the heat buildup during reentry. They had certainly been wrong about enough things already.

'When will the flight controls become effective?' Diederich asked.

'As soon as we hit the top of the atmosphere. Another few minutes.' Collins toyed with the useless control wheel. Shortly, the first molecules of air would begin to rub against the outside of the aircraft. That, in turn, would provide something for the controls to bite into. Much of the flight's outcome would depend on how Collins handled the controls those first few moments. 'I wish I had more data,' Collins said absently as he gazed down at his flight instruments. 'None of this equipment has been calibrated for what we're about to do.'

'I understand.' Diederich could offer little more, since the technical problems that faced the pilot were nearly beyond his comprehension. But he had repeatedly been witness to the fact that Donald Collins was an exceedingly capable man. If anyone could do it, Diederich felt that Collins could. 'Go on with your gut feelings.'

'Instincts don't mean much. Not in flying.'

'You're wrong.' Diederich leaned over to Collins. 'Mine don't, but yours sure as hell do. Instincts and gut feelings aren't magic. They're displays of subliminal knowledge. Your intuitions are based on a great deal of actual experience.'

'You're saying that I know more than I think I do?'

'Yes.'

'I hope so.' Collins looked back at his flight panel, then ran his tongue across his dry, cracked lips. Maybe Diederich was right, maybe his judgment and good sense that had seen him through so many years of flying hadn't left him after all. Maybe there was still hope. Collins tightened his grip on the control wheel.

'Three thirty-eight. Five minutes until maximum pressure,' Diederich announced as he peeked at the digital clock.

'Controls should respond any time now.' Collins fidgeted in his seat and tried to get himself in the best position possible. Even with a textbook-perfect reentry, there was bound to be a high level of aerodynamic forces involved, a measurable degree of unwanted gyrations. 'Get ready.' Collins placed his right hand on the throttle quadrant between the two pilot seats. His fingers seemed slightly less pained than they had a few minutes before.

'I'm ready.' Diederich cinched up his seat belt as tight as he could. He began to silently pray.

'Four minutes, thirty seconds.' No matter what happened, in less than five more minutes it would be over. If they were destined to die, it would happen quickly. There would be no lingering suffocation. Only a few seconds of searing heat, then complete disintegration. Not enough time to know what hit you.

Ben Robinson rushed up to the front console in the OPSCON and picked up the microphone. 'Donald. Listen to me carefully. I've got no time to explain. I'm going to give the microphone to one of our technicians, a man named Krause.' Robinson peeked over his shoulder to be certain that Krause was still there. He was. 'You've got to follow his instructions precisely.'

'Why? What the hell is he going to do for me?' Collins answered quickly, his voice more tight and high pitched than it had been earlier.

'Wing cooling. Krause has found a way to increase the flow.' Robinson stopped himself before he said more than he wanted to.

'That's difficult to believe.'

'I don't have time to explain. Please. Trust me.' Robinson looked at Krause. The saboteur had a neutral expression on his face, but something – the look in his eyes, the way he stood with his arms folded – was not in keeping with his words and promises. *What the hell am I doing?* For a brief instant Robisnon wondered if he hadn't bee duped, if he wasn't somehow helping Krause to

268

destroy the airliner instead of saving it. He had Krause's handwritten confession in his coat pocket, but he wondered if it would be admissible in a court of law. Maybe it wasn't – and maybe Krause already knew that.

Ralph Kennerdale stepped up to the console, took the microphone away from Robinson and pressed the transmit button. 'Please. Captain. I know you're entitled to a full and detailed explanation but there's not enough time left to give you one.' He looked at Krause and nodded briefly, the two men exchanging furtive glances. Kennerdale was glad to see that Krause had apparently come up with a method for stopping Captain Collins from destroying the airliner. The NASA chief turned his attention to the TV monitor on the front wall. The airliner had descended to the far corner of the screen. Visibly, it had shrunk to nearly nothing. It was almost out of view of the satellite camera, nearly back into the top of the atmosphere. 'NASA agrees with the plan formulated by United Aerospace,' Kennerdale transmitted, even though he had no idea of what Krause's plan was.

Robinson grabbed the microphone back. Just like Krause had said, he and Kennerdale obviously had some sort of arrangement between them. Robinson didn't know what to make of it, it was all happening too fast. 'Donald. Please. We don't have any time left,' he said as he pressed the transmit button.

'That's what I've been telling you people for the last two hours,' Collins answered.

Robinson glanced around the OPSCON. The TV camera in the far corner was aimed at him, but its red monitoring light was out. The TV studio was evidently still transmitting the satellite photo, and would probably continue to do so until there was nothing left to be seen. Then they'd turn on the OPSCON camera. Watts and Novak stood to the left of the camera and several NASA and TV technicians stood to the right. McBride and Becker had, in response to Robinson's orders, already gone downstairs. 'We've got to increase the flow of liquid hydrogen,' Robinson said into the microphone. Contrary to what Collins had deluded himself into believing, without Krause's help there was no chance at all with the reentry heat. Zero. 'Krause has a way to do it.'

There was a pause for several seconds before Collins came back

269

on the air. 'Okay, Ben. I hope to hell you know what you're doing. You've always been straight with me before.' Collins stopped speaking for a moment, but kept his microphone button pushed in. The sounds of heavy breathing echoed through the console speakers in the OPSCON for a while before he began to transmit again. 'Four minutes until the point of maximum reentry heat. Just to be sure that this is the right thing to do.'

'I'm sure.' Robinson handed the microphone to Krause. The young engineer immediately began to transmit a series of technical instructions.

Collins obeyed the instructions without question. 'Christ,' he transmitted after resetting the last of the circuit breakers that Krause had instructed him to activate. 'The cooling pressure is definitely increasing. Ninety pounds and climbing! One hundred!'

Krause turned to Robinson. 'It's working. Just like I told you.'

Robinson didn't answer. Instead, he picked up the console microphone. 'Keep reporting the pressure.'

'I can't. It's already top-scale, off the peg. It's reading something over one hundred and fifty.'

'Great.' *Christ.* Robinson wondered if the indication was accurate and, if it was, if the aircraft's plumbing and valve system could take that much pressure. 'Is everything else normal?'

'Yes.' Collins paused. 'No. Wait.' Several seconds ticked by. 'We're losing fluid. Liquid hydrogen. It's being dumped overboard out the wing-tip vents. I can see a thin line of continuous vapor behind the port wing.'

Robinson looked at the TV monitor, but the airliner was already out of range of the satellite camera. He spun around and faced Krause. 'What the hell happened?'

'Nothing bad. Really. It's part of the plan, part of the design.' Krause noticed that Kennerdale, Novak and Watts were huddled together in conference, their expressions angry and tense. Krause was repelled by the sight of the three of them. He was only sorry that he wouldn't be around when Robinson made public the confession that he had written denouncing them for attempting to obstruct the rescue for their own stupid, senseless reasons. Krause peeked at his wristwatch, then repositioned his body so that his leg with the cast on it was at a better, more comfortable angle.

'I hope you're right,' Robinson said in a threatening voice. 'For your sake.' He, too, had noticed the sudden change in Kennerdale. *What the hell is happening?*

'I've calculated the loss rate,' Collins added as he continued his transmission. 'If it doesn't increase any more . . . '

'It won't,' Krause said nervously in the background. 'I'm certain that it won't.'

' . . . then we've got enough liquid hydrogen to last at least fifteen minutes. That's more than enough.'

'Good. The flow rate is high enough to keep the reentry heat down.'

'I hope so. Three minutes and twenty seconds to go. I'll only transmit again if I've got a question. I'll be too busy to talk until we get through the point of maximum heat.'

'Good luck.' Robinson put down the microphone. His forehead was covered with cold sweat and his stomach lurched over and over as if it were him, not Collins, inside that rapidly falling aircraft. His ears had begun to ring and he felt suddenly lightheaded and nauseous. He knew what it was. He tightened his grip on the edge of the console. *Another attack. God Almighty.* A new wave of Ménière's swept over Robinson. He lowered his head and tried to close his eyes, but that only made things worse – the world began to spin even more rapidly. He thought for a moment that he might collapse. He kept his eyes fixed on one spot on the console as the doctor had taught him to do while he fought back the nausea. After a handful of seconds, the worst of the attack had passed.

'Please. You'd better come with me.'

'What?' Robinson raised his eyes. Krause stood behind him, ten feet away.

Krause motioned for Robinson to come toward him. 'Follow me. The safety of the flight depends on it.' There was a strange, agonized expression on Krause's face, as if he were about to say or do something that even he didn't want to. Krause began to walk rapidly away, the plaster cast on his leg clunking rhythmically against the linoleum floor.

'What in God's name are you talking about?' Robinson took a

deep breath to steady himself, then pushed himself away from the console and hustled toward the rear of the OPSCON. He followed the United Aerospace engineer most of the way down the rear corridor before he finally caught up. 'Stop. We're not going anywhere.'

'We have to.' Krause took the last few steps, then reached for the elevator button and pressed it. 'If you want to save the airliner, you have to follow me. We won't go very far.' The elevator door opened and he stepped inside.

'Get back here.' Robinson held his hand against the opened door.

Krause shook his head. 'No.' He glanced at his watch, then back at Robinson. Krause's face was bloodless white. 'In two minutes and fifty-five seconds from now,' he said, his words tumbling out rapidly, 'the airliner will pass the point of maximum dynamic pressure, the point of maximum reentry heat.'

'I know that.'

Krause held up a single trembling finger. 'One minute after that – give or take fifteen seconds – the airliner will explode.' He paused to allow the last word to sink in. 'That explosion will occur at three forty-four, Eastern standard time.' Krause gestured toward his watch for emphasis.

'You're bluffing.'

'No. I wish I was.' Krause shook his head in disbelief, as if it were someone else and not him who had made the last statement. 'We've got to hurry. There's not much time.' Krause had used the identical words and inflections that Robinson had used on him not ten minutes before. Krause leaned against the rear wall of the elevator as if he were too exhausted to stand. 'We can save the airliner if you come with me. Please. If you don't the airliner will explode.'

After a few seconds, Robinson stepped inside the elevator and allowed the doors to close. The two men rode in silence to the lower level. *What is Krause up to?* Robinson peeked at his own watch. In two and a half minutes the *Star Streak* would enter the zone of maximum reentry heat.

'I know what you're thinking,' Krause said as the elevator stopped and he stepped out. He headed toward the entrance door and walked as quickly as he could. 'The increased flow of liquid hydrogen will safely get the airliner past the point of maximum heat. That's true.' Krause opened the door and stepped outside. The midafternoon sun was bright and a continuous light breeze blew toward them. Krause hobbled along the sidewalk that lead away from Building 12. 'But the crew has no way to shut that flow of liquid hydrogen off. As that pilot has already reported, the excess is pouring out of the wing-tip vents. At three forty-four – three minutes from now – when the airliner reaches a dense-enough atmosphere, the liquid hydrogen will explode.'

'You're crazy.'

'I've made errors, but this is not one of them. Heat, fuel and air. That's all that's needed for an explosion. The only ingredient that's missing right now is the air. They'll have enough of that shortly.' When they reached the curve in the sidewalk, Krause looked at his watch again. 'This is far enough.'

'Make this fast.'

Krause closed his eyes, inhaled deeply, then looked at Robinson. Krause's eyes were moist, almost teary. 'You were right about a great many things. Sabotage. Ransom. An engineer at United Aerospace working alone.'

'But why?' Robinson had no idea what Krause was leading up to.

'Right from the beginning,' Krause continued without answering Robinson's question, 'there were two sabotage devices. Just like you guessed. But you gave me too much credit. I had, somehow, made a crucial mistake. A design mistake. Not only was the first device – the rocket engine lock-on circuit – supposed to activate more than two weeks ago, it was also supposed to be no more than a graphic warning, a display of what I was capable of. It was supposed to activate for only three seconds, then shut itself off.'

'Three seconds?'

Krause's face was etched with torment and pain. He nodded slowly. 'Somehow, I screwed it all up. I still don't know how. I never wanted to hurt anyone. I might've had a chance to discover my design mistake during the later checks I intended to do after I planted the device, but those were the checks that I never got

around to because of the gantry crane accident in the hangar.'
Krause looked down at the cast on his leg, then back at Robinson.

Dense atmosphere. Flammable liquid hydrogen vented overboard. Residual heat from reentry. There were enough elements in that combination for an explosion, if the proportions were right. They probably were – or soon enough would be. 'How do I get the liquid hydrogen to shut off?'

'I can't tell you. Not yet. I'll tell you at three forty-two. That'll give you one minute to get back to the building, then another minute to have Collins pull the proper circuit breakers.'

'Tell me now.'

'All I wanted was what was coming to me, what I deserved, what I had already earned. I can't go to jail, I couldn't stand being locked up like an animal. It's not my fault. I never wanted to hurt anyone.' Krause looked at Robinson with pleading, desperate eyes. 'When the first device didn't go off on schedule, I volunteered for the trip to Baltimore so that I could go up to Consolidated's New York maintenance base this weekend to take the devices out. I probably never would have put them back in, even if I found what my design errors were.'

'Tell me how to shut off the hydrogen.'

'At three forty-two, you'll have enough time to save the airliner. That also gives me enough time to get away. Because of my leg,' Krause said as he pointed at his cast, 'I'll need all the time I can get. Thank God that this place is in a residential area.' He pointed to the rows of houses in the distance. 'There's enough cars and people around to give me an easy way out.'

'I'll promise to give you a ten-minute head start if you tell me now.'

'No. I don't trust you enough.'

Robinson took a step backward, as if he were about to walk away.

'No. Stop,' Krause said sternly. 'Don't be foolish. There are over six hundred circuit breakers in that cockpit. You'll never guess the correct ones – they've got to be pulled in sequence. Please, do it my way. It's the only way.'

'Why should I trust you?' Robinson considered physically dragging Krause back to the OPSCON with him, but then dismissed the idea. Krause could not be reasoned with or threatened. He was right about one thing – it had to be done his way or not at all.

'You've got no choice. Neither one of us has any choices left. I'm telling you the truth. I never wanted to hurt anyone. All I wanted was what was coming to me.' Krause glanced nervously at his wristwatch. 'Fifty more seconds.'

'Tell me now.'

'No.' Krause fidgeted, then began to talk to fill the remaining time. 'The first device was only a warning, to get their attention. Once they recognized what I was capable of, I'd sell United Aerospace the blueprints of where the second device was for one million, six hundred thousand dollars. Not a penny more, not a penny less. Even at that price, it would be cheaper for them to pay me than to tear that aircraft completely apart trying to find that circuit.'

Robinson said nothing. He looked 50 feet beyond Krause toward the entrance gate, then glanced over his shoulder toward Building 12.

'You see,' Krause said, speaking more rapidly, his hands had begun to gesture in time with his words, 'that one million, six hundred thousand would have been my share of the licensing money. I had been cheated out of it when Nichols refused to put my name on the patent for the quality-control programming that I had created. United Aerospace has sold that programming concept all over the world.'

'What?'

'That quality-control idea was mine from the beginning. The design and execution were solely mine.' Krause took a step closer to Robinson, his eyes wide, his face contorted. 'I tried to be reasonable. All I asked Nichols for was half the patent. I told him I'd be glad to share it fifty-fifty with the company. He laughed at me. He said that I had no legal right to any of it. He said that any work I did as an employee belonged strictly to the company. It was as if I didn't exist at all, as if I were some kind of robot, some sort of slave. Nichols admitted that the programming concept had been mine, but he said that the company didn't owe me a thing for it. He said that I should be grateful for the five-thousand-

275

dollar bonus and the promotion.'

'But the second device . . . ?'

'The second device needed to be destructive. It was designed to operate during normal flight, when there was enough air over the wings to create an instant explosion. A mixture of liquid hydrogen and atmospheric oxygen would ignite by the normal heat of the aircraft's skin friction. I hated to do that, to plant an actual destructive device, but I had no choice. A hollow threat would have been no threat at all.'

'It's time.'

'Don't come toward me.'

'Tell me *now,* for chrissake!'

'Stand where you are.' Krause backed away several feet. He looked around. No one was in sight, and it was only 40 feet between him and the front gate. He took another step, then turned to Robinson. 'Navigation lights first, then one of the Pitot heaters. Circuit breaker numbers one-seventeen and two-sixty.' Krause began to move quickly toward the front gate before the last words were out of his mouth.

One-seventeen and two-sixty. Robinson turned away from Krause and ran full speed toward Building 12. He cut across the lawn, vaulted the short set of steps at the entrance to the building three at a time, then yanked open the door and dashed down the empty corridor. *One-seventeen and two-sixty. Navigation lights and Pitot heaters.*

Robinson rushed up to the elevator, then slammed his hand repeatedly against the button. The doors didn't open. Instead, he could hear the elevator motor begin to whine as the car slowly descended from the upper floor. The elevator was upstairs. *No time left.* Robinson turned from the elevator and bolted toward the narrow stairway at the rear of the corridor.

As he reached the first step, the combination of tension, physical exertion and rapid head movements had acted together to send out another wave of Ménière's symptoms. The long and shadowy corridor seemed to tilt one way, then the other as Robinson's faulty inner ear triggered an array of conflicting signals to his brain. Everything began to spin rapidly, as if he were on an out-of-control carousel.

Robinson's left foot missed the fourth step. He stumbled. His hand groped for the rail but couldn't find it. He fell heavily, then sprawled out motionless on the steep, narrow stairs. The left side of Robinson's head had hit hard against the metal edge of step number five.

Chapter Sixteen

WHEN BEN Robinson first opened his eyes, he couldn't tell if he had been unconscious for five seconds or five hours. He shook his head to clear it, then staggered to his feet on the dark, narrow stairway that led to the upper level of the OPSCON. Robinson grabbed tightly to the rail to steady himself, and found that the symptoms from the Ménière's disease had subsided enough to make it possible for him to stand upright.

The airliner will explode at three forty-four, give or take fifteen seconds. Robinson began to pull himself up the stairs. His legs dragged heavily and he barely managed to pick them up high enough to clear the edge of the next step. The left side of his head throbbed with pain. He could feel the warm flow of blood as it trickled out of the long, angular gash on his scalp and then down his left cheek. He had gone halfway up the staircase when he again stumbled and fell to his knees.

This time, Robinson managed to hang on to the rail when he fell. *Get up. Move your ass. No time left.* Robinson slowly pulled himself upright again. He took a deep breath, then continued to half-stagger, half-walk up the remainder of the staircase. He tried

278

once to look at his wristwatch, but it was too dark in the corridor for the watch to be seen clearly.

As Robinson stepped into the corridor at the top of the stairs, he heard loud voices and several shouts from inside the OPSCON. He was unable to tell whether they were shouts of joy or cries of grief. *Explode at three forty-four, give or take fifteen seconds. Pull them in sequence. Circuit breakers one-seventeen and . . .*

Robinson entered the rear of the OPSCON and rushed toward the front console where Novak, Kennerdale and Watts were.

'Where have you been? They're through it! Past the point of maximum heat!'

Robinson didn't answer. Instead, he looked at the panel clock. Three forty-three and thirty-nine seconds. 'Give me the microphone!'

'No.' Kennerdale scowled at Robinson and continued to hold the microphone close to his chest as if it were his own personal possession. 'We're on camera, for chrissake. Act like an adult. Wait your turn.'

'Face the other way,' Watts whispered. 'The side of your head is cut. You're bleeding on-camera.'

Robinson spotted the red monitor light on the TV camera in the corner of the OPSCON as it pointed directly toward them. 'Go to hell.' Robinson turned to Kennerdale and, with one powerful motion, shoved him aside and grabbed the microphone away.

'Stop! What are you doing?'

Robinson ignored them. Three forty-three and fifty-five seconds on the panel clock. *Circuit breakers one-seventeen and . . .* 'Donald!' he shouted as he pressed the transmit button. 'Do you read me?'

'Goddard, you're coming in garbled!'

Even with the distortion from the OPSCON speakers, Robinson could tell that Collins was under a high level of physical strain from the aerodynamic forces. 'Two circuit breakers!' he shouted as he pressed the transmit button. 'Pull them immediately! Number one-seventeen and . . .'

Robinson remembered that it was supposed to be one of the Pitot heaters, but he couldn't recall which one. There were eight

Pitot circuit breakers scattered across three different panels at the rear of the cockpit and unless he remembered the number of the correct one . . .

'One seventeen and . . . ' His head had filled with every conceivable, idiotic permutation of figures imaginable. Robinson tried to pry away Krause's last words from every other set of numbers – his birthday, his telephone number, his employee number, the aircraft's performance data – that he had ever used. The minute counter on the console clock blinked, then changed from three to four. *Three forty-four, give or take fifteen seconds.* 'Circuit breakers one-seventeen and . . . ' Still nothing. The numbers swarmed over him like locusts descending on a ripe field. As quickly as he pushed one nonsensical figure aside, another popped in to take its place. Forty-two, seven-four-one, two-zero-five-zero. They were everywhere, and they were all dead wrong.

Robinson closed his eyes and tried to coax the number to him. As if it were a flesh-and-blood creature with its own free will and volition, he tried to lure it by not pressing for it too hard.

Two-sixty. The number presented itself in his thoughts like a ghostly aberration that had elected to take shape and form. 'Two-sixty! Circuit breakers one-seventeen and two-sixty! Pull them in that order! Do it now!'

'What did he say? I can't hear him!'

'I don't know! I can't hear him either!'

'The hell with it!' Donald Collins took one more quick glance over his shoulder toward the front edge of the left wing. During the last several seconds it had turned in color from bright red to dull amber. The wing, which had reached a temperature of over two thousand degrees, had already begun to cool as they passed the point of maximum reentry heat. What worried Collins now was what he saw at the wing tip. 'The liquid hydrogen is still pouring out!' he shouted as loud as he could to get his voice above the incessant howl from the hypersonic wind that was only bare inches outside the cockpit. It was like driving a car at a hundred miles an hour with all the windows rolled down.

'That's what the gauge shows!' Diederich yelled back. He didn't know what else to say. He was too far from the side window to see outside and, besides, the heavy aerodynamic forces that pressed down on them made it difficult to move. Diederich stood with his hands heavily in his lap, his facial muscles distorted by the increased motions of the reentry as he strained to hear the words that came out of the cockpit speaker. They were muted, impossible to decipher – probably a combination of heat-induced radio interference plus the noises in the cockpit. 'I still don't understand him!'

'Me neither!' Collins allowed his voice to trail off as he wrestled with the flight controls, his attention fixed to the gauges on his flight panel. The altimeter continued to rapidly wind down from the top of its scale as the *Star Streak* passed through 250,000 feet. The airspeed indicator had also begun to creep back off its high-limit peg. They would soon be back within the ship's normal operating parameters. Even the noise in the cockpit seemed to have lessened. Collins listened closely as the radio voice transmitted again but it was no use, he still couldn't make it out. He grabbed his microphone. 'Goddard, you're coming in garbled!'

'Circuit breakers?' Diederich asked. He thought he might have caught a few of the words.

'Can't tell!' Collins raised his eyes and glanced out the front windshield. The view of the Earth's horizon had flattened considerably as they continued to fall back toward the atmosphere. The highest level of clouds – a blanket of flat white with isolated caps of billowy gray – was still far beneath them. According to NASA calculations, they were over the Eastern Pacific Ocean, not far from California.

Collins knew that in another few minutes they'd be low enough to ignite the four jet engines and turn the normal pressurization pumps back on. After that, he'd be able to bring the airliner in for what should basically be a routine landing. Diederich had been right, the descent into the atmosphere had been much less difficult than he thought, a great deal less violent than the launch had been. 'We'll make it!' Collins shouted above the cockpit noise that still remained, more for his own benefit than for Diederich's. *Liquid hydrogen.* Collins looked over his left shoulder again, toward the wing-tip vent. The continual overflow of the super-cool liquid hydrogen had become their only remaining abnormality. *Ignite the jet engines – ignite the liquid hydrogen.* 'God Almighty!' In a sudden, horrid flash of insight, Collins realized that when they finally got low enough to start their jet engines, they'd also be low enough to where the combustible liquid hydrogen might explode. 'We've got to stop the liquid hydrogen flow!'

Diederich pressed hard against the panel shutoff switch, but could see from the gauges that it hadn't worked. 'No use. It won't shut off!'

'Wait!' Collins pointed toward the cockpit speaker. 'They're still transmitting!' Collins heard a few partially garbled words, then silence. But the microphone at Goddard remained keyed, still on the air, even though no one was talking. 'He said something about one-seventeen.' It seemed as if the voice were Robinson's, and it also seemed as if he had stopped his last sentence midway. Collins looked down at the panel clock; it was a few seconds past three forty-four.

'Two-sixty!' the cockpit speakers suddenly blared. 'Circuit breakers one-seventeen and two-sixty! Pull them in that order! Do it now!'

Diederich sat bolt-upright and placed his hand on his seatbelt clamp. 'Should I . . . '

It was Robinson's tone, more than his words, that Collins reacted to because of the ingrained faith and trust he had in his friend. 'Yes.' The snatches of isolated words had begun to make sense. 'Fast! Circuit breakers one-seventeen and two-sixty! They're on the rear panel – pull them!'

Diederich ripped off his seat belt and dove toward the panel in the rear of the cockpit. He began to run his eyes frantically across the endless rows of black plastic switches, each with a numbered label beneath it. 'One-seventeen!' he shouted as he found the first switch and yanked it out. He continued to hunt for circuit breaker number 260.

Three forty-four and eight seconds. Robinson hardly dared to breathe as he turned his head to look around the OPSCON. Everyone seemed to be frozen in position, waiting, watching. The only apparent movement was on the front screen. The live satellite coverage displayed a closeup picture of Katie Graham's body as she continued to tumble, end-over-end, through space. With the airliner gone, there was nothing behind her except a deep and empty blackness speckled with brilliant stars.

Robinson forced himself to look back at the console clock. Three forty-four and twelve seconds. *The airliner will explode at three forty-four, plus or minus fifteen seconds.* Robinson bit into his lower lip and squeezed the microphone between his hands. *What the hell have I done? My fault.* It was too late to transmit any additional messages, too late for explanations. There was only enough time left to hope, to pray.

'One-seventeen! He's got that one!' Collins' shrill voice filled the OPSCON. A few people cheered, but most remained quiet. The only man in the room who knew full well the implication of what the circuit breakers meant remained the most silent of all.

The pulsing numbers on the digital console clock continued to change at their consistent pace. Thirteen seconds. Fourteen seconds.

'Wait! I think . . . ' Collins kept the transmitter keyed. Everyone in the OPSCON, everyone who sat at home in front of their TV sets could hear the background noise in the cockpit, the anguish in Collins' voice, his rapid, labored breathing.

Three forty-four and fifteen seconds. Time was up.

'He's got it out! Circuit breaker two-sixty is pulled!' Collins hesitated a brief instant before he transmitted again. 'The liquid hydrogen is shut off! Christ, yes I can see it! It's stopped!'

'That's it!' Robinson shouted, his booming voice carried to every corner of the room. 'They've made it!'.

The OPSCON exploded into a deafening chorus of cheers and shouts. Scores of people slapped each other on the back, many embraced. A few openly cried, tears of joy rolling down their grinning, smiling faces.

Robinson leaned against the center console, closed his eyes and let the perspiration-covered microphone slide out of his hands. 'God Almighty,' he said quietly. 'Thank you.'

'What, may I ask, was all that about?'

Robinson turned.

Kennerdale stood a few feet away, Watts and Novak beside him. 'I think we're entitled to an explanation,' Kennerdale said in a low voice. 'We'll be back on the air in a moment – what the hell am I supposed to say to the TV audience?' Without actually pointing, Kennerdale motioned toward the TV camera in the far corner of the OPSCON, its red monitoring light off.

'Ben? Do you read me?' Collins called.

Robinson turned away from Kennerdale, Novak and Watts. He snatched up the console microphone. 'Yes.' There was so much to say, he couldn't think of where to begin. 'Go ahead.'

'We're down to fifty thousand feet. All four jet engines have restarted. The normal pressurization pumps are on – the fresh air is incredible!' Collins laughed long and hard. 'I've got a vent blowing straight on my face.'

'I'll bet.' Robinson had all along imagined what Collins was going through, and he could now imagine equally how good he must feel.

'I'm contacting air traffic control on the other radio. I'll be back with you in a minute.'

'Okay.' Robinson turned back to Kennerdale. His smile faded quickly. 'What do you want?' Robinson had too many things to do – he had to contact the F.B.I. so they could start hunting for Krause – and he didn't want to waste any time with Kennerdale at that moment. But he knew that Kennerdale and his two friends had attempted to manipulate the rescue for their own purposes, and he intended to do something about it, too.

'Don't play big shot with me – this is still NASA, and I'm still in charge. I think we can easily find a way to do without your radio-operating skills.'

'Fine with me.' Robinson began to walk away.

'Wait.' Watts stepped forward to block Robinson's exit. 'Stay cool,' he said as he plastered his famous smile across his face, then nodded toward the TV camera. 'Don't blow the show now. America is watching.' The red light had been turned on; they were being broadcast, live. 'Why don't we do it this way,' Watts said as he maneuvered himself into a better camera position, his hand conspicuously on Robinson's shoulder. 'We'll have Mr. Robinson speak first. Then he can brief the audience – and us –

284

on the significance of the circuit breakers.'

'I don't have time.'

'Really? Why not?'

Robinson shrugged. At this point, he had no intention of telling anyone other than the F.B.I. about Krause – he didn't want to jeopardize their chances of finding the saboteur by saying too much publicly, and didn't want to jeopardize his own investigation of Kennerdale, Watts and Novak. 'Okay. I'll make a short statement about the circuit breakers.' Robinson figured he could make up something to satisfy everyone for the moment, then head for the police. One additional minute wouldn't make a difference; Krause was long out of the area anyway.

'I'll agree with that,' Kennerdale said. 'Especially the part about keeping it short.' Kennerdale watched as a TV technician placed a microphone on a stand a few feet in front of Robinson, then gestured to indicate that the sound system was live.

Robinson stepped up to the TV microphone and cleared his throat. As the camera focused directly on him, everyone in the OPSCON fell silent. The red light that showed that the camera was live glowed brightly. 'Ladies and gentlemen,' Robinson began as he faced the TV lens, 'as you already know, the airliner has descended safely into the atmosphere. It will only be a matter of time . . . '

'Ben? You still read me?'

Robinson reached over to the console and picked up the transmitter microphone. 'Go ahead,' he said, his voice being carried out on both the radio channel to the airliner and the TV hookup.

'Our flight has been cleared direct to Los Angeles. That's the closest large airport. We'll be on the ground in twenty minutes. Everything is going strictly routine, we should have no further problems.'

'That's great.'

'Right. It's about time.' Collins laughed. 'But before we get too low to speak to you directly,' he added as his voice turned serious again, 'put Krause on the radio. I want to thank him for the modification to the wing-cooling system. I'm sure that's what saved us. Is he the one who came up with the method of shutting it off?'

'Sort of.' *Krause was the saboteur.* Robinson took a deep breath, he wasn't sure of what to say next. He turned partway to avoid looking directly at Kennerdale and, as he did, allowed his eyes to wander off to the far corner of the lower level of OPSCON.

Alex Krause stood against the wall, an armed guard on one side of him, a well-dressed bullish-looking man on the other. Although he had never met him, Robinson knew that the man to Krause's left had to be the chief of Goddard security, Frank Schaefer. Robinson had, until that moment, forgotten about the telephone conversation with Schaefer a few hours before. *No one from United Aerospace gets past the front gate, not without your approval.*

Robinson turned quickly away. It was time for another command decision. Up until that moment, Robinson had been uncomfortable in his new job at United Aerospace, uncomfortable with the prospect of spending the rest of his life out of the cockpit. But suddenly he felt ready for anything, especially the challenges of his new position – a position that gave him a great many options. Robinson was thoroughly in control of his life again, the world had become his cockpit.

Robinson stepped closer to the TV microphone. Even though Krause had been caught, Robinson had no intention of allowing any of them – not Krause, not Kennerdale, Novak or Watts – to stay off the hook any longer. He owed that much to Donald Collins, to all those who had suffered onboard the airliner, and to those who had died. He owed it to the countless number of dedicated, conscientious employees of United Aerospace and Consolidated Airways who had suffered silently along with Collins and the rest.

Robinson saw that he had it within his power to see that justice would be done, long before the courts and the lawyers got hold of the case and mired things down in endless technicalities. Those technicalities might even allow some of the guilty people to avoid justice altogether. 'I don't know where Krause is,' Robinson transmitted to Collins, his voice simultaneously being picked up by the TV microphone and transmitted across the nation to the millions glued to their TV sets. 'He's not around.'

'Where could he be?' Collins asked. The surprise in his voice was evident, even through the flattened tones of the console speaker.

'I don't know.' Robinson faced the camera directly. 'But Krause did leave something.' With a hand that trembled almost too much to control, Ben Robinson glanced up at Kennerdale, Novak and Watts. He resisted the temptation to turn and face Krause. Instead, he reached into his coat pocket and took out the folded sheet of paper. Robinson could see those three names scribbled repeatedly across the sheet in several places. *Kennerdale. Novak. Watts.* 'It's some sort of note,' Robinson said as he slowed his speech pattern so the millions who watched in front of their TV sets would have no difficulty in understanding his every word. 'It's a handwritten message from Krause. A statement of some sort. I'll read it to you.'

NEL BESTSELLERS

T51277	'THE NUMBER OF THE BEAST'	*Robert Heinlein*	£2.25
T50777	STRANGER IN A STRANGE LAND	*Robert Heinlein*	£1.75
T51382	FAIR WARNING	*Simpson & Burger*	£1.75
T52478	CAPTAIN BLOOD	*Michael Blodgett*	£1.75
T50246	THE TOP OF THE HILL	*Irwin Shaw*	£1.95
T49620	RICH MAN, POOR MAN	*Irwin Shaw*	£1.60
T51609	MAYDAY	*Thomas H. Block*	£1.75
T54071	MATCHING PAIR	*George G. Gilman*	£1.50
T45773	CLAIRE RAYNER'S LIFEGUIDE		£2.50
T53709	PUBLIC MURDERS	*Bill Granger*	£1.75
T53679	THE PREGNANT WOMAN'S BEAUTY BOOK	*Gloria Natale*	£1.25
T49817	MEMORIES OF ANOTHER DAY	*Harold Robbins*	£1.95
T50807	79 PARK AVENUE	*Harold Robbins*	£1.75
T50149	THE INHERITORS	*Harold Robbins*	£1.75
T53231	THE DARK	*James Herbert*	£1.50
T43245	THE FOG	*James Herbert*	£1.50
T53296	THE RATS	*James Herbert*	£1.50
T45528	THE STAND	*Stephen King*	£1.75
T50874	CARRIE	*Stephen King*	£1.50
T51722	DUNE	*Frank Herbert*	£1.75
T51552	DEVIL'S GUARD	*Robert Elford*	£1.50
T52575	THE MIXED BLESSING	*Helen Van Slyke*	£1.75
T38602	THE APOCALYPSE	*Jeffrey Konvitz*	95p

NEL P.O. BOX 11, FALMOUTH TR10 9EN, CORNWALL

Postage Charge:
U.K. Customers 45p for the first book plus 20p for the second book and 14p for each additional book ordered to a maximum charge of £1.63.

B.F.P.O. & EIRE Customers 45p for the first book plus 20p for the second book and 14p for the next 7 books; thereafter 8p per book.

Overseas Customers 75p for the first book and 21p per copy for each additional book.

Please send cheque or postal order (no currency).

Name ....

Address ....

....

Title ....

While every effort is made to keep prices steady, it is sometimes necessary to increase prices at short notice. New English Library reserve the right to show on covers and charge new retail prices which may differ from those advertised in the text or elsewhere.(7)